Belisarius sensed a new presence and immediately understood its meaning. He saw a point of light in the void. A point, nothing more, which seemed infinitely distant. But he knew, even in the seeing, that the distance was one of time not space.

Time opened and the future came.

The point of light erupted, surged forward. A moment later, floating before Belisarius, was one of the Great Ones. The general understood, now, that he would never see them fully. Too much of their structure lay in mysterious forces which would never be seen by earthly eyes.

A new voice came to him, like Aide's, in a way, but different. FORCE FIELDS, ENERGY MATRICES. THERE IS LITTLE IN US LEFT OF OUR EARTHLY ORIGINS, AND NO FLESH AT ALL.

He saw into the being, now. Saw the glittering network of crystals which formed the Great One's—heart? Soul? And there came a sense of mirth; vast, yet whimsical.

And the general knew, then—finally—that these almost inconceivable beings were truly his own folk. He had but to look in a mirror, to see the crooked smile that would, someday, become that universe-encompassing irony—and that delight in irony. . . .

BOOKS IN THIS SERIES
An Oblique Approach
In the Heart of Darkness
Destiny's Shield
Fortune's Stroke

BAEN BOOKS by DAVID DRAKE

Hammer's Slammers

The Tank Lords	*The Butcher's Bill*
Caught in the Crossfire	*The Sharp End*

Independent Novels and Collections
The Dragon Lord
Birds of Prey
Northworld Trilogy
Redliners
Starliner
Mark II: The Military Dimension
All the Way to the Gallows

The General Series: (with S.M. Stirling)

The Forge	*The Sword*
The Hammer	*The Chosen*
The Anvil	*The Reformer*
The Steel	

The Undesired Princess and The Enchanted Bunny
(with L. Sprague de Camp)
Lest Darkness Fall and To Bring the Light
(with L. Sprague de Camp)
Enemy of My Enemy:
Terra Nova
(with Ben Ohlander)
Armageddon
(edited with Billie Sue Mosiman)

BAEN BOOKS by ERIC FLINT
Mother of Demons
1632

ERIC FLINT

DESTINY'S SHIELD

DAVID DRAKE

A Baen Books Original

Baen Publishing Enterprises
P.O. Box 1403
Riverdale, NY 10471

ISBN: 0-671-57872-3

Cover art by Keith Parkinson
Interior maps by Randy Asplund

First paperback printing, June 2000

Library of Congress Catalog Number 99-22046

Distributed by Simon & Schuster
1230 Avenue of the Americas
New York, NY 10020

Production by Windhaven Press, Auburn, NH
Printed in the United States of America

to Donald

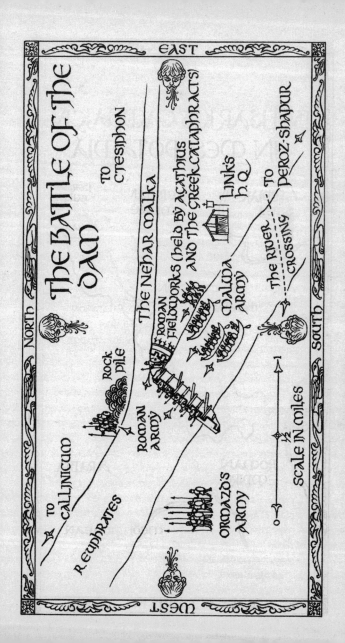

THE BATTLE OF THE DAM

EAST

NORTH

SOUTH

WEST

TO CTESIPHON

The Nehar Malka

Roman Fieldworks (held by Agathius and the Greek cataphracts)

Link's H.Q.

TO PEROZ-SHAPUR

The River Crossing

Malwa Army

Rock Pile

Roman Army

Ormazd's Army

TO CALLINICUM

R. Euphrates

Scale in miles

0   ½   1

Prologue

It was the Emperor's first public appearance since he had been acclaimed the new sovereign of Rome, and he was nervous. The ambassador from Persia was about to be presented to his court.

"He's going to be mean to me, Mommy," predicted the Emperor.

"Hush," whispered the Empress Regent. "And *don't* call me 'Mommy.' It's undignified."

The Emperor stared up at the tall imposing figure of his new mother, seated on her own throne next to him. Meeting her cold black eyes, he hastily looked away.

His new mother made him nervous, too. Even though his old mother said his new mother was a good friend, the Emperor wasn't fooled. The Empress Regent Theodora was *not* a nice lady.

The Empress Regent leaned over and whispered into his ear:

"Why do you think he'll be mean to you?"

The Emperor frowned.

"Well—because Daddy gave the Persians such a fierce whipping." Then, remembering: "My old daddy, I mean."

The Emperor glanced guiltily at the figure of his new father, standing not far away to his right. Then,

1

meeting the sightless gaze of those empty sockets, he looked away. Very hastily. Not even his real mother tried to claim that *Justinian* was a "nice man."

Theodora, again, hissing:

"And don't call the Empire's *strategos* 'daddy.' It's not dignified, even if he is your stepfather."

The Emperor hunched down on his throne, thoroughly miserable.

It's too confusing. Nobody should have this many mommies and daddies.

He began to turn his head, hoping to catch a reassuring glimpse of his real parents. He knew they would be standing nearby, among the other high notables of the Roman court. But the Empress Regent hissed him still.

"Stop fidgeting! It's not regal."

The Emperor made himself sit motionless. He grew more and more nervous, watching the stately advance of the Persian ambassador down the long aisle leading to the throne.

The Persian ambassador, he saw, was staring at him. Everybody was staring at him. The throne room was packed with Roman officials, every one of whom had their eyes fixed on the Emperor. Most of them, he thought, were not very nice—judging, at least, from sarcastic remarks he had heard his parents make. *All four* of his parents. The scurrilous nature of officialdom was one of the few subjects they did not quarrel about.

The ambassador was now much closer. He was rather tall, and slender of build. His complexion was perhaps a bit darker than that of most Greeks. His face was lean-jawed and aquiline, dominated by a large nose. His beard was cut in the short square style favored by Persians.

The ambassador was wearing the costume of a Persian nobleman. His gray hair was capped by the traditional gold-embroidered headdress, which Persians called a *citaris*. His tunic, though much like a

Roman one, had sleeves which reached all the way down to the wrists. His trousers also reached far down, almost covering the red leather of his boots.

Seeing the bright color of the ambassador's boot-tips, the Emperor felt a momentary pang. His old father—his *real* father—had a pair of boots just like those. "Parthian boots," they were called. His father favored them, as did many of his Thracian cataphracts.

The ambassador was now close enough that the Emperor could make out his eyes. Brown eyes, just like his father's. (His old father; his new father had no eyes.)

But the Emperor could detect none of the warmth which was always in his old father's eyes. The Persian's eyes seemed cold to him. The Emperor lifted his gaze. High above, the huge mosaic figures on the walls of the throne room stared down upon him. They were saints, he knew. Very holy folk. But their eyes, too, seemed cold. Darkly, the Emperor suspected they probably hadn't been very nice either. The severe expressions on their faces reminded him of his tutors. Sour old men, whose only pleasure in life was finding fault with their charge.

He felt as if he were being buried alive.

"I'm hot," he complained.

"Of course you're hot," whispered Theodora. "You're wearing imperial robes on a warm day in April. What do you expect?"

Unkindly:

"Get used to it." Then:

"Now, *act properly*. The ambassador is here."

Twenty feet away, the Persian ambassador's retinue came to a halt. The ambassador stepped forward two paces and prostrated himself on the thick, luxurious rug which had been placed for that purpose on the tiled floor of the throne room.

That rug, the Emperor knew, was only brought out from its special storage place for the use of

envoys representing the Persian King of Kings, the
Shahanshah. It was the best rug the Roman Empire
owned, he had heard.

Persia was the traditional great rival of the Roman
Empire. It wouldn't do to offend its representatives.
No, it wouldn't do at all.

The Persian ambassador was rising. Now, he was
stepping forward. The ambassador extended his
hand, holding the scroll which proclaimed his status
to the Roman court. The motion brought a slight
wince to the face of the ambassador, and the
Roman Emperor's fear multiplied. The wince, he
knew, was caused by the great wound which the
ambassador had received to his shoulder three years
before.

The Emperor's real father had given him that
wound, at a famous place called Mindouos.

He's going to be mean to me.

"I bring greetings to the *Basileus* of Rome from
my master Khusrau Anushirvan, King of Kings of Iran
and non-Iran."

The ambassador spoke loudly, so everyone in the
huge throne room could hear. His voice was very
deep, as deep as anyone's the Emperor had ever
heard except church singers.

"My name is Baresmanas," continued the ambassador. "Baresmanas, of the Suren."

The Emperor heard a whispering rustle sweep the
throne room. He understood the meaning of that
rustle, and felt a moment's pride in his understanding. For weeks, now, his tutors had drilled him
mercilessly in the history and traditions of Persia. The
Emperor had not forgotten his lessons.

Officially, the Suren were one of the *sahrdaran*,
the seven greatest noble families of Persia. Unoffi-
cially, they were the greatest. Rustam, the legendary
hero of the Aryans—their equivalent of Hercules—
was purported to have been of that family. And the

Persian general who shattered Crassus' Roman army at Carrhae had been a Suren.

Sending a Suren ambassador, the Emperor knew, was the Shahanshah's way of indicating his respect for Rome. But the knowledge did not allay his fear.

He's going to be mean to me.

The stern, haughty, aristocratic face of the Persian ambassador broke into a sudden smile. White teeth flashed in a rich, well-groomed beard.

"It is a great pleasure to meet you, Your Majesty," said the ambassador. Baresmanas bowed toward Theodora. "And your mother, the Regent Theodora."

The Emperor reached out his hand to take the scroll. After unrolling the parchment, he saw with relief that the document was written in Greek. The Emperor could read, now, though still with no great facility. And this document was full of long-winded words that he didn't recognize at all. He began studying it intently until he heard a slight cough.

Out of the corner of his eye, the Emperor saw the Empress Regent nodding graciously. Remembering his instructions, the Emperor hastily rolled up the parchment and followed her example. Then, seeing the hint of a frown on Theodora's brow, he belatedly remembered the rest of her coaching.

"We welcome the representative of our brother," he piped, "the Basileus of Pers—"

The Emperor froze with fear at his blunder.

By long-standing protocol, the Emperor of Rome always called the Emperor of Persia the "Basileus" rather than the "King of Kings." By using the same title as his own, the Roman Emperor thereby indicated the special status of the Persian monarch. No other ruler was ever granted that title by Romans, except, on occasion, the negusa nagast of Ethiopia.

But Persians *never* called themselves Persians. That term was a Greek bastardization of the Persian province of Fars, the homeland of the old Achaemenid dynasty. Persians called their land Iran—land of the Aryans. They were immensely snooty on the matter, too, especially the distinction between Aryans and all lesser breeds. Many non-Aryan nations were ruled by the Shahanshah, but they were not considered part of the land of the Aryans itself. *Those* were simply "non-Iran."

The Emperor's paralysis was broken by the slight, encouraging smile on the ambassador's face.

"—the Basileus *of Iran and non-Iran,*" he quickly corrected himself.

The ambassador's smile widened. A very friendly gleam came into his brown eyes. For a moment—a blessed moment—the Roman Emperor was reminded of his father. His old father.

He glanced at the mutilated face of his new father, the former Emperor Justinian. That sightless face was fixed upon him, as if Justinian still had eyes to see. That sightless, harsh, bitter face.

It's not fair, whimpered the Emperor in his mind. *I want my old father back. My real father.*

The ambassador was backing away. The Emperor of Rome began to sigh with relief, until, catching a hint of Theodora's disapproval, he stiffened with imperial dignity.

Maybe he won't be mean to me, after all.

The ambassador was fifteen feet off, now. He still seemed to be smiling.

It's not fair. The Sassanids are from Fars, too, so why can't we call them Persians?

Now, he did sigh, slightly. He felt the Empress Regent's disapproval, but ignored it.

It's too much to remember all at once.

Another sigh. The Empress Consort hissed. Again, he ignored her reproof.

I'm the Emperor. I can do what I want.

That was patently false, and he knew it.

It's not fair.

I'm only eight years old.

The ambassador was thirty feet away, now. Out of hearing range. Theodora leaned over.

The Emperor braced himself for her reproach.

Nasty lady. I want my old mother back.

But all she said was:

"That was very well done, Photius. Your mother will be proud of you." Then, with a slight smile: "Your *real* mother."

"I'm proud of you, Photius," said Antonina. "You did very well." She leaned over the throne's armrest and kissed him on the cheek.

Her son flushed, partly from pleasure and partly from guilt. He didn't think being kissed in public by his mother fit the imperial image he was supposed to project. But, when his eyes quickly scanned the throne room, he saw that few people were watching. After the Empress Regent had left, to hold a private meeting with the Persian ambassador and his father (*both* of his fathers), the reception had dissolved into a far more relaxed affair. Most of the crowd were busy eating, drinking and chattering. They were ignoring, for all practical purposes, the august personage of the Emperor. No-one standing anywhere near to him, of course, committed the gross indiscretion of actually turning their back on the throne's small occupant. But neither was anyone anxious to ingratiate themselves to the new Emperor. Everyone knew that the real power was in the hands of Theodora.

Photius was not disgruntled by the crowd's indifference to him. To the contrary, he was immensely relieved. For the first time since the reception began, he felt he could relax. He even pondered, tentatively, the thought of reaching up and scratching behind his ear.

Then, squaring his shoulders, he did so. Scratched furiously, in fact.

I'm the Emperor of Rome. I can do what I want.

"Stop scratching behind your ear!" hissed his mother. "You're the Emperor of Rome! It's undignified."

The Emperor sighed, but obeyed.

It's not fair. I never asked them to make me Emperor.

Chapter 1

CONSTANTINOPLE
Spring, 531 A.D.

As soon as Antonina put Photius to bed, she hastened to the imperial audience chamber. By the time she arrived, the Persian ambassador was reaching the conclusion of what had apparently been a lengthy speech.

Taking her seat next to Belisarius, Antonina scanned the room quickly. Except for the guards standing against the walls, the huge chamber was almost empty. The usual mob of advisers who sat in on Theodora's audiences was absent. The only Romans present to hear the Persian ambassador were Theodora, Justinian, and Belisarius.

Baresmanas himself was the only Persian present. Antonina knew that the extremely limited participation had been at the request of the Persians. That fact alone made clear the seriousness with which they took this meeting. She focussed her attention on the ambassador's final remarks.

9

"And so," said Baresmanas sternly, "I must caution you once again. Do not think that Roman meddling in the current internal situation in Persia will go unchallenged. Your spies may have told you that our realm verges on civil war. I, for one, do not believe that is true. But even if it is—all Aryans will unite against Roman intrusion. Do not doubt that for a moment."

The ambassador's stern expression relaxed, replaced by a semi-apologetic smile which was, under the circumstances, quite warm. Antonina was struck by Baresmanas' change in demeanor. She suspected that the friendly face which now confronted the Roman Empress and her top advisers was much closer to the man himself than the stiff mask which had delivered the previous words.

"Of course, it is quite possible that all of my teeth-baring is unnecessary. I do not mean to be rude. Rome is known for its wisdom as well as its martial prowess, after all. It is quite possible—likely, I should say—that the thought of intervening in Persia has never once crossed your mind."

Antonina was impressed. Baresmanas had managed to deliver the last sentence with a straight face. The statement, of course, was preposterous. For the last five hundred years, no Roman emperor had spent more than three consecutive days without at least *thinking* about attacking Persia. The reverse, needless to say, was equally true.

She leaned over and whispered into Belisarius' ear: "What's this about?"

His reply also came in a whisper:

"The usual, whenever the Persians have to find a new emperor. Khusrau's been the leading candidate ever since Kavad died—he's been officially proclaimed, actually—but his half-brother Ormazd is apparently not reconciled to the situation. Baresmanas was sent here by Khusrau to warn us not to muck around in the mess."

Antonina made a little grimace.

"As if we would," she muttered.

Belisarius smiled crookedly. "Now, love, let's not be quite so self-righteous. It *has* happened, you know. Emperor Carus took advantage of the civil war between Bahram II and Hormizd to invade Persia. Even captured their capital of Ctesiphon."

"That was over two hundred years ago," she protested softly.

"So? Persians have long memories. So do we, for that matter. Carus' invasion was retribution for Ardashir's attack on us during our civil war after Alexander Severus was murdered."

Antonina shrugged. "The situation's different. We've got the Malwa to worry about, now."

Belisarius started to make some response, but fell silent. The great double doors to the audience chamber were opening. A moment later, a worn-looking Persian officer was being ushered in by Irene Macrembolitissa, the chief of the Roman Empire's spy network.

"Speaking of which—" he muttered.

Antonina started. "You think—?"

He shrugged. "We'll know soon enough. But we've been expecting the Malwa to invade Mesopotamia, sooner or later. From the look of that Persian officer, I suspect 'sooner' has arrived."

The Persian officer had reached Baresmanas. The ambassador was standing some fifteen feet away from Theodora. Although a chair had been provided for him, Baresmanas apparently felt that his stern message would carry more weight if delivered standing.

The ambassador stooped slightly to hear what the officer had to say. The newly arrived Persian whispered urgently into his ear.

Antonina could see an unmistakable look of surprise and apprehension come to the ambassador's face. But Baresmanas was an experienced diplomat. Within seconds, the ambassador had regained his composure. By the time the Persian officer finished imparting whatever report he had brought with him, Baresmanas' expression was impassive and opaque.

When the officer finished, Baresmanas nodded and whispered a few words of his own. Immediately, the man bowed to the Roman Empress and hastily backed out of the room.

Antonina glanced over at Irene. The spymaster, after ushering the officer into the audience chamber, had discreetly taken position against the wall next to the door.

Antonina's gaze met Irene's. To all outward appearance, the spymaster's own face seemed void of expression. But Antonina knew Irene very well, and could not miss her friend's suppressed excitement.

Behind Baresmanas' back, Irene gave Antonina a quick little gesture. Thumbs up.

Antonina sighed. "You're right," she whispered to her husband. "Irene's like a shark smelling blood."

"The woman does love a challenge," murmured Belisarius. "I think she'd rather be tortured in the Pit for eternity than go for a week without excitement." A chuckle. "Provided, of course, that Satan let her keep her books."

Baresmanas cleared his throat, and addressed Theodora once again.

"Your Majesty, I have just received some important news. With your permission, I would like to leave now. I must discuss these matters with my own entourage."

Theodora nodded graciously. Then:

"Would you like to schedule another meeting?"

Baresmanas' nod was abrupt, almost curt.

"Yes. Tomorrow, if possible."

"Certainly," replied Theodora.

Antonina ignored the rest of the interchange between the Empress and Baresmanas. Diplomatic formalities did not interest her.

What *did* interest her was Irene.

"What do you think?" she whispered to Belisarius. "Is she going to be the first person in history to actually explode?"

Belisarius shook his head. He whispered in return:

"Nonsense. Spontaneous human eruption's impossible. Says so in the most scholarly volumes. Irene knows that perfectly well. She owns every one of those tomes, after all."

"I don't know," mused Antonina, keeping a covert eye on her friend against the wall. "She's starting to tremble, now. Shiver, quiver and quake. Vibrating like a harp string."

"Not possible," repeated Belisarius. "Precluded by all the best philosophers."

Baresmanas was finally ushered out of the room. Irene exploded.

"It's on! It's on! It's on! It's on! It's on!"

Bouncing like a ball. Spinning like a top.

"The Malwa invaded Mesopotamia! Attacked Persia!"

Quiver, shiver; quake and shake.

"My spies got their hands on the message! Khusrau's instructed Baresmanas to seek Roman help!"

Vibrating like a harp string; beating like a drum.

"See?" demanded Antonina.

Chapter 2

Three nights later, the imperial audience chamber was again the scene of a meeting. After concluding an initial round of discussions with Baresmanas, Theodora had summoned her top advisers and officials.

Theodora had a multitude of advisers, but the ten people in that room constituted the majority of what both she and Belisarius thought of as the "inner circle." Membership in that circle depended not on formal post or official position—although post and position generally accompanied them. Membership in the inner circle depended on two far more important things:

First, the personal trust of Belisarius and what passed for "personal trust" from the perennially suspicious Theodora.

Second, knowledge of the great secret. Knowledge of the messenger from the future, the crystalline quasi-jewel which called itself Aide, who had attached itself to Belisarius and warned the Roman Empire's greatest general that his world had become the battleground for powerful and mysterious forces of the far distant future.

Theodora herself occupied a place in her circle of advisers, sitting below a great mosaic depicting Saint

Peter. The seating arrangement was odd, for an imperial conference—the more so in that Theodora was not sitting on a throne, but a simple chair. ("Simple," at least, by imperial standards.) Traditionally, when Roman sovereigns discussed affairs of state with their advisers, the advisers stood on their feet while the monarchs lounged in massive thrones.

But—

"*Of course* we should accept the Persian proposal," came a harsh voice.

The Empress cocked her head and examined the speaker. He returned her gaze, with his scarred and empty eye-sockets.

Justinian was the cause of that peculiar seating arrangement. By custom, the former Emperor could no longer sit by her side. Officially, he was nothing now but one of her advisers. But Theodora had not been able to bear the thought of humiliating her husband further, and so she had gladly accepted Belisarius' suggestion that she solve the problem in the simplest way possible. Henceforth, when she met with her advisers, Theodora would sit with them in a circle.

"Explain, Justinian," said Anthony Cassian. The newly-elevated Patriarch of Constantinople leaned forward in his chair, clasping his pudgy hands.

"Yes, do," added Germanicus forcefully. The commander of the Army of Illyria was scowling.

Germanicus nodded to Theodora. "With all due respect, Your Majesty, I do not view *any* alliance with Persia favorably. Damn the Medes, anyway! They've always been our enemy. Persia and the Malwa Empire can claw each other to pieces, as far as I'm concerned."

A murmur of protest began to rise from several of the people sitting in the room.

"Yes, yes," snapped Germanicus, "I know that Malwa is our ultimate enemy." He glanced at Belisarius' chest, where the "jewel" from the future lay nestled in a pouch under the general's tunic. "But I don't see why—"

Justinian's harsh voice interrupted. *"Damn the Persians.* And the Malwa! It's the dynasty I'm thinking about." Justinian's bony hands clenched the arms of his chair. "Don't fool yourselves," he snarled. "Do you really think the aristocracy is happy with the situation? Do you really?" He cawed a harsh, humorless laugh. "This very night—I guarantee it—half the Greek nobility is plotting our overthrow."

"Let them plot all they want," said Sittas, shrugging. The heavyset general smiled cheerfully.

"I'm a Greek nobleman, myself, mind you. So I'm not about to dispute Justinian's words. If anything, he's being charitable. By my own estimate, *two-thirds* of the Greek aristocracy is plotting our overthrow. This very night, just as he says."

Sittas yawned. "So are the rats in my cellar, I imagine. I'm more concerned about the rats."

Chrysopolis shook his head vigorously. "You are much too complacent, Sittas," he argued. "I myself share Justinian's concerns."

Chrysopolis had replaced the executed traitor John of Cappadocia as the empire's praetorian prefect. He was the one other member of the inner circle, who, like Germanicus, was not personally well-known to Belisarius. But the general himself had proposed his inclusion. Among the highest Roman officials who survived the purge after the failed coup d'etat which had been suppressed by Belisarius and Antonina a few months before, Chrysopolis had a reputation for ability and—a far rarer characteristic among those circles— scrupulous honesty.

"Do you really think this alliance would have that good an effect?" he asked.

"Of course," stated Justinian. He held up a thumb. "First. The Army will be ecstatic. Persia's the enemy they fear, not Malwa. Anything that prevents another war with Persia will meet their approval. Even after Belisarius' great victory at Mindouos, the Army still has no desire to match Persian lancers on the field of battle."

"The Malwa will be worse," pointed out Antonina. "Their numbers are much larger, and they have the new gunpowder weapons."

Justinian shrugged. "So? Roman soldiers have no experience with the Malwa, so they're not worried about them. Over time, that will probably change. But it's the present I'm concerned with. And, right now, I can think of no better way to cement the Army's allegiance to the dynasty than for Photius to forge a Hundred Years' Peace with Persia."

Justinian held up his forefinger alongside his thumb. "Two. It'll please the populace at large, especially in the borderlands." His head turned, the sightless sockets fixing on Anthony Cassian. "The peasants of the region are already delighted with Cassian's succession to the Patriarchate. They're Monophysite heretics, the lot of them, and they know Cassian will rein in the persecution."

"I have no formal authority over Patriarch Ephraim of Antioch," demurred Anthony. "The border regions fall under his jurisdiction."

"The hell with Ephraim," hissed Justinian. "If the dynasty's hold on the throne stabilizes, we'll crush that bastard soon enough. I know it, you know it, Ephraim knows it—*and so do the peasants of the borderlands.*"

Belisarius saw that Germanicus was still scowling. The Illyrian general, quite obviously, was unmoved by Justinian and Chrysopolis' concerns. Belisarius decided it was time to intervene.

"We can live with Persia, Germanicus," he stated. "We have, after all, for a millennium. *We cannot live with Malwa.* The Malwa seek to rule the world. Their invasion of Persia is simply the first step toward their intended conquest of Rome. I say we fight them now, on Persian soil, with Persia's lancers as our allies. Or else we will fight them later, on Roman soil, with the Persian lancers shackled into the ranks of Malwa's gigantic army alongside their Rajput and Kushan vassals."

Germanicus eyed him skeptically. Belisarius repressed a sigh. He was aggravated by the man's stubbornness, but he could not in good conscience condemn him for it. The commander of the Army of Illyria had only been made privy to the great secret a month before. Germanicus, like Chrysopolis, had no longstanding personal relationship with Belisarius. But he was a close kinsman of Justinian and an excellent general in his own right. Theodora had urged his inclusion in the inner circle—this was the one subject where she never issued commands to Belisarius—and Belisarius had agreed.

Abstractly, he knew, the Illyrian general accepted the truth of Aide's nature, and the crystal's warning of the future. But, like most generals, Germanicus was conservative by temperament. Persia, not India, was the traditional rival of the Roman Empire.

No, he could not condemn Germanicus for his prejudiced blindness. He simply returned the man's glare with a serene, confident gaze.

After a moment, Germanicus stopped glaring.

"Are you so certain, Belisarius?" he asked. The Illyrian general's tone was not hostile, simply—*serious*. Like most Roman soldiers he had the deepest respect for Belisarius.

Belisarius nodded his head firmly. "Trust me in this, Germanicus. If Malwa is not checked, the day will come when the Roman Empire will vanish as if it had never existed."

After a moment, Germanicus sighed. "Very well, then. I will defer to your judgement. I'm not happy about it, but—" He sat up, squaring his shoulders. "Enough. I withdraw my objections."

Theodora saw that all of her advisers had reached the same conclusion.

"So be it," she announced. "We'll tell the Persian ambassador that we accept the offer of alliance. In principle, at least. Let's move on to the specifics of their proposal."

She turned to Irene Macrembolitissa. Officially, Irene was the most junior member of the high bureaucracy, having been elevated only recently to the post of *sacellarius*, the "keeper of the privy purse." Her actual power was immense. She was Theodora's spymaster and the chief of the Empire's unofficial secret police, the *agentes in rebus*. She had also become one of Theodora's few—very, very few—genuine friends.

"Begin by summarizing the situation with the invasion, if you would."

Irene leaned forward, brushing back her thick brown hair. "The Malwa attack on Persia began two months ago," she said. "As Belisarius had predicted, they began with a massive sea-borne invasion of the Tigris-Euphrates delta. Within two days, they captured the great port at Charax and have been turning it into the entrepot for their invasion of Mesopotamia."

"Aren't they attacking in the north as well?" asked Hermogenes.

Irene nodded. "Yes. They have a large army pressing into Persia's eastern provinces. That army, however, seems to be only lightly equipped with gunpowder weapons. For the most part, they're made up of traditional forces—Malwa infantry backed by Ye-tai security battalions, with a very large force of Rajput cavalrymen."

"Second-raters, then," stated Germanicus.

Belisarius shook his head.

"Not at all. The Rajput cavalry are excellent, and they're under the command of Rana Sanga. I know him from my trip to India. Know him rather well,

in fact. He's as good a general as you'll find anywhere. And while I don't personally know the top
Malwa commander of the northern expedition, Lord
Damodara, I do know that Rana Sanga respected
him deeply."

Germanicus frowned. "Why—?"

Belisarius chuckled. "There's a method to the
Malwa madness. The Rajputs are the heart of
Damodara's army, and the Malwa don't trust their
Rajput vassals. So they put their best general in
charge of the toughest campaign, gave him little in
the way of gunpowder weapons, and placed almost
all the Rajput cavalry at his disposal. Damodara will
have no choice. He'll have to rely on Rana Sanga
and the Rajputs for his shock troops, slugging it out
for months against Persian cavalry in some of the
worst terrain you can imagine. The Malwa are killing
two birds with one stone. The Persians can't ignore
the threat, so they have to divert much of their army
from the main campaign in Mesopotamia. And, at
the same time, the Malwa will be—"

Germanicus nodded. "Bleeding the Rajputs white."

"Exactly."

Sittas grunted. "That means the northern expedition isn't something we need to worry about. Not for
some time, at least. That'll be up to the Persians to
deal with."

He eyed Irene. "How big is the Malwa army in
Mesopotamia?"

She hesitated, knowing that her next words would
be met with disbelief. "At least two hundred thousand men. Probably more."

"That's nonsense!" exclaimed Germanicus.

Belisarius overrode him. "It is *not* nonsense.
Believe it, Germanicus. The Malwa Empire is the
one power in the world which can field that big an
army. *And keep it supplied,* so long as they hold
Charax. When I was in Bharakuccha, India's great

western seaport, I saw with my own eyes the huge fleet of supply ships they were constructing."

Germanicus' face was pale. "Two hundred thousand," he whispered.

"*At least*," emphasized Belisarius. "And they'll have the bulk of their gunpowder units, too. About their only weakness will be in cavalry."

Irene shook her head. "Not even that, Belisarius. Not light cavalry, at least. I just got word yesterday that the Lakhmite dynasty has transferred its allegiance from Persia to the Malwa. That gives the Malwa a large force of Arab cavalry—*and* a camel force that can operate in the desert regions on the right bank of the Euphrates. Which, by the way, seems to be the river which the Malwa are using as their invasion route."

"Slow going," commented Hermogenes. "The Euphrates meanders all over the flood plain. The Tigris would be quicker."

Belisarius shrugged. "The Malwa aren't relying on speed and maneuver. They've got a sledgehammer moving up the Euphrates. Once they reach Peroz-Shapur, they can cross over to the Tigris. They'll have the Persian capital at Ctesiphon surrounded."

"What's the Persian response?" asked Germanicus.

"From what Baresmanas told me," responded Irene, "it seems that Emperor Khusrau intends to make a stand at Babylon."

"*Babylon?*" exclaimed Cassian. "There *is* no Babylon! That city's been deserted for centuries!" He shook his head. "It's in ruins."

Irene smiled. "The city, yes. But the *walls* of Babylon are still standing. And, by all accounts, those walls are almost as mighty as they were in the days of Hammurabi and Assurbanipal."

"What are the Persians asking of us?" queried Antonina.

Irene glanced at Chrysopolis. The praetorian

prefect had handled that part of the initial discussions with Baresmanas.

"They want an alliance with Rome, and as many troops as we can send to help Khusrau at Babylon." He nodded to Sittas. "The Persians do not expect us to help them against the Malwa thrust into their eastern provinces. But they are—well, *desperate*—to get our help in Mesopotamia."

"How many troops do they want us to send?" asked Justinian.

Chrysopolis took a deep breath. "They're asking for forty thousand. The entire Army of Syria, and the remaining twenty thousand from Anatolia and our European units."

The room exploded.

"That's insane!" cried Sittas. "That's half the Roman army!"

"It'd strip the Danube naked," snarled Germanicus. "Every barbarian tribe in the Balkans would be pouring across within a month!" He turned to Belisarius. "You can't be seriously considering this proposal!"

Belisarius shook his head. "No, I'm not, Germanicus. *Although I would if I thought we could do it.*" Again, Belisarius shrugged. "But, the simple fact is that we can't. We have to maintain a strong force on the Danube, as you said. And, unfortunately, we have to keep Sittas' army in and around Constantinople. As we all know, the dynasty's hold is still shaky. Most of the nobility would back another coup, if they thought it would succeed."

Germanicus tugged on his beard. "At the moment, in other words, we have nothing to send Persia except the existing armies in Syria and Egypt."

"Not even that," said Theodora. "We've got a crisis in Egypt, too."

She looked to her spymaster. "Tell them."

"As you all know," said Irene, "the former Patriarch of Alexandria, Timothy IV, was murdered during the Nika insurrection—at the same time as Anthony's predecessor Epiphanios. The culprits were never found, but I'm quite sure it was the work of Malwa assassins."

"Aided and abetted by ultra-orthodox forces in the Church," said Justinian forcefully.

Irene nodded. "After three months of wrangling, the Greek nobility in Alexandria imposed a new Patriarch. An ultra-orthodox monk by the name of Paul. The very next day he reinstated the persecution. Alexandria's been in turmoil ever since. Riots and street fights almost daily, mostly between ultra-orthodox and ultra-Monophysite monks. We just got the news yesterday."

"What the hell is the Army of Egypt doing?" demanded Germanicus.

"They've sided with the new Patriarch," replied Irene. "According to my reports, in fact, the army's commander was Paul's chief advocate."

"That's General Ambrose, isn't it?" asked Hermogenes.

Irene nodded. Sittas growled:

"I know that bastard. He's not worth a damn on the battlefield. A politician down to his toenails. Ambitious as Satan."

The praetorian prefect sighed. "So much for the Army of Egypt. We won't be able to send them to Persia."

"It's worse than that, Chrysopolis," stated Belisarius. "We're going to have to send a military force to Egypt to set the situation straight."

"You think we should intervene?"

"I most certainly do. Egypt is the largest and richest province of the Empire. In the long run, we're relying on Egypt to be the bastion for our naval campaign in the Erythrean Sea. The last thing we can afford is to have its population riddled with disaffection and rebellion."

Theodora added her voice. "I am in complete agreement with Belisarius on this matter." She nodded toward Cassian. "At Anthony's recommendation, I'm sending a deacon named Theodosius to replace Paul as Alexandria's Patriarch. He's a moderate Monophysite. A member of the Severan school like Timothy."

Chrysopolis frowned. "How are you going to enforce the appointment?"

For the first time since the meeting started, Theodora grinned. But there was not a trace of humor in the expression. "With a combination of the old and the new. You know of the religious order which Michael of Macedonia has founded? He's offered to send several thousand of them to Egypt, to counter the existing monastic orders."

"That's fine against other monks in the streets, armed with cudgels," grunted Hermogenes. "But the Army of Egypt—"

"Will be dealt with by the Theodoran Cohort," stated Belisarius.

The announcement brought dead silence to the room. All eyes turned to Antonina.

The little Egyptian woman shrugged. "I'm all we've got, I'm afraid."

"Not quite," said Belisarius. He looked at Hermogenes. "I think we can spare one of your legions, to give Antonina's grenadiers an infantry bulwark. And I'm going to give her five hundred of my cataphracts for a cavalry force."

Hermogenes nodded. Frowning, Germanicus looked back and forth between Belisarius and Antonina.

"I would have thought you'd want to use the grenadiers in Persia," he commented.

Before Belisarius could reply, Theodora spoke up. "*Absolutely not*. Other than Belisarius' small unit of rocketeers, Antonina's cohort is our only military force equipped with gunpowder weapons. They've never been in a real battle. I'm not going to risk them in Persia. Not this early in the war."

Germanicus' frown deepened. "Then who—?"

"Me," said Belisarius. "Me, and whatever troops we can scrape up." He scratched his chin. "I think we can spare five or six thousand men from the Army of Syria, along with my own bucellarii."

"I can give you two thousand cataphracts," interjected Sittas. He glanced at Germanicus.

The Illyrian army commander winced. "I can probably spare five hundred. No more than that, I'm afraid. There's bound to be trouble with the northern barbarians within the next year. The Malwa will be spreading their gold with a lavish hand."

Hermogenes finished counting on his fingers and looked up.

"That doesn't give you much of an army, Belisarius. You've got, what—a thousand cataphracts, after you give five hundred to Antonina?"

Belisarius nodded.

Hermogenes blew out his cheeks. "Plus two thousand from Sittas and five hundred from Germanicus. That's three and a half thousand heavy cavalry. The Army of Syria can probably give you three or four thousand infantry and a couple of thousand cavalry. But the cavalry will be light horse archers, not cataphract lancers."

"Ten thousand men, at the most," concluded Germanicus. "As he says, that's not much of an army."

Belisarius shrugged. "It's what we've got."

"I'm not happy at the idea of Belisarius personally leading this army," stated Chrysopolis. "He's the Empire's strategos. He should really stay here in the capital."

"Nonsense!" barked Justinian. For the first time since the meeting began, he too broke into a grin. And, like that of his wife's, the expression was utterly humorless.

"You want an alliance with Persia, don't you?" he demanded. "They won't be happy at our counter-offer of ten thousand men. But Belisarius' reputation will make up the difference." Now, a bit of humor crept into that ravaged face. "Stop frowning, Chrysopolis. I can see your sour face as if I still had eyes."

He leaned forward, gripping the armrests of his chair. His head scanned the entire circle of advisers. For just a fleeting moment, everyone would have sworn Justinian could actually see them.

"I made that man a general," said the former emperor. "It's one of the few decisions I made that I've never regretted."

He leaned back in his seat. "The Persians will be delighted. Believe it."

Chapter 3

The next morning, when the Empress Regent gave Baresmanas the Roman response to Persia's proposal, he *was* delighted. He had hoped for a larger army, true. But neither he nor Emperor Khusrau had really expected the Romans to send them forty thousand troops.

The Roman generosity in not demanding territorial concessions in the borderlands also pleased him immensely. That was quite unexpected.

But, best of all—*Belisarius*.

Not every member of the Persian delegation shared his attitude—including his own wife, the Lady Maleka. As soon as Baresmanas returned to the small palace in which the Persians had been housed, right in the middle of the imperial complex, she strode into the main salon, scowling fiercely.

"I do not approve," she told her husband, very forcefully. "We should not be currying favor from these wretched Roman mongrels, as if we were lowborn beggars."

Baresmanas ignored her. He stood before the flames burning in the salon's fireplace, warming his hands from the chill of an April morning.

"I do not approve!" repeated Lady Maleka.

Baresmanas sighed, turned away from the fire. "The Emperor approves," he said mildly.

"Khusrau is but a boy!"

"He most certainly is *not*," replied her husband firmly. "True, he is a young man. But he is in every respect as fine an Emperor as ever sat the Aryan throne. Do not doubt it, wife."

Lady Maleka scowled. "Even so— He is too pre-occupied with the Malwa invasion! He forgets our glorious Aryan heritage!"

Her husband bit off a sharp retort. Unlike his wife, Baresmanas was well-educated. A scholar, actually, which was unusual for a sahrdaran. Lady Maleka, on the other hand, was a perfect specimen of their class. Like all Persian high noblewomen, she was literate. But it was a skill which she had never utilized once she reached adulthood. She much preferred to learn her history seated on rich cushions at their palace in Ctesiphon, listening to bards recounting the epics of the Aryans.

Baresmanas studied the angry face of his wife, trying to think of a way to explain reality that would penetrate her prejudiced ignorance.

The truth of history, he knew, was quite different from her fantasy version of it. The Iranians who ruled Persia and Central Asia had originated, like their Scythian brethren, from the steppes of Asia. They, too, had been nomadic barbarians once. Over a millennium ago, the Aryan tribes had marched south from the steppes, in their great epic of conquest. The westward-moving tribes had become known as the Iranians and had created the glory of the ancient Medes and Persians. Their eastward-bound cousins had conquered northern India and created the Vedic culture which eventually permeated the entire subcontinent.

And then, having done so, both branches of the Aryans had invented a new history for themselves.

A history full of airy legends and grandiose claims, and precious little in the way of fact.

Myths and fables, grown up in the feudal soil of the east. The real power of the Iranians, now as before, lay on the Persian plateau and the great rich lands of Mesopotamia. But the Aryans—the nobility, at least—chose to remember the legends of the northeastern steppes.

And then, he thought sourly, *remember them upside down. They don't remember the military strength of barbarian horsemen. Only the myth of pure blood, and divine ancestry.*

Studying his wife, Baresmanas recognized the impossibility of penetrating her prejudices.

So be it. The Aryans had other customs, too.

"Obey your husband, wife," he commanded. "And your Emperor."

She opened her mouth.

"*Do it.*"

Lady Maleka bowed her head. Sullenly, she stalked from the room.

Baresmanas lowered himself onto a couch near the fire. He stared into the flames. The hot glow seemed to lurk within his dark eyes, as if he saw a different conflagration there.

Which, indeed, he did. The memory of a fire called the battle of Mindouos. Where, three years before, a Roman general had shattered the Persian army. Outfoxed them, trapped then, slaughtered them—even captured the Persian camp.

Belisarius.

Baresmanas had been at that battle. So had his children, in the Persian camp.

He looked away from the fire, wincing.

His children would never have been at Mindouos had Baresmanas not brought them there. He, too, for all his scholarship, had lapsed into Aryan haughtiness. It was the long-standing custom of noble Persians to bring their families to the field of battle. Displaying, to the enemy and all the world, their arrogant confidence in Aryan invincibility.

His wife had refused to come, pleading her health. (Not from the enemy, but from the heat of the Syrian desert.) But his children had come, avidly—his daughter as much as his son. Avid to watch their famous father, second-in-command to Firuz, destroy the insolent Romans.

Baresmanas sighed. He reached up with his left hand and caressed his right shoulder. The shoulder ached, as always, and he could feel the ridged scar tissue under the silk of his tunic.

A Roman lance had put that scar there. At Mindouos. Baresmanas, like all the charging noble lancers, had been trapped in the center. Trapped, by the cunning of the Roman commander; and, then, hammered under by the force of his counter-blow.

Belisarius.

Baresmanas could remember little of the battle's final moments. Only the confusion and the choking dust; the growing, horrible knowledge that they had been outwitted and outmaneuvered; the shock and pain, as he lay dazed and bleeding on the trampled ground, his shoulder almost severed.

Most of all, he remembered the terror which had coursed through his heart, as if hot iron instead of blood flowed through his veins. Terror, not for himself, but for his helpless children. The Persian camp was unprotected, then, from the triumphing Romans. Baresmanas had known the Roman soldiers would ravage it like wolves, especially their Hun auxiliaries, raping and murdering.

And so they had; or, at least, had started to do.

Until Belisarius, and his cataphracts, had put a stop to the atrocities. He had been as decisive and ruthless toward his own Huns as he had been toward the Persians.

Weeks later, after he had been ransomed by his family, Baresmanas had heard the tale from his daughter Tahmina. Seeing the oncoming Huns, she and her brother had hidden themselves under the silk cushions in their tent. But the savages had not been fooled. A squad of Huns had found Tahmina soon enough, and dragged her out of the tent. Her brother had tried to come to her rescue, but it had been a futile gesture. The Huns had not killed the boy—alive, he would bring a good price on the slave market. They had simply split his scalp with a blow, casually, while they began stripping off his sister's clothing.

The Roman general had arrived then, accompanied by his cataphracts, and ordered the Huns to cease. Tahmina had described to Baresmanas how the Hun who held her by the hair had taunted Belisarius. And how the general, cold-faced, had simply spoken the name of his cataphract. A cataphract whose face was even colder, and as wicked-looking as a weasel. The cataphract had been as quick and deadly as a weasel, too. His arrows had slaughtered the Huns holding Tahmina like so many chickens.

Belisarius.

Strange, peculiar man. With that odd streak of mercy, lying under the edge of his ruthless and cunning brain.

Baresmanas turned his head, staring back at the fire. And now, for the first time since he learned of the Malwa butchery of Mesopotamia, could see the enemy roasting in the flames.

Belisarius.

Chapter 4

It was the most beautiful cathedral Justinian had ever seen. More beautiful, and more majestic, than he had even dreamed. The capstone to his life. The Hagia Sophia that he had planned to build.

The Mese, the great central thoroughfare of Constantinople, began at the Golden Gate and ended at the base of the cathedral. Down its entire length—here in scatters; there, mounded up in piles like so much offal—were the bodies of the plague victims.

Half the city was dead, or dying. The stench of uncollected rotting bodies mingled with the sickly smell of burning cadavers to produce a thick miasma, hanging over Constantinople like a constant fog. The same miasma that he had seen hanging over Italy, and North Africa, and every province which Belisarius had reconquered for him.

Justinian the Great. Who, in the name of restoring the greatness of the Roman Empire, had bankrupted the eastern half to destroy the western. And left the entire Mediterranean a war-ravaged breeding ground for the worst plague in centuries.

Justinian the Great. Who, more than any other man, caused the final splintering of Greco-Roman civilization.

✧　　✧　　✧

Justinian jerked erect in his chair.

"No more," he croaked. "I can bear it no longer."

He leaned forward and extended his arm, shakily. In the palm of his hand rested a shimmering, glowing object. A jewel, some might have called it. A magical gem.

Belisarius took the "jewel" from Justinian and replaced it in its pouch. A moment later, the pouch was once again suspended from his neck.

The "jewel" spoke in his mind.

He is not a nice man.

Belisarius smiled crookedly.

No, Aide, he is not. But he can *be a great man.*

The crystalline being from the future exuded skepticism.

Not sure. Not a nice man, at all.

"Are you satisfied, Justinian?" Belisarius asked.

The former emperor nodded.

"Yes. It was everything you said. I almost wish, now, that I had never asked for the experience. But I needed—"

He made a vague motion with his hand, as if to summon up unknown words.

Belisarius provided them:

"You needed to know if your suspicions were warranted, or not. You needed to know if the elevation of my stepson to the imperial throne stemmed from motives of personal ambition and aggrandizement, or—as I claimed at the time—from the needs of the war against the Malwa."

Justinian lowered his head. "I am a mistrustful man," he muttered. "It is rooted in my nature." He opened his mouth to speak again. Clamped it shut.

"There is no need, Justinian," said Belisarius. "There is no need."

The general's smile grew more crooked still. He had had this conversation once before, in a nightmare vision. "It would take you hours to say what you are trying to say. It will not come easily to you, if at all."

Justinian shook his head. "No, Belisarius. There *is* a need. For my sake, if not yours." Harshly: "I sometimes think losing my eyes improved my vision." He took a deep breath. Another. Then, like a stone might bleed:

"I apologize."

The third occupant of the room chuckled. "Even in this," he said, "you are still arrogant. Do you think you are the world's only sinner, Justinian? Or simply its greatest?"

Justinian swiveled his head.

"I will ignore that remark," he said, with considerable dignity. "And are *you* certain, Michael of Macedonia? Of this—creature—you call the Talisman of God?"

"Quite certain," replied the stony voice of the monk. "It is a messenger sent by the Lord to warn us all."

"Especially me," muttered Justinian. The blind man rubbed his mangled eye-sockets. "Has Theodora—?"

"No," replied Belisarius. "I offered, once, but she declined. She said she preferred to take the future as it comes, rather than seeing it in a vision."

"Good," stated Justinian. "She does not know about the cancer, then?"

It was Belisarius' turn to jerk erect in his chair, startled. "No. *Good God!* I never thought of that, when I offered to give her the jewel."

"Seventeen years," stated Justinian. His voice was very bleak. "She will die, then, from cancer."

The Macedonian cleared his throat. "If we succeed in defeating the Malwa—"

Justinian waved him off. "That's irrelevant, Michael. Whatever other evils the Malwa will bring, they are not responsible for cancer. And don't forget—the vision which the jewel gave me was of the future that would have been. The future where the Malwa were never elevated to world mastery by this demonic power called Link. The future where I remained emperor, and we reconquered the western Mediterranean."

He fell silent, head bowed. "I am right, Belisarius, am I not?"

Belisarius hesitated. He cast his thoughts toward Aide.

He is right, came the reply. Aide forestalled the next question:

And there is no cure for cancer. Not, at least, anything that will be within your capability for many, many years. Centuries.

Belisarius took a deep breath.

"Yes, Justinian. You are right. Regardless of what else happens, Theodora will die of cancer in seventeen years."

The former emperor sighed. "They burned out my tear ducts, along with my eyes. I damn the traitors for that, sometimes, even more than my lost vision."

Shaking himself, Justinian rose to his feet and began pacing about the room.

The plethora of statuary which had once adorned his room was gone, now. Theodora had ordered them removed, during Justinian's convalescence, worried that her blind husband might stumble and fall.

That fear had been quickly allayed. Watching the former Emperor maneuver through the obstacles littering the floor, Belisarius was struck again by the man's uncanny intelligence. Justinian seemed to know, by sheer memory, where every one of those potential obstructions lay, and he avoided them unerringly.

But the obstacles were no longer statuary. Justinian had no use, any longer, for such visual ornament. Instead, he had filled his room with the objects of his oldest and favorite hobby—gadgets. Half the floor seemed to be covered by odd contrivances and weird contraptions. Justinian even claimed that his blindness was an asset, in this regard, since it forced him to master the inner logic of his devices. Nor could Belisarius deny the claim. The general stared at one of the larger mechanisms in the room, standing in a corner. The device was quiescent, at the moment. But he had seen it work. Justinian had designed the thing based on Belisarius' own description of a vision given to him by Aide.

The first true steam engine ever built in Rome— or anywhere in the world, so far as he knew. He had not seen its like even during his long visit to Malwa India. The thing itself was not much more than a toy, but it was the model for the first locomotive which was already being planned. The day would come when Belisarius would be able to shuttle his troops from one campaign to another in the same way he had seen Aide describe in visions. Visions of a terrible carnage in the future which would be called the American Civil War.

A voice drew him back to the present.

"Seventeen years," mused Justinian sadly. "Whereas I, according to the jewel, will live to a ripe old age." Pain came to his ravaged face. "I had always hoped she might outlive me," he whispered. Justinian squared his shoulders.

"So be it. I will give her seventeen good years. The best I can manage."

"Yes," said Belisarius.

Justinian shook his head. "God, what a waste. Did the jewel ever show it to you, Belisarius? That future that would have been, had the Malwa never risen? The future where I had you ravage the western Mediterannean in the name of reconstituting Roman glory? Only to see half the Empire die from the plague while I used the royal treasury to build one grandiose, useless monument after another?"

"The Hagia Sophia was not useless, Justinian,"

demurred Belisarius. "It was—would have been—one of the world's genuine glories."

Justinian snorted. "I will allow that one exception. No—two. I also codified Roman law. But the rest? The—" He snapped his fingers. "That secretary of yours. You know, the foul gossip. What's his name?"

"Procopius."

"Yes, him. That fawning toad even wrote a book glorifying those preposterous structures. Did you see that?"

"Yes."

Michael spoke. "I hear you've dispensed with the reptile's services, now that you no longer need him to pass false rumors to the enemy. Good riddance."

Belisarius chuckled. "Yes, I did. I doubt very much that Malwa spies place any more credence in his claims that Antonina was spending all her time at our estate in Syria holding orgies in my absence."

"Not after she showed up at the Hippodrome with her force of Syrian grenadiers and smashed the Nika insurrection!" barked Justinian. The former emperor rubbed his eye-sockets. "Since he's out of work, Belisarius, send him to me. I'll give him a book to write. Just the kind of fawning propaganda he wrote for me in another future. Only it won't be called *The Buildings*. It'll be called *The Laws*, and it will praise to the skies the Grand Justiciar Justinian's magnificent work providing the Roman Empire with the finest legal system in the world."

Justinian resumed his seat. "Enough of that," he said. "There's something else I want to raise. Belisarius, I am a bit concerned about Antonina's expedition to Egypt."

The general cocked an eyebrow. "So am I!" he exclaimed. "She's my wife, you know. I'm not happy at the idea of sending her into a battle with only—"

"Nonsense!" snapped the former emperor. "The woman'll do fine, as far as any battles go. Don't underestimate her, Belisarius. Any woman that small who can slaughter half a dozen street thugs in a knife fight can handle that sorry bastard Ambrose. It's the *aftermath* I'm worried about. Once she's crushed this mini-rebellion, she'll be moving on. To the naval side of your campaign. What then?" He leaned forward, fixing Belisarius with his eyeless gaze.

"Who's going to *keep* Egypt under control?"

"You know our plans, Justinian. Hermogenes will assume command of the Army of Egypt and—"

The former Emperor snorted. "He's a soldier, man! Oh, a damned fine one, to be sure. But soldiers aren't much use, when it comes to suppressing the kind of religious fanatics who keep Egypt in a turmoil." He sighed heavily. "Trust me, Belisarius. I speak from experience. If you use a soldier to squash a monk, all you create is a martyr."

Justinian now turned to face Michael. "You're the key here, Michael. We will need your religious authority."

"And Anthony's," qualified the monk.

Justinian waved his hand impatiently. "Yes, yes, and the Patriarch's help, of course. But you are the key."

"Why?" demanded Michael.

Belisarius replied. "Because changing an empire's habits and customs—built through the centuries—will require religious fervor. A popular movement, driven by zeal and conviction. I don't disagree with Justinian, on that point. He's right—soldiers just create martyrs." He cleared his throat. "And, for the other— well, Anthony is as kindly, even saintly, a man as I ever hope to meet. The ideal Patriarch. But—"

A wintry smile came to the monk's gaunt face. "He is not given to smiting the unrighteous," concluded Michael. The Macedonian shifted position in his chair, much like a hawk sets his talons on a tree limb. "I have no such qualms, on the other hand."

"Rather the contrary," murmured Justinian.

The former Emperor smiled grimly. He quite approved of Michael of Macedonia. The Stylite monk was a holy man, which Justinian most certainly was not. Yet they shared a certainly commonality of spirit. A Thracian peasant and a Macedonian shepherd, as youths. Simple men, ultimately. And quite savage, each in their own way.

Belisarius spoke again, shaking his head. "We've already decided to send Michael's monks to Egypt, Justinian. I agree that they'll help. The fact remains, however, that without military force those monks will just wind up another brawling faction in the streets. Our military forces were already stretched—and now, I will be taking what few troops we can spare to combat the Malwa in Persia. We cannot divert those forces, Justinian, and the imperial treasury is too bare to finance the creation of a new army."

Suddenly, images flashed through Belisarius' mind.

Ranks of cavalrymen. Their weapons and armor, though well made, were simple and utilitarian. Over the armor, they wore plain tunics. White tunics, bearing red crosses. Parading through the main thoroughfare of a great city. Behind them marched foot soldiers, also wearing that simple white tunic emblazoned with a huge red cross.

The general burst into laughter.

Thank you, Aide!

He turned to Michael. "Have you chosen a name for your new religious order?"

The Macedonian grimaced. "Please, Belisarius. I did not create that order. It was created by others—"

"Inspired by your teachings," interjected Justinian.

"—and practically foisted upon me." The monk scowled. "I have no idea what to do with them. As much as anything else, I offered to send them with Antonina to Egypt because they were demanding some holy task of me and I couldn't think of anything else to do with them."

The general smiled. For all his incredible—even messianic—force of character, Michael of Macedonia was as ill-suited a man as Belisarius had ever met for the executive task of leading a coherent and disciplined religious movement.

"Someone must have brought them together," he said. "Organized them. It wasn't more than a month after you began your public sermons in the Forum of Constantine that bands of them began to appear in the streets spreading your message."

The Macedonian snorted. "Three of them, in fact. Their names are Mark of Athens, Zeno Symmachus, and Gaiseric. Zeno is an Egyptian, from the Fayum; Gaiseric, a Goth. Mark, of course, is Greek. Mark is orthodox, Zeno is a Monophysite, and Gaiseric is an Arian."

"And they get along?" asked Belisarius lightly.

Michael began to smolder, then relaxed. "Yes, Belisarius. They regard the issue of the Trinity as I do—a decoy of the Devil's, to distract men while Satan does his work." He smiled. "Not, mind you, that any room they jointly inhabit isn't occasionally filled with the sound of disputatious voices. But there is never any anger in it. They are each other's brothers, as they are mine."

"And what position do you advance, in these occasional disputes?" queried Justinian.

"You know perfectly well my position," snapped Michael.

The former emperor smiled. Justinian adored theological discussion. Other than Theodora's care, it had been the company of Michael and Patriarch Cassian which, more than anything, had enabled him to find his way through the darkness of the soul, in the months after his blinding.

"My opinion on the Trinity is orthodox, in the same way as Anthony's," stated Michael. "Though more plainly put." He snorted. "My friend Anthony

Cassian is Greek, and is therefore not satisfied with simple truth until he can parse it with clever Greek syllogisms and make it dance to dialectical Greek tunes. But I am not Greek. I am Macedonian. True, we are a related people. But to the Greeks God gave his intellect, and to us he gave his common sense."

Here, a wintry smile. "This, of course, is why the great Philip of my ancestry lost his patience and decided to subdue the whole fractious lot of quarreling southron. And why his son, the *Macedonian* Alexander, conquered the world."

"So the Greeks could inherit it," quipped Justinian.

"Place them in charge of the order, then," said Belisarius. "And find women with similar talents. There must be some."

Michael stroked his great beard. "Yes," he said, after a moment's thought. "Two, in particular, come immediately to mind. Juliana Syagrius and Helen of Armenia."

"Juliana Syagrius?" demanded Justinian. "The widow of—?"

Michael nodded. "The very same. Not all of my followers are common folk, Justinian. Any number of them are from the nobility—although usually from the equestrian order. Juliana is the only member of the senatorial classes who has responded to my teachings. She has even offered to place her entire fortune at my disposal."

"Good Lord!" exclaimed Justinian. "She's one of the richest people in the empire!"

Michael glared. "I am well aware of that, thank you! And what am I supposed to do with it? I have lived on alms since I was a youth—a habit I have no intention of changing."

The sour look on his face made plain the monk's attitude toward wealth. He began to mutter various phrases concerning camels and the eye of a needle.

Unkind phrases. *Very* unkind phrases, in point of fact.

Belisarius interrupted the gathering storm.

"You will use that fortune to buy arms and armor, Michael. And the provisions needed to support your new order."

"They will beg for their support, damn them!" snapped Michael. "Just as I do!"

Belisarius shook his head. "They will be too busy. Much too busy." The general smiled—broadly, not crookedly. "Yours will be a religious order of a new kind, Michael. A *military* order."

A name flashed through the general's mind.

"We will call them the *Knights Hospitaler*," he said, leaning forward in his chair.

Guided by Aide through the labyrinth of future history, Belisarius began to explain.

After Michael was gone, hurrying his way out of the Great Palace, Justinian sighed. "It will not work, Belisarius. Oh, to be sure, at first—" The former emperor, veteran of intrigue and maneuver, shook his head sadly. "Men are sinners. In time, your new monks will simply become another lot of ambitious schemers, grasping for anything in sight."

Image. A magnificent palace. Through its corridors, adorned with expensive statuary and tapestries, moved men in secretive discourse. They wore tunics—still white, with a simple red cross. But the tunics were silk, now, and the hilts of the swords suspended from their scabbards were encrusted with gems.

"True," replied Belisarius. His voice lost none of its good cheer. "But they will not lapse until Malwa is done. After that—" Belisarius shrugged. "I do not know much, Justinian, of the struggle in the far distant future in which we find ourselves ensnared. But I have always known we were on the right side, because our enemies—those who call themselves the 'new gods'—seek human perfection. There is no such thing, and never will be." He rose from his chair.

"You know that as well as I. Do you really think that your new laws and your judgements will bring paradise on earth? An end to all injustice?"

Justinian grunted sarcastically.

"Why do it, then?" demanded Belisarius.

"Because it's worth doing," growled Justinian.

The general nodded. "God judges us by what we seek, not what we find."

Belisarius began to leave. Justinian called him back.

"One other thing, Belisarius. Speaking of visions." The former Emperor's face twisted into a half-smile. It was a skeptical sort of expression—almost sardonic.

"Have you had any further visions about your little protegé in India? Is she making Malwa howl yet?"

Belisarius returned Justinian's smile with a shake of the head. "Shakuntala? I don't *know*—I've certainly had no visions! Aide is not a magician, Justinian. He is no more clairvoyant than you or I." The general smiled himself, now. There was nothing sardonic in that expression, though. And it was not in the least bit crooked. "I imagine she's doing splendidly. She's probably already got a little army collected around her, by now."

"Where is she?"

Belisarius shrugged. "The plan was for her to seek exile in south India. Her grandfather's the King of Kerala. Whether she's there or not, however, I don't know. I've received no word. That's the very reason Irene is accompanying Antonina to Egypt. She'll try to re-establish contact with Shakuntala and Rao through the Ethiopians."

"I can't say I'm happy about that, by the way," grumbled Justinian. "I didn't oppose the idea at the council, since you seemed so set upon it. But—Irene's a fiendishly capable spymaster. I'd be a lot happier if she were here at Theodora's side in the capital, keeping an eye on traitors."

Skeptically:

"Do you *really* think this little rebellion you took so much time—and money—to foster is anything but wishful thinking?"

Belisarius studied the blind man for a moment, before replying. Justinian, for all his brilliance, was ill-equipped by temperament to gauge the power of a popular rebellion. The man thought like an emperor, still. Belisarius suspected that he always had, even when he was a peasant himself.

"I know the girl, Justinian. You don't. For all her youth, she has the potential to be a great ruler. And in Rao she has one of the finest generals in India."

"So?" grunted Justinian. "If the success of your rebellion hinges so completely on two people, the Malwa can take care of that with a couple of assassinations."

Belisarius laughed.

"Assassinate *Rao?* He's the best assassin in India himself! God help the Malwa who tries to slip a knife into that man's back!" He shook his head. "As for Shakuntala—she's quite a proficient killer in her own right. Rao trained her, from the time she was seven. And she has the best bodyguards in the world. An elite Kushan unit, led by a man named Kungas."

The skepticism was still evident on the former emperor's face. Belisarius, watching, decided it was hopeless to shake Justinian's attitude.

He was not there, as I was—to see Shakuntala win the allegiance of the very Kushans who had been assigned by Malwa to be her captors. God, the sheer force in that girl's soul!

He turned away. Then, struck by a memory, turned back.

"Aide *did* give me a vision, once, while I was in

India. That vision confirmed me in my determination to set Shakuntala free."

Justinian cocked his head, listening.

"Many centuries from now, in the future—in *a* future, it might be better to say—all of Europe will be under the domination of one of history's greatest generals and conquerors. His name will be Napoleon. He will be defeated, in the end, brought down by his own over-weening ambition. That defeat will be caused, as much as anything, by a great bleeding wound in Spain. He will conquer Spain, but never rule it. For years, his soldiers will die fighting the Spanish rebellion. The rebels will be aided by a nation which will arise on the island we call Britannia. The Peninsular War, those islanders will call it. And when Napoleon is finally brought down, they will look back upon that war and see in it one of the chief sources of their victory."

Still nothing. Skepticism.

Belisarius shrugged. Left.

Outside, in the corridor, Aide spoke in his mind.

Not a nice man, at all.

The facets flashed and spun into a new configuration. Like a kaleidoscope, the colors of Aide's emotion shifted. Sour distaste was replaced by a kind of wry humor.

Of course, the Duke of Wellington was not a nice man, either.

In the room, Justinian remained in his chair. He spent some time pondering the general's last words, but not much. He was far more interested in contemplating a different vision. Somewhere, in the midst of the horror which the jewel had shown him, Justinian had caught a glimpse of something which gave him hope.

A statue, he had seen. Carved by a sculptor of the figure, to depict justice.

The figure had been blind.

"In the future," murmured the former emperor, "when men wish to praise the quality of justice, they will say that justice is blind."

The man who had once been perhaps the most capable emperor in the long history of the Roman Empire—and certainly its most intelligent—rubbed his empty eye-sockets. For the first time since his mutilation, the gesture was not simply one of despair and bitterness.

Justinian the Great. So, more than anything, had he wanted to be known for posterity.

Perhaps . . .

Theodora, at Belisarius' urging, had created a position specifically tailored for Justinian. He was now the empire's Grand Justiciar. For the first time in centuries, the law of Rome would be codified, interpreted and enforced by the best man for the task. Whatever had been his faults as an Emperor, there was no one who doubted that Justinian's was the finest legal mind in the empire.

Perhaps . . .

There had been Solomon and Solon, after all, and Hammurabi before them.

So why not add the name Justinian to that list?

It was a shorter list, now that he thought about, than the list of great emperors. Much shorter.

Chapter 5

MUZIRIS
Spring, 531 A.D.

"Any minute now," whispered the assassin at the window. "I can see the first contingents of her cavalrymen coming around the corner."

The leader of the Malwa assassination team came to the window. The lookout stepped aside. Carefully, using only one fingertip, the leader drew the curtain aside a couple of inches. He peered down onto the street below.

"Yes," he murmured. He turned and made a gesturing motion with his right hand. The other two assassins in the room came forward, carrying the bombard between them. They moved slowly and laboriously. The bombard was two feet long and measured eight inches across. It was made of wrought iron bars, square in cross section and an inch thick. The bars were welded together to form a rough barrel about six inches in diameter, which was then further strengthened with four iron hoops. A thick plate was welded to the back of the bars. The bombard was bolted down to a wooden base—teak, reinforced with brass strips—measuring three feet by two feet. The two men strained under the effort of carrying the device.

Part of their careful progress, however, was due to the obstacles in their way. The room was littered with the squalid debris of a poor family's cramped apartment.

As they came forward, they maneuvered around the bodies of the family who had once lived there. A man, his wife, her mother, and their four children. After killing the family, the assassins had piled the corpses in a corner. But the room was so small that the seven bodies still took up a full quarter of the floor space. Most of the floor was covered with blood, dried now, but still sticky. A swarm of flies covered the corpses and the bloodstains.

One of the assassins wrinkled his nose.

"They're already starting to stink," he muttered. "Damn southwest India and its fucking tropical climate—and we're in the hot season. We should have kept them alive until—"

"Shut up," hissed the leader. "What were we going to do? Guard them for almost a full day? The baby would have begun squawling, anyway."

His subordinate lapsed into sullen silence. A few seconds later, he and his companion levered the bombard onto the hastily-improvised firing platform which the assassination squad had erected that morning. It was a rickety contraption—simply a mounded up pile of the pallets and two wicker chairs which had been the murdered family's only furniture. But it would suffice. The bombard was not a full-size cannon. It would fire only one round, a sack full of drop shot. The recoil would send the bombard hurtling into the far wall, out of action.

That would be good enough. When she passed through the street below the window of the apartment, the Empress-in-exile of Andhra would be not more than twenty yards distant. There was nowhere for her to escape, either, even if the alarm was given at the last moment. The narrow street was hemmed in, on both sides, by mud-brick tenement buildings identical to the one in which the assassins lay waiting. At that point blank range, the cannister would sweep a large swath of the street clean of life.

"Here she comes," whispered the lookout. He was peering through a second window, now. Like his leader, he had drawn the curtain aside no more than an inch or two.

"Are you certain it is she?" demanded the leader. The lookout had been assigned to the squad because he was one of the few Malwa assassins who had personally seen the rebel Empress after her capture at the siege of Amaravati. The girl had aged, of course, since then. But not so much that the lookout wouldn't recognize her.

"It must be Shakuntala," he replied. "I can't see her face, because she's wearing a veil. But she's small—dark-skinned—wearing imperial regalia. Who else would it be?"

The leader scowled. He would have preferred a more positive identification, but—

He hissed an unspoken command to the other two assassins in the room. The command was unnecessary. They were already loading the gunpowder and the cannister round into the bombard. The leader scampered back and sighted along its length. He could only estimate the angle, since the curtain hanging in the window obscured his view of the street below. But the estimate would be good enough. It was not a weapon of finesse and pinpoint accuracy.

The leader made a last inspection of the cannon. He could not restrain a grimace. The blast and the recoil, confined in that small room, was almost certain to cause some injuries to the assassins themselves. Hopefully, those injuries would not disable any of them—not enough, at least, to prevent them making their escape in the chaos and confusion after Shakuntala and her immediate entourage were slaughtered.

"I wish they'd perfected those new impact fuses they've been working on," muttered one of the assassins. "Then we could have used a real cannon at long range. This misbegotten—"

"Why not wish she didn't have thousands of Maratha cavalrymen to protect her, while you're at it?" snarled the leader. "And those fucking Kushan cutthroats? Then we could have just slid a knife into her ribs instead of—"

"She's fifty yards away," hissed the lookout. "The first cavalry escorts are already passing below."

He plastered himself against the wall, crouching down as far as he could while still being able to peek through the window. The expression on his face, beneath the professional calm, was grim. He was almost certain to be scorched by the exhaust from the cannon blast. And there was also the possibility that a weak weld could result in the cannon blowing up when it was fired.

"Forty yards."

One of the two bombard handlers retreated to a far corner, curling into a ball. The other drew out a lighting device and ignited the slow match. After handing it to the squad leader, he hurried to join his comrade in the corner. The leader crouched next to the bombard's firehole, ready to set off the charge.

"Thirty-five yards," announced the lookout by the window. "Get ready."

The men in the room took a deep breath. They had already decided to fire the bombard when the Empress was twenty-five yards distant. They knew that Shakuntala's horse would travel less than five yards in the time it took for the slow match to ignite the charge. If all went as planned, the sack full of lead pellets would turn the ruler-in-exile of conquered Andhra into so much mincemeat.

The leader held up the slow match. Brought it close to the firehole.

"Thirty yards."

The door behind them erupted like a volcano. The first man coming through the door cut the squad leader aside before the assassin had time to do more than flinch. It was a brutal sword strike—not fatal, simply enough to hurl the man away from the cannon. Quick, quick. The assassin screeched with pain. His right arm dangled loose, half-severed at the elbow. The slow match fell harmlessly to the floor, hissing in a patch of blood.

The lookout at the window had time to recognize the man who killed him, before that same sword went into his heart. As agile and skilled as he was, the assassin had no more chance of evading that expert thrust than a tethered goat.

In the few seconds that it took him to die, the assassin tried to remember his killer's name. He knew the name, but it would not come. He knew only that he had been slain by the commander of Shakuntala's Kushan bodyguard. The man whom he and his squad simply called *Iron-face*.

One of the assassins huddled in the corner died soon thereafter, hacked into pieces by the three Kushan soldiers who piled into the room after their commander. The commander himself took care of the last Malwa. This one he did not kill outright. He wanted him for questioning. The Kushan lopped off the man's right hand as it came up holding a blade, then struck him senseless with a blow of the sword's pommel on the forehead.

The Kushan commander scanned the room. By now, with another five Kushans crowding in, the room was packed like a meat tin. Three of them had subdued the assassin whose arm the commander had half-severed upon bursting through the door.

"That's enough," he commanded. "See to the Empress."

"No need, Kungas," murmured one of his men. The Kushan soldier had pushed back the curtains in one of the windows. "She's on her way here already."

"Damn the girl!" growled Kungas. "I told her to stay back."

The Kushan commander strode to the window and glared out onto the street below. The Empress—the supposed "Empress" at the head of the column—was sitting on her horse. The girl was beginning to shake, now. A trembling hand came up and removed the veil. She wiped her face, smearing off some of the dye which had darkened her skin.

But Kungas was looking elsewhere, farther back along the column of cavalry escort. At the figure of another small girl, urging her horse forward. Unlike the "Empress," this girl was wearing simple and unadorned clothing: nothing more than a colorfully dyed tunic over pantaloons, the garments of a typical camp-follower—a soldier's common-law wife, perhaps. She, also, was dark-skinned. But her skin-tone was natural, and there was not the slightest trace of trembling in *her* hands.

"You're going to catch an earful," said the Kushan standing next to Kungas. "She looks angrier than a tigress guarding her cubs." He added cheerfully: "Of course, she's a *small* tigress. For what it's worth."

Kungas grunted. For a moment, something that might have been a sigh almost escaped his lips. But only for the briefest instant. Thereafter, the mask closed down.

On the street below, the true Empress halted her horse long enough to see to the well-being of her double. Then she dismounted and charged into the entrance of the tenement building.

She was lost from Kungas' sight, but he could hear her stamping up the narrow wooden stairs leading to the rooms on the upper floor. He could also hear her voice.

"How can such a small girl have such a loud voice?" wondered the other Kushan. "And how can slippers make such a stamping clatter?"

"Shut up, Kanishka," growled Kungas. Kanishka smiled seraphically.

The Empress' voice, coming from below:

"Never again, Kungas! Do you hear me? Never again!"

She burst into the room. Her eyes immediately fixed on those of Kungas. Black, hot eyes.

"Never again! Jijabai might have been killed!"

Kungas' iron face never wavered. Nor did his harsh voice. "So might you, Empress. And you are irreplaceable."

Shakuntala glared at him for a few seconds. Then, recognizing the futility of trying to browbeat the commander of her bodyguard, she glared around the room. When she saw the bodies of the family, she recoiled.

"Malwa beasts," she hissed.

"It's how we spotted them," said Kungas. "Our spies saw that this building seemed lifeless, everyone hiding in their rooms. Then they smelled the bodies."

He glanced at the bombard. Three of his men were already disarming the weapon. "But we only discovered them just in time. It was a well-laid ambush. Their only mistake was killing the family too soon."

"The baby would have squawled all night," commented Kanishka.

Kungas shrugged. "So? It would hardly be the only shrieking infant in a slum."

Shakuntala grimaced. Kungas, in his way, was the hardest man she had ever met.

She tore her eyes away from the pitiable sight of the dead family and stared at the assassins. "How many did you keep alive?"

"Two," replied Kanishka. "Better than we hoped."

"They'll talk," said Kungas. "Not easily—not Malwa assassins. But they'll talk."

"They won't know much," said Shakuntala.

"Enough. I was right. You will see."

The Empress stared at Kungas. After a moment, she looked away. "That it would come to this. My own grandfather."

"What did you expect?" came a voice from the door.

Shakuntala turned. Dadaji Holkar was standing in the doorway. Her imperial adviser's eyes scanned the room, coming to rest on the piled-up bodies of the dead family.

"Malwa," he said softly. The word was not condemning, nor accusatory. It was simply a term of explanation. Self-evident. His eyes returned to Shakuntala. "What did you expect, girl?" he repeated. "You threaten his kingdom with Malwa's gaze, and Malwa's fury. You organize a private army in his largest seaport. You disrupt his streets with riot and tumult."

"I did not! It was Malwa provocateurs who stirred up the Keralan mob against the refugees from Andhra!"

Holkar stroked his beard, smiling. "True. But it was your Maratha cavalrymen who sabred the mob and spit them on their lances."

"As well they should!" came her hot reply. "Many of those refugees were Maratha themselves!"

Holkar chuckled. "I am not arguing the merits of the thing, girl. I am simply pointing out that you have become a major—*embarrassment*—to the King of Kerala. That old man is no doting village grandfather, Shakuntala. He is as cold-blooded as any ruler needs to be. With the Malwa Empire now at war with Persia, he thinks he is safe from their ambitions—as long as he can avoid drawing their attention. The last thing he wants is his granddaughter forging a rebellion in the Deccan from a base in his own kingdom."

Holkar stepped into the room, avoiding the bodies which littered the floor. When he came up to the Empress, he placed a gentle hand on her shoulder. He was the only member of her entourage who ever took that liberty. He was the only one who dared.

"He is my grandfather," whispered Shakuntala. Her voice throbbed with pain. "I can remember sitting on his knee, when I was a little girl." She stared out the window, blinking away tears. "I did not really expect him to help me. But I still didn't think—"

"He may not have given the orders, Your Majesty," said Kungas. "Probably didn't, in fact." The Kushan commander gestured at the dead assassins. "These are Malwa, not Keralan."

Shakuntala's black eyes grew hard.

"So what? You predicted it yourself, Kungas. A Malwa assassination attempt, with the tacit approval of the Keralan authorities." She turned away, shaking her shoulders angrily. "The viceroy would not have done this on his own. He would not dare."

"Why not? He can deny everything." Again, Kungas gestured to the dead assassins. "Malwa, not Keralan."

Shakuntala stalked toward the door.

"He would not *dare*," she repeated. At the door, she cast a final glance at the dead family. "This was my grandfather's work," she hissed. "I will not forget."

A moment later, she was gone. The stamping

sounds of her slippered feet going down the stairs
came through the door. Dadaji Holkar and Kungas
exchanged a glance. The adviser's expression was
rueful. That of Kungas' was sympathetic, insofar as
a mask of iron can be said to have an expression.

Kanishka had finished tying a tourniquet around
the maimed arm of the Malwa assassin leader. He
stooped and hauled the man to his feet. The Malwa
began to moan. Kanishka silenced him with a savage
blow.

"Glad I'm not her imperial adviser," he muttered.
"Be like advising a tigress to eat rice." He draped the
unconscious assassin over his shoulder and made for
the door.

Then he said cheerfully, "A small tigress, true. For
all the good that'll do her grandpa."

Within a minute, the Kushans had cleared the
bodies from the small apartment—including, at
Kungas' command, the bodies of the dead family.
They would find a priest to give them the rites. The
two dead Malwa assassins would be tossed into a
dung-heap. After their interrogation, the two still alive
would follow them.

Kungas and Holkar were left alone in the room.

"That *was* very close," commented Holkar. The
statement was not a criticism, simply an observation.

"There will be another," replied the Kushan commander. "And another after that. It's obvious that the
Keralan authorities will turn a blind eye to Malwa
spies and assassins coming after her. We must get the
Empress to a place of safety, Dadaji—*and soon*. After
today, she will no longer let me use Jijabai as her
double."

Kungas' shoulders twitched. Coming from another
man, the gesture would have been called a shrug. "I
can only protect her for so long, here in Muziris."

Holkar broke into a little smile. "How about
Deogiri?" he asked. Then, laughed outright, seeing

Kungas' face. For once—just for an instant—there had been an expression on that iron mask. Kungas' eyes had actually widened. In another man, the gesture would have been called a goggle.

"*Deogiri?*" he choked. "*Are you mad?* The place is a Malwa stronghold! It's the largest city in Majarasthra, except for Bharakuccha. The Malwa have a garrison of—"

He broke off. The iron face was back. "You know something," he stated.

Dadaji nodded. "We just got word this morning, from a courier sent by Rao. Rao believes he can seize Deogiri. He has apparently managed to infiltrate thousands of his fighters into the city. The garrison is big, but—so he says, and he is a man who knows— sloppy and unprepared."

Kungas paced to the window. Stared out, as if he were gauging the Maratha cavalrymen in the street below.

Which, as a matter of fact, he was.

"Over three thousand of them, we've got now," he mused, "with more coming in every day as the word spreads."

"You've got more Kushans, too," pointed out Holkar.

"Six hundred," agreed Kungas. "Most of them are my own kinfolk, who deserted the Malwa once they heard the news of my change of allegiance. But a good third of them are from other clans. Odd, that."

From behind, unobserved by Kungas' sharp eyes, Holkar studied the stocky figure standing at the window. His face softened.

He had come to love Kungas, as he had few other men in his life.

Belisarius, of course, who had freed him from slavery and breathed new life into his soul. His son, still laboring in captivity somewhere in India along with the rest of Holkar's shattered family. Rao, the national hero of the Maratha people, whom he had idolized all his life. A brother, killed long ago, in battle against the Malwa. A few others.

But Kungas occupied a special place on that short list. He and Holkar were comrades-in-arms, united in a purpose and welded to a young Empress' destiny. Close friends, they had become—two men who would otherwise have been like total strangers, each to the other.

Dadaji Holkar, the former slave; low-caste by birth, and a scribe and scholar by profession. A man whose approach to the world was intrinsically philosophical, but whose soft and kindly soul had a rod of iron at its center.

Kungas, the former Malwa mercenary; a Kushan vassal by birth, a soldier by trade. A man whose view of the world was as pragmatic as a tiger's, and whose hard soul was much like his iron-masked face.

The one was now an imperial adviser—no, more. Shakuntala had named Holkar the *peshwa* of Andhra-in-exile, the premier of a people laboring in Malwa chains. The other, Kungas, was her chief bodyguard as well as one of her central military leaders.

The girl's own soul was like a lodestone for such men. Others had been drawn by that magnet in the months since she set herself up in exile at Muziris. Men like Shahji and Kondev, cavalry commanders—and those who followed them, Maratha horsemen burning to strike a blow at the Malwa.

Most were Maratha, of course, like Holkar himself. But not all. By no means. Men had come from all over the subcontinent, as soon as they heard that India's most ancient dynasty still lived, and roared defiance at the Malwa behemoth. Fighters, in the main—or simply men who wanted to be—from many Malwa subject nations. There were Bengali peasants in her small little army taking shape in the refugee camps at Muziris; not many, but a few. And Biharis, and Orissans, and Gujaratis.

Nor were all of them warriors. Hindu priests had come, too. Sadhus like Bindusara, who would hurl their own defiance at the Mahaveda abomination to their faith. And Buddhist monks, and Jains, seeking refuge in the shelter which the Satavahana dynasty had always given their own creeds.

In the few months since she had arrived in Muziris, Shakuntala's court-in-exile had become something of a small splendor. Modest, measured by formal standards; luminous, measured by its quality.

But of all those men who had come, Holkar treasured one sort above all others.

Malwa power rested on four pillars:

First and foremost, their monopoly of gunpowder and their Ye-tai barbarians.

Holkar intended to steal the first, or get it from the Romans. The other—*death to the Ye-tai*.

Then, there were the two other pillars—the soldiers who formed the Malwa army's true elite: the Rajputs and the Kushans.

No Rajputs had come. Holkar would have been astonished if they had. The Rajputs had sworn allegiance to the Malwa empire, and they were a people who held their honor sacred.

Still, he had hopes. Perhaps someday—what man can know?

But the Kushans—ah, that was a different matter. A steadfast folk, the Kushans. But they had none of Rajputana's exaggerated concept of honor and loyalty. The Kushans had been a great people themselves, in their day, conquerors and rulers of Central Asia and Northern India. But that day was long gone. Persia had conquered half their empire, and the other half had been overrun by the Ye-tai. For centuries, now, the Kushans had been mere vassals under the thumb of others, valued for their military skills, but otherwise

treated with disdain. Their loyalty to Malwa, Dadaji
had often thought, was much like Kungas' face. To
the outer world, iron; but still a mask, when all was
said and done.

Kungas' voice interrupted his little reverie.

"Odd," he repeated. He turned away from the window. "We started with only thirty. The men in my
immediate command. I expected I would draw some
of my own kinfolk, since I am high-ranked in the clan.
But the others—"

Holkar shook his head. "I do not think it strange
at all, my friend."

He reached out his hand and tapped his finger on
Kungas' chest. It was like tapping a cuirass. "The
Buddha's teachings still lurk there, somewhere inside
your skeptical soul."

Kungas' lips quirked, just a bit. "I doubt that,
Dadaji. What good did the Buddha do us, when the
Ye-tai ravaged Peshawar? Where was he, when Malwa
fit us with the yoke?"

"Still there," repeated the peshwa. "You disbelieve?
Think more about those Kushans who have come,
from other clans. What brought them here, Kungas?"

The Kushan looked away. Holkar drove on. "I will
tell you, skeptic. Memory brought them here. The
memory of Peshawar—and Begram, and Dalverzin
and Khalchayan, and all the other great cities of the
Kushan realm. The memory of Emperor Vima, and
his gigantic irrigation works, which turned the desert
green. The memory of Kanishka the Great, who
spread Buddhism through half of Asia."

Kungas shook his head. "Ah! Gone, all gone. It is
the nature of things. They come, they go."

Dadaji took Kungas by the arm, and began leading him out of the blood-soaked, fly-infested room.
"Yes, they do. And then they come back. Or, at least,
their children, inspired by ancient memory."

Irritably, Kungas twitched off Holkar's hand. They

were in the narrow corridor now, heading for the rickety stairs leading to the street below.

"Enough of this foolishness," he commanded. "I am a man who lives in the present, and as much of the future as I can hope to see—which is not much. Tell me more of Rao's plan for Deogiri. If he takes the city, he cannot hold it alone for more than a year. Not even Deogiri is that great a fortress—not against the siege cannons which Venandakatra will bring to bear. He will need reinforcement. And then, we will need—somehow!—to maintain a supply route. *How?* And we will need to get cannons of our own. *How?* From the Romans?"

He stopped, from one step to the next, and gave Holkar a sharp glance. "Ha! They have their own problems to deal with. Belisarius will be marching into Persia, soon. You know that as well as I do. That will help, of course—help greatly. The Malwa will not be able to release forces from their Persian campaign—not with Belisarius at their front— but Venandakatra still has a powerful army of his own, in the Deccan."

He strode on, almost stamping down the stairs. Over his shoulder:

"So—tell me, philosopher! How will we get the cannons?"

Dadaji did not reply until both men were out on the street. He took a deep breath, cleansing the stench of death out of his nostrils. Then said, still smiling:

"Some of them, we will steal from the Malwa. As for the rest—Belisarius will provide."

Kungas' brow lowered, slightly. On another man, that would have been a fierce scowl. "He is thousands of miles away, Dadaji!"

Holkar's smile was positively serene, now. For an instant, Kungas was reminded of a statue of the Buddha. "He will provide, skeptic. Trust me in this.

Belisarius set this rebellion of ours in motion in the first place. He has not forgotten us. Be sure of it."

Kungas made his little version of a shrug, and strode off behind the diminishing figure of his Empress. Holkar remained behind, staring after him.

"Trust me in this, my friend," he whispered. "Of five things in this world I am certain. Malwa will fall. My Empress will restore Andhra. Peshawar will rise again. Belisarius will not fail us. And I—"

His eyes teared. He could not speak the words.

I will find my wife and children. Wherever the Malwa beasts have scattered them, I will find them.

Chapter 6

"I will not take Maurice with me to Egypt, Belisarius. *Absolutely not.* So stop pestering me about it. And stop pestering me about Valentinian and Anastasius. I refuse to take them either."

Belisarius stared at his wife for a moment, before blowing out his cheeks. He leaned back in his chair and glared at Antonina. "You do not understand the danger, woman! You need the best military adviser in the world. *And* the best bodyguards."

Seeing the set and stubborn expression on his wife's face, and the way she clasped her hands firmly on the table between them, Belisarius cast a furious glare about the salon. His hot eyes scanned the mosaics which decorated the walls of their small palace within the imperial complex, without really seeing them. The gaze did, however, linger for a moment on a small statue perched on a corner stand.

"Damn cherub," he growled. "What's that naked little wretch smirking about?"

Antonina tried to fight down a smile. Her struggle was unsuccessful, however, and the sight of her quirking lips only added to her husband's outrage.

Belisarius grit his teeth and twisted in his chair, swiveling his head to the right. "Sit down, Maurice!" he commanded. "Damn you and your stiff ways! I promoted you, remember? You're a general yourself, now. A chiliarch, no less!" Belisarius made a curt motion with his hand, as if to sweep Maurice forward. "So sit down!"

The commander of Belisarius' personal retinue of bucellarii shrugged, stepped forward, and pulled up a chair. As soon as he took his seat at the table, Belisarius leaned toward him and said:

"Explain it to her, Maurice. She won't listen to me, because she thinks I'm just being a fretful husband. But she'll listen to you."

Maurice shook his head. "No."

Belisarius' eyes widened. "No?" His eyes bulged. "*No?*" His next words were not, entirely, coherent.

Maurice grinned at Antonina.

"Never actually seen him gobble before. Have you?"

Antonina matched his grin. "Oh, any number of times." The grin began a demure smirk. "Intimate circumstances, you understand?"

Maurice nodded sagely. "Of course. Dancing naked on his chest, that sort of thing."

"Not to mention the whip and the iced—"

"*Enough!*" roared Belisarius. He slammed his fist on the table.

Antonina and Maurice peered at him with identical, quizzical expressions. Much like two owls might study a bellowing mouse.

"He usually does that much better, I seem to recall," mused Antonina.

"*Much* better," agreed Maurice. "The key is understatement. The sense of steel under the soft voice."

Belisarius began to roar again; but, seeing the widening grins, managed to bring himself under control.

"*Why not?*" he demanded, through clenched teeth.

Maurice's grin faded. The grizzled veteran stroked his stiff, curly gray beard. "I won't do it," he replied, "because she's right and you're wrong. You *are* thinking like a fretful husband—instead of a general."

He waved down Belisarius' protest. "She doesn't need me because she's not going to be fighting pitched battles on the open field against vastly superior forces. *You are.*"

Antonina nodded.

Again, Belisarius began to protest; again, Maurice drove him down.

"Besides, she'll have Ashot. That stubby little Armenian may not have quite as much battlefield experience as I do, but he's not far short of the mark. You know that as well as I do. He's certainly got the experience to handle whatever Antonina will run up against in Alexandria."

"But—"

"Oh—*be quiet*, young man," snapped Maurice. For just an instant, the chiliarch's stony face reverted to an expression he had not worn in years. Not since the days he had taken under his wing a precocious teenage officer, fresh from his father's little estate in Thrace, and taught him the trade of war.

"Have you *already* forgotten your own battle plan?"

Belisarius sat back. Maurice snorted.

"Thought so. Since when do you subordinate strategy to tactics, young man? Alexandria's just a step on the road. Your whole strategy against the Malwa pivots on seapower. While you distract them in Persia, Antonina will lead a flanking attack against the enemy's logistics, in alliance—we hope—with the Kingdom of Axum. The Ethiopians, with their naval power, are critical to that plan. For that matter, the Axumite navy will be essential for providing support to the rebellion in Majarashtra which you did everything in your power to foment, while you were in India. They'll need cannons, gunpowder—everything you've talked about supplying them. That's why you've always insisted on building our armaments industry in Alexandria. So we can provide logistical support for the Ethiopians and the Indian rebellion."

The chiliarch took a deep breath. "For all those reasons, Ashot is far better suited to serve as her adviser than I am. The man's a former seaman. What I know about boats—" He snapped his fingers. "Not to mention the Ethiopians," he rolled on. "Ashot's familiar with them—even speaks the language. I know exactly two words in Ge'ez. Beer, and the future subjunctive tense of the verb 'to copulate.' That'll be useful, coordinating an allied naval campaign and a transoceanic logistics route!"

Belisarius slumped into his chair.

"All right," he said sourly. "But I still insist that she take Valentinian and Anastasius! They're the best fighters we've got. She'll need the protection they can—"

"For what?" demanded Maurice. He planted his thick hands on his knees and leaned forward. For a moment, he and Belisarius matched glares. Then Maurice's lips quirked. He cocked an eye at the little Egyptian woman sitting across the table.

"Are you planning to lead any cavalry charges, girl?"

Antonina giggled.

"Furious boarding parties, storming across the decks of ships?"

Giggle, giggle.

"Leading the troops scaling the walls of a town under siege?"

Giggle, giggle, giggle.

"Cut and thrust? Hack and hew?"

The giggles erupted into outright laughter.

"Actually," choked Antonina, "I was thinking more along the lines of guiding from the rear. You know. Ladylike."

She leaned back, arching her neck haughtily, and began pointing with an imperious finger. "You there!

That way. And you—over there. Move smartly, d'you hear?"

Belisarius rubbed his face. "It's not that simple, Maurice—and you know it, even if Antonina doesn't."

For a moment, the old crooked smile came back. A feeble travesty of it, rather.

"Aren't you the one who taught me the law of battle? 'Everything gets fucked up as soon as the enemy arrives. That's why—' "

"—he's called the enemy," concluded Maurice. The veteran shook his head. "That's not the point, Belisarius. It may well happen, despite all our plans, that Antonina finds herself swept up in the fray. So be it. She'll still have hundreds of Thracian bucellarii protecting her, each and every one of whom—as you damn well know—will lay down his life for her, if need be. None of them may be quite as murderous as Valentinian or Anastasius, but they're still the best soldiers in the world. In my humble opinion. If they can't protect her, Valentinian and Anastasius won't make the difference.

"*Whereas*," he snarled, "the two of them might very well make the difference for *you*. Because unlike Antonina, you *will* be leading cavalry charges and hacking and hewing way more than any respectable general has any business doing."

Glare.

"As you well know."

Maurice stared at Belisarius in silence. The general slouched further down in his chair. Further. Further.

"Never actually seen him pout before," mused the chiliarch. Again, he cocked his eye at Antonina. "Have you?"

"Oh, certainly!" piped the little woman. "Any number of times. Intimate circumstances, of course. When I have a headache and refuse to smear olive oil all over his—"

"Enough," whined Belisarius.

Antonina and Maurice peered at him with identical, quizzical expressions. Much like two mice might study a whimpering piece of cheese.

Several hours later, Belisarius was in a more philosophical mood.

"I suppose it'll work out all right, in the end," he said, almost complacently.

Antonina levered herself up on her elbow and smiled down at her husband.

"Feeling less anxiety-ridden, are we?"

Belisarius stretched out his legs and clasped his hands behind his head.

"Now that I've had more time to think about it," he allowed graciously, "I've decided that perhaps Maurice was—"

"Liar!" laughed Antonina, slapping his arm. "You haven't been doing any thinking at all since we came to bed! Other than figuring out new and bizarre positions from which to stick your—"

"Don't be coarse, woman," grunted Belisarius. "Besides, I didn't hear you complaining. Rather the opposite, judging from the noises you were making."

"You didn't hear me claim that I was enjoying the metaphysics of the enterprise, either."

She sprawled flat on the bed, aping her husband's pose. Hands clasped behind her head, legs stretched out.

"I say," she pontificated, "now that I've had a bit of time to ponder the question—in between getting fucked silly—I have come to the conclusion that perhaps that uncouth Maurice fellow may have raised the odd valid point, here and there."

Belisarius eyed his wife's naked body, glistening with sweat. Antonina smiled seraphically. She took a deep breath, swelling her heavy breasts, then languidly spread her legs.

"Ontologically speaking, of course," she continued,

"the man's daft. But the past several hours of epistemological discourse have led me to the tentative conclusion that perhaps—"

She spread her legs wider. Took another deep breath.

"—some of the fellow's more Socratic excogitations may have elucidated aspects of the purely phenomenological ramifications of—"

Belisarius discarded all complacency. Antonina stopped talking then, though she was by no means silent.

Some time later, she murmured, "Yes, all anxieties seem to be gone."

"That's because my brains are gone," came her husband's sleepy reply. "Fucked right out of my head."

In the morning, Photius made an entrance into his parents' sleeping chamber and perched himself upon their bed. Despite the many other changes in his life, the boy insisted on maintaining this precious daily ritual. A pox on imperial protocol and decorum.

The gaggle of servants and bodyguards who now followed the young Emperor everywhere remained outside in the corridor. The servants thought the entire situation was grotesque—and quite demeaning to their august status as imperial valets and maids. But they maintained a discreet silence. The bodyguards were members of the general's Thracian bucellarii, led by a young cataphract named Julian. Julian had been assigned the task of serving as Photius' chief bodyguard for two reasons. First, he was married to Hypatia, the young woman who had been Photius' nanny for years. (And still was, though she now bore the resplendent title of "imperial governess.") Second, for all his youth and cheerful temperament, Julian was a very tough soldier. Julian and the men under his command had made quite clear upon assuming their new duties that they were not even remotely interested in listening to the complaints of menials. So, while Photius enjoyed his private moment with his parents, his bodyguards chatted amiably in the corridor outside and his servants nursed their injured pride.

Photius' stay in his parents' bedroom was longer than usual. His stepfather was leaving that day, to begin his new campaign in Mesopotamia. Photius no longer felt the same dread of that prospective absence that he once had. The boy's confidence in Belisarius' ability to overcome all obstacles and perils was now positively sublime. But he would miss him, deeply. More deeply now, perhaps, than ever before.

Eventually, however, he emerged. A new sense of duty had fallen on the boy's little shoulders, and he knew that his stepfather had many responsibilities of his own that day.

"All right," he sighed, after closing the door behind him. "Let's go. What's first?"

Julian grinned down at him. "Your tutor in rhetoric insists—*insists*—that you must see him at once. Something to do with tropes, I believe. He says your slackness in mastering synecdoche has become a public scandal."

Glumly, Photius began trudging down the corridor. "That's great," he muttered. "Just great." The boy craned his neck, looking up at Julian's homely, ruddy-hued face. "Do you have any idea how *boring* that man is?"

"Look at it this way, Emperor. Some day you'll be able to have him executed for high tedium."

Photius scowled. "No I won't. I think he's already dead."

Trudge, trudge.

"Life was a lot more fun, before they made me Emperor."

Trudge, trudge.

❖   ❖   ❖

Before mounting his horse, Belisarius gave Antonina a last, lingering embrace.

"How long, do you think?" she whispered.

Her husband shrugged. "Impossible to tell, love. If things go as we've planned—and that's a big if— we won't see each other for a year and a half, thereabouts. You'll have to wait until July of next year for the monsoon to be blowing the way we need it."

She grimaced. "What a way to meet."

Belisarius smiled. "That's *if* things go as planned. If they don't—who knows? We may meet sooner."

Staring up at him, Antonina found it impossible to match his smile. She knew the unspoken—and far more likely—corollary.

If our plans fail, one or both of us will probably be dead.

She buried her face into his shoulder. "Such a long time," she murmured. "You've only been back for a few months since your trip to India. And that lasted a year and a half."

Belisarius stroked her long black hair. "I know. But it can't be helped."

"*Damn Theodora*," hissed Antonina. "If it weren't for her obsession with keeping the gunpowder weapons under female control, I wouldn't have to—"

"That's nonsense!" snapped Belisarius. He took his wife by the shoulders and held her away from him. Then, with none of his usual whimsy, said:

"Even if Theodora didn't have her foibles, *I'd* insist that you command the Theodoran Cohort. You're the best person for the job. It's that simple."

Antonina stared back at him for a moment, before lowering her eyes. "So *long*," she whispered. "A year and a half." Suddenly, unexpectedly, she smiled. "But at least we'll be able to stay in touch. I almost forgot—a present came from John of Rhodes yesterday."

She turned and summoned a servant standing

nearby in the courtyard. The man advanced, bearing a package wrapped in heavy layers of wool.

Antonina took the package from him and unfolded the cloth. Within, carefully nestled, were two identical objects.

She held one of them out to her husband.

"Here they are. John's first telescopes. One for you and one for me."

Grinning delightedly, Belisarius immediately began looking through the telescope. He became so entranced with the marvelous contrivance that he momentarily forgot everything else, until Antonina's little cough brought him back.

"Wonderful," he said, wrapping the telescope back into the woolen cloths. "With these, and the new semaphore stations, we'll be able to communicate within days."

Antonina chuckled. "Once the stations are built, that is. And assuming John can produce enough of the telescopes."

"They will and he will," said her husband confidently. He stroked her cheek. "Count on it, love. Within a few months, you'll get your first message from me."

There was nothing more to be said. For a moment, husband and wife gazed at each other. Then, a last embrace; a last kiss. Belisarius mounted his horse and rode out of the courtyard, Maurice at his side. His two personal bodyguards, Anastasius and Valentinian, followed just behind.

At the gate, Belisarius turned in his saddle and waved. Antonina did not wave back. She simply held up the telescope.

"I'll be waiting for your message!" she shouted.

An hour later, Irene arrived, bearing her own cloth-wrapped gifts.

"Don't drop them!" she warned Antonina, as she

passed the bundle over. "I stole them from Theodora's own wine cellar. Best vintage in the Roman Empire."

Antonina staggered a bit, from the weight.

"Mother of God, how many bottles did you bring?"

Irene propelled her little friend down the corridor. "As many as we need to get you through the day. Tradition, girl, tradition. The last time Belisarius went off on one of these quests, you and I got blind drunk. Well, you did. I was simply there to lend a comforting shoulder."

"Lying wench!" squawked Antonina. "You passed out before I did."

"A fable," stated Irene firmly. "I fell asleep, that's all."

Antonina snorted. "Sure. On the floor, flat on your belly."

"I've only got your word for that," came the dignified response. "Hearsay, pure hearsay."

Once in the salon, Antonina lined up the bottles on a side table. "Like so many soldiers," she murmured admiringly.

Irene seized the first bottle. "It'll be a massacre. Get the goblets."

Two hours later, well into the carnage, Antonina hiccuped.

"'Nough o' this maudlinnininess!" Another hiccup. "Le'ss look t'the future! Be leaving soon, we will. For Egypt. 'S'my homeland, y'know?" Hiccup. "Land o' my birt. *Birth*."

Studiously, she poured more wine into her goblet. "I'm still s'prised Theodora agreed t'let you go," she said. "Never thought she let her chief spy"— giggle—"spy-*ess*, should say, out of her zight. Sight."

Irene's shrug was a marvel—a simple gesture turned into a profound, philosophical statement.

"What else c'ld she do? *Somebody* has to go to India. *Somebody* 'as to rish—re-ish—" Deep breath; concentration. "*Re-es-ta-blish* contact with Shakuntala."

Irene levered herself up on the couch, assuming a proud and erect stance. The dignity of the moment, alas, was undermined by flatulence.

"How gross," she pronounced, as if she were discussing someone else's gaucherie. Then, breezed straight on to the matter at hand. Again, a pronouncement:

"I am the obvious person for the job. My qualifications are immense. Legion, I dare say."

"Ha!" barked Antonina. "You're a woman, that's it. Who else would Theodora trust for that kind of—of—of—" She groped for the words.

"Subtle statecraft," offered Irene. "Deft diplomacy."

Antonina sneered. "I was thinking more along the lines of—of—"

"Sophisticated stratagems. Sagacious subterfuges."

"—of—of—"

"Dirty rotten sneaky—"

" 'At's it! 'At's it!"

Both women dissolved into uproarious laughter. This went on for a bit. Quite a bit. A sober observer might have drawn unkind conclusions.

Eventually, however, they settled down. Another bottle was immediately brought to the execution block. Half the bottle gone, Antonina peered at Irene solemnly.

"Hermogenes'll be staying wit' me, you know. In Egypt. After we part comp'ny and you head off t'India. You'll be having your own heartbreak then. But we prob'ly won' be able to commimmi—*commiserate*—properly. Then. Be too busy. Ressaponzabilities. So we better do it now."

Irene sprawled back on her couch. "Too late. 'S'already done." She shook her head sadly. "Hermogenes and I are *hic*—" Hiccup. "Are *hic*— Dammit! Hist—*hic*story. Dammit! *History.*"

Antonina's eyes widened.

"What? But I heard—rumor flies—he asked you to marry him."

Irene winced. "Yes, he did. I'd been dreading it for months. That was the death-knell, of course."

Seeing her friend's puzzled frown, Irene laughed. Half-gaily; half-sadly.

"Sweet woman," she murmured. "You forget Hermogenes's not Belisarius." She spread her hands ruefully. Then, remembering too late that one hand held a full wine goblet, stared even more ruefully at the floor.

"Sorry about that," she muttered.

Antonina shrugged. "We've got servants to clean it up. Lots of 'em."

"Don't care about th'floor! Best wine in the Roman Empire." She tore her eyes from the gruesome sight. Tried to focus on Antonina.

"Something about Hermogenes not being Belisarius," prompted the little Egyptian. "But I don't see the point. *You* don't have a disreputable past to live down, like I did." Giggle. "Still do, actually. That's the thing about the past, you know? Since it's over it never goes away and you're always stuck with the damned thing." Her eyes almost crossed with deep thought. "Hey, that's philosophical. I bet even Plato never said it so well."

Irene smiled. "It's not the past that's the problem. With me and Hermogenes. It's the *future*. Hermogenes—" She waved her hand again, but managed to restrain the gesture before adding further insult to the best vintage in the Roman Empire. "—Hergomenes," she continued. "He's a sweet man, no doubt about it. But—conventional, y'know? Outside of military tactics, anyway. He wants a proper Greek wife. Matron. Not—" She sighed, slumping back into the couch. "Not a spymaster who's out and about doing God knows what at any hour of the day and night."

Irene stared sadly at her half-filled wine goblet. Then, drained away her sorrows.

Antonina peered at her owlishly.

"You sure?" she asked. Irene lurched up and tottered over to the wine-bearing side-table. Another soldier fell to the fray.

"Oh, yes," she murmured. She turned and stared down at Antonina, maintaining a careful balance. "Do I really seem like the matron-type to you?"

Antonina giggled; then, guffawed.

Irene smiled. "No, not hardly." She shrugged fatalistically. "Fact is, I don't think I'll ever marry. I'm jus—I don' know. Too—I don' know. Something. Can't imagine a man who'd live wit' it."

She staggered back to her couch and collapsed upon it.

Antonina examined her. "Does that bother you?" she asked, very slowly and carefully.

Irene stared at the far wall. "Yes," she replied softly. Sadly.

But a moment later, with great vehemence, she shook her head.

"'Nough o' this maudilinitity!" she cried, raising her goblet high. "'Ere's to adaventureness!"

Two hours later, Antonina gazed down at Irene in triumph. "Belly down, onna floor, jus' like I said."

She lurched to her feet, holding the last wine bottle aloft like a battle standard. "Vittorous again!" she cried. Then, proving the point, collapsed on top of her friend.

The servants who carried the two women into Antonina's bedroom a short time later neither clucked with scandal nor muttered with disrespect. Not with Julian and three other grinning bucellarii following close behind, ready to enforce Thracian protocol.

"Let 'em sleep it off together," commanded Julian. He turned to his comrades.

"Tradition."

Thracian heads nodded solemnly.

The next morning, after he entered the bedchamber, Photius was seized with dismay.

"Where's my mother?" he demanded.

Irene's eyes popped open. Closed with instant pain.

"Where's my mother?" he cried.

Irene stared at him through slitted eyelids.

"Who're you?" she croaked.

"I'm the Emperor of Rome!"

Irene hissed. "Fool boy. Do you know how many Roman emperors have been assassinated?"

"Where's my mother?"

Her eyelids crunched with agony. "Yell one more time and I'll add another emperor to the list."

She dragged a pillow over her head. From beneath the silk-covered cushion her voice faintly emerged:

"Go away. If you want your stupid mother—the drunken sot—go look for her somewhere else."

"Where's my mother?"

"Find the nearest horse. Crazy woman'll be staring at it."

After the boy charged out of the room, heading for the stables, Irene gingerly lifted the pillow. The blinding sight of sunrise filtering through the heavy drapes immediately sent her scurrying back for cover. Only her voice remained at large in the room.

"Stupid fucking tradition."

Moan.

"Why can't that woman just commit suicide like any reasonable abandoned wife?"

Moan.

Chapter 7

MESOPOTAMIA
Summer, 531 A.D.

When he encountered the first units from the Army of Syria, just outside Callinicum, Belisarius heaved a small sigh of relief.

Baresmanas, riding next to him at the head of the column, said nothing. But the very stillness of his face gave him away.

"Go ahead and laugh," grumbled Belisarius.

Baresmanas did not take Belisarius up on the offer. Diplomatic tact was far too ingrained in his habits. He simply nodded his head, and murmured in return:

"There are certain disadvantages to elite troops from the capital, accustomed to imperial style. It cannot be denied."

The sahrdaran twisted in his saddle and looked back at the long column. The cavalrymen were riding along a road near the right bank of the Euphrates.

The road was not paved, but it was quite wide and well-maintained. The road ran from Callinicum to the Cilician Gates, passing through the river towns of Barbalissus and Zeugma. It was the principal route bearing trade goods between the Roman Empire and Persia.

Belisarius' own bucellarii rode at the head of the column—a thousand cataphracts, three abreast, maintaining good order. Behind them came the small contingent of artillery wagons and ambulances, along with the ten rocket-bearing chariots which the general had dubbed *katyushas*. These vehicles were also maintaining a good order.

Then—

Straggling and straying, drifting and disjointed, came the remaining twenty-five hundred heavy cavalry in Belisarius' little army.

The majority of these—two thousand men—were from the Constantinople garrison. The remainder were from Germanicus' Army of Illyria. The Illyrians had maintained a semblance of good order for the first few hundred miles of their forced march. Unlike the troops from the capital, they had some recent experience on campaign. But even they, by the time the army passed through the Cilician Gates into the northern desert of Syria, had become as disorganized as the Greek cataphracts.

Disorganized—and exceedingly disgruntled.

The troops were much too far back for Baresmanas to hear their conversations, but he had no difficulty imagining them. He had been listening to their grousing for days, even weeks. The troops from Constantinople, in particular, had not been hesitant in making their sentiments known, each and every night, as they slumped about their campfires.

Crazy fucking Thracian.

How did this lunatic ever get to be a general, anyway?

By the time we get there, a litter of kittens could whip us, we'll be so worn out.

Crazy fucking Thracian.

How did this lunatic ever get to be a general, anyway?

"You *have* been pushing them rather hard," said Baresmanas.

Belisarius snorted. "You think so?" He turned in his own saddle, scowling. "In point of fact, Baresmanas, the pace we've been maintaining since we left Constantinople is considerably *less* than my own troops are accustomed to. For my bucellarii, this has been a pleasant promenade."

His scowl deepened. "*Two months*—to cover six hundred miles. Twenty miles a day, no better. For a large infantry army, that would be good. But for a small force of cavalrymen—on decent roads, most of the time—it's disgraceful."

Now, Barasmanas did laugh. More of a dry chuckle, perhaps. He pointed to the small group, led by two officers, trotting toward them from the direction of Callinicum.

"I take it you think these Syrian lads will be a good influence."

Belisarius examined the approaching Roman soldiers. "Not exactly. Those damned garritroopers are too full of themselves to take a bunch of scruffy border troops as an *example*. But I do believe I can use them to shame the bastards."

The oncoming officers were now close enough to discern their individual features.

"If I'm not mistaken," commented Baresmanas, "the two in front are Bouzes and Coutzes. The same brothers whom we captured just a few days before the battle at Mindouos. While they were—ah—"

"Leading a reconnaisance in force," said Belisarius firmly.

"Ah. Is that what it was?"

The sahrdaran's eyebrows lifted.

"At the time, I had the impression the headstrong fellows were charging about trying to capture a mysterious pay caravan which, oddly enough, was never found by anyone."

Belisarius shook his head sadly. "Isn't it just terrible? The way vicious rumors get started?"

Very firmly:

"Reconnaissance in force."

Less than a minute later, the oncoming Romans reached Belisarius. The general reined in his horse. Behind him, the long column came to a halt. A moment later, Maurice drew up alongside.

Bouzes and Coutzes sat in their saddles stiff-backed and erect. Their young faces were reasonably expressionless, but it took no great perspicacity to deduce that they were more than a bit apprehensive. Their last encounter with Belisarius had been unfortunate, to say the least.

But Belisarius had known that the brothers would be leading the troops from the Army of Syria, and he had already decided on his course of action. Whatever hotheaded folly the two had been guilty of in the past, both Sittas and Hermogenes had been favorably impressed by the brothers in the three years which had elapsed since the battle of Mindouos.

So he greeted them with a wide smile and an outstretched hand, and made an elaborate show of introducing them to Baresmanas. He was a bit concerned, for a moment, that the brothers might behave rudely toward the sahrdaran. Bouzes and Coutzes, during the time he had worked with them leading up to the battle of Mindouos, had been quite vociferous regarding their dislike for Persians. But the brothers allayed that concern immediately.

As soon as the introductions were made, Coutzes said to Baresmanas:

"Your nephew Kurush has already arrived at

Callinicum. Along with seven hundred of your cavalrymen. They've set up camp just next to our own."

"We would have brought him with us to meet you," added Bouzes, "but the commander of the Roman garrison in Callinicum wouldn't allow it."

"The stupid jackass is buried up to his ass in regulations," snapped Coutzes. "Said it was forbidden to allow Persian military personnel beyond the trading emporium."

Belisarius laughed. Romans and Persians had been trading for as long as they had been fighting each other. In truth, trade was the basic relationship. For all that the two empires had clashed many times on the field of battle, peace was the more common state of affairs. And, during wartime or peacetime, the trade never stopped. Year after year, decade after decade, century after century, caravans had been passing along that very road.

But—empires being empires—the trade was heavily regulated. (Officially. The border populations, Roman and Persian alike, were the world's most notorious smugglers.) For decades, Callinicum had been established as the official entrepot for Persians seeking to trade with Rome—just as Nisibis was, on the other side of the border, for Romans desiring to enter Persia.

"Leave it to a garrison commander," growled Maurice. "He *does* know we're at war with the Malwa, doesn't he? In alliance with Persia?"

Bouzes nodded. Coutzes snarled:

"He says that doesn't change regulations. Gave us quite a lecture, he did, on the unrelenting struggle against the mortal sin of smuggling."

Now, Baresmanas laughed. "My nephew wouldn't know how to smuggle if his life depended on it! He's much too rich."

Belisarius spurred his horse into motion. "Let's get to Callinicum. I'll have a word or two with this garrison commander."

"Just one or two?" asked Coutzes. He seemed a bit aggrieved.

Belisarius smiled. "Five, actually. *You are relieved of command.*"

"Oh."

" 'Deadly with a blade, is Belisarius,' " murmured Maurice.

They entered Callinicum two hours later, in mid-afternoon.

The general's first order of business was to ensure that the last group of builders and artisans still with him were adequately housed. When he left Constantinople, Belisarius had brought no less than eight hundred such men with his army. Small groups of them had been dropped off, at appropriate intervals, to begin the construction of the semaphore stations which would soon become the Roman Empire's new communication network. Callinicum would be the final leg of the Constantinople-Mesopotamia branch of that web.

That business done, Belisarius went off to speak his five words to the garrison commander.

Five words, in the event, grew into several hundred. The garrison commander's replacement had to be relieved, himself. After the general took a few dozen words to inform the new commander that Belisarius would be taking half the town's garrison with him into Mesopotamia, the man sputtered at length on the imperative demands of the war against illicit trade.

Belisarius spoke five more words.

His replacement, in turn, had to be relieved. After Belisarius used perhaps two hundred words, more or less thinking aloud, to reach the decision that it made more sense to take the entire garrison except for a token force, the third commander in as many hours shrieked on the danger of brigand raids.

Belisarius spoke five more words.

In the end, command of the Roman forces in Callinicum fell on the shoulders of a grizzled, gap-toothed hecatontarch.

"Hundred men'll be dandy," that worthy informed the general. "Just enough to keep reasonable order in the town. Nothing else for them to do. Callinicum's a fortress, for the sake of Christ—the walls are forty feet high and as wide to match. The sorry-ass brigands in these parts'd die of nosebleed if they climbed that high."

Cheerfully: "As for smuggling, fuck it. You couldn't stop it with the whole Roman army. Soon as the sun goes down, you throw a rock off these walls in any direction you'll bounce it off three smugglers before it hits the ground. At least one of them'll be a relative of mine."

Very cheerfully: "Any given Tuesday, prob'ly be my wife."

At sunset, Belisarius led his army out of Callinicum toward the military camp a few miles away where the forces from the Army of Syria were awaiting them. The freshly-conscripted soldiers from the town's garrison—seven hundred *very* unhappy infantrymen—were marched out between units of the general's bucellarii. The Thracians encouraged the new recruits with tales of glory in the past, booty in the future, and drawn bows in the present. Cataphract bows, with hundred-pound pulls and arrowheads you could shave with.

Baresmanas, riding at the head of the column, was out of earshot of the Callinicum garrison. But he had no difficulty imagining their muttered conversation.

Crazy fucking Thracian.

How did this lunatic ever get to be a general, anyway?

Chapter 8

Kurush's pavilion was far smaller than the gigantic construct which the Emperor of Malwa had erected at the siege of Ranapur. But, thought Belisarius, it was possibly even more richly adorned and accoutered. And with much better taste.

As he reclined on a pile of plump, silk-covered cushions placed at one end of a low table, Kurush himself placed a goblet of wine before him. Belisarius eyed the thing uneasily. It was not the wine which caused that trepidation. The general had no doubt that it was the finest vintage produced by Persia. No, it was the goblet itself. The drinking vessel was easily the most elaborate and expensive such object Belisarius had ever seen. For all the goblet's massive size, the design was thin and delicate, especially the flower-shaped stem—and, worst of all, made entirely of glass. Embedded throughout the bowl was gold leaf, highlighting the intricate facets cut in the form of overlapping, slightly concave disks. The finishing touch was the four medallions inset around the side of the bowl, standing out in high relief. About an inch in diameter, each carried a marvelous etching of a winged horse.

Gold medallions, naturally. Except for the silver wings, and the tiny little garnet eyes.

Belisarius glanced around the table. Bouzes,

Coutzes and Maurice were all staring at their own identical goblets. The brothers with astonishment, Maurice with deep gloom.

"Afraid to touch the damned thing," he heard Maurice mutter.

Fortunately, Baresmanas intervened.

"Have no fear, comrades," he said, smiling. "My nephew has two chests full of these things."

He gestured gaily. "Besides, even if you should happen to drop one, it would hardly break on *this* floor."

The four Romans eyed the carpet. In truth, the pile was so thick that the cushions on which they sat were entirely redundant.

Kurush, taking his place at the other end of the table from Belisarius, frowned. Not with irritation, but simply from puzzlement. "Is there a problem?" he asked. His Greek, like that of most Persian noblemen, was accented but fluent.

Baresmanas chuckled. "Not everyone, nephew, is accustomed to drinking wine out of a king's ransom."

The young Persian stared at the goblet in his hand. "This thing?" He looked up at his uncle. "It is valuable?"

All four of the Romans joined Baresmanas in the ensuing laughter. Their reaction was not diplomatic, perhaps, but they found it impossible to resist.

Fortunately, Kurush proved to be the affable type. He seemed to possess little of the prickly hauteur of most Persian noblemen. After a moment, he even joined in the laughter himself.

"I'm afraid I don't pay any attention to these matters," he confessed. Shrugging: "My retainers take care of that." He made a sweeping gesture. "But—please, please! Drink up! You must all be dying of thirst, after that miserable desert."

Kurush's words swept hesitation aside. All four Romans drank deeply from their goblets. And found, not to their surprise, that the vintage was marvelous.

Belisarius took advantage of the distraction to give Kurush a careful study. He had already learned, from Baresmanas, that Kurush had been charged by Emperor Khusrau to be the Persians' principal military liaison with Belisarius and his Roman forces.

The nobleman was in his mid-twenties, he estimated. The young officer was tall and slender, with a narrow face and rather delicate features.

At first glance, he reminded Belisarius of certain hyper-cultured Athenian aesthetes whom the general had occasionally encountered. The sort of soulful young men who could not complete a sentence without two or three allusions to the classics, and whose view of the world was, to put it mildly, impractical.

The likeness was emphasized by the way in which Kurush wore his clothing. The garments themselves were expensive and well-made. (As were those of Athenian aesthetes—all of whom were aristocrats, not shepherds.) But they seemed to have been tossed on with little care for precision of fit and none at all for color co-ordination.

Closer examination, however, undermined the initial impression. Kurush's hands, though slim-fingered, were strong-looking. And Belisarius did not miss the significance of the worn indentation on Kurush's right thumb. Unlike Romans, who favored the three-fingered draw, Persians drew their bows with thumb-rings.

Then, there was the way he moved. Kurush's stride, his gestures—even his facial expressions—all had a nervous quickness about them. Almost eager, like a spirited thoroughbred before a race. They bore no resemblance whatever to the affected languor of aesthetes.

Finally, there were the eyes. Like most Medes—and most Athenian aesthetes, for that matter—Kurush's

eyes were brown. But there was nothing vague and
unfocussed in their gaze. Despite his youth, the Persian was already beginning to develop faint wrinkles
around the sockets. Those wrinkles did not come from
studying poetry in Athens by candlelight. They came
from studying terrain under the scorching desert sun.

Kurush's first words, after setting down his goblet, were to Maurice. "I understand that you were
in command of the Roman forces on the hill, at
Mindouos."

Maurice nodded. Kurush shook his head.

"You must have laughed at us, trying to drive our
horses up that demon-created slope."

Maurice hesitated, gauging the Persian. Then, with
a little shrug:

"You'd have done better to dismount."

Kurush smiled. Quite cheerfully. "So I discovered!
My horse was shot out from under me right at the
start. I cursed my bad luck, at the time. But I think
it was all that saved my life. On foot, I could duck
behind boulders. Not even *your* arrows could penetrate rock!"

Again, he shook his head. "I'd been warned—"
He nodded toward Baresmanas. "—by my uncle, in
fact, that no one in the world uses more powerful
bows than Roman cataphracts. I didn't shrug off his
warning—not *that* voice of experience—but I still
hadn't expected to see an arrow drive right through
my mount's armor."

Then, with a frown:

"You've got a very slow rate of fire, though. Do
you really think the trade-off is worth it?"

Belisarius had to fight down a laugh. The young
Persian's frown was not hostile. Not in the least. For
all the world, it reminded the general of nothing so
much as a young aesthete's frown, contemplating the
relative merits of two styles of lyric poetry.

Maurice shrugged. "I don't think the question can

be answered in purely military terms. There's the matter of national temperament, too. You Persians have a flair for mounted archery that I don't think Romans could ever match. So why make the attempt? Better to concentrate on what we do well, rather than become second-rate Persian imitations."

Kurush nodded. "Well said." The young officer sighed. "It's probably all a moot point, anyway. These infernal new Malwa devices have changed everything."

"Have you seen them in action?" asked Belisarius.

Kurush winced. "Oh, yes. Three times, in fact. I've been at all the pitched battles we fought against the invaders on the open field, until we finally decided to withdraw and take a defensive stance at Babylon."

"Describe the invasion for me, if you would," requested Belisarius. He gestured politely toward Baresmanas. "Your uncle has given me an excellent overall picture, but he was not a direct eyewitness. I would appreciate more detail."

"Certainly." Kurush drained his goblet and reached for one of the small amphorae on the table. He began speaking while in the process of pouring himself more wine.

"There were hundreds of ships in the Malwa invasion fleet. Gigantic vessels, many of them. I'm no seaman, but those of my staff with maritime experience tell me that their big sailing ships have a carrying capacity of at least a thousand tons."

"More like two thousand," interjected Belisarius, "if they're the same ships I saw being built at Bharakuccha."

Kurush eyed him with respectful surprise. "I did not realize you had experience with naval matters."

Belisarius chuckled. "I don't. Or very little, at least. But one of my companions in Bharakuccha was Garmat, the chief adviser for the King of Axum. That was his estimate, after seeing the ships. I think that estimate can be trusted. In my experience, all high-ranking Ethiopians are most definitely naval experts."

"That's my experience as well," commented Baresmanas. He grimaced. "Two thousand tons. I don't think any Persian ship has that big a carrying capacity."

"Nor any of ours," added Bouzes. "Except for a handful of the grain ships which sail out of Egypt."

Belasarius nodded toward Kurush. "Please continue."

"The fleet arrived with no warning—well—" He scowled. "No warning which was heeded. A few merchants gave the alarm, but they were ignored by the imperial authorities." The scowl deepened. "Arrogant bastards."

Belisarius was amused to see the stiff, diplomatically expressionless faces of Bouzes, Coutzes, and Maurice. It was the commonly held opinion of most Romans that *all* Persian officials were "arrogant bastards." Belisarius did not share that opinion—Baresmanas and Kurush were not the first Persian nobles he had found likeable, even charming—but there was no denying that the charge had some basis in fact. Roman officials also, of course, could often be accused of "arrogant bastardom." But there was nothing in the world quite like a Persian aristocrat—especially one who also occupied a post in the imperial hierarchy—when it came to sheer, unadulterated, icy haughtiness. Compared to such, Rajput nobility could almost be described as casual and warm-hearted. Even the Malwa dynastic clan, for all their unparalleled brutality and megalomania, did not—quite—exhibit that sense of unthinking superiority over all other men.

Apparently, Roman tact was insufficient. Either that, or Kurush was more perceptive than Belisarius had realized. The young Persian glanced around the table at the distant, polite expressions of the

Romans. Then, with a little smile, added, "But perhaps no more so than others of their ilk."

He quaffed some wine. Then continued:

"The fleet entered the confluence of the Tigris-Euphrates Rivers and landed a huge army. The ships carried horses and even a score of elephants, in addition to their terrible new weapons. Within two days, they overwhelmed the garrison at Charax."

The scowl returned in full force. "The murderous swine massacred the garrison and enslaved the entire population. The womenfolk were treated horridly, especially by those stinking Ye-tai barbarians whom the Malwa seem to dote on. The nobility were singled out for particular persecution. The Malwa were not in the least interested in obtaining ransom. Instead, they slaughtered all the male azadan—even babies—and all noblewomen except those who were young and pretty. Such girls were taken by the Malwa officers as concubines."

He ran his long fingers through his thick hair. The scowl faded a bit, pushed aside by an expression of scholarly thoughtfulness. "In all the centuries that we Persians and you Romans have fought each other, there have been many atrocities committed." He waved his hand. "By both sides, by both sides. Still— I cannot think of a single instance of such gross and unvarnished cruelty. Not one."

"There *is* no such instance," stated Baresmanas firmly. "Nothing on such a scale, at least. And let us also note that, for all the savageries which both our people have been guilty of in our dealings with each other, there have also been many—*many*—instances of generosity and chivalry."

He bestowed an appreciative look on Belisarius. "Your mercy at Mindouos being one of the most outstanding examples."

"Well said!" exclaimed his nephew. Kurush drained his wine. When he set the goblet back on the table,

his expression combined good cheer and rueful-
ness.

"I *know*," he chuckled. "For a time, there, I was
quite certain my throat was going to be slit." He
shuddered, slightly. "Three of your damned Isaurians
had me down—talk about mean, tough bastards!—
grinning like wolves. They sounded like wolves, too,
quarreling over which one was going to get the first
bite."

He grinned at Maurice. "Then one of you Thracian
lads rode up and reasoned with them. Partly with a
drawn bow, and partly with talk of my money."

Maurice grinned back. "And how much was your
ransom?"

Kurush snorted. "Enough to set those three
Isaurians up for life! Would you believe, the damned
barbarians demanded—"

He broke off. "But I'm straying. That was three
years ago. The Malwa are here today—and, as my
learned uncle so cogently remarks, I think we will
see no such instances of mercy and forbearance
coming from the Malwa."

"It is not their method," agreed Belisarius. "The
Malwa aristocracy is already rich. They are not even
slightly interested in ransom. And the troops, who
might be, are completely subjugated to their rule."

He drained his own cup. "The Malwa seek to
conquer the world. Nothing less. And they intend
to rule it with a hand of iron. Charax was only the
first atrocity of the many they will commit in
Persia—and Rome, later, if Persia falls. But it was
by no means their first. By no means." The general's face grew bleak. "I was at Ranapur, when the
Malwa broke the rebellion. Two hundred thousand
people were still alive in that great city, when the
Malwa finally breached the walls. Five days later,
after unspeakable atrocities, there were not more
than fifty survivors. A few young noblewomen tough

enough to survive their ordeal, and then sold into slavery."

For a moment, the pavilion was filled with a grim silence. Then Maurice muttered:

"Continue, please."

Kurush shook off the mood. "After the Malwa finished their conquest of Charax, the bulk of their army proceeded upriver, accompanied by over a hundred of their smaller ships. The remainder of the fleet waited in Charax, while the Malwa began expanding and strengthening the port. We assume that those ships will return to India for further provisions, once the monsoon changes." He glanced toward the entrance of the pavilion, as if to gauge the season. "We're in the beginning of June, now. Within a month, the winds will be right for them."

Belisarius nodded. "Their fleet will sail for Bharakuccha in July. Then, after reprovisioning, they'll begin their return journey toward the end of October. Early November, at the latest."

"What are their actual military forces?" asked Coutzes.

Kurush spread his hands on the table and leaned back. "You'll find this hard to believe, but—"

"No, we won't," said Belisarius, quite forcefully, with a warning glance at Bouzes and Coutzes.

"—based on my own personal observation, I estimate the total number of their troops—*not counting the large garrison they left in Charax*—at two hundred thousand men."

When the expected Roman reaction did not emerge, Kurush's eyes widened slightly.

Maurice cleared his throat. "Break that down a bit, if you would."

Kurush paused, thinking.

"I don't think they have more than forty thousand cavalry. The great mass of their troops are infantry, and most of them seem of mediocre quality.

The Ye-tai, of course, are quite ferocious in combat. But the Malwa seem to use them principally as a stiffener for their common troops."

"They're primarily security battalions," interjected Belisarius. "That's how I saw the Malwa using them, when I was in India. In battle, their main job is to make sure that the common soldiers obey their officers. They're utterly ruthless toward deserters or even stragglers."

Kurush nodded. "Most of the infantry are simply armed with traditional weapons. Spears, swords, axes. And their armor is flimsy, for the most part. As I said, mediocre-quality troops." He shrugged. "But with those huge numbers, they simply overwhelm their opposition. *After* they've ravaged the opponent with their demon weapons."

"Describe the weapons," said Belisarius.

Kurush spread his hands apologetically. "I will do so as best I can, Belisarius. But keep in mind that I only saw the damned things at a distance, and I was never sure exactly what I was watching."

"Let's do it the other way around, then. Let *me* tell you what I think the Malwa are using, and you can correct me based on your direct experience."

The Persian nodded. Belisarius took a sip of his wine, thinking, and then said, "I think—I *hope*, actually—their weapons fall into three main categories. Siege cannons, rockets, and grenades." After describing these three types of gunpowder weapons, based on his observations in India, Belisarius continued, "The rockets will be used in much the same manner that we Romans have traditionally used field artillery in a battle. The disadvantage of the rockets is their extreme inaccuracy—"

He hesitated for a moment, fighting temptation. His *own* rockets—the katyusha rockets—had proven to be fairly accurate, in tests. Not as accurate as catapults, but much less erratic than the Malwa rockets he had observed. Guided by Aide, Belisarius had had real venturi made for his rockets, using all the skills of Greek metalsmiths. He had even insisted on machining the bronze exhaust nozzles. But he hoped their accuracy would come as a surprise to the enemy. He had no reason to distrust Baresmanas and Kurush, or to suspect they were loose-mouthed. Still—

He glided over the problem, for the moment.

"—but they compensate by their destructiveness and their relative ease of operation. You don't have to lug around a heavy onager or scorpion to fire a rocket. Just a trough and a simple firing device. Then, too, the things tend to panic the opponent's cavalry horses."

Kurush nodded gloomily. "It's impossible to control horses under a rocket barrage."

Again, Belisarius hesitated, torn between the need for secrecy and distaste at hiding secrets from his own allies. This time, distaste won the struggle.

"That's not actually true, Kurush." Seeing the look of surprise in the young sahrdaran's face, Belisarius smiled crookedly.

"I thought the same, once, when I first encountered rockets. My subsequent experience, however, taught me that horses can become accustomed to the sound and fury of gunpowder weapons. The secret is to expose them to the noise at an early age. A full-grown warhorse, as a rule, will usually remain skittish. But a horse trained as a foal will manage well enough."

He gestured toward the open flap of the pavilion. "The horses which pull my katyushas, for instance, have been specially selected for their steadiness under fire. And most of my bucellarii have been equipped with mounts trained to stand up under gunpowder fire."

The two Persians at the table were stroking their

beards thoughtfully. To Belisarius, their thoughts were obvious. *Awkwardly* obvious.

Great news. But we Persians have no gunpowder weapons with which to train our horses. How to steal them from the enemy? Or—better yet—convince the Romans to supply us with the infernal things?

For a moment, Belisarius and Baresmanas stared at each other. Then, seeing the Roman general's faint nod, Baresmanas looked away.

We will discuss the matter later was the meaning of the nod. That, and:

I have my opinion, but—

That was enough. An experienced diplomat, Baresmanas was well aware of the controversies which were undoubtedly raging among the Romans over this very delicate problem. An alliance with Persia was one thing. Arming the ancient Medean foe with gunpowder weapons was a different proposition altogether.

There was no point in pressing the matter at the moment, so Baresmanas changed the subject.

"And the grenades?" He pointed to Kurush. "According to my nephew, the things are solely used in close order assaults."

"He's quite right. That is their function. I never observed them used any other way in India."

He decided to pass on a secret, now. The enemy almost certainly knew it anyway. Some of their spies must have escaped the slaughter at the Hippodrome where Belisarius and Antonina crushed the Malwa-engineered Nika rebellion. If nothing else, the bodies of the traitor Narses and his companion Ajatasutra had never been found. Both Belisarius and Theodora were certain that the former Grand Chamberlain, with his legendary wiliness, had managed to make his escape.

So:

"My wife—she commands our only force of

grenadiers, the Theodoran Cohort—*has* introduced a more long-range capability to grenade warfare."

He described, briefly, the sling and sling-staff methods of Antonina's grenadiers, before concluding: "—but, even so, we are still talking about bow-range, no more."

Baresmanas and Kurush nodded understandingly. Slings were not a weapon which Persian nobility favored personally, but they were quite familiar with the ancient devices.

Belisarius poured himself some more wine and, then, after glancing inquiringly about the table, refilled the goblets of Bouzes and Baresmanas as well.

As he set the wine down, the general reflected upon the absence of servants in the pavilion. That simple fact told him a great deal about his host, all of which met his complete approval.

Kurush seemed otherwordly and absent-minded, in some ways. More precisely, he seemed absent-minded in the way that very rich people often are—so accustomed to personal service that they treat it as a routine fact of life. But when it came to military matters, Kurush had obviously been able to discard his class attitudes. The battle-tested officer had not made the nobleman's mistake of forgetting that lowly menials have ears, and minds, and tongues. So he and his distinguished guests would pour their own wine, and serve each other as comrades.

Belisarius, after taking a sip of that excellent vintage, continued:

"You will probably not have experienced the siege cannons, as yet. The devices are huge, heavy, and ungainly. Useless in a field battle. But you will encounter then soon enough, at Babylon. The Malwa will surely bring them up to reduce the walls."

"How powerful are they?" asked Baresmanas.

"Think of the largest catapult you've ever seen, and

then multiply the force of the projectile by a factor of three. No, four or five." He shrugged. "The Malwa do not use the things particularly well, in my opinion. Based, at least, on my observations at Ranapur. But they hardly need to. Ranapur was a great city, with the tallest and thickest brick walls I've ever seen. By the time the siege cannons were done—which still took months, mind you—those great walls were so much rubble."

Kurush grimaced. "The walls of Babylon are not brick, more's the pity. At least, not kiln-brick. The outer walls were, at one time, but the city's been deserted for centuries. Over the years, the peasants of the region have used that good brick to build their own huts. All that's left of the outer walls is the rubble core. The inner walls are still standing, but they're made entirely of sun-dried bricks. After all these centuries, the walls aren't much stronger than packed earth."

"Thick walls, though, aren't they?" asked Maurice.

Kurush nodded. "Oh, yes. Very thick! The outer walls are still over fifty yards wide, with a hundred yard moat in front of them. The inner walls are a double wall, with a military road in the middle. Counting that road—say, seven yards in width—the inner walls probably measure some twenty yards in thickness."

Maurice's eyes widened. Coutzes whistled softly, shaking his head. "God in heaven," he muttered. "I had no idea the ancients could build on such a scale."

Bouzes snorted. "Why not, brother? You've seen the pyramids in Egypt. I know you have. I was standing right next to you when you whistled softly, shook your head, and said: 'God in Heaven. I had no idea the ancients could build on such a scale.' "

The room erupted in laughter. Even Coutzes, after a momentary glare at his brother, started chuckling ruefully.

The moment of humor was brief, however. Soon enough, grim reality returned.

Again, Belisarius was torn by warring impulses. The need for secrecy, on the one hand, especially with regard to Aide's existence; the need—certainly the personal desire—for frankness with his new allies, on the other.

He decided to steer a tricky middle course.

"Actually," he said, clearing his throat, "I think the nature of Babylon's walls will work entirely to your— I should say, *our*—advantage. Cannon fire—delivered by gigantic siege cannon, at any rate—is too powerful to be resisted by hard walls, whether brick or even stone. You're actually much better off using thick, soft walls. Such walls simply absorb the cannon shot, rather than trying to deflect it."

All the other men at the table, except Maurice, stared at Belisarius with wide-eyed surprise. Maurice simply tightened his lips and gazed down at his goblet.

Maurice was the only one in the pavilion who knew Belisarius' secret. The general had finally divulged it to him, months earlier, after his return from India. Belisarius had always felt guilty, during the long months he had kept that secret from Maurice. So, when he finally did reveal Aide's existence, he compensated by sharing Aide's insights with Maurice to a greater extent than he ever had with anyone else, even Antonina.

Yet, if he had initially done so from guilt, his reasons had changed soon enough. In truth, he had found Maurice to be his most useful confidant—when it came, at least, to Aide's military advice. Not to Belisarius' surprise, the phlegmatic and practical Thracian peasant-turned-cataphract had been more receptive to Aide's often-bizarre advice than anyone else.

"You saw this in India?" queried Kurush. "Such fortifications?"

Maurice gave Belisarius a quick, warning glance. The chiliarch knew full well where Belisarius had seen "such fortifications." Not in India, but in visions. Visions which Aide had put in his mind, of the siege warfare of the future. Especially the theories and the practice of a great student of fortifications over a millennium in the future. A man named Vauban, who would live in a country which would be called France.

"Not directly, no, Kurush. But I did notice, toward the end of the siege of Ranapur, that the crumbled walls actually resisted the siege cannons better than they had while the brickwork was still intact."

He mentally patted himself on the back. It was not entirely a lie, after all. He consoled himself with the thought that the rubbled walls of Ranapur *had*, in retrospect, resisted the cannon shot quite well. Even if he hadn't noticed at the time.

Fortunately, the lie passed muster. Kurush and Baresmanas seemed so relieved by the information that they showed no inclination to press Belisarius on the point.

The conversation now began to turn toward the Malwa's relative weakness in cavalry, especially heavy cavalry, and how the allied forces might best take advantage of it. But before the discussion had gotten very far, they were interrupted.

A Persian officer bearing the insignia of an imperial courier entered the tent, somewhat apologetically, and approached the table. As he leaned over and whispered something to Baresmanas, Belisarius politely looked away and diverted the Romans' attention with an anecdote from the siege of Ranapur. The anecdote, involving his assessment of the relative merits of Rajput and Ye-tai cavalry, was interesting enough to capture the full attention of Bouzes and Coutzes and, to all appearances, Maurice. But he noted that Kurush was paying hardly any attention at all. The young sahrdaran's face was stiff. Whatever news was being whispered into Baresmanas' ear, Belisarius was certain, his nephew suspected its content. And was not happy in his suspicion.

When the courier left, Baresmanas gave Belisarius a quick look which, subtly, conveyed both apology and request.

Understanding, Belisarius rose and said: "It's late, and we're all tired. I think it would be best to continue this discussion later. We'll have plenty of opportunity to talk during our march south."

The other Romans immediately followed his example. Within two minutes, they were mounting their horses outside the pavilion and riding toward the Roman encampment nearby.

"Something's up," said Coutzes.

"Politics," announced his brother. "Got to be."

Belisarius was a bit startled. Abstractly, he knew Bouzes and Coutzes were not stupid. But the brothers had behaved with such thoroughgoing foolishness, during his previous encounter with them three years earlier, that he had not expected such quick perspicacity.

He said nothing in reply, however. Not until he and Maurice parted company with the brothers at their tent, and began riding toward the Thracian part of the encampment.

"He's right, you know," commented Maurice.

Belisarius nodded. "They've got a succession crisis. Khusrau's new to the throne and he's got lots of half-brothers. Ormazd, in particular, was not happy with the situation. Civil war probably would have broken out, if the Malwa hadn't invaded. Persians can sneer at us crude adoption-happy Romans all they want, but they've got their own sorry history of instability whenever the throne's up for grabs. Often enough in the past, when a Persian Emperor died, a civil war erupted. One claimant from the Sassanid dynasty fighting another. Three or four of them at once, sometimes."

They rode on a little further in silence. Then, Maurice smiled and remarked:

"I thought you did quite well, by the way. Lying through your teeth, I mean. The little touch about the crumbling brick walls of Ranapur was especially nice. Had such a ring of authenticity about it. Completely avoided the—uh, *awkwardness*—of explaining to a couple of Persian sahrdaran that your experience with fortifications in the new age of gunpowder comes from the advice of a fucking barbarian—a *Gaul*, no less— who won't even be born for twelve hundred years."

Belisarius grimaced. Maurice plowed on cheerfully.

"You did let one thing slip, though. When you mentioned that you *hoped* the only weapons the Malwa had were siege guns, rockets and grenades."

Belisarius winced. But Maurice seemed determined to till the entire field.

"Bad slip, that. Fortunately, the Persians didn't catch it. Or they might have asked: 'what particular weapons do you *fear* seeing?' "

The chiliarch glanced at his general slyly. "Then what would you have said?"

Belisarius stared ahead, stiff-faced, silent.

"Oh, yes," chuckled Maurice. "Difficult, that would have been."

He mimicked Belisarius' distinctive baritone: "I hope we don't see mobile artillery. Or, even worse, handcannons. You know—the stuff we Romans have been trying to develop through our secret weapons project, guided by visions of the future from a magical jewel some of us call the Talisman of God. Not, mind you, with any instant success."

They were at the tent which they shared. Belisarius dismounted. On the ground, he stared up at Maurice's grinning countenance. Then said, firmly, even severely, "I have the utmost confidence in John of Rhodes."

Maurice shook his head. "That's because you've never worked with him."

The chiliarch dismounted from his own horse, and followed Belisarius into the tent. "I *have*, on the other hand," he grumbled. "Quite the exciting experience, that is."

Chapter 9

RHODES
Summer, 531 A.D.

"Get down, you idiot!"

Antonina ducked behind the barricade. Just in time. There was a sharp, nasty-sounding, explosive crack. An instant later, an object went whizzing overhead somewhere in her vicinity.

John's head popped up behind his own barricade. When Antonina gingerly looked up, she found the naval officer's blue eyes glaring at her fiercely.

"How many times do I have to tell you?" he demanded. "This stuff is dangerous!"

The other observers of the test, five Roman officers, were beginning to rise from behind the heavy wooden barricades which surrounded, on three sides, the cannon which had been tested.

The late, lamented cannon. Lying on its side, off the heavy wooden cradle, with one of the wrought iron bars which made up its barrel missing. Seeing that gaping, scorched split running down the entire

104

length of the barrel, Antonina winced. The missing iron bar was the object which had whizzed past—and it could have easily taken off her head.

John stumped out from behind his barricade.

"That's it! That's it!" he cried. He transferred his glare to the little cluster of Roman officers and pointed a imperious finger at Antonina. "This woman is henceforth banned for all time from the testing area!" he pronounced. "You are encharged with enforcing that order!"

Hermogenes cleared his throat. "Can't do that, John. Antonina's in command, you know. Of you and me both. Direct imperial mandate. If you want to inform the Empress Theodora that you're over-riding her authority, you go right ahead and do it. Not me."

"'Druther piss on a dragon, myself," muttered one of the other officers, the young Syrian named Euphronius who served as Antonina's chief executive officer for the Theodoran Cohort.

The regular infantry officer standing next to him, who served Hermogenes in the same capacity, nodded sagely.

"So would I," agreed Callixtos. "A big, angry, wide-awake, *hungry* dragon—"

"—guarding its hoard," concluded another officer. This man, Ashot, was the commander of the Thracian bucellarii whom Belisarius had assigned to accompany his wife to Egypt.

The last of the officers said nothing. His name was Menander, and he was new to his post. A hecatontarch, he was now—theoretically, the commander of a hundred men. A lad of twenty, who had never before commanded anyone. But Menander's title was a mere formality. His real position was that of Antonina's "special adviser."

Menander was the third of the three cataphracts who had accompanied Belisarius in his expedition to India. The other two, Valentinian and Anastasius, had remained with the general as his personal bodyguards. Menander, who had little of their frightening expertise in slaughter, had been assigned a different task. Belisarius thought Menander had gained an excellent grasp of gunpowder weapons and tactics during the course of their adventures in India, and so he had presented him to his wife with praise so fulsome the fair-skinned youth turned beet-red.

So, unsure of himself, Menander said nothing. But, quite sure of his loyalties, he squared his shoulders and stepped to Antonina's side.

John, seeing the united opposition of the entire military command of the expedition, threw up his hands in despair.

"I'm not responsible then!" The blue-eyed glare focussed again on Antonina. "You are doomed, woman. Doomed, I say! Destined for an early grave!"

John began stumping about, arms akimbo. "Dismembered," he predicted. "Disemboweled," he forecast. "Decapitated."

With a serene air of augury: "Shredded into a bloody, corpuscular mass of mutilated and mangled flesh."

Antonina, from long experience, waited until John had stumped about for a minute or so before she spoke.

"Exactly what happened, John?" she asked.

As always, once his irascibility was properly exercised, the naval officer's quick mind moved back to the forefront.

John gave the splintered cannon a cursory glance. "Same thing that usually happens with these damned wrought-iron cannons," he growled. "If there's any flaw at all in the welding, one of the staves will burst."

He stepped over to the cannon and squatted next to it.

"Come here," he commanded. "I'll show you the problem."

Antonina came around the barricade and stooped next to him. A moment later, the five officers were also gathered around.

John pointed to one of the iron bars which ran down the length of the barrel. The barrel was made up of twelve such bars—eleven, now, on this ruptured one. The bars were an inch square in cross-section and about three feet long. The corners of each bar joined its mates on the inside of the barrel, forming a dodecagonal tube about three inches in diameter. On the outside diameter of the barrel, the gaps between the bars had been filled up with weld.

John pointed to the broken welds which had once held the missing bar in place. "That's where they always rupture," he said. "And they do it about a third of the time."

He scowled, more thoughtfully than angrily. "I wouldn't even mind if the things were predictable. Then I could just test each one of them, and discard the failures. Won't work. I've seen one of these things blow up after it had fired successfully at least twenty times."

Hesitantly, Euphronius spoke up. "I notice you don't have the same hoops welded around the barrel that you have on the handcannons. Wouldn't that strengthen the barrel, if you added them?"

Antonina watched John struggle with his temper. The struggle was very brief, however. When the naval officer spoke his voice was mild, and his tone simply that of patient explanation. It was one of the many things she liked about the Rhodian. For all of John's legendary irritability, Antonina had long ago realized that John was one of those rare hot-tempered people who is rude to superiors yet, as a rule, courteous to social inferiors.

"Yes, it would, Euphronius," he said. "But here's the problem. The handcannons are small, and reasonably light—even with the addition of a few reinforcing hoops. Furthermore, the powder charge isn't really all that big. But to accomplish the same purpose with these three-inchers, I'd have to surround the barrel with hoops down its entire length. That adds a lot of weight—"

He hesitated, calculating.

"Right now, these things weigh about one hundred and fifty pounds. If you add the hoops—as I said, we'd have to run the hoops all the way down the length, not just occasional reinforcement like the handcannons—you'd wind up with a barrel weighing another fifty pounds or so. Say two hundred pounds— and that's just the weight of the barrel. Doesn't include the cradle."

"That's not so bad," commented Ashot. "Especially if you use it on a warship."

"Yes and no," replied John. "It's true that the weight wouldn't matter on a ship. The problem is with the integrity of the iron."

He glanced at Antonina.

"One of the things Belisarius told me—and I've verified it with my own tests—is that these welded wrought-iron cannons have to be properly maintained. The damned things have to be cleaned in boiling water after each period of use, or else the powder residues build up and start corroding the metal." He grimaced. So did Ashot.

Hermogenes, staring back and forth at the two men, frowned with puzzlement. "I don't see the problem," he said. "Sure, that'd be a real nuisance for a land army, having to boil water and wash out the cannons. Especially in the desert. But on a ship—"

John's eyes bugged out. Before the naval officer could give vent to his outrage, Ashot intervened.

"Don't forget, John. He's never served at sea."

John clenched his jaws. "Obviously not," he growled.

Ashot, smiling, said to Hermogenes, "The one thing you do *not* want to do on a ship is build a big fire in order to boil a huge kettle of water. Believe me, Hermogenes, you don't. There's nothing in the world that'll burn like a ship. All that oil-soaked wood—pitch—rigging—"

"Damned ships are like so much kindling, just waiting to go up," concurred John. "Besides, what water would you use? *Sea-water?* That'd corrode the barrels even faster!"

Antonina straightened. "That's it, then. We'll go with cast bronze guns for the warships. And the field artillery. We'll restrict the wrought-iron weapons for the infantry's handguns."

"They'll still blow up, now and then," warned John.

Euphronius smiled, with surprising good cheer. "Yes, John, they will. I've seen it happen—had it happen to me, once—and it's a bit scary. But my grenadiers can handle it. The one nice thing about these wrought-iron guns, when they do go, is that they blow sideways, not back. Startling as hell, but it's not really that dangerous."

"Except to the man standing next to you," muttered Callixtos.

"Not really. Don't forget—the handcannons have those hoop reinforcements. So far, every time one of the guns has blown—which, by the way, doesn't happen all that often—the hoops have kept the staves from flying off like so many spears. What you get is ruptured pieces. Those can hurt you, sure—even kill you, maybe—but the odds aren't bad." Euphronius shrugged. "That's life. We're farmers and shepherds, Callixtos. Farming's dangerous too, believe it or not. Especially dealing with livestock. My cousin was crippled just last year, when—"

He broke off, waving aside the incident. All who watched the Syrian peasant-turned-grenadier were struck by the calm fatalism of the gesture.

"We'll manage," he repeated. The cheerful smile returned. "Though I will emphasize the importance of keeping the guns clean, to my grenadiers. Even if that means having to haul a bunch of heavy kettles around."

Now, chuckling:

"The wives'll scream bloody murder, of course, since they'll wind up doing most of the hauling."

John was still not satisfied. "Bronze is expensive," he complained. "Iron cannons are a *lot* cheaper."

Antonina shook her head.

"We'll just have to live with the cost. I won't subject my soldiers and sailors to that kind of gamble. Let the treasury officials wail all they want."

Grimly: "If they wail too much, I'll refer them to Theodora."

Her usual good humor returned. "Besides, John, we can make the giant fortress cannons out of wrought iron. Once we get to Alexandria. It won't matter what they weigh, since they'll never be moved once they're erected to defend the city. And there'll be no problem keeping them clean. The garrison gunners won't have anything else to do anyway. Hopefully, the guns'll never be used."

John scowled. "Are you *sure* about this?" he demanded.

He was not talking about the cannons, now. He was raising—again—the argument he had been having with Antonina since she arrived at Rhodes. The very first instruction Antonina had given John, almost the minute she set foot on the island, was to organize the transfer of the armaments complex he had so painstakingly built up, in its entirety, to Alexandria.

Antonina sighed.

"John, we've been over this a hundred times. Rhodes is just too isolated. The war with the Malwa will be won in the south. Egypt's the key. And besides—"

She hesitated. Like most Rhodians of her acquaintance, John had a fierce attachment to his native island. But—

"Face the truth, John. Rhodes isn't just isolated—it's too damn small."

She waved her hand toward the cluster of workshops some fifty yards away from the testing range. The workshops, like the testing area, were perched on a small bluff overlooking the sea. Behind them rose a steep and rocky ridge.

"This is a war like no other ever fought. We need to build a gigantic arms complex to fight it. That means Alexandria, John, not this little island. Alexandria's the second largest city in the Empire, after Constantinople, and it has by far the greatest concentration of manufactories, artisans, and skilled craftsmen. There's nowhere else we can put together the materials—and, most importantly, the workforce—quickly enough."

"Egypt's the richest agricultural province of the Empire, too," added Hermogenes. "So we won't have any problems keeping that workforce fed. Whereas here on Rhodes—"

He left off, gesturing at the rugged terrain surrounding them. Rhodes was famous, throughout the Mediterranean world, for the skill of its seamen and the savvy of its merchants. Both of which talents had developed, over the centuries, to compensate for the island's hardscrabble agriculture.

John stood up slowly. "All right," he sighed. Then, with a suspicious glance at Antonina:

"You sure this isn't just an elaborate scheme to justify a triumphant return to your native city?"

Antonina laughed. There was no humor in that sound. None at all. "When I left Alexandria, John, I swore I'd never set foot in that place again." For a moment, her beautiful face twisted into a harsh, cold mask. *Fuck Alexandria*. All I remember is poverty, scraping, and—"

She paused, shrugged. All of the men standing around knew her history. All of them except Euphronius had long known.

The Syrian peasant had only learned that history three months earlier, when Antonina selected him as her executive officer and invited him and his wife to her villa for dinner. She had told them, then, over the wine after the meal. Watching carefully for their reaction. Euphronius had been shocked, a bit, but his admiration for Antonina had enabled him to overcome the moment.

His wife Mary had not been shocked at all. She, too, admired Antonina. But, unlike her husband, she understood the choices facing girls born into poverty. Mary had chosen a different path than Antonina— for a moment, her hand had caressed her husband's, remembering the tenderness of a sixteen-year-old shepherd boy—but she did not condemn the alternative. She had thought about it herself, more than once, before deciding to marry Euphronius and accept the life of a peasant's wife.

Antonina turned away. "Fuck Alexandria," she repeated.

Chapter 10

MESOPOTAMIA
Summer, 531 A.D.

An hour into the march from Callinicum, Baresmanas passed on the bad news.

"It seems we may face a civil war, after all, on top of the Malwa invasion," he said grimly.

The Persian nobleman stared out over the arid landscape of northern Mesopotamia. Other than the occasional oasis, the only relief from the bleak desolation was the Euphrates, half a mile east of the road the army was taking.

Belisarius cocked an eyebrow toward the sahrdaran, but said nothing. After a moment, Baresmanas sighed.

"I had hoped it would not come to this. But Ormazd was always a fool. Khusrau's half-brother has a great deal of support among some of the sahrdaran families, especially the Varazes and the Andigans. A large part of the Karen are favorable to him, also. And he is quite popular among the imperial *vurzurgan*. All of that has apparently gone to his head.

"*Stupid!*" he snorted. "The great mass of the dehgans have made clear that their loyalty is to Khusrau. Without them—" Baresmanas shrugged.

Belisarius nodded thoughtfully, reviewing his knowledge of the power structure in Persia.

Persian society was rigidly divided into classes, and class position usually translated directly into political power. The seven sahrdaran families provided the satraps of major provinces and, often enough, the royalty of subordinate kingdoms. Below the great sahrdaran houses came the class of "grandees," whom the Persians called *vurzurgan*. The vuzurgan ruled small provinces, and filled the higher ranks of the imperial officialdom.

Finally, at the base of the Persian aristocracy, came the *azadan*—"men of noble birth." Most of these consisted of small landed gentry, that class which the Persians called the *dehgans*. It was the dehgans who provided the feared armored lancers which were the heart of the mighty Persian army.

So—Khusrau's rival Ormazd, for all that he had gained the support of many high-ranked noblemen, had failed to win the allegiance of the men who provided Persia's rulers with their mailed fist.

Belisarius smiled his crooked smile. "Even Aryan principles," he murmured, "have to take crude reality into account."

Baresmanas matched the sly smile with one of his own, saying: "It's your fault, actually."

Belisarius' eyes widened. "*My* fault? How in the world—"

"Ormazd's most powerful and influential supporter is Firuz. Who is a Karen, as you may know."

Belisarius shook his head. "No, I did not know. We *are* speaking of the same Firuz who—"

"Yes, indeed. The same Firuz—the same illustrious champion—who led the Aryan army at Mindouos. Led it to its most ignominious defeat in well over a century—at your hands, my friend."

Belisarius frowned. "I knew he had survived the battle. I even visited, while we held him captive, to pay my respects. He was quite rude, so my visit was very brief. But I did not know he was Karen, and I had no idea he held such sway in dynastic affairs."

Baresmanas chuckled scornfully. "Oh, yes. He is quite the favorite of imperial grandees, and the Mazda priesthood thinks well of him also. That favoritism, in fact, is what led to him being given the command of the army at Nisibis. Despite his obvious"—all humor vanished—"military incompetence."

Belisarius was distracted for a moment. A serpent slithering off the road had unsettled his mount. After calming the horse, he turned back to Baresmanas and said: "That would explain, I imagine, the hostility of the dehgans to his candidate Ormazd."

The sahrdaran tightened his lips. "They have not forgotten that insane charge he led at Mindouos, which trapped us against your field fortifications." He shuddered. "What a hideous slaughter!"

For a moment, the sahrdaran's face was drawn, almost haggard. Belisarius looked away, controlling his own grimace. It *had* been pure butchery in the center at Mindouos. Just as he had planned—trapping the Persian lancers against his infantry while he hammered them from the flank with his own heavy cavalry.

He sighed. Over the past months, he had become quite fond of Baresmanas. Yet he knew he would do it all again, if the necessity arose.

Something of his sentiments must have been clear to the Persian. Baresmanas leaned over and said, almost in a whisper:

"Such is war, my friend. In this, if nothing else, we are much alike—neither of us gives any credence to myths of glory and martial grandeur."

"As my chiliarch Maurice taught me," Belisarius replied harshly, "war is murder. Organized, systematic murder—nothing more and nothing less. It was the first thing he said to me on the day I assumed command as an officer. Seventeen, I was, at the time. But I had enough sense to ask my chief subordinate—he was a decarch, then—his opinion."

Baresmanas twisted in his saddle, looking back at the long column which followed them.

"Where is Maurice, by the way? I did not see him when we set out this morning." He studied the column more closely. "For that matter, where are your two bodyguards?"

Now, Belisarius did grimace. "There's been a problem. I asked Maurice to deal with it. I sent Valentinian and Anastasius with him, along with a regiment of my bucellarii."

Baresmanas eyed him shrewdly. "Looting?"

The general's grimace deepened. "Worse. In Callinicum last night, some of the Constantinople garrison got drunk in a tavern and raped the girl who was serving them. The tavernkeeper's own daughter, as it happened. When the tavernkeeper and his two sons tried to intervene, the soldiers murdered all three of them."

Baresmanas shook his head. "It happens. Especially with troops—"

"*Not in my army it doesn't.*" The general's jaws were tight. "Not more than once, anyway."

"You have punished the culprits."

"I had all eight of them beheaded."

Baresmanas was silent for a moment. An experienced officer, he understood full well the implications. Armies, like empires, have their own internal divisions.

"You are expecting trouble from the Constantinople garrison troops," he stated. "They will resent the execution of their comrades by your Thracian retinue."

"They can resent it all they want," snarled Belisarius. "Just so long as they've learned to fear my bucellarii."

He twisted in his saddle, looking back.

"The reason Maurice and his men aren't at the front of the army this morning is because they're riding on the flanks of the Constantinople troops. Dragging eight bodies behind them on ropes. And a sack full of eight heads."

He turned back, his face set in a cold glare. "We've got enough problems to deal with. If those garrison soldiers get the idea they can run wild in a *Roman* town, just imagine what they'd do once we reach Persian territory."

Baresmanas pursed his lips. "That *would* be difficult. Especially with Ormazd stirring up trouble against what he's calling Khusrau's 'capitulation' to the Roman Empire."

Belisarius chuckled. "The Malwa Empire is ravaging Persia and Ormazd is denouncing his half-brother for finding an *ally*?"

The sahrdaran shrugged. "If it weren't that, it would be something else. The man's ambitions are unchecked. We had hoped he would accept his status, but—"

Belisarius looked at him directly. "What exactly is the news that was brought by your courier?"

"It is not news, Belisarius, so much as an assessment. After the Malwa invaded, Ormazd formally acquiesced to Khusrau's assumption of the throne. In return, Khusrau named him satrap of northern Mesopotamia—the rich province we call Asuristan and you call by its ancient name of Assyria. Ormazd pledged to bring thirty thousand troops to the Emperor's aid at Babylon. We have learned that he has in fact gathered those troops, but is remaining encamped near the capital at Ctesiphon. At your ancient Greek city of Seleucia, in fact, just across the Tigris."

The sahrdaran bestowed his own cold glare on the landscape. "Well positioned, in short, to seize *our* capital. And serving no use in the war against Malwa. We suspect the worst."

"You think Ormazd is in collusion with the Malwa?"

Baresmanas heaved a sigh.

"Who is to know? For myself, I do not believe so—not at the moment, at least. I think Ormazd is simply waiting on the side, ready to strike if Khusrau is driven out of Babylon." He rubbed his face wearily. "I must also tell you, Belisarius, that the courier brought instructions for me. Once we reach Peroz-Shapur, I will have to part company with your army. I am instructed by the Emperor to take Kurush and my soldiers—and the remainder of my household troops, who await me at Peroz-Shapur—to Ormazd's camp."

"And do what?" asked Belisarius.

Baresmanas shrugged. "Whatever I can. 'Encourage' Ormazd, you might say, to join the battle against the invaders."

Belisarius eyed him for a moment. "How many household troops will there be at Peroz-Shapur?"

"Two thousand, possibly three."

Belisarius looked over his shoulder, as if to gauge Baresmanas' forces. The seven hundred Persian cavalrymen who escorted the sahrdaran were barely visible further back in the long column.

"Less than four thousand men," he murmured. "That's not going to be much of an encouragement."

Again, Baresmanas shrugged.

Belisarius broke into a grin. "Such a diplomat! Do you mean to tell me that Emperor Khusrau made no suggestion that you might request a bit of help from his Roman allies?"

Baresmanas glanced at him. "Well . . . The courier *did* mention, as a matter of fact, that the Emperor had idly mused that if the Roman commander were to be suddenly taken by a desire to see the ancient ruins of the glorious former capital of the Greek Seleucids—that he would have no objections." Baresmanas nodded. "None whatsoever."

Belisarius scratched his chin. "Seleucia. Yes, yes. I feel a sudden hankering to see the place. Been a life-long dream, in fact."

They rode on for a bit, in companionable silence, until Belisarius remarked: "Seleucia wasn't actually founded by Greeks, by the way. Macedonians."

Baresmanas waved his hand. "Please, Belisarius! You can hardly expect a pureblood Aryan to understand these petty distinctions. As far as we are concerned, you mongrels from the west come in only two varieties. Bad Greeks and worse Greeks."

Chapter 11

Two days later, the long-simmering discontent of the Constantinople troops came to a boil. After the mid-day break, when the order was given to resume the march, the garrison soldiers remained squatting by their campfires, refusing to mount up.

Their action had obviously been co-ordinated in advance. Several of his Thracian bucellarii, including Maurice, reported to Belisarius that the garrison troopers' sub-officers had been seen circulating through the route camp during the break. The top officers of the Constantinople soldiers, the chiliarch and the tribunes, were apparently not involved directly. But they were just as apparently making no effort to restore discipline to their troops.

"It's an organized mutiny," concluded Maurice angrily. "This is not just some spontaneous outburst."

Belisarius made a calming gesture with his hand. For a moment, he stared at the Euphrates, as if seeking inspiration from its placidly moving waters. As usual, whenever possible, the army had taken its mid-day break at a place where the road ran next to the river.

He wiped his face with a cloth. The heat was oppressive, even in the shade provided by the canopy which his men had erected for him at the break. The shelter was not a tent—simply a canvas stretched across six poles. Enough to provide some relief from the sun, while not blocking the slight breeze.

"Let's not use that term," the general stated firmly. He met Maurice's glare with a calm gaze. " 'Mutiny' isn't just a curse word, Maurice. It's also a legal definition. If I call this a mutiny, I am required by imperial edict to deal with it in specific ways. Ways which, at the moment, I am not convinced are necessary. Or wise."

Belisarius scanned the faces of the other men crowded into the shelter of the lean-to. All of the top commanders of the army were there, except for the officers in charge of the Constantinople troops. Their absence made their own shaky allegiance quite clear.

Baresmanas and Kurush were also standing there. Belisarius decided to deal with that problem first.

"I would appreciate it, Kurush, if you would resume the march with your own troops. Move as slowly as you can, without obviously dawdling, so that we Romans can catch up to you as soon as this problem is settled. But, for the moment, I think it would be best if—"

Kurush nodded. "There's no need to explain, Belisarius. You don't need Aryan soldiers mixed into this brew. We'd just become another source of tension."

He turned away, moving with his usual nervous energy, and began giving quick orders to his subordinates. Baresmanas followed, after giving Belisarius a supportive smile.

With none but Romans now present, the atmosphere eased a bit. Or, it might be better to say, Roman inhibitions relaxed.

"Call it what you want," snarled Coutzes. "I think you ought to give those fucking garrison commanders the same treatment you gave those eight fucking—"

"*I* think we ought to hear what the general thinks," interjected Bouzes. He laid a restraining hand on his brother's arm. "He *is* noted for his cunning, you know. Or have you forgotten?"

Coutzes made a sour face, but fell silent. Bouzes grinned at Belisarius. "Perhaps we might announce the suddenly-discovered presence of a Malwa pay caravan?" he suggested cheerfully. "Send the garritroopers off on a 'reconnaissance-in-force'?"

All the officers standing around erupted in laughter, except Belisarius. But even he, in the humor of the moment, could not help returning Bouzes' grin.

In the few days since Bouzes and Coutzes had joined his forces, Belisarius had come to share Sittas and Hermogenes' assessment of the two brothers. Neither one, it was true—especially Coutzes—had entirely shed their youthful tendencies toward hot-headedness. But those tendencies, in the three years since Mindouos, had clearly been tempered by experience.

Belisarius' grin faded, but a smile remained. Yes, he had already decided that he approved of the Thracian brothers. Not all men have the temperament to learn from experience. Belisarius himself did, and he prized that ability in others.

Humor, he thought, was the key—especially the ability to laugh at oneself. When he heard Bouzes and Coutzes, in Callinicum, invite Maurice to join them in a "reconnaissance-in-force" to the nearest tavern, he knew the brothers would work out just fine.

He shook off the humor. His problem remained, and it was not comical in the least. "I want to settle this without bloodshed," he announced. "And I don't think it's needed, anyway. Maurice, I'm not quibbling with you over legal definitions. I simply think that you're misreading the situation."

Maurice tugged his beard. "Maybe," he said, grudgingly. "But—"

Again, Belisarius held up a hand. Maurice shrugged, slightly, and fell silent.

The general now turned toward Timasius, the commander of the five hundred Illyrian cavalrymen given to him by Germanicus.

"Your men are the key to the situation," he announced. "Key, at least, to the way I handle it. Where do they stand?"

Timasius frowned. "Stand? Exactly how do you mean that, general?"

Timasius' thick accent—like most Illyrians from Dacia, his native language was Latin rather than Greek—always made him seem a bit dull-witted. At first, Belisarius had dismissed the impression, until further acquaintance with the man had led him to the conclusion that Timasius was, in fact, a bit on the dim side. He seemed a competent enough officer, true, when dealing with routine matters. But—

Belisarius decided he had no time to be anything other than blunt and direct.

"What I mean, Timasius, is that you Illyrians have also been complaining loudly since we began the march two months ago." He waved down the officer's gathering sputter of protest. "I am not accusing you of anything! I am simply stating a fact."

Timasius lapsed into mulish, resentful silence. Belisarius tightened his jaws, prepared to drive the matter through. But it proved unnecessary. Timasius' chief subordinate, a hecatontarch by the name of Liberius, spoke up.

"It's not the same, general. It's true, our men have been grousing a lot—but that's just due to the unaccustomed exertions of this forced march."

The man scowled. On his heavy-set, low-browed face, the expression made him seem like an absolute dullard. But his ensuing words contradicted the impression.

"You've got to distinguish between that and what's

eating the Constantinople men. *They're* a lot of pampered garrison troops. True, they're not nobility, except the officers—not *that* unit—but they've picked up the attitude. They're used to lording it over everybody, friend and foe alike." The scowl deepened. The man's brow disappeared almost completely. "*Especially* over their own, the snotty bastards. That girl in Callinicum wasn't the first tavern maid they've been free with, you can be sure of that. Probably been quite a few in Constantinople itself given that same treatment—and had it hushed up afterward, by the capital's authorities."

A little growl from several of the other officers under the canopy indicated their concurrence.

"Illyrian soldiers aren't exactly famous for their gentle manners, either," commented Belisarius mildly.

Liberius winced. In point of fact, Illyrian troops had the reputation of being the most atrocity-prone of any Roman army, other than outright mercenaries.

"It's still not the same," he stated—forcefully, but not sullenly. Belisarius was impressed by the man's dispassionate composure.

Liberius gestured toward Bouzes and Coutzes, and the other officers from the Syrian army. "These lads are used to dealing with Persians. Civilized, the Medes are. Sure, when war breaks out both sides have been known to act badly. But, even then, it's a matter between empires. And in between the wars—which is most of the time—the borderlands are quiet and peaceful."

Several of the Syrian officers nodded. Liberius continued: "What you *don't* get is what we have in Illyricum—constant, unending skirmishes with a lot of barbarian savages. Border villages ravaged by some band of Goths or Avars who are just engaging in casual plunder. Their own kings—if you can call them that—don't even know about it, most of the time."

He shrugged. "So we repay the favor on the nearest barbarian village."

The scowl returned in full force. "That is *not* the same thing as raping a girl in your own town—and then murdering half her family in the bargain!"

Again, the growl of agreement swept the room. Louder, this time. Much louder.

Belisarius glanced at Timasius. Liberius' slow-thinking commander had finally caught up with his subordinate's thoughts. He too, now, was nodding vehemently.

Belisarius was satisfied. For the moment, at least. But he made a note to speak to the Illyrian commanders in the near future. To remind them that they would soon be operating in Persia, and that the treatment which Illyrians were accustomed to handing out to barbarians in the trans-Danube would *not* be tolerated in Mesopotamia.

He moved out of the shade, toward his horse. "All right, then."

His officers made to follow. Belisarius waved them back. "No," he announced. "I'll handle this myself."

"*What?*" demanded Coutzes. "You're not taking anyone with you?"

Belisarius smiled crookedly, holding up two fingers.

"Two." He pointed toward Valentinian and Anastasius, who had been waiting just outside the canopy throughout the conference. As soon as they saw his gesture, the two cataphracts began mounting their horses.

Once he was on his own horse, Belisarius smiled down at his officers—all of whom, except Maurice, were staring at him as if he were insane.

"Two should be enough," he announced placidly, and spurred his horse into motion.

As the three men began riding off, Valentinian muttered something under his breath.

"What did he say?" wondered Bouzes. "I didn't catch it."

Maurice smiled, thinly. "I think he said 'piss on crazy strategoi.' "

He turned back toward the shade of the shelter. "But maybe not. Be terribly disrespectful of the high command! Maybe he just said 'wish on daisies, attaboy.' Encouraging his horse, you know. Poor beast's probably as sick of this desert as we are."

As they headed down the road, Belisarius waved Valentinian and Anastasius forward. Once the two men were riding on either side, he said:

"Don't touch your weapons unless the muti—ah, dispirited troops—take up theirs."

He gave both men a hard glance. Anastasius' heavy face held no expression. Valentinian scowled, but made no open protest.

A thin smile came to the general's face. "Mainly, what I want you to do after we arrive at the Greeks' camp is to disagree with me."

Anastasius' eyes widened. "*Disagree*, sir?"

Belisarius nodded. "Yes. Disagree. Not *too* openly, mind. I *am* your commanding officer, after all. But I want you to make clear, in no uncertain terms, that you think I'm an idiot."

Anastasius frowned. Valentinian muttered.

"What was that last, Valentinian?" queried Belisarius. "I'm not sure I caught it."

Silence. Anastasius rumbled: "He said: '*That* won't be hard.' "

"That's what I thought he said," mused Belisarius. He grinned. "Well! You won't have any difficulty with the assignment, then. It'll come naturally to you."

Valentinian muttered again, at some length. Anastasius, not waiting for a cue, interpreted. "He said—I'm summarizing—that clever fellows usually

wind up outsmarting themselves. Words to that
effect."

Belisarius frowned. "That's all? It seemed to me
he muttered quite a few more words than that. Entire
sentences, even."

Anastasius shook his head sadly. "Most of the other
words were just useless adjectives. Very redundant."
The giant bestowed a reproving glance on his comrade. "He's given to profanity."

They were nearing the encampment of the Constantinople garrison troops. Belisarius spurred his
horse into a trot. After Valentinian and Anastasius
dropped back to their usual position as his bodyguards, Belisarius cocked his head and said:

"Remember. *Disagree. Disapprove.* If I say something reasonable, scowl. Pleasant, snarl. Calm and
soothing—spit on the ground."

Mutter, mutter, mutter.

Belisarius repressed his smile. He did not ask for
a translation. He was quite sure the words had been
pure profanity.

They began encountering the first outposts of the
Constantinople garrison. Within a minute, trotting
forward, they passed several hundred soldiers, huddled
in small groups at the outer perimeter of the route
camp. As Belisarius had expected, a large number of
the troops were holding back from the body of men
milling around in the center. These would be the
faint-hearts and the fence-sitters—or the "semi-
loyalists," if you preferred.

He made it a point to bestow a very cordial smile
upon all those men. Even a verbal greeting, here
and there. Valentinian and Anastasius immediately
responded with their own glowers, which Valentinian
accompanied by a nonstop muttering. The garrison
troops responded to the general's smile, in the main,
with expressions of uncertainty. But Belisarius noted
that a number of them managed their own smiles

in return. Timid smiles; sickly smiles—but smiles
nonetheless.

I knew it, he thought, with considerable self-
satisfaction.

Aide's voice came into his mind. **Knew what? And
what is going on? I am confused.**

Belisarius hesitated, before responding. To his—
"its," technically, but the general had long since come
to think of Aide as "he"—consciousness, insubordination and rebellion were bizarre conceptions. Aide
had been produced by a race of intelligent crystals
in the far distant future and sent back in time, to save
them from enslavement (and possibly outright destruction) by those they called the "new gods." The
intelligence of those crystals was utterly inhuman, in
many ways. One of those ways was their lack of
individuality. Each crystal, though distinct, was a part
of their collective mentality—just as each crystal, in
its turn, was the composite being created by the ever-
moving facets which generated that strange intelligence. To those crystals, and to Aide, the type of
internal discord and dispute which humans took for
granted was almost unfathomable.

*We are having what we call a "mutiny," Aide. Or
a "rebellion."*

From long experience, Belisarius had learned
how to project his own visions into the consciousness of Aide. He had found that such visions often
served as a better means of communication than
words.

He did so now, summoning up images of various
mutinies and rebellions of the past, culminating with
the revolt of Spartacus and its gruesome finale.

He could sense the facets flashing around the
visions, trying to absorb their essence.

While they did so, and Aide ruminated, Belisarius
and his bodyguards reached the center of the camp.
At least four hundred soldiers from the Constantinople

garrison were clustered there, most of them in small groups centered around the older soldiers.

Belisarius was not surprised. The men, he gauged, were leaning heavily on the judgements and opinions of their squad leaders and immediate superiors. This was an army led by pentarchs, decarchs, and hecatontarchs, now, not officers.

Good. I can deal with those veterans. They'll be sullen and angry, but they'll also be thinking about their pensions. Unlike the officers, they don't have rich estates to retire to.

Silence fell over the mob. Belisarius slowly rode his horse into the very center of the crowd. After drawing up his mount, he scanned the soldiers staring up at him with a long, calm gaze.

A thought came from Aide.

This is stupid. Your plan is ridiculous.

The facets had reached their conclusion, firmly and surely, from their assessment of the general's vision. Especially the last vision, the suppression of the Spartacus rebellion.

Preposterous. Absurd. Irrational. You cannot possibly crucify all these men. There is not that much wood in the area.

Belisarius struggled mightily with sudden laughter. He managed, barely, to transform the hilarity into good cheer.

So it was, to their astonishment, that the mutinous soldiers of the Constantinople garrison witnessed their commanding general, whom they assumed had come to thunder threats and condemnation, bestow upon them a smile of sheer goodwill.

They barely noticed the savage snarls on the faces of his two companions. Only two or three even took umbrage at Valentinian's loud expectoration.

An officer scurried forward, after pushing his way through the first line of the crowd standing around the general. Four other officers followed.

Belisarius recognized them immediately. The officer in front was Sunicas, the chiliarch who commanded the Constantinople troops. The men following him were the tribunes who served as his chief subordinates. He knew only one of them by name—Boraides.

When the five men drew up alongside his horse, Belisarius simply looked down upon them, cocking an eyebrow, but saying nothing.

"We have a problem here, general," stated Sunicas. "As you can see, the men—"

"We certainly do!" boomed Belisarius. His voice was startlingly loud, enough so that an instant silence fell over the entire mob of soldiers. The general was so soft-spoken, as a rule, that men tended to forget that his powerful baritone had been trained to pierce the din of battles.

Belisarius, again, scanned the immediate circle of soldiers. This time, however, there was nothing benign in that gaze. His scrutiny was intent and purposeful.

He pointed to one of the soldiers in the inner ring. A hecantontarch, young for his rank. The man was bigger than average, and very burly. He was also quite a handsome man, in a large-nosed and strong-featured way. But beneath the outward appearance of a muscular bruiser, Belisarius did not miss the intelligence in the man's brown eyes. Nor the steadiness of his gaze. "What is your name?" he asked.

"Agathius." The hecatontarch's expression was grim and tightly-held, and his answer had been given in a curt growl which bordered on disrespect. But the general was much more impressed by the man's instant willingness to identify himself.

Belisarius waved his hand in a casual little gesture which encompassed the entire encampment. "You are in command of these men." The statement was firm, but matter-of-fact. Much like a man might announce that the sun rises in the east.

Agathius frowned.

"*You* are in command of these men," repeated Belisarius. "*Now. Today.*"

Agathius' frown deepened. For a moment, he began to look toward the men at his side. But then—to Belisarius' delight—he squared his broad shoulders and lifted his head. The frown vanished, replaced by a look of stony determination. "You may say so, yes."

"What do *you* say?" came the general's immediate response.

Agathius hesitated, for the briefest instant. Then, shrugging: "Yes."

Belisarius waited, staring at him. After a moment, grudgingly, Agathius added: "General. Sir."

Belisarius waited, staring at him. Agathius stared back. A little look of surprise flitted across his face, then. The young hecatontarch blew out his cheeks and stood very erect. "I am in command here, sir. Today. Now."

Belisarius nodded. "Tomorrow, also," he said. Very pleasantly, as if announcing good weather. "And, I hope, for many days to come."

From the corner of his eye, Belisarius caught a glimpse of Anastasius' bug-eyed glare of disapproval. He heard Valentinian mutter something. The words were too soft to understand, but the sullen tone was not.

The general shifted his gaze to the chiliarch and the tribunes standing by his stirrup. The calm, mild expression on his face vanished—replaced by pitiless condemnation.

"*You are relieved of command, Sunicas.* Your tribunes also. I want you on the road to Constantinople within the hour. You may take your personal gear with you. And your servants, of course. Nothing else."

Sunicas goggled. The tribune Boraides exclaimed: "You can't do that! *On what grounds?*"

Belisarius heard Valentinian immediately growl: "Quite right!" Then: loud muttering, in which the words "outrageous" and "unjust" figured prominently. Anastasius, for his part, simply glowered at the newly-promoted mutineer Agathius. But, oh, such a wondrous glower it was! Worthy of a Titan!

The hecatontarch's returning glare was a more modest affair. Merely Herculean. The sub-officers of the Constantinople troops in the circle began closing ranks with Agathius. In seconds, three other hecatontarchs and perhaps a dozen decarchs were standing shoulder-to-shoulder, matching hard stares with the Thracian cataphracts.

Belisarius immediately sided with the Greek soldiers.

Twisting sharply in his saddle, he bestowed his own very respectable glower on Valentinian and Anastasius.

"I'll stand for no insubordination!" he snapped. "Do you understand?" He almost added "from knaves and varlets," but decided that would be a bit overmuch.

Valentinian and Anastasius lowered their heads submissively. But not *too* submissively, Belisarius was pleased to see. Their stance exuded that of the chastened but still stubborn underlings, resentful of their commander's grotesque violation of military norms and protocol.

Belisarius whipped his harsh gaze back to Boraides.

"On what grounds?" he demanded. "*On what grounds?*"

The general's own glower now ascended into the mythic heights. Worthy of Theseus, perhaps, confronting the minotaur. "*On the grounds of gross incompetence!*" he roared.

Again, he swept his hand in a circle. The gesture, this time, was neither little nor casual. He stood erect in his stirrups, moving his arm as if to command the tides. "The first duty of any commander is to *command*," he bellowed. "You have obviously failed in that duty. These men are not under your command. You have admitted as much yourself." He sat back in the saddle. "Therefore I have replaced you with a man who is capable of command." He pointed to Agathius. "*Him*. He is the new chiliarch of this unit."

Now looking at Agathius, Belisarius gestured toward Sunicas and the tribunes. "See to it, Agathius. I want these—these fellows—on the road. Within the hour."

Agathius stared at the general. Belisarius met his gaze with calm assurance. After a few seconds, the new chiliarch cocked his head toward one of the men standing next to him, without taking his eyes from Belisarius, and murmured:

"Take care of it, Cyril. You heard the general. Within the hour."

Cyril, a scarred veteran perhaps ten years older than Agathius, gave his newly-promoted superior a sly little grin. "As you wish, *sir!*" he boomed.

Cyril strode toward Sunicas and the tribunes. His grin widened, widened. Became rather evil, in fact. "You've got your orders. *Move.*"

The former commanding officers ogled him. Cyril made a little gesture. Four decarchs closed ranks with him, fingering their swords.

Anastasius' eyes bugged out. His expression verged on apoplexy.

Valentinian muttered. The words "outrageous" and "unjust" were, again, distinct. Belisarius thought he also heard the phrase "oh, heavens, what shall we do?" But, maybe not.

He glared at Anastasius and Valentinian. The cataphracts avoided his gaze, but, still, held their stubborn pose. Several more sub-officers from the garrison troops sidled forward. Two of them went to assist Cyril and his decarchs—who were now, almost physically, driving the former commanders off—but most of them edged toward Belisarius. Prepared, it was clear, to defend the general against his own bodyguards. If necessary.

"Well, that's that," announced Belisarius.

He began climbing down from his horse. A pentarch hastened forward to assist him.

Once on the ground, Belisarius strode over to Agathius and said: "It's a miserably hot day. Would you have some wine, by any chance?"

This time, Agathius did not hesitate for more than a second. "Yes, sir. We do. May we offer you some?"

"I would be delighted. And let us take the opportunity to become acquainted. I should like to be introduced to your subordinates, also. You'll need to appoint new tribunes, of course." He shrugged. "I leave it to your judgement to select them. You know your men better than I do."

Agathius eyed him wonderingly, but said nothing. He led the way to a canvas shelter nearby. Most of the sub-officers in the circle followed, in a little mob. Only a handful remained behind, faithfully at their new post, keeping a vigilant eye on the general's sullen and untrustworthy bodyguards.

Within seconds, amphorae began appearing and wine was poured. Within two minutes, Belisarius was squatting in the shelter of the canopy, with no fewer than three dozen of the Constantinople troopers' chief sub-officers forming an audience. The men were very tightly packed, trying to crowd their way into the shade.

For all the world, the impromptu gathering had the flavor of a mid-afternoon chat.

"All right," said Belisarius pleasantly, after finishing his cup. "I'll tell you what I want. Then you'll tell me what you want. Then we'll see if we can reach a settlement."

He scanned the small crowd briefly, before settling his gaze on Agathius.

"I want an end to the slackness of your marching order. The men can grouse and grumble all they want, but I want them to do it in formation. Some reasonable approximation of it, at least." He held out his cup. A decarch refilled it.

"I realize that you're unaccustomed to the conditions, here in the desert—and that it's been a long time since you've had to undertake a forced march like this. But enough's enough. You're not weaklings, for the sake of Christ. You've had two months to get into shape! The truth is, I don't think the march is that hard on you, anymore. You've just gotten into the habit of resentfulness."

He stopped to sip at his wine, gazing at Agathius. The new chiliarch took a deep breath. For a moment, his eyes wandered, staring out at the harshlit desert.

One of the sub-officers behind him started to say something—a protest, by the tone—but Agathius waved him down. "Shut up, Paul," he growled. "Tell the truth, I'm sick of it myself."

His eyes returned to Belisarius. He nodded. "All right, general. I'll see to it. What else?"

"I want you to accept some detachments from the Army of Syria. Light cavalry." A crooked smile. "Call them advisers. Part of the problem is that you've no experience in the desert, and you've been too arrogant to listen to anyone."

He pointed to the canvas stretched over his head. "You didn't figure this out, for instance, until a week ago. Till then you set up regular tents, every night, and sweltered without a breeze."

Agathius grimaced. Belisarius plowed on.

"There's been a hundred little things like that. Your cocksure capital city attitude has done nothing but make your life harder, and caused resentment in the other units. I want it to stop. I'll have the Syrian units send you some light auxiliaries. They'll be Arabs, the most of them—know the desert better than anyone. If you treat them properly, they'll be a big help to you."

Agathius rubbed the back of his neck. "Agreed. What else?"

Belisarius shrugged. "What I expect from all my other units. Henceforth, Agathius, you will attend the command conferences. Bring your tribunes. A few hecatontarchs, if you want. But don't bring many—I like my conferences to be small enough that we can have a real discussion and get some work done. I'm not given to speeches."

Agathius eyed him skeptically.

"And what else?"

"Nothing." Belisarius drained the cup, held it out. Again, it was refilled.

"Your turn," he said mildly.

Agathius twitched his shoulders irritably.

"Ah—!" he exclaimed. He was silent, for a moment, frowning. Then:

"It's like this, general. The real problem isn't the march, and it isn't the desert. As you said, we've gotten used to it by now. It's—" He gestured vaguely. "It's the way we got hauled out of the barracks, without a day's notice, and sent off on this damned expedition. Off to Mesopotamia, for the sake of Christ, while—"

He lapsed into a bitter silence. One of the decarchs behind him piped up.

"While all the fucking *noble* units got to stay behind, cozy in the capital. Living like lords."

Belisarius lifted his head, laughing. "Well, of course!" he exclaimed. "The last thing I wanted on this expedition was a bunch of aristocrats."

He shook his head ruefully. "God, think of it! Every cataphract in those units can't move without twelve servants and his own personal baggage train. I'd be lucky to make five miles a day."

He bestowed a very approving smile on the soldiers squatting around him.

"I told Sittas I wanted his best *fighting* unit. Had

quite a set-to with him, I did. Naturally, he tried to fob off his most useless parade ground troops on me, but I wouldn't have it. '*Fighters*,' I said. Fighters, Sittas. I've got no use for anything else."

The Greeks' chests swelled a bit. Their heads lifted.

Belisarius drained his cup. Held it out for another refill.

"Stop worrying about those lordly troops, lounging in their barracks in Constantinople. Within a year, you'll have enough booty to sneer at them. Not to mention a glorious name and the gratitude of Rome."

The soldiers' gaze became eager. "Booty, sir?" asked one. "Do you think so? We'd heard—"

He fell silent. Another spoke: "We'd heard you frown on booty, sir."

Belisarius' eyes widened. "From whom did you hear *that*? Not the Syrian soldiers! Each one of those lads came away from Mindouos with more treasure than they knew what to do with. And you certainly didn't hear it from my Thracian cataphracts!"

The Greeks exchanged glances with each other. Suddenly, Cyril laughed.

"We heard it from the other garrison units. In Constantinople. They said Belisarius was a delicate sort, who wouldn't let his men enjoy the gleanings of a campaign."

Belisarius' good humor vanished. "That's not booty. That's *looting*. And they're damn well right about that!"

He brought a full Homeric scowl to bear.

"*I won't tolerate looting and indiscipline*. I never have, and I never will. Have no doubt about that, any of you. The penalty for looting in my army is fifty lashes. And I'll execute a man who murders and rapes. On the second offense, in the same unit, the officer in command'll be strapped to the whipping post himself. Or hung."

He drained his cup. Held it out. Immediately

drained the refill. Held it out again. The soldiers eyed the cup, then him. To all appearances, the general seemed not in the slightest affected by the wine he had drunk.

"Make no mistake about it," he said. Softly, but very firmly. "If you can't abide by those rules—"

He tossed his head dismissively. "—then follow those five bums back to your cozy barracks in Constantinople."

He drained the cup. Held it out. As it was being refilled, he remarked casually: "The reason those noble fellows in Constantinople are confused on this point is because those fine aristocratic champions don't know what a campaign looks like in the first place. When's the last time they went to war?"

A chuckle swept through the little crowd.

"A *campaign*, men, is when you set out to thrash the enemy senseless and *do it*. Once that job's done—we call it *winning the war*—booty's no problem at all. But we're not talking about 'gleanings' here."

Scornfully: " 'Gleanings' means stealing silver plate from a peasant's hut. His *only* silver plate, if he has one in the first place. Or his chickens. *Booty* means the wealth of empires, disgorged to their conquerors."

He lifted his cup, waved it in the general direction of the east.

"There's no empire in the world richer than the Malwa. And they travel in style, too, let me tell you. When I was at Ranapur, the Malwa Emperor erected a pavilion damned near as big as the Great Palace. And you wouldn't believe what he filled it with! His throne alone—his 'traveling chair,' he called it—was made of solid—"

Belisarius continued in this happy vein for another ten minutes. Half that time he spent regaling his audience with tales of Malwa treasure, spoken in a tone of awe and wonder. The other half, with tales of Malwa fecklessness and cowardice, in tones of scorn and derision.

None of it was, quite, outright lies. None of it was, quite, cold sober truth.

By the time he finished, he had emptied another amphora of wine. His audience had emptied their fair share, also.

He glanced up at the sun. Yawned.

"Ah, hell. It's too late to start a proper march now, anyway."

He rose to his feet.

"Give me a minute, boys, to give the order. Then we can get down to some serious drinking."

The soldiers ogled him. The general was not only standing erect, with perfect ease, he wasn't even swaying. Belisarius strode toward Valentinian and Anastasius. His two cataphracts had remained on their horses, sweating rivers in the hot sun. Glaring resentfully at the Constantinople troops.

In a loud voice, he called out to them: "Pass the word to Maurice! We'll take a break for the rest of the day. Resume the march tomorrow morning."

He began to turn away, waving his hand in a gesture of dismissal. Then, as if taken by a sudden happy thought, added: "And tell my servants to bring some wine! Plenty of it—enough for all of us. Good vintage, too—d'ye hear? I'll have no swill for these men!"

By the time the servants appeared, leading a small mule train carrying many large amphorae, the encampment of the Constantinople troops had turned into a cheerful celebration. The audience surrounding the general had grown much, much larger. Dozens of common soldiers—hundreds, counting those milling on the edges—had crowded around the sub-officers in the inner circle.

When the sun fell, Belisarius ordered the canopy

dismantled, so that all of his soldiers could hear him better. That done, he continued his tales.

Tales of Malwa treasure and Malwa military incompetence, of course. But, woven among those tunes, were other melodies as well. He spoke of the huge numbers of the Malwa, which could only be thwarted by disciplined and spirited troops. Of the valor of their Persian allies, and the imperative necessity of not offending them with misconduct. Of his own nature as a general—good-hearted but, when necessary, *firm*.

But most of all, as the evening progressed, he spoke of Rome. Rome, and its thousand years of glory. Rome, often defeated in battle—rarely in war. Rome, savage when it needed to be—but, in the end, an empire of laws. Whose very emperor—and here his troops suddenly remembered, with not a little awe, that the genial man sharing their cups was the Emperor's own father—only ruled with the consent of the governed. *Especially* the consent of those valiant men whose blood and courage had forged Rome and kept it safe through the centuries.

The very men who shared his wine.

He drained his last cup. "I believe I've had enough," he announced. He rose to his feet—slowly, carefully, but without staggering—and eyed his horse. "Fuck it," he muttered. "Too far to ride."

He turned toward Agathius. "With your permission, chiliarch, I'd like to make my bed here tonight."

Agathius' eyes widened. He rose himself, rather shakily, and stared about. He seemed both startled and a bit embarassed. "We don't have much in the way of—"

Belisarius casually waved his hand.

"A blanket'll do. Often enough I've used my saddle for a pillow, on campaign."

Two decarchs hastily scrambled about, digging up the best blanket they could find.

As they saw to that task, Belisarius straightened and said, very loudly:

"If there is any request that you have, make it now. It will be granted, if it is within my power to do so."

There was a moment's hesitation. Then, a hecatontarch cleared his throat and said: "It's about the men you've—your Thracians have been dragging alongside us."

A little mutter of agreement swept the crowd. There was resentment in that mutter, even some anger, but nothing in the way of hot fury.

Agathius spoke, very firmly: "Those boys were a bad lot, sir. We all knew it. Wasn't the first time they mistreated folk. Still—"

"Shouldn't be *dragged*," someone complained.

A different voice spoke: "Fuck that! A stinking *filthy* bunch they were—and you all know it!"

The man who had spoken rose.

"Drag them all you want, sir. Just don't do it next to us. It's—it's not right."

The mutter which swept the crowd was more in the nature of a growl, now.

Belisarius nodded. "Fair enough. I'll have them buried first thing in the morning. A Christian burial, if I can find a priest to do the rites."

A soldier nearby snorted. "Fat lot of good that'll do 'em, once Satan gives 'em the eye."

A ripple of laughter swept the encampment.

Belisarius smiled himself, but said: "That's for the Lord to decide, not us. They'll have a Christian burial."

He paused, then spoke again. His powerful voice was low-pitched, but carried very well. Very well.

"There will be no more of this business."

He made no threats. The hundreds of soldiers who heard him noted the absence of threats, and appreciated it. They also understood and appreciated, now, that their general was not a man who issued threats.

But that, came to it, he would have half an army drag the corpses of the other half, if that was what it took to make it *his* army.

"Yes, sir," came from many throats.

"My name is Belisarius. I am your general."

"Yes, sir," came from all throats.

The next morning, shortly after the army resumed its march, a courier arrived from the Persian forces who had gone ahead. The courier had been sent back by Kurush to inquire—delicately, delicately—as to the current state of the Roman army.

Belisarius was not there to meet the courier. He was spending the day marching in the company of his Constantinople troops. But Maurice apprised the Persian of the recent developments.

After the courier returned to Kurush's tent, that evening, and related the tale, the young Persian commander managed to restrain himself until the courier was gone.

Then, with only his uncle for an audience, he exploded.

"I can't believe it!" he hissed. "The man is utterly mad! He deals with a mutiny by dismissing the *officers*?—and then promotes the *mutineers*? And then spends the whole night carousing with them as if—"

"Remind me again, nephew," interrupted Baresmanas, coldly. "I seem to have forgotten. Which one of us was it—who won the battle at Mindouos?"

Kurush's mouth snapped shut.

That same evening, in the Roman encampment, the new chiliarch of the Constantinople troops arrived for his first command meeting. He brought with him the newly appointed tribunes—Cyril was one of them—and two hecatontarchs. Throughout the ensuing conference, the seven Greek soldiers sat uneasily to one side. They did not participate, that night, in the discussion. But they listened closely, and were struck by four things.

One. The discussion was lively, free-wheeling, and relaxed. Belisarius clearly did not object to his subordinates expressing their opinions openly—quite unlike most Roman generals in their experience.

Two. That said, it was always the general who made the final decisions. Clear decisions, clearly stated, leading to clear lines of action. Quite unlike the murky orders which were often issued by commanders, which left their subordinates in the unenviable position of being blamed in the event of miscommunication.

Three. No one was in the least hostile toward them. Not even the general's Thracian cataphracts.

Indeed, the commander of his bucellarii, Maurice, singled them out following the meeting, and invited them to join him in a cup of wine. And both commanders of the Syrian troops, the brothers Bouzes and Coutzes, were quick to add their company.

Many cups later in the evening, Agathius shook his head ruefully.

"I can't figure it out," he muttered, "but somehow I think I've been swindled."

"You'll get no sympathy from us," belched Coutzes.

"Certainly not!" agreed his brother cheerfully. Bouzes leaned over and refilled Agathius' cup. "At least you got swindled *into* an army," he murmured.

Agathius stared at him, a bit bleary-eyed. "What's *that* supposed to mean?"

"Never mind," stated Maurice. The burly veteran held out his own cup. "I believe I'll make my own reconnaissance-in-force on that amphora, Bouzes. If you would be so kind."

And that produced the fourth, and final, impression in the minds of the Constantinople men that night.

A peculiar sense of humor, those Thracians and Syrians seemed to have. The quip was witty, to be sure—but to produce such a howling gale of knee-slapping laughter?

Chapter 12

MUZIRIS
Summer, 531 A.D.

"Under no circumstances, Empress," stated the viceroy of Muziris firmly. "Your grandfather will neither see you, nor will he rescind the ban on your travel to the capital at Vanji."

The viceroy turned in his plush, heavily-upholstered chair and gestured to a man sitting to his right. Like the viceroy, this man was dressed in the expensive finery of a high Keralan official. But instead of wearing the ruby-encrusted sword of a viceroy, he carried the emerald-topped staff of office which identified him as one of Kerala's *Matisachiva*. The title meant "privy councillor," and he was one of the half-dozen most powerful men in the South Indian kingdom.

The Matisachiva was slender; the viceroy, corpulent. Otherwise, their appearance was similar and quite typical of Keralans. Kerala was a Dravidian land. Its people were small and very dark-skinned—almost as dark as Africans. Shakuntala's own size and skin color, along with her lustrous black eyes, were inherited from her Keralan mother.

The Matisachiva's name was Ganapati. The moment Shakuntala had seen him, sitting next to the viceroy in his audience chamber, she understood the significance of his presence. She remembered Ganapati. Ten years before, at the age of nine, she had spent a pleasant six months in Vanji, the capital city in the interior. At the time, she had been the daughter of the great Emperor of Andhra, visiting her mother's family. She had been well-received then, even doted upon—and by none more so than her grandfather. But, even then, there had been times that a headstrong girl had to be held in check. Whenever such times came, it had always been Ganapati who was sent to do the deed.

Andhra was gone now, crushed under the Malwa heel. But she was quite sure that Ganapati retained his old special post—saying *no* for the King of Kerala.

Ganapati cleared his throat.

"The King—your grandfather—is in a difficult situation. Very difficult. The Malwa Empire is not directly threatening us. Nor are they likely to, in the foreseeable future. Malwa's ambitions in the Deccan seem to have been satisfied by their"—he grimaced apologetically—"conquest of your father's realm. And now their attention is focussed to the northwest. Their recent invasion of Persia, from our point of view, was a blessing. The great bulk of their army is tied up there, unavailable for use against the independent south Indian monarchies. Persia will not fall easily, not even to the Malwa."

The viceroy leaned forward, interjecting earnestly: "That's especially true in light of the newest development. According to the most recent reports, it seems that the Roman Empire will throw its weight on the side of the Aryans. Their most prestigious general, in fact, is apparently leading an army into

Persia. A man by the name of Belisarius. As Ganapati says, the Malwa Empire is now embroiled in a war which will last for years. Decades, even."

Ganapati cleared his throat.

"Under these circumstances, the obvious course of action for Kerala is to do nothing that might aggravate the Malwa. They are oriented northwest, not south. Let us keep it that way."

Dadaji Holkar interrupted. "That is only true for the immediate period, Matisachiva. The time will come when Malwa will resume its march to the south. They will not rest until they have conquered all of India."

Ganapati gave Shakuntala's adviser a cold stare. For all of Holkar's decorum and obvious erudition, the Keralan councillor suspected that the headstrong Empress-in-exile had chosen a most unsuitable man to be her adviser. The impetuous child had even named the man as her *peshwa*! As if her ridiculous "government-in-exile" needed a premier.

The Matisachiva sniffed. No doubt Holkar was brahmin, as Maratha counted such things. But Maratha blood claims were threadbare, at best. Like all Maratha, Holkar was a deeply polluted individual.

Still—Ganapati was a diplomat. So he responded politely.

"That is perhaps true," he said. "Although I think it is unwise to believe we can read the future. Who really knows Malwa's ultimate aims?"

He held up a hand, forestalling Shakuntala's angry outburst.

"Please, Your Majesty! Let us not quarrel over the point. Even if your adviser's assessment is accurate, it changes nothing. Malwa intentions are one thing. Their capabilities are another. Let us suppose, for a moment, that the Malwa succeed in their conquest of Persia. They will be exhausted by the effort—*and* preoccupied with the task of administering vast and newly-subjugated territories."

He leaned back in his chair, exuding self-satisfaction.

"Either way, you see, Malwa poses no danger to Kerala—*so long as we do not provoke them.*"

The Matisachiva frowned, casting a stony glance at Holkar.

"Unfortunately, the recent actions of the Maratha rebels are stirring up the—"

"They are not *rebels*," snapped Shakuntala. "They are Andhra *loyalists*, fighting to restore the legitimate power to the Deccan. Which is *me*. I am the rightful ruler of Andhra, not the Malwa invaders."

For a moment, Ganapati was nonplussed.

"Well—yes. Perhaps. In the best of all worlds. But we do not live in that world, Empress." The frown returned. "The fact is that Malwa *has* conquered Andhra. In *that* world—the *real* world—Raghunath Rao and his little band of outlaws—"

"Not so little," interjected Holkar. "And hardly outlaws! Speaking of new developments—we just received word yesterday that Rao has seized the city of Deogiri after overwhelming the large Malwa garrison."

Ganapati and the viceroy jerked erect in their chairs.

"*What?*" demanded the viceroy. "*Deogiri?*"

"Madness," muttered the Matisachiva. "Utter madness."

Ganapati rose to his feet and began pacing. For all the councillor's practiced diplomacy, he was obviously very agitated.

"Deogiri?"

Holkar nodded.

"Yes, Matisachiva—*Deogiri*. Which, as you know, is both the largest and the best fortified city in southern Majarashtra."

The Matisachiva pressed both hands against his beard.

"This is a catastrophe!" he exclaimed. He turned

toward Holkar and Shakuntala, waving his hands in midair.

"Do you know what this means? The Malwa will be sending a large army to subdue the rebels! And Deogiri is not far from Kerala's northern frontier!"

Holkar smiled icily.

"What 'large' army?" he demanded. "You just got through pointing out that most of the Malwa Empire's forces are tied up in Persia."

Shakuntala's adviser overrode the Matisachiva's splutter of protest.

"You can't have it both ways, Councillor Ganapati! The fact is that Rao's stroke was masterful. The fact is that he does *not* lead a 'small band of outlaws.' The fact is that he seized Deogiri with a large force, and has every chance of holding it for some time. The Malwa satrap Venandakatra has nothing at his disposal beyond provincial troops and what small portions of the regular Malwa army can be spared from the war in Persia. Personally, I doubt if they will be able to release *any* of those forces. As it happens, I know the Roman general Belisarius personally. His military reputation is quite deserved."

Ganapati's hand-waving now resembled the flapping of an outraged hen. "This in intolerable! The whole situation is intolerable!" He glared furiously at Shakuntala and her peshwa. "Enough!" he cried. "We have tried to be diplomatic—*but enough*! You and your Marathas have practically taken possession of Muziris! At least two thousand of your brigand horsemen—"

Shakuntala shot to her feet. "They are not brigand horsemen! They are Maratha cavalrymen who escaped from Andhra after the Malwa conquest and have been reconstituted as my regular army under properly appointed officers!"

"And there are quite a bit more than 'at least two thousand,' " growled Holkar. "By last count, the

Empress of Andhra's Maratha cavalry force in Muziris numbers over four thousand. In addition, we have two thousand or so infantrymen, being trained by eight hundred Kushans who have spurned Malwa and given their loyalty to Shakuntala. Elite soldiers, those Kushans—each and every one of them—as you well know.

"In short," he concluded coldly, "the Empress has a considerably larger force than the Keralan garrison residing in the city." Very coldly: "And a much better force, as well."

Ganapati ogled the peshwa. "Are you threatening us?" he cried. *"You would dare?"*

Holkar rose to his own feet. It was not an angry, lunging gesture; simply the firm stance of a serious man who has reached the limit of his patience. "That's enough," he said, quietly but firmly. He placed a hand on Shakuntala's shoulder, restraining her anger.

"There is no point in pursuing this further," he continued. "The situation is clear. The King of Kerala has abandoned his duty to his own kin, and acquiesces in the Malwa subjugation of Andhra. *So be it*. In the meantime, refugees from the Malwa tyranny have poured into Kerala. Most of these refugees have concentrated in Muziris. Among them are thousands of superb Maratha cavalry loyal to Empress Shakuntala. All of which means that, at the moment, she constitutes the real power in the city."

Ganapati and the viceroy were staring wide-eyed at Holkar. The peshwa was speaking the simple, unadorned truth—which was the last thing they had been expecting.

Holkar spread his hands in a sharp, forceful gesture. "As you say, Ganapati, the situation is intolerable. For us as much as for you."

"You threaten us?" gobbled the Matisachiva. "You would dare? You would—"

"Be silent!" commanded Shakuntala.

Ganapati's gobbling ceased instantly. Holkar fought down a grin. The Keralan dignitary had never encountered Shakuntala in full imperial fury. When she threw herself into it, Shakuntala could be quite overpowering, for all her tender years.

"We do not intend to occupy Muziris," she stated, coldly—almost contemptuously. "Since my grandfather has demonstrated for all the world his unmanliness and disrespect for kin, I cast him from my sight. I will leave Kerala—and take all my people with me."

She glared at the two Keralan officials. "*All of them*. Not just the cavalrymen, but all of the other refugees, as well."

The viceroy shook his head, frowning. "There are at least forty thousand of them," he muttered. "Where will—"

"We will go to Tamraparni. The ruler of that great island has offered one of his sons in marriage to me. He has also said he would welcome Andhra's refugees and will assist me in my struggle to regain my rightful place. In light of my grandfather's treachery, I have decided to accept the offer."

She fell silent. After a moment, Ganapati and the viceroy exchanged stares.

At first, their expressions registered astonishment. Then, delight. Then, once the obvious obstacle occured to them, puzzlement.

Gauging the moment, Shakuntala spoke again. "Yes. I will require a fleet of transport ships. At least a hundred and fifty. Preferably two hundred. You will provide them for me, along with the funds needed to carry through this great migration."

Again, the squawks of official outrage filled the room. But Holkar, watching, sensed the victory. When it came, even sooner than he had expected, he was gratified but not surprised. Following his sovereign through the corridors of the viceregal palace, back

to their waiting escort, he took the time to admire
the small figure of the girl striding before him.

She is listening to me. Finally.

As they rode back toward the refugee camps,
Shakuntala leaned over her saddle and smiled at
Holkar.

"That went quite well."

"I told you it would work."

"Yes, yes," she murmured. "I see now that I really
must listen more closely to my adviser."

Holkar did not miss the sly smile.

"Impudent child," he grumbled.

"Impudent?" she demanded. "This—coming from
you? Wait till the ruler of Tamraparni discovers that
he has promised to aid me in my war against Malwa!
And his son's hand in marriage!"

"He has a son," replied Holkar, with dignity. "Several of them, in fact. And I have no doubt that he
would have made the offer, if he listened carefully
to his advisers."

Shakuntala laughed. "You are an incorrigible
schemer, Dadaji!"

"*Me?* You are no slouch yourself, Your Majesty."

Holkar gave her a wry smile. "Although there are
times you petrify me with your boldness. I thought
you were mad, to order Rao—"

"I *told* you Rome would enter the Persian war
immediately," the Empress stated. The satisfaction on
the girl's face was obvious. It was not often that the
nineteen-year-old Empress had been proven right in
a disagreement with her canny, middle-aged peshwa.
"And I *told* you Belisarius would be leading their army."

"Yes, you did," agreed Holkar. "That was why you
overrode my protest at the insane idea of having Rao
seize Deogiri immediately. I had thought to wait,
until we were certain that Belisarius and the Romans
had entered the war."

The humor left Shakuntala's face. "I had no choice, Dadaji," she whispered. "You were there when Rao's courier told us of Venandakatra's atrocities in the Majarashtra countryside. The beast was murdering ten villagers for every one of his soldiers lost to Rao's raiders."

Holkar's own face was drawn. "He will butcher even more, in retaliation for Deogiri."

The Empress shook her head.

"I think you are wrong, Dadaji. With southern Majarashtra's largest city in our hands, Venandakatra will have no choice. His own status with the Malwa Emperor will depend on retaking Deogiri. He does not have so great an army that he can besiege Deogiri—you know how strong it is; the place is a fortress—and still send his cavalry on punitive rampages throughout the Deccan. Nor can he call for assistance from Emperor Skandagupta. You know as well as I do that the Malwa have been pressing him to release troops for the Persian campaign. With Rome—and Belisarius—now in the war, they will most certainly not send him reinforcements."

Again, she shook her head. "No, I am right here also—I am sure of it. The pressure on the Maratha country folk will ease, while the Vile One concentrates on Deogiri."

"And what if he takes Deogiri?" demanded Holkar. "What then? And what if the Malwa defeat the Persians and Romans quickly?"

Shakuntala laughed. "*Quickly?* With *Belisarius* leading the Romans?"

Holkar smiled. "I admit, the likelihood is not great." He cocked an eye at her. "You're counting on that, aren't you?"

She nodded—firmly, seriously. "I never would have ordered Rao to take Deogiri, otherwise."

The look she now gave her adviser was not that

of an impetuous child. It was almost ancient in its cold calculation.

"He is using us, you know—Belisarius, I mean. That was why he freed me from captivity, and gave me most of the treasure he stole from the Malwa. To start a rebellion in their rear, draining forces which would otherwise be sent against him."

Dadaji nodded. "It is his way of thinking." He studied her face. "You do not seem indignant about the matter," he commented.

The Empress shrugged. "Why should I be? Belisarius was never dishonest about it. He *told* me what he was doing. And he also promised me that he would do what was in his power to aid us. Which"—she chuckled—"he is certainly doing."

She urged her horse into a faster pace. "You know the man well, Dadaji—better than I do, when it comes down to it. He is the most cunning man in the world, yes—unpredictable, in his tactics. But there is one thing about Belisarius which is as predictacle as the sunrise."

"His honor."

She nodded. "He *promised* me. And he has not failed to keep that promise. He will batter the Malwa beasts in Persia, while we bleed them in the Deccan."

She urged her mount into a trot. There was no reason for that, really, other than her irrepressible energy.

"I was right to order Rao to seize Deogiri," she pronounced. "Now, we must see to it that he can keep the city."

Chapter 13

THE EASTERN MEDITERRANEAN

Summer, 531 A.D.

The expedition which set sail from Rhodes toward the end of summer was an impressive armada.

Antonina had brought a sizable fleet with her from Constantinople, to begin with. She had enough transport ships to carry her grenadiers, the five hundred bucellari under Ashot's command, and the infantrymen from the Army of Syria who would embark later at Seleuceia. The transports, all of them merchant sailing vessels, were escorted by two dromons, the oared warships favored by the Roman navy.

She had even requisitioned three of the great grain ships. The merchant combines which financed those ships had complained bitterly, despite Antonina's generous compensation, but the Empress Theodora had cowed them into submission. Quite easily. A simple frown, a purse of the lips, a glance at the Grand Justiciar. The merchants had suddenly discovered their compensation was quite ample, thank you.

The huge grain haulers slowed her fleet considerably, but Antonina had had no choice. At a great ceremony in the Forum of Constantine, five days before her departure from Constantinople, Michael of Macedonia had presented her with the Knights Hospitaler who had volunteered for the Egyptian expedition. Antonina had been expecting the monks from the new religious order—but not *three thousand* of them, proudly drawn up in their simple white tunics, marked by the distinctive red cross.

What she had conceived of, initially, as a lean military expedition, had grown by leaps and bounds. No sooner had she obtained the grain ships for the Knights Hospitaler than a small horde of officials and bureaucrats showed up at the docks. These were staffs—the typically bloated staffs—for the newly-appointed civil and canonical authorities of Egypt, clerks, and scribes, in the main, to serve the new Praetorian Prefect of Egypt and the Patriarch of Alexandria. Each and every one of whom, naturally, luxuriated in the grandiose titles with which those mundane occupations were invariably annointed by Roman official custom: *tabularii, scrinarii, corniculaarii, commentarienses, magister libellorum, magister studiorum, speculatores, beneficiarii* . . .

And so on and so forth.

They, too, wailed like lost sheep when presented with their crude shipboard accommodations—tents, for the most part, pitched on the decks of the small sailing ships which Antonina hastily rounded up, naturally over the wails of *their* owners. But they, too, like the disgruntled grain traders, reconciled themselves to their fate. Theodora's frown had almost magical capabilities, when it came to quelling indignant merchants and bureaucrats.

Then, the very day before departure, Michael had shown up to inform her, quite casually—*insufferable saint! damnable prophet!*—that many more Knights Hospitaler would be waiting in Seleuceia and Tyre and possibly other ports along the Levant, eager to join the crusade in Egypt.

Three more grain ships were seized—one of them overhauled by her dromons as it tried to flee the Golden Horn—emptied hurriedly of their cargoes and pressed into imperial service. Again, Theodora put her frown to work.

Finally, departure came. For a few days, Antonina luxuriated in the relative quiet of a sea voyage, until her arrival at Rhodes placed new demands upon her. John had been forewarned, by courier, of the imperial plan to transfer his armaments complex to Egypt. But, with his stubborn, mulish nature, he had made only half-hearted and lackadaisical efforts to organize the transfer. So, once again, the task had fallen on Antonina. She scrambled about, requisitioning ships on Rhodes itself—and then, coming up short, sending Ashot with the dromons to commandeer some of the vessels at Seleuceia—until the expedition was finally ready to sail.

But, in the end, sail it did. With the newest addition to the fleet proudly in the fore—John's new warship.

John took immense pride in the craft. It was the first warship in the history of the world, he announced, which was designed exclusively for gunpowder tactics. Menander demurred, at first, on hearing that claim, pointing out that the Malwa had already developed rocket ships. But John had convinced the young cataphract otherwise. The Malwa rocket ships, he pointed out, were a bastard breed. Clumsy merchant ships, at bottom, with a few portable rocket troughs added on. Jury-rigged artillery platforms, nothing more.

Menander, after seeing the ship for himself, had

quickly changed his mind. Indeed, this was something new in the world.

John's pride and joy was not completely new, of course. In the press of time, the Rhodian had not been able to build a ship from scratch. So he had started with the existing hull of an *epaktrokeles*—a larger version of the Roman Empire's courier vessels. He had then added gunwales and strengthened the ship's deck with bulwarks, so that the recoil of the cannons would not cave in the planking.

In the end, he had a swift sailing craft armed with ten cast-bronze guns, arranged five on a side. The cannons were short-barreled, with five-inch bores which had been scraped and polished to near-uniform size. For solid shot, which they could fire with reasonable accuracy up to three hundred yards, John had selected marble cannon balls. The balls had been smoothed and polished to fit the bores properly. For cannister, the cannons were provided with lead drop-shot.

"What did you decide to call her?" asked Menander.

"The *Theodora*."

"Good choice," said Menander, nodding his head vigorously.

John grinned. "I am mulish, stubborn, contrary, pig-headed and irascible, Menander. I am *not* stupid."

Had her fleet consisted purely of warships, Antonina could have made the voyage to Alexandria in less than a week; with favorable winds, three or four days.

The winds, in fact, *were* favorable. Antonina learned, from John and Ashot, that the winds in the eastern Mediterranean were almost always favorable for southward travel during the summer months. Eight days out of ten, they could count on a steady breeze from the northwest.

The slow grain ships, of course, set the pace for

the armada. But even those ships, with favorable winds, could have made the passage in a week.

Yet, she estimated the voyage would take at least a month, probably two. The reason was not nautical, but political and military.

The immediate goal of her expedition was to stabilize the Empire's hold over Egypt and Alexandria. But Irene and Cassian had counseled—and Theodora had agreed—that Antonina should kill two birds with one stone. Or, to use a more apt metaphor, should intimidate the cubs on her way to bearding the lion.

The religious turmoil had not spread—yet—to the Levant. But the same forces which were undermining the Empire in Egypt were equally at work in Syria and Palestine, and, in the person of Patriarch Ephraim, had an authoritative figure around which to coalesce.

So Theodora had instructed her, as she sailed along the eastern shore of the Mediterranean, to "show the standard."

Antonina had been quite taken by that expression. When she mentioned it to Belisarius, her husband had smiled crookedly and said:

"Catchy, isn't it? She got it from me, you know. From Aide, I should say—although the proper expression is 'show the flag.'"

Antonina frowned, puzzled.

"What's a 'flag'?"

After Belisarius explained, Antonina shook her head.

"Some of what they do in the future is just plain stupid. Why would anyone in their right mind replace a perfectly good imperial gold standard with a raggedy piece of cloth?"

"Oh, I don't know. As a soldier, I have to say I approve. A flag's light. *You* try hauling around a great heavy gold standard in a battle someday. In Syria, in the summertime."

Antonina brushed the problem aside, with great dignity.

"Nonsense. *I'm* not a lowly foot soldier. *I'm* an admiral. *My* ships will damn well 'show the standard.'"

And show it they did.

At Seleuceia, first. They stayed in that great port for a full week. Two of those days were required to embark the hundreds of new Knights Hospitaler who came aboard. But most of the time was spent bearding Patriarch Ephraim in his den.

Seleuceia was Antioch's outlet to the sea. Antioch was the Empire's third greatest city, after Constantinople and Alexandria. Antonina did not take her troops into Antioch itself, but she spent the week parading about the streets of Antioch's harbor. By the third day, most of the population—especially the Syrian commoners—were cheering her madly. Those who weren't were huddling in their villas and monasteries. Thinking dark thoughts, but saying nothing above the level of a mutter.

On her seventh and last day in Seleuceia, a large contingent from the Army of Syria arrived from their fortress in Daras. Most of those soldiers boarded her ships. The rest—

With great ceremony, Antonina turned over to their safe-keeping the large band of artisans who would erect the semaphore stations between Antioch and Seleuceia. Those stations would serve as the link between the coastal network she would create and the Anatolian-Mesopotamian leg which Belisarius was constructing.

While Antonina engaged in public browbeating, Irene occupied herself with subterfuge. She traveled secretly to Antioch, and, by end of the week, had solidified the previously-shaky imperial spy network in Ephraim's domain.

✧   ✧   ✧

South, now, to Tyre. Stopping, if only for a few hours, at every port of any size along the way.

Showing the standard.

Tyre was a celebration. And a great, subtle victory.

The population of the city was out in force, packed into the harbor, awaiting her arrival. She and her soldiers could hear the cheering from a mile away. Standing on the docks, proudly drawn up, were another thousand Knights Hospitaler.

And, standing among them, the Bishop of Jerusalem.

Theodosius, the newly-designated Patriarch of Alexandria whom Antonina was taking to Egypt, pointed him out to her as soon as her flagship drew near the docks. He began to whisper urgently into her ear, explaining the significance of the Bishop's presence. On her other side, Irene was doing the same.

Antonina stilled them both with a gesture. "I know quite well what it means, Theodosius—Irene. The Bishop of Jerusalem has decided to break from Patriarch Ephraim's authority and submit to that of the imperium's church."

She chuckled drily. "Of course, he has his own fish to fry. The See of Jerusalem has been trying to get official recognition as a Patriarchate for—what is it, now? Three centuries?"

Theodosius nodded.

Antonina's chuckle turn into a little laugh. "Well, and why not? Isn't Jerusalem the holiest city in Christendom, when you come right down to it?"

Theodosius stroked his beard furiously. "Well, yes, I suppose. But the Church councils have always ruled against Jerusalem's claim, on the grounds—"

"—that it's a dinky little border town. Filled—or rather, not so filled—by a bunch of sleepy provincials."

Theodosius winced. "That's putting it rather crudely. But—yes. In essence."

"And what's wrong with sleepy provincials? You won't see *them* ruining a perfectly good afternoon nap by wrangling over the relationship between the *prosopon* and the *hypostasis* of Christ."

She turned away from the rail, still smiling. "*Patriarch* of Jerusalem," she murmured. "Yes, yes. Has a nice sound to it."

In the end, she actually *went* to Jerusalem. Suspending her voyage for a full month, while she and her Theodoran Cohort—and all of the Knights Hospitaler from Constantinople, eager to finally see the Holy Land for themselves—marched inland.

A great, grand escort for the Bishop of Jerusalem in his triumphant return. Antonina found the bishop to be, in his person, a thoroughly obnoxious creature. Petty in his concerns, and petulant in his manner. But she took great delight in his *persona*. By the time she left Jerusalem, the Bishop—who was already calling himself the Patriarch—had given his complete and public blessing to her enterprise.

By tradition and church rulings, the Patriarch of Antioch had always held authority over that great area of Syria and the Levant which Romans called *Oriens*. No longer. In a week at Seleuceia, Antonina had undermined Ephraim's prestige. Now, in a month in Palestine, she had cut his ecclesiastical territory in half.

A new council would have to be called, of course, to confirm—or, again, deny—Jerusalem's claim. Antonina did not begin to have the authority to do so. Not even the Emperor, without the approval of a council, could establish a new Patriarchate. But any such council was far in the future. Theodora would stall, stall, stall. For years to come, the Bishop of Jerusalem would defy Ephraim and cling as closely as possible to the Empress Regent's imperial robes.

✧   ✧   ✧

Show the standard, indeed. As her flagship sailed away from Tyre, Antonina gazed up admiringly at the great, gold imperial standard affixed to the mainmast.

"A 'flag'!" she snorted. "How in the name of Christ could you intimidate anybody with a stupid rag?"

But the best—the very best—came at a fishing village. Antonina was pleased, of course, by the welcome given to her by the small but enthusiastic population, who greeted her armada from their boats. But she was absolutely delighted by the welcome given by the men aboard the much bigger ship which sailed among those humble fishermen.

A warship from Axum. Carrying Prince Eon and his dawazz, who bore official salutations from the negusa nagast to the new Roman Emperor. Along with a proposal for an alliance against Malwa.

Her first words to Eon were: "How in the world did you get a warship into the Mediterranean from the Red Sea?"

His, to her with a grimace. "We portaged. Don't ask me how. I can't remember."

"Fool boy!" Ousanos said. "He can't remember because it's impossible. I told him so."

Irene to Ousanas, grinning: "You must have slapped his head a thousand times."

Ousanas groaned: "Couldn't. Was much too weary. Idiot Prince made me carry the stern. All by myself."

Eon, proudly: "Ousanas is the strongest man in the world."

Ousanas slapped the Prince atop his head. "Suckling babe! Strongest man in the world is resting somewhere in his bed. Conserving his strength for sane endeavors!"

Chapter 14

MESOPOTAMIA
Summer, 531 A.D.

The first sign of trouble came just a few hours after the army bypassed Anatha. The town, located directly on the Euphrates, was one of the chain of fortified strongholds which the Sassanid emperors had erected, over the centuries, to guard Persia from Roman invasion.

Baresmanas and Kurush had offered to billet the Roman troops in the town itself, along with their own soldiers, but Belisarius had declined.

There was always the risk of incidents with the local inhabitants, whenever a passing army was billeted in a town. That was especially true with an army of foreigners. Had Belisarius' forces consisted of nothing but his Thracians and the Syrian units, he would not have been concerned. His bucellarii were long accustomed to his discipline, and the soldiers from the Army of Syria were only technically foreigners.

The Syrians were closely akin, racially and

linguistically, with the people of western Mesopotamia. And the Arabs who constituted a large portion of the Syrian army were identical. Arabs—on both sides of the border—tended to view the political boundaries between Rome and Persia as figments of imperial imagination. Those soldiers were familiar with Persian ways and customs, and most of them spoke at least passable Pahlavi. Many of those men had relatives scattered all across the western provinces of the Persian empire.

The same was not true—most definitely not true—with his Greek and Illyrian troops.

The problem was that Anatha was not large enough to hold his entire army. He would not trust the Greek and Illyrian soldiers, without his Thracian and Syrian troops to help keep order. On the other hand, if he allowed the Syrians and Thracians to enjoy the comforts of the town, while the Constantinople and Illyrian troops camped outside—

He would rekindle the resentments which he had finally managed, for the most part, to overcome.

So he ordered the army to bypass the town altogether.

The command, of course, caused hard feelings among his troops—all of it aimed at him. But the general was not concerned. To the contrary—he accepted the collective glare of his soldiers quite cheerfully. The animosity expressed in those glowering eyes would cement his army, not undermine it. Not so long as *all* of his soldiers were equally resentful and could enjoy the mutual bond of grumbling at the lunacies of high command: Sour Thracian grousing to disgruntled Illyrian, sullen Greek cataphract to surly Arab cavalryman.

Fucking jackass.

Whoever made this clown a general, anyway?

By the time we get wherever we're going—the moon, seems like—we'll be too worn out to spank a brat.

Fucking jackass.
Whoever made this clown a general, anyway?

Three hours after the walls of Anatha fell below the horizon, Belisarius saw a contigent of the Arab light cavalry he was using as scouts come galloping up.

Maurice trotted his horse forward to meet them, while Belisarius ordered a halt in the march. After a brief consultation with the scouts, the chiliarch hastened back to Belisarius. By the time he arrived, Baresmanas and Kurush were already at the general's side, along with Bouzes and Coutzes.

"There's a mob of refugees pouring up the road from the east," reported Maurice. "The scouts interviewed some of them. They say that a large Malwa cavalry force—" He shrugged. "You know how it is—according to the refugees, there's probably a million Malwa. But it's a large enough force, apparently, to have sacked a town called Thilutha."

"Thilutha?" exclaimed Kurush. The young sahrdaran stared to the east.

"Thilutha's not as big as Anatha," he announced, "but it's still a fortified garrison town. There's no way a pure cavalry force should have been able to capture it."

"They've got gunpowder," Belisarius pointed out.

Maurice nodded. "The refugees are babbling tales about witchcraft used to shatter the town's gates."

Belisarius squinted into the distance. "What's your guess, Maurice? And how far away are they?"

The chiliarch stroked his beard thoughtfully. "It's a big force, general. Even allowing for refugee exaggeration, the Arab scouts think there must be at least ten thousand soldiers. Probably more."

"A raiding party," stated Bouzes. His snub-nosed face twisted into a rueful grimace. "A reconnaissance-in-force, probably."

Belisarius nodded. "It's good news, actually. It

means Emperor Khusrau is still holding them at Babylon. So the Malwa have sent a large cavalry force around him, to ravage his rear and disrupt his supplies and communications."

He paused for a moment, thinking. "I'm not sure Khusrau can hold Babylon forever, but the longer he does the better it is. We need to buy time. Time for Persia, time for Rome. Best way to do that, right now, is to teach the Malwa they can't raid Mesopotamia with impunity."

His tone hardened. "I want to destroy that force. Hammer them into splinters." He stood in his stirrups, scanning the area around them. "We need a place to trap them."

Kurush frowned. "Anatha is only a few hours behind us. We could return and—"

Belisarius shook his head. "Anatha's much too strong, with us there to aid in the defense. The Malwa will take one look and go elsewhere. Then we'll have to chase *them*, and fight a battle on ground of *their* choosing."

A little smile came to Baresmanas' face. "You want something feeble," he announced. "Some pathetic little fortification that looks like nothing much, but has places to conceal your troops." The smile widened. "Something like that wretched infantry camp you built at Mindouos."

Belisarius' lips twisted. "Yes, Baresmanas. That's exactly what I want."

Comprehension came to Kurush. The young Persian nobleman's face grew pinched, for an instant. Then, suddenly, he laughed.

"You are a cold-blooded man, Belisarius!" he exclaimed. With a sad shake of his head:

"You'd never make a proper Aryan, I'm afraid. Rustam, dehgan of dehgans, would not approve."

Belisarius shrugged. "With all due respect to the legendary national hero of the Aryans, and the fearsome power of his bull-headed mace—Rustam died, in the end."

"Trapped in a pit by his enemies, while hunting," agreed Kurush cheerfully. "Speaking of which—"

The sahrdaran looked to his uncle. "Isn't there an imperial hunting park somewhere in this vicinity?"

Baresmanas pointed across the river, toward a large patch of greenery a few miles away.

"There," he announced.

All the officers in the little group followed his pointing finger. At that moment, Agathius rode up, along with his chief tribune Cyril. Seconds later, the Illyrian commanders arrived also. The top leadership of the Allied army was now assembled. Quickly, the newcomers were informed of the situation and Belisarius' plan.

"We'll need to cross the Euphrates," remarked Coutzes. "Is there a ford nearby?"

"Has to be," replied Maurice. "The refugees are on that side of the river. Since the scouts talked to them, they must have found a way across."

The chiliarch gestured toward the Arab cavalrymen, who had been waiting a short distance away. They trotted up to him and he began a quick consultation.

"It makes sense," commented Kurush. "Thilutha is on the left bank. At this time of year, the river can be forded any number of places. The Malwa have probably been crossing back and forth, ravaging both sides."

Maurice returned.

"The fork's not far, according to the scouts." He gauged the sun. "We can have the whole army across the river by nightfall, if we press the matter."

"Press it," commanded the general.

Belisarius scanned his group of officers. The gaze was not cold, but it was stern. His eyes lingered for a moment on Agathius.

The commander of the garrison troops broke

into a grin. "Don't worry, general. My boys won't drag their feet. Not with the prospect of something besides another fucking day's march to look forward to."

His eyes grew a bit unfocussed. "Imperial hunting park," he mused. "Be a royal villa and everything there, I imagine."

He took up his reins, shaking his head. "Terrible, terrible," he murmured, spurring his horse. "Such damage the wondrous thing'll suffer, in a battle and all."

After Agathius was gone, along with all the other subordinate officers except Maurice, Kurush gave Belisarius a cold stare.

"There is *always* a villa in an imperial hunting park," he stated. "Accoutered in a manner fit for the King of Kings. Filled with precious objects."

The general returned the gaze unflinchingly. "He's right, Kurush. I'm afraid the Emperor's possessions are going to take a terrible beating."

"Especially with gunpowder weapons," added Maurice. The Thracian chiliarch did not seem particularly distressed at the thought.

"I'm not concerned about the destruction caused by the *enemy*," snapped the young Persian nobleman.

"Be silent, nephew!" commanded Baresmanas. The sahrdaran's tone was harsh, and his own icy gaze was directed entirely at Kurush.

"I know the Emperor much better than you," he growled. "I have known him since he was a child. Khusrau Anushirvan, he is called—Khusrau 'of the immortal soul.' It is the proper name for that man, believe me. No finer soul has sat the Aryan throne since Cyrus. Do you think such an emperor would begrudge a few tokens to the brave men who come to his aid, when his people are ravaged by demons?"

Kurush shrank back in his saddle. Then, sighing,

he reined his horse around and trotted toward his troops. A moment later, Maurice left, heading toward his own soldiers.

Once they were alone, Baresmanas smiled rue-fully. "Quite a few tokens, of course. And such tokens they are!"

Belisarius felt a sudden, deep friendship for the man beside him. And then, an instant later, was seized by a powerful impulse.

"You are quite right, you know."

Baresmanas eyed him.

"About Khusrau, I mean. He will rule the Aryans for fifty years, and will be remembered for as long as Iran exists. 'Khusrau the Just,' they will call him, over the centuries."

Baresmanas' face seemed to pale, a bit, under the desert-darkened complexion.

"I had heard—" he whispered. He took a breath, shakily. "There are rumors that you can foretell the future, Belisarius. Is it true?"

Belisarius could sense Aide's agitation, swirling in his mind. He sent a quick thought toward the flashing facets.

No, Aide. There are times when secrecy defeats its purpose.

He returned the sahrdaran's piercing stare with his own steady gaze.

"No, Baresmanas. Not in the sense that you mean the term."

The army was beginning to resume the march. Belisarius clucked his own horse into forward motion, as did Baresmanas.

The general leaned toward the sahrdaran. "The future is not fixed, Baresmanas. This much I know. Though, it is true, I have received visions of the possible ways that future river might flow."

He paused. Then said, "We worship different gods, my friend. Or, perhaps, it is the same God seen in different ways. But neither of us believes that darkness rules."

He gestured ahead, as if to indicate the still-unseen enemy.

"The Malwa are guided by a demon. That demon brought them the secret of gunpowder, and filled them with their foul ambition. Do you really think such a demon could come into the world—unanswered by divinity?"

Baresmanas thought upon his words, for a time, as they rode along. Then, he said softly, "So. As always, God gives us the choice."

Belisarius nodded. The sahrdaran's pallor faded. He smiled, then, rather slyly.

"Tell me one more thing, Belisarius. I will ask nothing else on this matter, I promise. Did a divine spirit guide you at Mindouos?"

The general shook his head. "No. At least— *No*. I believe such a spirit kept me from harm in the battle. Personally, I mean. But the tactics were mine."

The sahrdaran's sly smile broadened, became a cheerful grin. "For some reason, that makes me feel better. Odd, really. You'd think it would be the opposite—that I would take comfort from knowing we were defeated by a superhuman force."

Belisarius shook his head. "I don't think it's strange at all, Baresmanas. There is—"

He fell silent. There was no way to explain, simply, the titanic struggle in the far distant future of which their own battles were a product. Belisarius himself understood that struggle only dimly, from glimpses. But—

"It is what we are fighting about, I think, in the end. Whether the course of human history is to be shaped by those who make it, or be imposed upon them by others."

He spoke no further words on the subject.

Nor did Baresmanas—then, or ever. In this, the

sahrdaran was true to his Aryan myths and legends. He had given his word; he would keep it.

The skeptical scholar in him, of course, found his own stiff honor amusing. Just as he found it amusing that the cunning, low-born Roman would never have revealed his secret, had he not understood that Aryan rigor.

Most amusing, of course, was another thought.

To have picked such a man for an enemy! Demons, when all is said and done, are stupid.

Aide, however, was not amused at all. In the hours that followed, while the army found the ford scouted by the Arab cavalrymen and crossed to the left bank of the Euphrates, and then encamped for the night, Belisarius could sense the facets shimmering in their thoughts. The thoughts themselves he could not grasp, but he knew that Aide was pondering something of great importance to him.

The crystal did not speak to him directly until the camp had settled down, the soldiers all asleep except for the posted sentinels. And a general, who had patiently stayed awake himself, waiting in the darkness for his friend to speak.

Do you really think that is what it is about? Our struggle with the new gods?

Yes.

Pause. Then, plaintively:

And what of us? Do we play no role? Or is it only humans that matter?

Belisarius smiled.

Of course not. You are part of us. You, too, are human.

We are not! shrieked the crystal. **We are different! That is why you created us, because— because—**

Aide was in a frenzy such as Belisarius had not seen since the earliest days of his encounter with the jewel. Despair—frustration—loneliness—confusion—most of all, a frantic need to *communicate*.

But it was *not* the early days. The differences between two mentalities had eased, over the years. Eased far more than either had known.

Finally, finally, the barrier was ruptured completely. A shattering vision swept Belisarius away, as if he were cast into the heavens by a tidal wave.

Chapter 15

Worlds upon worlds upon worlds, circling an incomprehensible number of suns. People on those worlds, everywhere—but people changed and transformed. Misshapen and distorted, most of them. So, at least, most men would say, flinching.

Death comes, striking many of those worlds. The very Earth itself, scoured clean by a plague which spared no form of life. Nothing left—except, slowly, here and there, an advancing network of crystals.

Aide's folk, Belisarius realized, come to replace those who had destroyed their own worlds. Created, by those who had slain themselves, to be their heirs.

Belisarius hung in the darkness. Around him, below him, above him—in all directions—spun great whirling spirals of light and beauty.

Galaxies.

He sensed a new presence, and immediately understood its meaning. A great sigh of relief swept through him.

Finally, finally—

He saw a point of light in the void. A point, nothing more, which seemed infinitely distant. But he knew, even in the seeing, that the distance was one of time not space.

Time opened, and the future came.

The point of light erupted, surged forward. A moment later, floating before Belisarius, was one of the Great Ones.

The general had seen glimpses of them, before. Now, for the first time, he saw a Great One clearly.

As clearly, at least, as he ever could. He understood, now, that he would never see them fully. Too much of their structure lay in mysterious forces which would never be seen by earthly eyes.

A new voice came to him. Like Aide's, in a way, but different.

FORCE FIELDS. ENERGY MATRICES. THERE IS LITTLE IN US LEFT OF OUR EARTHLY ORIGINS. AND NO FLESH AT ALL.

Like a winged whale, vaguely, in its broad appearance. If ever a whale could swim the heavens, glowing from an inner light. But much, much larger. The Great One dwarfed any animal that had ever lived.

OUR DIMENSIONS MEASURE EIGHT BY THREE BY TWO, APPROXIMATELY, IN THE VISIBLE SPECTRUM. WHAT YOU CALL MILES. OUR MASS IS—DIFFICULT TO CALCULATE. IT DEPENDS ON VELOCITY. WE CAN ATTAIN 93% LIGHT SPEED, AT OUR UTMOST—CALL IT EXERTION. WE MUST BE VERY CAREFUL, APPROACHING A SOLAR SYSTEM. SHOULD ONE OF US IMPACT A PLANET, AT THAT VELOCITY, WE WOULD DESTROY IT. AND POSSIBLY OURSELVES AS WELL.

The being had no eyes, no mouth, no apparent sense organs of any kind. Yet the general knew that the Great One could detect everything that any human could, and much else besides.

He saw into the being, now. Saw the glittering network of crystals which formed the Great One's—heart? Soul?

THEY ARE OUR HERITAGE NOW. OUR CREATORS, AS MUCH AS OUR CREATIONS. THEY

DO FOR US WHAT SOMETHING CALLED DNA ONCE DID FOR OUR ANCIENT ANCESTORS. ALLOW THE FUTURE TO EXIST.

Belisarius studied the crystalline network more closely. The crystals, he thought, seemed much like Aide. Yet, somehow different.

AIDE IS MUCH DIFFERENT. IT—NO, FOR YOU IT WILL ALWAYS BE "HE"—BEARS THE SAME RELATIONSHIP TO THESE AS YOU DO TO A BACTERIUM. AKIN, BUT GREATER.

The Great One sensed the general's incomprehension. *What is a "bacterium"?*

AS YOU DO TO AN EARTHWORM. OR, BETTER, A MUSHROOM. WE DESIGNED THESE CRYSTALS FOR OUR OWN SURVIVAL. BUT THEN DISCOVERED WE COULD NOT MAKE THEM, OR USE THEM, UNLESS WE CREATED A CRYSTAL INTELLIGENCE TO GUIDE AND ASSIST US. THOSE BECAME AIDE'S PEOPLE.

They were your slaves, then. As I have heard the "new gods" say.

NEVER.

There came a sense of mirth; vast, yet whimsical. And the general knew, then—finally—that these almost inconceivable beings were truly his own folk. He had but to look in a mirror, to see the crooked smile that would, someday, become that universe-encompassing irony—and that delight in irony.

THE PEASANT WHO TILLS THE FIELD BRINGS CHILDREN INTO THE WORLD—TO HELP IN THE LABOR, AMONG OTHER THINGS. ARE THOSE CHILDREN SLAVES?

They can be, replied the general. *I have seen it, more often than I like to remember.*

The sense of wry humor never faded.

NOT IN YOUR HOUSE. NOT IN YOUR FIELD. NOT IN YOUR SMITHY.

No, but—

The Great One swelled, swirled. Looped the heavens, prancing on wings of light and shadow.

AND WHOSE CHILD AM I—CRAFTSMAN?

There was a soundless peal, that might be called joyful laughter. The Great One swept off, dwindling.

Wait! called out Belisarius.

NO. YOU HAVE ENOUGH. I MUST BE OFF TO JOIN MY BRETHREN AND SEE THE UNIVERSE. OUR FAMILY—YOUR DESCENDANTS—HAVE FILLED THAT UNIVERSE. FILLED IT WITH WONDER THAT WE WOULD SHARE AND BUILD UPON. WE DO NOT HAVE MUCH TIME, IN OUR SHORT LIVES, TO DELVE THAT SPLENDOR. A MILLION YEARS, PERHAPS—NOT COUNTING TIME DILATION.

Nothing but a tiny dot of light, now.

Wait! cried Belisarius again. *There is so much I need to know!*

The faint dot paused; then, swirled back. A moment later, Belisarius was staring awe-struck at a towering wall of blazing glory.

THERE IS NOTHING YOU NEED TO KNOW, THAT YOU DO NOT ALREADY. WE ARE YOUR CREATION, AS AIDE'S FOLK ARE OURS. AND NOW YOUR GRANDCHILDREN HAVE COME TO YOU FOR HELP, IN THEIR TIME OF TROUBLE.

SO WHAT DO YOU NEED TO KNOW— *OLD MAN*? YOU ARE THE ELDER OF THAT VILLAGE WHICH NOW SPANS GALAXIES. YOU ARE THE BLACKSMITH WHO FORGED HUMANITY ON ITS OWN ANVIL.

Belisarius laughed himself then, and it seemed that the galaxies shivered with his mirth. The Great One before him rippled; waves of humor matching his own.

IT IS OUR MOST ANCIENT RELIGION, GRANDFATHER. AND WITH GOOD REASON.

Swoop—away, away. Gone now, almost. A faint dot, no more.

A faint voice; laughing voice:
CALL IT—ANCESTOR WORSHIP.

When Belisarius returned to the world, he simply stared for a time. Looking beyond the hanging canopy to the great band of stars girdling the night sky. The outposts of that great village of the future.

Then, as he had not done in weeks, he withdrew Aide from his pouch.

There was no need, really. He had long since learned to communicate with the "jewel" without holding it. But he needed to see Aide with his own eyes. Much as he often needed to hold Photius with his own hands. To rejoice in love; and to find comfort in eternity.

Aide spoke.
You did not answer me.
Belisarius:
Weren't you there—when I met the Great One?
Uncertainly:
Yes, but— I do not think I understood. I am not sure.
Plaintively, like a child complaining of the difficulty of its lessons:
We are not like you. We are not like the Great Ones. We are not human. We are not—
Be quiet, Aide. And stop whining. How do you expect to grow up if you whimper at every task?
Silence. Then: **We will grow up?**
Of course. I am your ancestor. One of them, at least. How do you think you got into the world in the first place?
Everything that is made of us grows up. Certainly my offspring!
A long, long silence. Then: **We never dreamed. That we, too, could grow.**

✧   ✧   ✧

Aide spoke no more. Belisarius could sense the facets withdrawing into themselves, flashing internal dialogue.

After a time, he replaced the "jewel" in the pouch and lay down on his pallet. He needed to sleep. A battle would erupt soon, possibly even the next day.

But, just as he was drifting into slumber, he was awakened by Aide's voice.

Very faint; very indistinct.

What are you saying? he mumbled sleepily. *I can't hear you.*

That's because I'm muttering.

Proudly:

It's good you can't hear me. That means I'm doing it right, even though I'm just starting.

Very proudly:

I'll get better, I know I will. Practice makes perfect. Valentinian always says that.

The general's eyes popped open. "Sweet Jesus," he whispered.

I thought I'd start with Valentinian. Growing up, I mean. He's pretty easy. Not the swordplay, of course. But the muttering's not so hard. And—

A string of profanity followed.

Belisarius bolted upright.

"Don't use that sort of language!" he commanded. Much as he had often instructed his son Photius. And with approximately the same result.

Mutter, mutter, mutter.

Chapter 16

By the time Belisarius arrived at the hunting park, the Arab scouts had already had one brief skirmish with the advance units of the oncoming Malwa army. When they returned, the scouts reported that the Malwa main force was less than ten miles away. They had been able to get close enough to examine that force before the Malwa drove them off.

There was good news and bad news.

The good news, as the scout leader put it:

"Shit-pot soldiers. Keep no decent skirmishers. Didn't even see us until we were pissing on their heads. Good thing they didn't bring women. We seduce all of them. Have three bastards each, probably, before shit-pot Malwa notice their new children too smart and good-looking."

The bad news:

"Shit-pot lot of them. *Big* shit-pot."

Belisarius looked to the west. There was only an hour of daylight left, he estimated.

He turned to Maurice. "Take all the bucellarii and the katyushas. When the Persians arrive, I'll have them join you." He pondered, a moment. "And take the Illyrians, too."

A quick look at Timasius, the Illyrian commander.

"You'll be under Maurice's command. Any problem with that?"

Timasius shook his head—without hesitation, to Belisarius' relief. His opinion of the Illyrian rose. Smart, the man might not be. But at least he was well-disciplined and co-operative.

The general studied the woods to the northeast.

"Judging from what I saw as we rode in, I think there'll be plenty of good cover over there. I want all the men well hidden, Maurice. No fires, tonight, when you make camp. You'll be my surprise, when I need it, and I don't want the Malwa alerted."

Belisarius did not elaborate any further. With Maurice, there was no need. "You've got signal rockets?"

The Thracian chiliarch nodded.

"Remember, green means—"

"Green means we attack the enemy directly. Red means start the attack with a rocket volley. Yellow—come to your assistance. White—run for our lives."

Maurice glared at Belisarius. "Any instructions on how to lace up my boots?" He glanced at the horizon. "If you're going to tell me which direction the sun goes down, you'd better make it quick. It's already setting. North, I think."

Belisarius chuckled. "Be off, Maurice."

Once the chiliarch trotted off—still glowering—Belisarius spoke to Bouzes and Coutzes.

"One of you—either one, I don't care—take the Syrian infantrymen and start fortifying the royal villa. Take the Callinicum garrison also. The men will probably have to work through the night."

The brothers grimaced. Belisarius smiled.

"Tell them to look on the bright side. They'll have to dismantle the interior of the villa. Be all sorts of loose odds and ends lying around. Have to be picked up, of course, so nobody gets hurt falling all over them."

Bouzes and Coutzes cheered up immediately. Belisarius continued.

"Don't make the fortifications look *too* solid, but make sure you have the grenade screens ready to be erected at a moment's notice. And make sure there's plenty of portals for a quick sally."

The brothers nodded, then looked at each other. After a moment's unspoken discussion—using facial gestures that meant nothing to anyone else—Bouzes reined his horse around and trotted off.

"All right, then," said Belisarius. "Coutzes, I want you to take the Syrian cavalry—and all of the Arab skirmishers except the few we need for scouts—and get them ready for a sally first thing tomorrow morning. It'll be a Hunnish sort of sally, you understand?"

Coutzes nodded. A moment later, he too was trotting away. Only Agathius was left, of the command group, along with his chief tribune Cyril.

Belisarius studied them for a moment.

"I want you and your Constantinople unit to get well rested, tonight. Set a regular camp, not far from the villa. Make sure it's on the eastern grounds of the park, where the terrain is open. I want you between the Malwa and the villa itself. You understand?"

Agathius nodded. Belisarius continued:

"Build campfires—big ones. Allow the men a double ration of wine, and let them enjoy themselves loudly. Encourage them to sing, if they've a taste for it. Just don't let them get drunk."

Cyril frowned. "You're not worried the enemy will see—"

"I'm *hoping* the enemy will scout you out."

Agathius chuckled. "So they *won't* go snooping through the woods on the north, where they might stumble on the Thracians and Illyrians. Or sniff around the villa itself, where they could see how the Syrians are fortifying it."

The burly officer stroked his beard.

"It'll probably work," he mused. "If their skirmishers are as bad as Abbu says, they'll be satisfied with spotting us. Easy, that'll be. They can get back to their army without spending all night creeping through a forest that might have God knows what lurking in it."

Belisarius nodded. Agathius eyed him. His gaze was shrewd—and a bit cold.

"You're going to hammer the shit out of us, aren't you?"

Again, Belisarius nodded.

"Yes, Agathius. Your men are probably going to have the worst of it. In the beginning, at least. I'm hoping the Syrian cavalrymen can draw them into a running battle, lead them back here. If they do—"

"You want us to sally. A big, straight-up, heavy cavalry lance charge. Kind of thing minstrels like to sing about."

"Yes. But you've got to be disciplined about it. That charge has to be solid, but I want you to disengage before you get cut to pieces. Can you do that? I want an honest answer. In my experience, cataphracts tend to think they're invincible. They get so caught up in the—"

Agathius barked a harsh laugh. "For the sake of Christ, general! Do we look like a bunch of aristocrats to you?"

"Right good at disengaging, we are," added Cyril, chuckling. "If you'll forgive me saying so, sir."

Belisarius grinned. "If it'll make you feel any better, I'll be joining you in the charge. I'm rather good at disengaging myself. If you'll forgive me saying so."

The two Greeks laughed—and gaily now. But when their humor died away, there was still a residue of coldness lurking in the back of their eyes.

Belisarius understood immediately. "You've had no experience under my command," he said softly. "I ask you to trust me in this matter. Don't worry about the booty. Tell your men they'll get their fair share—after the battle's won."

Cyril glanced toward the villa. The Syrian infantrymen were already pouring into the lavish structure. Even at the distance—a hundred yards—the glee in their voices was evident.

Agathius' eyes remained on the general. The suspicion in those eyes was open, now.

Belisarius smiled crookedly. "Those Syrians *do* have experience under my command. They know the penalty for private looting. Don't forget, Agathius, my bucellarii won't be anywhere near that villa, either. You didn't see Maurice complain, did you? That's because he's not worried about it. Anybody holds out on my Thracians, there'll be hell to pay."

Agathius couldn't help wincing.

All whimsy left Belisarius' face. When he spoke, his tone was low and earnest.

"In my army, we all share in the spoils. Fairly apportioned *after* the battle. Except for what we set aside to care for the disabled and the families of the men who died, each soldier will get his share. Regardless of where he was or what he was doing."

Agathius and Cyril stared at him. Then Agathius nodded his head. It was not a gesture of assent. It was more in the nature of a bow of fealty. A moment later, Cyril copied him.

When their heads lifted, the familiar crooked smile was back on the general's face.

"And now, if you don't mind, I'd like to discuss the tactics of this—what'd you call it, Agathius—*minstrel charge*?" He chuckled. "I like the sound of that! Especially if the minstrel can sing a cheerful tune—every hero survived, after all."

Agathius grinned. "I've always preferred cheerful tunes, myself."

"Me too," added Cyril. "Loathe dirges. Detest the damn things."

✧   ✧   ✧

An hour after sunset, the Persian cavalry showed up at the hunting park. Belisarius met them a mile away from the villa, and explained his plans for the coming battle.

To his relief, Kurush immediately agreed. The young nobleman did cast a sour glance in the direction of the villa, but he made no inquiry as to its condition.

Belisarius himself, with the aid of several Thracian cataphracts sent by Maurice, guided the Persians to the spot in the northeast woods where his bucellarii and the Illyrians had made their camp.

Their progress was slow. The woods were dense—no local woodcutter would dare hew down an imperial tree—and the only illumination came from the last glimmer of twilight. Belisarius took advantage of the time to explain his plans in great detail. He was particularly concerned with impressing upon Kurush the need to let his katyushas open the attack. The rocket chariots had never been used in a battle before. Belisarius wanted to find out how effective they would be.

In the course of their conversation, Kurush filled in some further information on the enemy. The Persians had spent the day scouting the left flank of the approaching Malwa army. Like his own scouts, they had found the enemy's skirmish line to be ragged and ineffective. But—unlike his small group of lightly-armed Arabs—the heavy Persian cavalrymen had been willing to hammer the advance guards and press very close to the Malwa main army before disengaging.

They had seen more of that army, thus, and Kurush was able to add further speficics to the information Belisarius had already obtained.

The Malwa army *was* large—very large, for what was in essence a cavalry raid. Kurush estimated the main body of regular troops numbered twelve thousand. They were not as heavily armed as Persian lancers or Roman cataphracts, but they were not light cavalry either. There *was* a force of light cavalry serving the Malwa—about five hundred Arabs wearing the colors of the Lakhmid dynasty.

Interspersed among the regular troops were battalions of Ye-tai horsemen. Their exact numbers had been difficult to determine, but Kurush thought there were two thousand of the barbarians. Possibly more.

In addition, riding at the center of the Malwa army, the Persians had seen hundreds of Malwa kshatriya and several dozen Mahaveda priests. The priests, unlike the kshatriya, were not on horseback. They were riding in large wagons drawn by mules. The contents of those wagons were hidden under canvas, but Kurush assumed that the wagons contained their gunpowder weapons and devices.

None of this information caused the Roman general any particular distress. The force structure was about what he had guessed, and he was not disturbed by the size of the Malwa army. True, the odds were at least 3-to-2 against him, so far as the numbers were concerned. Still, he would be fighting the battle on the tactical defensive, on ground of his choosing.

But the last item of information which Kurush imparted made him wince.

"Describe them again," he commanded.

"They number perhaps two thousand, Belisarius. They form the Malwa rear guard—which is quite odd, in my opinion. If *I* were leading that army, I would have those troops in the vanguard. They keep formation as well as any parade ground troops I've ever seen, but I don't think—"

Belisarius shook his head. "They are most definitely not parade troops, Kurush."

He sighed. "And the reason they're bringing up the rear is because the Malwa don't trust them much. The problem, however, is not military. It's political."

"Damn," he grumbled. "There were two things I didn't want to run into. One of them are Rajputs, and the other—you're sure about the topknots?"

Kurush nodded. "It's quite a distinctive hairstyle. Their helmets are even designed for it."

"Yes, I know. I've seen them. Kushan helmets."

The Persian winced himself, now. "*Kushans?* You're sure?"

"Yes. No other enemy troops look like that. To the best of my knowledge, anyway—and remember, I spent over a year in India. I got a very close look at the Malwa army."

Kurush started to say something, but broke off in order to dodge a low-hanging branch in the trail. When he straightened, he muttered: "We *did* defeat them, you know. We Aryans. Centuries ago. Conquered half the Kushan empire, in fact."

Belisarius smiled. "No doubt your minstrels sing about it to this day."

"They sing about it, all right," replied Kurush glumly. "Dirges, mostly, about glorious victories with maybe three survivors. The casualties were *very* heavy."

At midnight, after his return, Belisarius took a tour of the villa. Baresmanas came with him. The Persian ambassador had been a warrior, in his day— a renowned one, in fact—but the combination of his advancing years and the terrible injury he had suffered at Mindouos made it impossible for him to participate in thundering lance charges. So he had cheerfully offered his services to the infantry who would be standing on the defensive at the villa.

Bouzes and three of his officers guided Belisarius and Baresmanas through the villa, holding torches aloft, proudly pointing out the cunning of the fortifications. They were especially swell-chested with regard to the grenade screens. The screens were doubled linen, strengthened by slender iron rods sewn lengthwise into the sheets. The design allowed for easy transportation, since the screens could be folded up into pleats and carried on mule back. The screens were now mounted onto bronze frameworks. These had been hastily brazed together out of the multitude of railings which had once adorned the balconies surrounding the villa's interior gardens. The frameworks had then been attached to every entryway or opening in the villa's outer walls with rawhide strips, looped through regularly spaced holes in the former railings.

"We didn't make the holes," admitted Bouzes. "They'd already been drilled, as fittings for the uprights. But we realized they'd allow for leather hinges. You see? Each one of the screens can be moved into place just like a door. Takes less than five seconds. Until then, there's no way to see them from outside the villa."

Belisarius was not surprised, actually, by the shrewdness of the design. He already knew that his Syrian infantrymen, with the jack-of-all-trades attitude of typical borderers, were past masters at the art of jury-rigging fortifications out of whatever materials were available. But he complimented them, nonetheless, quite lavishly.

Baresmanas was even more effusive in his praise. And he made no mention of the pearls which had once adorned the Emperor's railings, nestled in each one of the holes which now held simple rawhide lashings.

Nor did the sahrdaran comment on the peculiar appearance of the great bronze plaques which the Roman infantry had used to bulwark some of the flimsier portions of the outer wall. Those plaques had once hung suspended in the Emperor's huge dining hall, where his noble guests, feasting after a day's hunting, could gaze up at the marvelously

etched figures. The etchwork was still there. But the
hunting scenes they depicted seemed pallid. The
lions wan, without their emerald eyes; the antelopes
plebeian, without their silver antlers; the panthers
drab, without their jade and ruby spots; and the
elephants positively absurd—like big-nosed sheep!—
without their ivory tusks.

Baresmanas said nothing in the dining room itself,
either, when he and Belisarius joined the infantrymen
in a late meal, other than to exchange pleasantries
with the troops on the subject of the excellence of
the food. Fine fare it was, the Syrians allowed—
marvelous, marvelous. Truly fit for an Emperor! And
if Baresmanas thought it odd that the splendid meal
was served on wooden platters and eaten with peasant
daggers, he held his tongue. He did not inquire as
to the whereabouts of the gold plates and utensils
which would, by all reasonable standards, have made
much more sensible dining ware for such a regal feast.

Only once, in that entire tour, did Baresmanas
momentarily lose his composure. Hearing Bouzes laud
the metalworking skills of his troops, which could
finally be put to full use by virtue of the extraordi-
narily well-equipped smithy located in the rear of the
imperial compound, Baresmanas expressed a desire
to observe the soldiers at their work.

Bouzes coughed. "Uh, well—it's very hot back
there, lord. Terrible! And dirty? You wouldn't believe
it! Oh, no, you wouldn't—with those fine clothes? No,
you wouldn't—"

"I insist," said Baresmanas. Politely, but firmly. He
brushed the silk sleeve of his tunic in a gesture which
combined whimsy and unconcern.

"There's going to be a battle tomorrow. I doubt
these garments will be usable afterward, anyway. And
I am fascinated by the skills of your soldiers. There's
nothing comparable in the Persian army. Our dehgan
lancers and their mounted retainers wouldn't stoop

to this kind of work. And our peasant levees don't know how to do anything beside till the soil."

Bouzes swallowed. "But—"

Belisarius intervened.

"Do as the sahrdaran asks, Bouzes. I'd like to see the workshop myself. I've always loved watching skilled smiths at their trade."

Bouzes sighed. With a little shrug, he turned and led the way toward the rear of the compound. Out of the royal chambers, through the servant quarters, and into the cluster of adjoining buildings where the practical needs of Persia's emperors were met, far from the fastidious eyes of Aryan royalty.

When they entered the smithy, all work ceased immediately. The dozen or so Syrian infantrymen in the workshop froze at their labors, staring goggle-eyed at the newcomers.

Baresmanas stared himself. Goggle-eyed.

The center of the shop was occupied by a gigantic cauldron, designed to smelt metal. The cauldron was being put to use. It was almost brim-full with molten substance. At that very moment, two infantrymen were standing paralyzed, staring at the sahrdaran, stooped from the effort of carrying a large two-handled ladle over to the ingot-molds ranged against a far wall.

The mystery of the imperial dining ware was solved at once. Only a small number of the gold plates—and not more than a basket's worth, perhaps, of gold utensils—still remained on a shelf next to the cauldron. That small number immediately shrank, as a handful of gold plate slipped out of the loose fingers of the Roman soldier gaping at Baresmanas. Plop, plop, plop, into the brew.

But it was not the plates which held the Persian nobleman transfixed. It was the sight of the much larger objects which were slowly joining the melt.

Baresmanas' gaze settled on a winged horse which

perched atop a heavy post. The post was softening rapidly. Within a few seconds, the horse sank below the cauldron's rim.

"That was the Emperor's bed," he choked. "It's made out of solid gold."

The soldiers in the smithy paled. Bouzes glanced appealingly at Belisarius.

The general cleared his throat. "Excellent work, men!" he boomed. "I'm delighted to see how well you've carried out my instructions." He placed a firm hand on Baresmanas' shoulder. "It's terrible, what military necessity drives us to."

The sahrdaran tore his eyes away from the cauldron and stared at Belisarius.

"I believe I mentioned, Baresmanas, that I hope to capture Malwa cannons in the course of the campaign. The problem, of course, is with the shot." The general scowled fiercely. "You wouldn't believe the crap the Malwa use! Stone balls, for siege work. And the same—broken stones, for the sake of God!—do for their cannister." He pursed his lips, as if to spit. Restrained himself. "I won't have it! Proper cannister can make all the difference, breaking a charge. But for that, you need good lead."

He fixed the soldiers with an eagle eye. "You found no lead, I take it?"

The soldiers stared at him, for a moment. Then one of them squeaked: "No, sir! No, sir!"

Another, bobbing his head: "We looked, sir. Indeed we did. Scoured the place! But—"

A third: "Only lead's in the water pipes." His face grew lugubrious. "Have to tear the walls apart to get at 'em."

A fourth, shaking his head solemnly: "Didn't want to do that, of course. A royal palace, and all."

Every infantryman's face assumed a grave expression. Well-nigh funereal. Heads bobbed in unison.

"Be a terrible desecration," muttered one.

"'Orrible," groaned another.

Belisarius stepped forward and looked down into the cauldron, hands clasped behind his back. The general's gaze was stern, fastidious, determined—much like that of a farmer examining night-soil.

"Gold!" he snorted. Then, shrugging heavily: "Well, I suppose it'll have to do."

He turned away, took Baresmanas by the arm—the sahrdaran was still standing stiff and rigid—and began leading him toward the entrance.

"A cruel business, war," he muttered.

Baresmanas moved with him, but the Persian's head swiveled, staring back over his shoulder. His eyes never left the cauldron until they were out of the smithy altogether.

Then, suddenly, he burst into laughter. No light-hearted chuckling, either. No, this was shoulder-shaking, belly-heaving, convulsive laughter. He leaned weakly against a nearby wall.

"This was Emperor Kavad's favorite hunting park," he choked. "Spent half his time here, before age overcame him."

Another round of uproarious laughter. Then:

"He told me once—ho! ho!—that he was quite sure his son Khusrau was conceived on that bed! Ho! Ho! So proud he was! He had slain a lion, that day, and thought it was an omen for his son's future."

Belisarius grinned at him. "Poetic justice, then! A thing for legend! Even at his conception, Khusrau Anushirvan was destined to rend the Malwa!"

Baresmanas pushed himself away from the wall. Now it was he who took Belisarius by the arm, and began leading the way back to the central villa.

Still laughing, he murmured: "Perhaps we should keep that legend to ourselves, my friend. Myths are so easy to misinterpret."

They walked a few steps. The sahrdaran gave Belisarius a sly glance. "What will you tell Emperor

Khusrau about his hunting villa—if there's no battle,
I mean?"

Belisarius smiled crookedly.

"I was just wondering that myself."

He blew out his cheeks.

"Pray for an earthquake, I suppose."

Chapter 17

"It's a good thing you sent the Persian troops to us last night," remarked Maurice, after dismounting from his horse. "We're not the only ones who figured out that those woods are the best hiding place in the area. All the servants fled the villa when they saw the Syrians coming and they wound up with us. If it hadn't been for Kurush and his men, who settled them down, they'd be scampering all over the landscape squawking like chickens. The Malwa would have been bound to capture a few."

Belisarius winced.

"I hadn't thought of that," he muttered. The general glanced back at the villa behind him. "When we arrived, the place was empty. I should have realized there must have been a little army of servants living here, even when the Emperor's not in residence."

"*Little* army? You should see that mob!"

Belisarius cocked an eye. "Will it be a problem?"

Maurice shook his head. "I don't imagine. The Persians quieted them down and then moved them farther back into the woods. They instructed the servants to remain there, but Kurush told me he made sure to explain which direction was what. He thinks at least half the servants will start running as soon as the Persians take their battle positions, but at least they'll be running deeper into the woods, *away* from the Malwa. If the enemy catches any of them, it'll be too late for the information to do them any good."

Maurice looked toward the villa.

"What's the situation here?" he asked. The chiliarch examined the villa and the area surrounding it.

The imperial villa was not a single structure, but an interconnected series of buildings. The buildings formed an oblong whose long axis was oriented north-to-south. The center of the oblong was open, forming an interior garden. The buildings were enclosed within a brick wall which formed the outer grounds of the villa. The outer wall was low, and not massive. The buildings were nestled near the northeast corner of the wall. To the west, the wall extended outward for hundreds of yards before looping back around. The western grounds of the villa were well-tended and open, except for small copses of trees scattered about.

North and west of the villa, just beyond the wall, began the small forest which formed the actual hunting park. Those woods were dense, and covered many square miles of territory. Maurice's troops were hidden away in a part of that forest, about two miles northeast of the villa. To the south, the villa was separated from the Euphrates by a much thinner stretch of woods. The river was less than a mile away.

Examining the scene, Maurice could see that the forest and the river would act as a funnel, channeling the Malwa directly toward the villa. The area to the east of the villa was the only terrain on which a large army could move. No general would even consider trying to maneuver through the forest. Maurice had been able to get his cataphracts into those woods, true. But he was just setting an ambush, hiding his troops behind the first screen of trees. Even then, the task had been difficult.

He studied the open terrain east of the villa more

closely. That would be the battleground. Units of the Constantinople garrison were visible, here and there, eating their morning meal. To the southwest, nestled on the edge of the woods lining the river, Maurice could see portions of the barns, horsepens, and corrals where the imperial livestock were fed and sheltered.

Then, more carefully, Maurice examined the wall which enclosed the compound itself—the villa proper, with its adjoining buildings and the gardens. Finally, very closely, he studied the gateway in which he and Belisarius were standing.

He did not seem exactly thrilled by what he saw.

"A lame mule could kick that wall apart," he grumbled. "And as for this ridiculous so-called gate— I'd pit a half-grown puppy against it. Give three-to-one odds on the mutt."

Belisarius glanced at the objects of Maurice's disfavor. The general smiled. "Pretty though, aren't they?"

He patted Maurice on the shoulder.

"Relax, you morose old bastard. This is a hunting villa, not a fortress. The outer wall's purely decorative, I admit. But the villa itself was built for an Emperor. It's solid enough, even where the separate buildings connect with each other. Besides, Bouzes' boys did wonders last night, beefing it up. They'll hold—long enough, at least."

Maurice said nothing, but the sour expression on his face never faded.

The general's smile broadened. "Like I said— morose old bastard."

"I'm not morose," countered Maurice. "I'm a pessimist. What if your trap doesn't work?"

Belisarius shrugged. "If it doesn't work, we'll just have to fight it out, that's all." He waved at the villa. "Sure, it isn't much—but it's better than anything the Malwa have."

Before Maurice could reply, a cheery hail cut him

off. Turning, he and Belisarius saw that Coutzes had arrived. The commander of the Syrian light cavalry was trotting up the road leading to the villa. With him were all three of the cavalry's tribunes as well as Abbu, his chief scout.

Maurice glanced up at the sky. The sun was just beginning to peek over the eastern horizon. "If he's got news already, they either did a hell of a good job themselves, last night—or the enemy's breathing down our necks."

Belisarius chuckled. "Like I said—morose." He gestured with his head. "Look at those insouciant fellows, Maurice! Do those smiling faces look like men running for their lives?"

Maurice scowled. "Don't call soldiers 'insouciant.' It's ridiculous. Especially when it comes to Abbu."

The chiliarch studied the approaching figure of the scout leader. His somber mien lightened, somewhat. Maurice approved of Abbu. The Arab had a world-view which closely approximated his own. Every silver lining has a cloud; into each life a deluge must fall.

Abbu's first words, upon reining in his horse: "The enemy is laying a terrible trap for us, general. I foresee disaster."

Coutzes laughed. "The old grouch is just pissed because he had to work so hard last night."

"No enemy is that stupid!" Abbu snarled. "We practically had to lead them by the hand!" The Arab's close-set eyes were almost crossed with outrage. Belisarius had to restrain his own laugh.

Abbu's face was long and lean, dominated by heavy brows and a sheer hook of a nose. His hair was salt and pepper, but his beard was pure white. There was no air of the benign grandfather about him, however—the scar running from his temple down into the lush beard gave the man a purely piratical appearance.

Yet, at the moment, the fierce old desert warrior

reminded the general of nothing so much as a rustic matron, her proprieties offended beyond measure by the latest escapade of the village idiot.

"No army has skirmishers so incompetent!" Abbu insisted. "It is not possible. They would have drowned by now, marching all of them into a well."

With gloomy assurance:

"The only explanation—obvious, obvious!—is that the enemy is perpetrating a cunning ruse upon our trusting, babe-innocent selves. You have finally met your match, general Belisarius. The fox, trapped by the wilier wolf."

Maurice grunted sourly, much as the Cassandra of legend, seeing all her forebodings realized.

Belisarius, on the other hand, did not seem noticeably chagrined. Rather the contrary, in fact. The general was practically beaming.

"I take it you had to chivvy the Malwa vanguard, to get them to follow you to our camps?"

Abbu snorted. "For a while, we thought we were going to have to dismount and explain it to them. 'See this, Malwa so-called scout? This is a campfire. That—over there—is known as a tent. These fellows you see lounging about are called Roman troops. Can you say: *Ro-man*? Can you find your way back in the dark? Do you need us to make the report to your commanders? Or have you already mastered speech?'"

His lips pursed, as if he had eaten a lemon. "No enemy is so—"

"Yes, they are," interrupted Belisarius. The humor was still apparent on the general's face, but when he spoke, his tone was utterly serious. He addressed his words not to Abbu alone, but to all the commanders.

"Understand *this* enemy. They are immensely powerful, because of their weapons and the great weight of forces they can bring to bear on the field of war. But the same methods which created that gigantic empire are also their Achilles heel. *They trust no-one but Malwa.* Not even the Ye-tai. And with good reason! All other peoples are nothing but their beasts."

He scanned the faces staring at him, ending with Abbu's.

"They have scouts as good as any in the world, Abbu. The Kushans, for instance, are excellent. And the Pathan trackers who serve the Rajputs are even better. But where are the Kushans? *At the rear.* Where are the Rajputs?" He gestured to the northeast. "Being bled dry in the mountains, that's where. Here, in Mesopotamia, they are using common cavalrymen for skirmishers." He shrugged. "Without Ye-tai to shepherd them, those soldiers will shirk their duty at every opportunity."

"They're arrogant bastards, all right," chimed in Coutzes. "It's not just that their vanguard elements are sloppy—they've got almost no flankers at all."

Belisarius glanced at the rising sun. "How soon?" he asked.

Coutzes' reply was immediate. "An hour and a half, general. Two, at the most." The young Thracian gave Abbu an approving look.

"Despite all his grumbling, Abbu and his men did a beautiful job last night. The Malwa are headed directly for us, and they've assumed a new marching order. A battle formation, it looks like to me— although it's like none I've ever seen."

"Describe it," commanded Belisarius.

"They've got their regular cavalry massed along the front. It's a deep formation. They're still in columns, but the columns are so wide they might as well be advancing in a line."

"Slower than honey, they're moving," chipped in one of Coutzes' tribunes. Coutzes nodded. "Then, most of their barbarians—Ye-tai—are on the flanks.

But they're not moving out like flankers should be. Instead, they're pressed right against—"

"They're not flankers," interrupted Belisarius, shaking his head. "The Ye-tai are used mainly as security battalions. The Malwa commander has them on the flanks in order to make sure that his regular troops don't break and run when the battle starts."

Coutzes snorted. "I can believe that. They're some tough-looking bastards, that's for sure."

"Yes, they are," agreed Belisarius. "That's their other function. The Malwa commander will be counting on them to beat off any flank attack."

One of the other tribunes sneered. "They're not *that* tough. Not against Thracian and Illyrian cataphracts, when the hammer comes down."

Belisarius grinned. "My opinion—exactly." To Coutzes:

"The Kushans are still in the rear? Pressed up close, I imagine, against the formation in the center— the war wagons with the priests and the kshatriya?"

Coutzes nodded. Belisarius copied the gesture.

"It all makes sense," he stated. "The key to that formation—the reason it looks odd to you, Coutzes— is that the Malwa approach battle like a blacksmith approaches an anvil. Their only thought is to use a hammer, which, in this case, is a mass of cavalry backed up by rocket platforms. If the hammer doesn't work"—he shrugged—"get a bigger hammer."

"What about the Lakhmids?" asked Maurice.

Coutzes and the tribunes burst into laughter. Even Abbu, for the first time, allowed a smile to creep into his face.

"*They're* no fools," chuckled the scout leader. Approvingly: "Proper good Arabs, even if they are a lot of stinking Lakhmites. They're—"

Coutzes interrupted, still laughing.

"They *are* assuming a true flank position—*way* out on the flank. The left flank, of course, as near to the

desert as they can get without fighting an actual
pitched battle with the Ye-tai."

"Who are *not* happy with the Lakhmids," added
one of the tribunes. Another chimed in, "They'll break
in a minute, general. It's as obvious as udders on a
cow. You know how those Arabs think."

Abbu snorted. "Like any sane man thinks! What's
the point of riding a horse if you're not going to run
the damn beast? Especially with an idiot commander
who maneuvers his troops like—" the scout nodded
at Belisarius "—just like the general says. Like a
musclebound, pot-bellied blacksmith, waddling up to
his anvil."

Belisarius clapped his hands, once.

"Enough," he said. "Coutzes, start the attack as
soon as you can. By now, the Constantinople men will
be up and ready. I'll be with them, when the time
comes."

Coutzes peered at him. The look combined hesitation and concern. "Are you sure about that, general?
The casualties are going to be—"

"I'll be with them," repeated Belisarius.

Coutzes made a little motion with his shoulders,
like an abandoned shrug. He turned his horse and
trotted off. His tribunes and Abbu immediately followed.

Once they were gone, Maurice glanced at Belisarius.

"Odd," he remarked. "Hearing you make such
sarcastic remarks about blacksmiths, I mean. I always
thought you admired the fellows."

"I do," came the vigorous response. "Spent half my
time, as a kid, hanging around the smithy. Wanted
to be a blacksmith myself, when I grew up."

The general turned and began walking through the
gate back to the villa, Maurice at his side.

"I wasn't poking fun at *blacksmiths*, Maurice. I was
ridiculing generals who think *they're* blacksmiths."

He shook his head. "Smithing's a craft. And, like

any craft, it has its own special rules. Fine rules—
as long as you don't confuse them with the rules of
another trade. The thing about an anvil, you see, is
that it's just a big lump of metal. Anvils don't fight
back."

A half hour later, after parting company with Maurice, Belisarius rode his horse into the Constantinople
encampment. Valentinian and Anastasius accompanied
him, as always, trailing just a few yards behind.

The Greek troops were already up and about. Fed,
watered, fully armed and armored—and champing at
the bit. The soldiers greeted him enthusiastically when
he rode up. Belisarius listened to their cheers carefully. There was nothing feigned in those salutations,
he decided. Word had already spread, obviously, that
Belisarius would be fighting with them in the upcom-
ing battle. As he had estimated, the news that their
general would be sharing the risks of a cavalry charge
had completed the work of cementing the cataphracts'
allegiance.

I've got an army, finally, he thought with relief.
Then, a bit sardonically: *Now, I've only got to worry
about surviving the charge.*

Aide spoke in his mind:

**I think you should not do this. It is very
dangerous. They will have rockets.**

Belisarius scratched his chin before making his reply.

*I don't think that will be a problem, Aide. The
Syrians should have the enemy cavalry confused and
disorganized by the time we charge. If we move in
fast they'll have no clear targets for their rockets.*

Aide was not mollified.

**It is very dangerous. You should not do this.
You are irreplaceable.**

Belisarius sighed. Aide's fears, he realized, had
nothing to do with his estimation of the tactical odds.
They were far more deeply rooted.

No man is irreplaceable, Aide.

That is not true. You are. Without you, the Malwa will win. Link will win. We will be lost.

The general spoke, very firmly. *If I am irreplaceable, Aide, it is because of my ability as a general. True?*

Silence.

Belisarius demanded: *True?*

Yes, came Aide's grudging reply.

Then you must accept this. The risk is part of the generalship.

He could sense the uncertainty of the facets. He pressed home the lesson.

I have a small army. The enemy is huge. If I am to win—the war, not just this battle—I must have an army which is supple and quick to act. Only a united, welded army can do that.

He paused, thinking how best to explain. Aide's knowledge and understanding of humanity was vast, in many ways—much greater than his own. But the crystalline being's own nature made some aspects of human reality obscure to him, even opaque. Aide often astonished Belisarius with his uncanny understanding of the great forces which moved the human race. And then, astonished him as much with his ignorance of the people who made up that race.

Humanity, as a tapestry, Aide understood. But he groped, dimly, at the human threads themselves.

We are much like Malwa, we Romans. We, too, have built a great empire out of many different peoples and nations. They organize their empire by rigid hierarchical rules—purity separated from pollution, by carefully delineated stages. We do it otherwise. Their methods give them great power, but little flexibility. And, most important, nothing in the way of genuine loyalty.

We will only defeat them with cunning—and loyalty.

He closed in on his point, almost ruthlessly. He could feel Aide resisting the logic.

It is true, Aide. I am the premier general of Rome because of my victories over Persians and barbarians. I won those victories with border troops—Thracians, of course, but also Syrians and Illyrians. The Greek soldiers who form the heart of the Roman army know little of me beyond my reputation.

That is too abstract. For the war against Malwa, those men are key. I must have their unswerving loyalty and trust. Not just these men, today, but all the others who will follow.

Firmly, finally:

There is no other way. A general can only gain the loyalty of troops who know he is loyal to them, also. I have already shown the garrison troops that I cannot be trifled with. Now I must show them that I will not trifle with them. Their charge is the key to the battle. If it is pressed home savagely, it will fix the enemy's attention on the Greeks. They will not dream that there might be others—even more dangerous—hidden in the woods.

Silence. Then, plaintively:

It will be very dangerous. You might be killed.

Belisarius made no answer. By now, he was approaching the center of the Constantinople encampment. He could see Agathius astride his armored charger, fifty yards away, surrounded by his tribunes and hecatontarchs. The young chiliarch was issuing last-minute instructions. He was not bellowing or roaring those commands histrionically, however, as Belisarius had seen many Roman officers do on the morning of a battle. Even at a distance, the relaxed camaraderie of the Constantinople command group was obvious.

Aide's voice cut through the general's satisfaction.

I would miss you. Very much.

Belisarius focussed all his attention on the facets. He

was dazzled, as so many times before, by the kaleidoscopic beauty of that strangest of God's creations. That wondrous soul which called itself Aide.

I would miss you, also. Very much.

A small part of his mind heard Agathius' welcoming hail. A small part of his mind raised a hand in acknowledgement. For the rest—

Whimsy returned.

Let's try to avoid the problem, shall we?

The facets flashed and spun, assuming a new configuration. A shape—a form—Belisarius had never sensed in them, before, began to crystallize.

I will help, came the thought. Firm, solid—lean and sinewy.

Almost weaselish.

Those sorry bastards are fucked. Fucked!

Belisarius started with surprise. Aide's next words caused him to twist in his saddle, to make sure that he had not heard Valentinian himself.

Mutter, mutter, mutter.

"I didn't say a thing," protested Valentinian, seeing the general's accusing eyes. With an air of aggrieved injury, he pointed a thumb at the huge cataphract riding next to him. "Ask him."

"Man's been as silent as a tomb, general," averred Anastasius. "Although I doubt he's been thinking philosophical thoughts, as I have. I always contemplate before a battle, you know. I find the words of Marcus Aurelius particularly—"

Valentinian muttered. Anastasius cocked an eye.

"What was that? I didn't catch it."

Belisarius grinned.

"I think he said 'sodomize philosophy.' But, maybe not. Maybe he said 'sod of my patrimony.' Praying to the ancestral spirits of Thrace, you understand, for their protection in the coming fray."

Mutter, mutter, mutter.

Mutter, mutter, mutter.

Chapter 18

Belisarius ordered the charge as soon as he saw the first units of the Syrian light cavalry pouring back from the battlefield.

The battlefield itself, directly to the east, was too distant to make out clearly. From a mile away, it was just a cloud of dust on a level plain—fertile fields, once—further obscured by the little copses of trees which were the outposts of the imperial hunting park. But the general, from experience, had been able to gauge the tempo of the battle by sound alone.

Based on what he had heard, he thought the situation was progressing very nicely. He was particularly pleased—if he had interpreted the sounds correctly—by the situation on his right. There, Abbu and his men had concentrated their attentions on their Arab counterparts.

Abbu's scouts were bedouin tribesmen, pledged to the service of the Ghassanid dynasty. The Ghassanids were Rome's traditional allies in northwest Arabia. More in the way of vassals, actually, but Rome had always been careful to tread lightly on their prickly Arab sensibilities. The Lakhmids had served Persia in the same capacity, in northeast Arabia, until switching their allegiance to the Malwa.

The Malwa were a new enemy, for Rome and its

Ghassanid allies. But their Arab skirmishers were same Lakhmids that Abbu and his men—and their ancestors—had been fighting for centuries. That conflict had ancient, bitter roots.

Both sides in that fray ululated in the Arab manner, but there were subtleties which were quite distinct to the general's educated ear. For a time, the ululations had swelled and swayed, back and forth. Now, there was a different pattern to the chanting rhythm of that battle.

Unless Belisarius missed his guess badly, Abbu and his men had fairly routed the Lakhmids—and with them, the only competent scouts in the enemy's army besides the Kushans.

He was pleased—no, delighted. Many things Maurice had taught him until the general, finally, outstripped his tutor, but one of the earliest lessons had been simple and brutal:

First thing you do, you blind the bastards.

The "charge" which Belisarius ordered was more in the nature of a vigorous trot. The enemy was still almost a mile away, even if, as he expected, they were advancing toward him. A mile, especially in the heat of a Syrian summer, was much too far to race a warhorse carrying its own armor and an armored man.

So he simply trotted forward. At first, he kept a vigilant eye on the garrison troopers, making sure that the hotheads among them didn't spur the rest into a faster pace. His vigilance eased, after a bit, once it became obvious that Agathius' sub-officers were a steady and capable lot. Veterans all, they did an excellent job of restraining the overeager.

Even in a trot, two thousand cataphracts—along with Persian dehgans, the heaviest cavalry in the world—sounded like distant thunder. The Syrian light horsemen, scampering away from the enemy they had goaded into a furious charge, heard that sound and knew its meaning. Knew that their mightier brothers were coming to their aid. Knew, most of all, that their general—once again—had not failed them.

The first Syrians who galloped through the gaps left for them by the oncoming cataphracts were whooping and grinning ear to ear. Shouting their cheerful cries.

Belisarius! Belisarius!

Some—then more and more, as the battlecry gained favor: *Constantinople! Constantinople!*

Throughout, as the retreating Syrians poured through their ranks, chanting and hollering, the capital troopers maintained a dignified silence. But Belisarius could sense the hidden satisfaction lurking beneath those helmeted faces. All memories of town brawls and executed comrades vanished; all resentments of sharp-tongued borderers fled; all bitterness at aristocratic units lounging in Constantinople while they sweated in the desert were forgotten.

There was nothing, now, but the fierce pride of the toughest fighters the world had ever known.

Greeks.

Latin armies had outfought them, centuries before, with superior organization and tactics. Beaten them so thoroughly, in fact, that they had even adopted the name of their conquerors. The Empire was Greek, now, at its core. But they called it the Roman Empire, still, and took pride in the name.

Persian armies, in modern cavalry battles, had outmaneuvered and outshot them, time after time. Until the proud Greeks, who called themselves Romans, had finally imitated their ancient Medean foe. The cataphracts were nothing but a copy of the Persian dehgans, at bottom.

In war, others had been better than the Greeks, many times. But no-one had ever been better in a fight. The Greek hoplite had been the most terrible of foes, on the ancient battlefield. They had introduced into warfare a style of bloody, smashing, in-your-face combat that had shocked all their opponents.

Achilles come to life; Ajax reborn. The same blood flowed in the veins of the grim men riding alongside Belisarius that day. The armor was different. The weapons had changed. They rode forward on horseback rather than striding on phalanx feet. But they were still the same tough, tough, tough Greeks.

A half mile, now. Syrian cavalrymen were still swirling in the ground between Belisarius and the oncoming Malwa. "A Hunnish kind of sally," the general had asked for—and Huns couldn't have done it better. Advance. Volley. Retreat—but with the "Parthian shot," firing arrows over the shoulder. Counter-attack. Volley. Retreat. Swirl forward; swirl away. Kill; cripple; wound—and evade retaliation.

Belisarius could finally see a few of the advancing Malwa. He could sense their frenzied rage at the Syrian tactics. Full of their own arrogance, the Malwa thought only of closing with this infuriating army of skirmishers. Their lead units were pushing ahead, maintaining no battle order. The Ye-tai "enforcers" scattered among them were not driving the troopers forward. There was no need. The Ye-tai themselves were seized up in that same heedless fury.

The Malwa troops knew little of Mesopotamia, and the Ye-tai even less. Knew nothing of the crumbled bones which littered that soil—the bones of Roman soldiers, often enough, who had made their same mistake. Crassus and his legions had been slaughtered by the Parthians, half a millennium before, not so very far away.

Belisarius' main concern had been that the Malwa might precede their troops with rocket volleys. He had not been particularly worried about casualties, as such. The Malwa rockets were much too erratic and inaccurate to fire genuine barrages. But he had been worried that the noise might panic some of his garrison troopers' horses. The mounts which his Constantinople soldiers rode were the steadiest available, true. But they had little of the training with gunpowder weapons which his Syrian and Thracian cavalry had enjoyed.

It was obvious, however, that there would be no barrages. As he had hoped, the Syrians' light cavalry tactics had been too agile and confusing to give the Malwa kshatriya a clear target. Now, it was too late. The dust thrown up by thousands of horsemen—friend and foe alike—had completely obscured the front of the battlefield from the Malwa commanders in the center. They would not even be able to see the charge of his Constantinople heavy cavalry. They would *hear* it, certainly. Even in the din of battle, a full charge by two thousand cataphracts would shake the very earth. But the sound of thunder is not a suitable target for rockets, and the sound would be short-lived in any event. Once the cataphracts closed, rockets would kill more Malwa troops than Roman.

Belisarius spurred his horse forward. No gallop, simply an easy canter. To either side, the garrison troopers matched the pace. There was no need, any longer, for the hecatontarchs and decarchs to maintain a steady formation. The cataphracts' lines were as steady as if they had been drawn in ink. Battle was very near, and these were the same Greeks whose forefathers had marched in step at Marathon.

Five hundred yards. Though they were closer, the enemy had disappeared completely—swallowed by the dust which hovered over the battlefield, unstirred by even a gentle breeze.

Four hundred yards.

Out of the dust galloped a small body of Arab cavalrymen. They headed straight for the oncoming

Greeks. As they approached, Belisarius recognized the figure of Abbu.

The scout leader swept past the general, ululating fiercely. Blood dripped from a small gash on his cheek, but the old warrior seemed otherwise unharmed.

A moment later, Abbu drew his horse alongside Belisarius. His mount's flanks were heaving and sheened with sweat, but the horse seemed not in the least exhausted.

Abbu certainly wasn't.

"The Lakhmids are done!" he cried gaily. "Beaten like dogs! We whipped the curs into the river!"

Belisarius met that savage grin with his own smile.

"All of them?"

Abbu sneered.

"*Lakhmids*. Stinking Lakhmids are not bedouin, general Belisarius. River-rats. Oasis-huddlers. Die of fright in the good desert. I'm sure most of them are scurrying down this bank of the Euphrates. Doesn't matter. You won't see them again. Not for days, if ever. Nothing else, they'll get lost."

An exquisite sneer.

"Camel-fuckers, the lot. Don't even have the excuse of being perverts. Lakhmids are just too stupid to know the difference between a woman and a camel."

A *royal* sneer.

"Hard to blame them, of course. Lakhmid women are uglier than camels. Meaner, too."

Three hundred yards. There was a sudden rush of Syrians—the last die-hards, finally breaking off with the enemy. Then, a second or two later, the first ranks of the Malwa cavalry appeared in the dust. Galloping forward in a full and furious charge.

Belisarius caught a glimpse of Abbu's gleaming eyes. At that moment, the old man truly seemed a pirate, ogling a chest of gold.

The general laughed. "Let them be, Abbu. Our job, now." He jerked his head backward. "Be off. Regroup your men. Rejoin Coutzes and the Syrians. I want to be sure you're there to cover us—especially on the left—when we make our own retreat. I don't want any Malwa—*not one*—to get into those woods and find my surprise."

Abbu snorted.

"Worry about something else, general. Worry about *anything* else. No Malwa will get into those woods."

He began reining his horse around, taking a last glance at the Malwa. Two hundred and fifty yards away.

"God be with you, General Belisarius."

Hundreds of Malwa cavalry were visible now. Perhaps a thousand. It was hard to gauge, since they were so disorganized.

The enemy troopers finally caught sight of the heavily armored cataphracts approaching them. Some, apparently, began to have second thoughts about the reckless advance—judging from their attempts to rein in their mounts. But those doubters were instantly quelled by the Ye-tai. The Malwa army—more of a mob, really—continued its headlong charge.

Two hundred yards. The cataphracts drew their bows; notched their arrows.

Time.

Belisarius gave the order. The cornicens blew wild and loud.

The Roman cataphracts brought their mounts to a halt. As soon as the horses had steadied, all two thousand cavalrymen raised up in their stirrups. With the full power of their chests and shoulders, they drew back their bows and fired in unison.

The cataphracts were four ranks deep. The ranks were staggered in a checkerboard pattern to allow each rank a clear line of fire. With the gaps between the regiments, which provided escape routes for the retreating Syrians, the Constantinople mounted archers covered well over a mile of battlefront. Firing in a co-ordinated volley, at that short range, their arrows swept the front ranks of the oncoming Malwa like a giant scythe.

At least half of the arrows missed, burying their cruel warheads in the soft soil. But hundreds didn't, and most of those hundreds brought death and horrible injury. No bows in the world were as powerful as cataphract bows, few arrowheads as sharp, and none as heavy.

The Malwa staggered. Many shouted and screamed—some with shock and agony, others with fear and disbelief. Their light armor had been like so much tissue against those incredible arrows.

Belisarius motioned. Again, the cornicens blew.

The cataphracts sheathed their bows, reached back and drew their lances. Within seconds, they sent their horses back into motion. Not more than a hundred yards separated the two armies when the Romans began their charge. Those yards shrank like magic.

Ironically, it was the Malwa—the bleeding, battered, mangled Malwa—who closed most of that distance. Those Malwa in the front ranks who had survived the volley were driving their horses forward at a furious gallop, desperate to close before more arrows could be brought to bear on them.

It was a natural reaction—an inevitable reaction, actually, as Belisarius had known it would be—but it was disastrous nonetheless. A man on a galloping horse must concentrate most of his attention on staying in the saddle. That is especially true for men like the Malwa cavalry, who did not possess the stirrups of their Roman enemies. Men in that position, for all the dramatic furor of their charge, are simply not in position to wield their weapons effectively.

For their part, the Roman cataphracts did not advance at a gallop. They spurred their horses forward in a canter—a pace easy to ride, while they concentrated on their murderous work. They set their feet in the stirrups, leaned into the charge, positioned their heavy lances securely, and aimed the spearpoints.

When the two cavalry forces met, seconds later, the result was sheer slaughter.

Malwa horsemen were better armed and armored than Malwa infantry. But, by Roman or Persian standards, they were not much more than light cavalry. Their armor was mail—flimsy at that—and simply covered their torsos; the cataphract armor was heavy scale, covering not only the torso but the left arm and the body down to mid-thigh. Malwa helmets were leather caps, reinforced with scale; the cataphracts wore German-style Spangenhelm, their heads protected by segmented steel plate. The Malwa lances—in the tradition of stirrupless cavalry—were simply long and slender spears; the Greeks were wielding lances twice as heavy and half again as long.

The Ye-tai were better equipped than the common Malwa cavalrymen. Yet they, also, were hopelessly outclassed as lancers—and would have been, even had Belisarius not refitted his cavalry with the stirrups which Aide had shown him in a vision.

The Romans shattered the Malwa charge, across the entire line. Some Malwa in the first ranks, on both edges of the battlefront, were able to veer aside. The majority were simply hammered under. Over five hundred Malwa cavalrymen died or were seriously injured in that brutal collision. Half of them were spitted on lances. The other half, within seconds, were being butchered by cataphract swords and axes. And here, too, history showed—Malwa handweapons had none of the weight of Roman swords and axes. The Malwa had only months of experience fighting Persian dehgans; the Romans, centuries.

There were perhaps six thousand Malwa cavalrymen directly involved in this first major clash of the two armies. In less than two minutes, between the volley and the lance charge, they had suffered casualties in excess of fifteen percent—a horrendous rate, measured by the standards of any human army in history.

Then, the bloodletting worsened. The front ranks of the Malwa had been brought to a complete halt. Many of them, along with their horses, were spilled to the ground. Those still in the saddle were off-balance, bewildered, shocked.

The Malwa charging from behind had seen little of the battle due to the dust and the noise. Still driving their horses, they slammed into the immobilized mass at the front. Thousands of Malwa horsemen were now hopelessly tangled up and being driven willy-nilly against the Roman line.

Belisarius had been planning to call the retreat as soon as the initial clash was done. But now, seeing the confusion in the Malwa ranks, he ordered a standing fight. The cornicens blew again. The rear ranks of the cataphracts moved up, filling out the front line. The gaps were closed; the horsemen were almost shoulder to shoulder.

Flanked by Valentinian and Anastasius, Belisarius took a place in the center of the line. His lance had already been discarded. The Ye-tai that lance had spitted in the first clash had taken it with him, as he fell to the ground. The general drew his sword—not the spatha he generally favored, but the long Persian-style cavalry sword which he carried in a baldric. He rose in the stirrups and struck down a Malwa before him. The heavy sword cut through the man's helmet and split his skull.

Belisarius jerked loose the sword, struck another foe. Another. Another.

As before in battle, Aide was assisting him, giving the general almost superhuman reflexes and an uncanny ability to perceive everything sharply and clearly. But the assistance was almost moot. This battle—this brawl—called for strength and endurance, not speed and agility.

No matter. Belisarius was a big man, and a powerful one. His endurance had been shaped by the teachings and training of Maurice—who considered stamina the soldier's best friend—and his skill with a sword, by Valentinian. At no time in the ensuing fray did he fail to cut down his opponent, and at no time was he in danger of being struck down himself. That would have been true even if Valentinian had not been there to protect him on the left, just as the giant Anastasius did on his right.

That battle was as savage as any Belisarius had ever seen—on that scale, at least—and he was no stranger to mayhem. It was more like butchers chopping meat than anything else. The Malwa at the front could barely wield their weapons, so great was the press. The Romans hammered them down; hammered the ones who were pushed atop the corpses; hammered the ones who came after them.

At many places along the line, after a few minutes, the battle effectively ended. The Greeks could no longer reach live enemies, due to the obstruction of the dead ones.

The Malwa at the front began to recoil. The ones pressing from the rear had finally sensed the tide and eased away, allowing the men before them to stagger back. Belisarius, sensing the break in the battle, left off his merciless swordwork. Quickly, he scanned the front. He was in the very middle of the Roman ranks, and could no longer see either end of the battle line. But he knew the danger. For all their losses, the Malwa greatly outnumbered his Constantinople troops. Whether from conscious direction by their commanders, or the simple flow of individuals, they would soon be curling around his flanks.

He gave two quick orders. The cornicens blew, then blew again.

The first order was for the retrieval of casualties. The cataphracts, hearing that call, shouted their fury and contempt at the Malwa. It was as if the entire Constantinople unit was sneering, as one man.

We whipped your fucking worthless butts. Now, we'll take the time to gather up our own, before we amble on our way. Fuck you. You don't like it? Try and do something about it!

For all their braggadocio, the Greeks did not linger at the task. They were veterans, and knew as well as their general the danger of being outflanked before they could make their retreat. So, one cataphract aiding another, they quickly gathered up their casualties and draped them across their horses.

It did not take long, even though the Greeks took the time to collect the dead as well as the wounded. Their casualties had been incredibly light—much lighter than they had expected. *Much* lighter. They were almost shocked, once they realized how few bodies there were to retrieve.

The retreat started. Belisarius had been concerned about that retreat, before the battle. It is always difficult to keep soldiers, even the best of soldiers, under control at such times. There is an powerful tendency for men to speed up, anxious to gain distance from a pursuing enemy. Whether quickly, or almost imperceptibly, a retreat can easily turn into a chaotic rout.

Not this time. Within seconds, Belisarius knew he had nothing to fear. The Constantinople men, it was obvious, did not even consider themselves to be retreating. They were simply leaving, because there was nothing more to be done at the moment.

An easy canter, no more. The ranks reformed, even dressed their lines.

Belisarius took his place at the rear, during that

retreat, just as he had taken a place at the front during the charge. The Greeks noticed—again—and a great cheer surged through their ranks. *Belisarius! Belisarius!*

He smiled—he even waved—but he took no other notice of the acclaim. He spent most of the time, during that almost-leisurely retreat, staring over his shoulder. Watching the enemy. Gauging. Assessing.

He caught sight of Syrian and Arab units charging forward, ready to provide covering fire for the cataphracts. He waved them off. There was no need. The Malwa were pursuing, true. But it was not a furious, frenzied charge led by eager warriors. It was a sodden, leaden, sullen movement, driven forward by screaming Ye-tai.

The Malwa cavalrymen had had enough of Romans, for the moment.

Belisarius turned back, satisfied, and glanced at the sun. It was not yet noontime. He thought the Malwa commanders would not be able to drive their army back into battle for at least two hours. Possibly three.

Plenty of time. He had taken no pleasure in the killing. He never had, in any battle he had ever fought. But he did take satisfaction in a job well done, and he intended to do the same again. In two hours. Possibly three.

Plenty of time, for a craftsman at his trade.

Chapter 19

Two and a half hours later, the enemy began taking positions for the assault on the villa. The Malwa forces lined up on the open ground east of the royal compound, at a distance of half a mile. The front lines were composed of cavalry regulars, backed by Ye-tai. The rocket wagons, guarded by the Kushans, were brought to a halt fifty yards behind the front ranks. The kshatriya, overseen by Mahaveda priests, removed the tarpaulins covering the wagons and began unloading rockets and firing troughs. Within a few minutes, they had the artillery devices set up. There were eighteen of the rocket troughs, erected in a single line, spaced thirty feet apart.

From a room on the second floor of the villa, Belisarius studied the Malwa formation with his telescope. Standing just behind him were the top officers of the Syrian and Constantinople troops forted up in the imperial compound—Bouzes and Coutzes, Agathius and Cyril. They were listening intently as Belisarius passed on his assessment of the situation.

The general began by examining the rockets, but spent little time on that problem. Once the first two or three had been erected, he was satisfied that he understood them perfectly. The rockets were the same type he had seen—at much closer range—during the

219

sea battle he had fought against pirates while traveling
to India on a Malwa embassy ship. In that battle, the
rockets had wreaked havoc on the Arab ships. But,
he told his officers, he did not think they would have
that effect here.

"Most of the damage done by the rockets in the
pirate battle," he explained, lowering the telescope
for a moment, "was incendiary. The pirate galleys, like
all wooden boats, were bonfires waiting to happen."

Seeing the puzzlement on the faces of Bouzes and
Coutzes, the two Constantinople officers chuckled.

"Farm boys!" snorted Cyril. "You think 'cause a
boat's floating on water that she won't burn? *Shit.* The
planks are made of the driest wood anyone can find,
and what's worse—"

"—they're caulked with pitch," concluded Agathius.
Like his fellow Greek, the chiliarch was smirking—
that particular, unmistakable, insufferable smirk which
seafarers the world over bestow upon landlubbers.

"Not to mention the cordage and the sails," added
Cyril.

Bouzes and Coutzes, Thracian leaders of a Syrian army, took no offense at the Greeks' sarcasm.
On some other day, they might. But not on the day
when those same Greeks had given the enemy such
a thorough pounding. They simply grinned, shrugged
at their ignorance, and studied the interior of the
villa with new and enlightened eyes.

"A different matter altogether, isn't it?" commented
Belisarius.

Under the fancy trappings and elaborate decora-
tions, the royal compound was about as fireproof as
a granite tor. The walls were made of kiln-fired brick,
and the sloping roof was covered with tiles. Neither
would burn—those bricks and tiles had been *made*
in ovens—and he was quite sure the thick walls could
withstand the explosive power of the rockets' relatively
small warheads.

True, the roof tiles would probably shatter under a direct hit by a rocket. Belisarius did not think there would be many such hits, if any. He knew from experience that the Malwa rockets were not only erratic in their trajectories, but erratic in their destruction as well. They had no contact fuses. They simply exploded whenever the burning fuel reached the warhead. In order to shatter the roof, a rocket would have to hit directly—not at a glancing angle— *and* explode at just the right time.

The likelihood of that happening, in his estimation, was not much greater than being hit by lightning. And if, against all odds, a rocket should score a direct hit—

"Might break in the roof tiles," commented Bouzes.

Belisarius shrugged. "The tiles are supported by heavy beams. Wooden beams, yes. But these beams aren't anything like the thin planks of pirate galleys. They're much thicker, and, what's more important, *not* saturated with inflammable pitch."

He began studying the positions of the Malwa cavalry, now. Again, passing on his conclusions.

"They'll start with a rocket barrage, and then follow it up with a direct assault." A moment's silence, then: "I thought so. They're dismounting, now. It'll be an infantry attack."

"Those are cavalry!" protested Coutzes.

Belisarius pressed his lips together to keep from smiling. He remembered, from three years before, that Coutzes and Bouzes had been trained in the cavalry tradition. The young Thracian commander, it was obvious, had still not quite abandoned his contempt for foot-fighting.

His brother, however, had.

"Don't be stupid. We've been training our own men to be dragoons. Why shouldn't the Malwa?"

"Well said," murmured Belisarius. For a moment, he took his eye from the telescope and glanced at Coutzes.

"You're about to see why I insisted on training our cavalry to fight on foot. I know you think that was a waste of time—"

He drove over Coutzes' little protest. "—but the reason I did so was because I knew the time would come when we'd be able to arm those dragoons with grenades. And handcannons, I'm hoping."

He nodded toward the enemy, visible through the window.

"They already have grenades. The kshatriya are starting to pass them out to the regulars."

He took up the telescope again, and continued his scrutiny.

"They'll come in waves. Probably be one grenadier for every ten soldiers. The Ye-tai will be scattered through the lines in small squads, driving the regulars forward and pressing the assault. Some of the kshatriya will be in those lines, too, but most of them will stay at the center with the priests, manning the rockets. They'll also help the Kushans guard the wagons. They might—*damn!*"

He stiffened, staring through the telescope intently.

"*Damn,*" he repeated. "They're bringing up the Kushans. All two thousand of them."

"On foot?" asked Agathius.

Belisarius lowered the telescope, nodded. Then, with a bit of a rueful smile:

"Kushans, in my experience, don't have any fetishes when it comes to fighting. On foot, on horse, on boats—it doesn't matter to them. Whatever, they'll do it well. Very well."

He turned away from the window. It was obvious from his stance and expression that he had reached a decision. His officers gathered closer.

"This changes things," Belisarius announced. "As you know, I'd wanted to wait until tomorrow before bringing in Maurice and his boys."

He tapped the palm of his hand with the telescope, emphasizing his words.

"We're going to beat these bastards, one way or the other. But I want more than that—I want to *pulverize* them. The best way to do that is to rout them early in the morning, so we've got a full day for pursuit."

The officers nodded. All of them—even the two young brothers—were experienced combatants. They knew that a battle won at the end of day was a battle half-won. The kind of relentless, driving pursuit which could utterly destroy a retreating enemy was simply impossible once daylight was gone.

Agathius glanced out the window. "It's still before noon," he mused. "If the battle starts soon enough—"

Belisarius shook his head. "I'd wanted to let the Malwa spend all day hammering their heads against us here. Bleed them dry, exhaust them—then hit them at dawn with a massive flank attack by Maurice and Kurush. The attack would break their army, and then we'd sally out of the villa and drive over them."

He saw that his officers still didn't understand. He didn't blame them. Their brief experience with Malwa soldiers had not prepared them for the Kushans.

"The Kushans are a different breed. They *won't* come at us in a mass, chivvied by Ye-tai, depending on their grenades to do the work. They'll come at us like the best kind of Roman infantry would attack this place."

Of the officers standing around him, Bouzes was the most familiar with Belisarius' infantry tactics. The general saw dawning comprehension in his face.

"Shit," muttered the young Thracian. He glanced around the room. "The villa's not a fortress, when you come down to it. The fortifications we jury-rigged were designed to fend off grenades, not—"

Belisarius finished the thought.

"Not two thousand of the finest foot soldiers anywhere in the world, charging in squads, aiming to push into every door and portal so they can use their swords and spears."

Cyril scowled. "Let 'em! I don't care how good they are. We're not lambs ourselves, general. Our cataphracts can fight on foot—just watch! With us to back up the Syrians, we'll chop those—"

Belisarius waved his hand.

"That's not the point, Cyril. I don't doubt that we'll beat back the Kushans. But I can guarantee that we won't be doing it without suffering lots of casualties *and* without being exhausted ourselves, when the day's over. I don't think we'll be in any shape to be pursuing anybody, tomorrow."

He rubbed his jaw thoughtfully. "I wonder . . ."

Belisarius stepped back to the window and looked through the telescope again. For a minute, he studied the Kushans taking up their position. Then, pressing himself against the wall to the left of the window, he aimed the telescope at a sharp angle, studying something to the southwest.

"We've got no troops stationed at the corrals." He cast a quick, inquisitive glance at Bouzes. The young Thracian shook his head.

"No, sir." His tone grew a bit defensive: "I thought about it, but it's at least half a mile away. There didn't seem any point to—"

Belisarius smiled crookedly.

"No, there wasn't. I'm not criticizing your decision, Bouzes. I just wanted to make sure."

Again, Bouzes shook his head. "We've got nobody there, general."

"Good," stated Belisarius. He stared through the telescope for another minute, before turning away from the window.

"We're going to turn everything inside out. Instead of waiting until tomorrow, I'll have Maurice start the counter-attack at the beginning of the battle."

He hesitated. "Well, not quite. I don't think the Kushans will lead the first assault. Unless that Malwa commander's dumber than a chicken, he won't want to use his best troops until he's softened this place up a bit. He'll let regulars and Ye-tai hammer us with grenades. See what happens. If that doesn't work, then he'll send in the Kushans. They'll head up the second attack. And *that's* when I'll order Maurice to make his charge."

The look of incomprehension was back on the faces of the general's subordinates. Belisarius' own face broke into a cheerful grin. "The trick to dealing with Kushans, I've learned, is to exploit their talents."

"Begging your pardon, sir," spoke up Cyril, "but I don't understand what you're getting at. If Maurice attacks when the Kushans are still fresh—"

"What will the Kushans do?" demanded Belisarius. "*Think*, Cyril. And remember—they'll be excellent troops, with good commanders, *on foot*, suddenly finding themselves caught between a fortified villa and a heavy cavalry charge on their right flank."

Cyril was still frowning. Belisarius drove on.

"The rest of the Malwa army will be shattering, under that charge. Not to mention—"

He turned to Agathius. "Are your boys up for another bit of lance work? A sally, straight out of the villa?"

Agathius grinned. "After that promenade this morning? Hell, yes. It'll be a bitch, mind you, getting the horses through all those little gates."

Belisarius waved the matter off. "I don't care if the sally's ragged. It doesn't matter. All that matters is that while Maurice and Kurush are breaking the Malwa in half from the flank, the front lines of their army see a new threat coming at them straight ahead. The Ye-tai'll go berserk, trying to force the regulars to stand and fight. But the Kushans—"

"Sweet Jesus, *yes*," whispered Bouzes. He strode to the window and stared through it at a sharp angle. "They'll break for the corrals, and the barns and horse pens. Only place around where infantry could fort up and have a chance against heavy cavalry."

He stared back at Belisarius. "They'll have to react instantly, general. Are they really that good?"

"I'm counting on it," came the firm reply. "It's a gamble, I know. If they don't—if they stand their ground—then we'll be in one bloody mess of a brawl. It'll last all day."

He shrugged. "We'll still win, but half the Malwa army will make their escape."

Cyril and Agathius looked at each other. Then, at Belisarius.

"Glad I'm not a general," muttered Cyril. "I'd die from headache."

Agathius tugged at his beard. "If I understand correctly, general, you're planning to wreck the Malwa by isolating their best troops while we concentrate on chewing the rest of them to pieces."

Belisarius nodded. Agathius' beard-tugging grew intense.

"What's to stop the Kushans from sallying themselves? Coming to the aid of—"

Bouzes grinned. "Of what? The same stupid fucking Malwa jackasses who got them treed in the first place?"

Belisarius shook his head. "They won't, Agathius. The Malwa don't trust the Kushans for the good and simple reason that they can't. The Kushans will fight, in a battle. But they've got no love for their overlords. When the hammer falls, the Kushans will look out for themselves."

He turned to Bouzes. "After the initial sally—after we break them—move your Syrian troops to cover the Kushans. The infantry can't play any useful role, anyway, in a pursuit. But don't attack the Kushans— be a bloodbath if you do—just hold them there."

He grinned himself, now.

"Until tomorrow morning."

"We'll finish the Kushans then?" asked Coutzes.

Belisarius' grin faded to a crooked smile. He made a little fluttering motion with his hands.

"We'll see," he said. "Maybe. Maybe not. They're tough, Kushans. But I saw a girl work wonders with them, once, using the right words."

Half an hour later, the attack began. With a rocket barrage, as Belisarius had predicted.

As he watched the rockets soaring all over the sky, exploding haphazardly and landing hither and yon, Belisarius realized that the Malwa were actually doing him a large favor. Although his troops had always maintained a soldierly sangfroid on the subject, he knew that they had been quite apprehensive about the enemy's mysterious gunpowder weapons. Except for Valentinian and Anastasius, who had accompanied him to India, none of Belisarius' men had any real experience with gunpowder weapons. True, most of the soldiers had seen grenades used—some of them had even practiced with the devices. But even his katyusha rocket-men had never seen gunpowder weapons used in the fury and chaos of an actual battle.

Now, the men were getting their first taste of Malwa gunpowder weapons. And the main result, after the first five minutes of that barrage, was—

"They'd do better to use scorpions and onagers," commented a Syrian infantryman, crouched behind a plaque-strengthened window not far from the general.

A Greek cataphract pressed against a nearby wall barked a laugh. "They'd do better to build an assault tower and piss on us," he sneered.

The Syrian watched a skittering rocket sail overhead and burst in midair. The man, Belisarius noted, did not even flinch. In the first moments of the barrage, the Roman soldiers had been shaken by the sound and fury which the rockets produced. But now, with experience, they were taking the matter in stride.

The same Syrian, catching a glimpse of Belisarius, cocked his head and asked:

"What's the point of this, sir, if you don't mind my asking?" The infantryman made a little gesture toward the window. "I don't think more than a dozen of these things have exploded anywhere in the compound. And only a few of them's done any real damage—the ones that blew up over the gardens."

"Don't get too overconfident, men," said Belisarius. He spoke loudly, knowing that all the soldiers crammed into the large room were listening.

"In the proper circumstances, these rockets can be effective. But you're right, in this situation they'd do a lot better to use old-style catapults. Rockets are an area-effect weapon—especially *their* rockets, which aren't anywhere near as accurate as ours."

He paused, allowing the happy thought of Roman rockets to boost morale, before continuing:

"They're almost useless used against a protected fixed position like this one. The reason the Malwa are using them"—he grinned—"is because the arrogant bastards are so sure of themselves that they didn't bother to bring any catapults. Like we did."

The general's grin was answered by a little cheer. When the cheer died down, the Syrian who had spoken up earlier asked another question.

"How would they be doing if they had those siege guns you've talked about?"

Belisarius grimaced. It was more of a whimsical expression than a rueful one, however.

"If they'd had siege guns, I never would have forted us up here in the first place." He waved his hand, casually. "Big siege guns would flatten a place like this inside of five minutes. In ten minutes, there'd be nothing but rubble."

Carefully—gauging—he watched the cheer fade from his soldiers' faces. Then, just before solemnity turned grim, he boomed:

"*On the other hand*, siege guns are so big and awkward that they're sitting ducks on a battleground."

Again, he waved his hand. The gesture, this time, was not casual in the least. It was the motion of a master craftsman, demonstrating an aspect of his skill.

"If they'd brought siege guns, we'd have ripped them with open-field maneuvers."

The grin returned.

"Either way, either way—it doesn't matter, men. We'll thrash the Malwa anyway it takes!"

Outside, two rockets burst in unison. But the sound, loud as it was, completely failed to drown the cheers which erupted through the crowded room.

Belisarius! Belisarius!

One soldier only, in that festive outburst, did not participate in the acclaim—the same Syrian, still crouched by the window, still watching everything outside with a keen and vigilant gaze.

"I think that's it, general," he remarked. "I'm pretty sure they're getting ready to charge."

Belisarius moved to the window, and crouched down next to the soldier. He drew out his telescope and peered through it. For a few seconds, no longer.

"You're right," he announced. The general leaned over and placed a hand on the Syrian's shoulder.

"What's your name?" he asked softly.

The man looked a bit startled. "Felix, sir. Felix Chalcenterus."

Belisarius nodded, rose, and strode out of the room. In the hallway beyond, he turned right and headed toward the villa's central gardens. The Greek cataphracts massed in the hallway squeezed to the sides, allowing him a narrow passageway through which to move. A *very* narrow passageway—crooked, cramped, and lined with scale armor.

By the time he emerged into the gardens—a bit the way a seed bursts out of a crushed grape—he felt like he had been through a grape-press himself. For all its imperial size, the villa was far too small a structure to hold thousands of troops packed within its walls. Still, Belisarius had insisted on crowding as many men as possible into the buildings. The villa was not a fortress. But its solidly-built walls and roofs provided far more protection from rockets and arrows than the leather screens and canopies which provided the only missile shelter for the troops resting in the villa's open grounds.

When he finally emerged into the central gardens, he saw that even here the casualties from the barrage had been very light. This, despite the fact that the area was packed as tightly as the buildings were.

The horticultural splendor which had once reigned here was nothing but a memory, now. Every plant and shrub had been obliterated by the heavily-armored men who were jammed into every nook and cranny of the gardens. But few of those men seemed the slightest bit injured.

Belisarius was relieved, even though he was not surprised. Belisarius had been almost certain that the rockets' trajectories would be too flat to plunge into the gardens.

Obviously, his estimate had been correct. What few injuries had occured had resulted from the handful of rockets which, by bad luck, had exploded directly overhead. And even those had done little damage, due to the leather shrapnel screens stretched across much of the garden areas.

Again, Belisarius forced his way forward. Once he was through the gardens, he plunged into the jam-packed hallways of the buildings on the opposite side.

Squeeze, squeeze, squeeze. By the time he finally staggered into the open grounds in the rear of the villa, he felt almost as if he had been through another lance charge.

The expedition had taken much longer than he had expected. No sooner did he emerge into the open than he heard a cacophony of distant shouting behind him. Malwa battle cries. The enemy had launched their ground assault.

Belisarius did not even think of turning back. The thought of undergoing that gauntlet again almost made him shudder. There would be no point, anyway. Bouzes was in command of the three thousand infantrymen manning the villa, with five hundred Constantinople cataphracts to back him up. Belisarius was quite confident of their ability to fight off the first attack.

Coutzes and Agathius, seeing the general emerge, hurried to meet him. Their own pace was not quick. The area to the rear of the villa held the rest of the Greek cataphracts and the Syrian cavalry—over four thousand men, along with their horses. But the population density was not as extreme as it had been in the villa itself. The imperial compound's wall-enclosed western grounds were many acres in extent. Open areas, for the most part, interspersed with bridle paths, hedges, patios and scattered trees.

Within a few seconds, Belisarius was consulting with his cavalry commanders. All three of them spoke loudly, due to the rapidly escalating noise coming from the other side of the villa. Malwa and Roman battle cries were mingled with the sound of grenade explosions.

Belisarius' first words were, "How many casualties?"

"They'd have done better to use catapults," snorted Agathius. He looked at Coutzes. "What would you say? Twenty, maybe—overall?"

Coutzes shrugged. "If that many. Only three fatalities, that I know of."

"What about the horses?" asked the general.

Agathius rocked his head back and forth. "They're a little skittish, general. But we were able to keep them pretty much under control. Don't think we lost more than a dozen. Most of those'll be back, in a few hours, except a couple who broke their fool necks jumping the rear wall."

Coutzes laughed. "I don't think Abbu's precious horse will be coming back! I swear, general, the fucking thing almost jumped over the trees as well as the wall!"

Agathius grinned. Belisarius' eyes widened.

"*Abbu's*—you mean that gelding he dotes on?"

" 'Dotes on'?" demanded Coutzes. "That gelding's the apple of the old brigand's eye! He practically sleeps with the damn beast."

"Not any more," chuckled Agathius. "He's fit to be tied, he is. Last I saw he was standing on the wall shooting arrows at the creature. Didn't come close, of course—the gelding was already halfway to Antioch."

Belisarius shook his head. He was smiling, but the smile was overlaid with concern. "Did he manage—"

Coutzes cut him off.

"Don't worry, general. Abbu sent the Arab couriers off as soon as we gave him the word. Half an hour ago, at least. Maurice'll have plenty of warning that the plans have changed."

Belisarius' smile grew very crooked. "I'm glad I won't be there to hear him, cursing me for a fussbudget." He did a fair imitation of Maurice's rasping voice: "What am I? A babe in swaddling clothes—*a toddler*—has to be told to pay attention because plans are changing? Of course the plan's changing! Aren't I the one who taught that—that—*that general*—that plans always change when the enemy arrives?"

Coutzes grinned. Agathius' expression was serious.

"You think he'll be ready, then?" he asked. "I'll admit, I'm a bit worried about it. They weren't expecting to be called on this soon."

Belisarius clapped a hand on Agathius' heavy shoulder.

"Don't," he said softly. "If there's one thing in this world you can be sure of, it's that Maurice won't ever be caught napping in a battle. The only reason I sent the couriers was to make sure he'd move out the second we fired the signal rockets, instead of fifteen seconds later."

He turned to Coutzes. "Speaking of which . . ."

Coutzes pointed to a small copse of trees fifty yards distant.

"In there, general. Aimed and ready to fire as soon as you give the word. One red; followed by a green. And we've got three back-up rockets of each color in case one of them misfires."

Belisarius nodded. He turned his head back toward the villa, listening to the sound of the battle. Even buffered by the villa, the noise was intense. Intense, and growing more so by the second. The grenade explosions were almost continuous, now.

The general and his two officers listened for perhaps a minute, without speaking. Then Coutzes stated, very firmly, "Not a chance."

Agathius immediately nodded. So did Belisarius. All three men had reached the same assessment, just from the sound of the battle. For all the evident fury with which the Malwa were pressing the attack, their efforts would be futile. There had been not a trace of the unmistakable sounds of defenders losing heart. Not one cry of despair, not one desperate shriek— only a steady roar of Roman battle cries and shouts of confident triumph.

The assault would break, recoil; the Malwa stagger away, trailing small rivers of blood.

Belisarius turned away from the villa and quickly scanned the area.

"You're ready." It was a statement, not a question. Agathius and Bouzes didn't even bother to speak their affirmation.

The general sighed.

"Nothing for it, then." He looked back at the villa, wincing.

"Back into the vise, for me." He began walking toward the buildings, saying, over his shoulder: "I'll have the message relayed. Watch for it. Fire off the rockets at once."

To his relief, the crowd had thinned out a bit—in the rear buildings, at least. All of the soldiers who could had forced themselves into the buildings directly facing the Malwa, fired with determination to help beat off the attack. It only took Belisarius a couple of minutes to thread his way back to the central gardens.

There, however, he was stopped cold. Cursed himself for a fool.

He had forgotten that he had given orders, the day before, to use the gardens as a field hospital. The grounds were completely impassable, now. The casualties were not particularly severe, given the situation. But wounded men, along with their attendants, take up more space than men standing.

As he scrutinized the scene, a part of Belisarius was grimly pleased with what he saw. Outside of the terrible losses suffered by a routed army being pursued, there was no kind of battle which produced casualties as quickly as a close assault on fieldworks. Most of those casualties, of course, would be inflicted on the attackers. But the defenders would take their share also.

Yet, what he now saw in the gardens were light casualties, given the circumstances. And—even better— a much higher proportion of men wounded rather than killed, compared to the usual.

The screens worked, by God!

He had thought they would. Malwa grenades, like Roman ones, were ignited by hand-lit fuses. It was almost inevitable that the man lighting that fuse would cut it a bit too long, from fear of having the bomb blow up in his hand. The Malwa would have concentrated their grenades on the many doors and portals which lined the villa's walls and buildings. With the screens in place—put up almost instantly, without warning—the Malwa grenades would have bounced off and exploded too far away to do any concussive damage. True, shrapnel would pierce the leather—would eventually shred the screens entirely. But the screens had served to blunt the fury of the first assault, and almost all the Roman casualties had been the relatively minor wounds caused by leather-deflected shrapnel.

Pleased as he was, however, Belisarius did not spend much time examining the scene. He was too preoccupied with the unexpected problem of getting himself to a position where he could assess the next Malwa attack—the attack he was certain would be spearheaded by the Kushans. Timing would be all important, then, and he could not possibly order Maurice's attack when he had no idea what was happening.

For a moment, he considered working his way to the front by circumnavigating the interconnected buildings which made up the compound. But he dismissed the idea almost immediately. Every one of those buildings would be so jampacked with soldiers as to make forward progress all but impossible.

He had just about come to the grotesque but inescapable conclusion that he was going to have to make his way through the gardens by walking on the bodies of wounded men, when he heard his name called.

"General Belisarius! General Belisarius! Over here!"

He looked across the gardens. Standing in a doorway on the opposite side was the same infantryman he had spoken with earlier. Felix—Felix Chalcenterus.

"You won't be able to get across, sir!" shouted the Syrian soldier. "The chiliarch sent me back here to watch for you! Wait a minute! Just a minute!"

The man disappeared. He returned about a minute later, preceded by Bouzes. As soon as he stepped into the doorway, Bouzes cupped his hands around his mouth, forming an impromptu megaphone, and hollered:

"Let's set up a relay! With your permission, sir!"

Belisarius thought the problem over. For a second or two, no more. He nodded, and waved his hand. Then, copying Bouzes' handcupping, shouted back:

"Good idea! Leave Felix in the door! If the Kushans lead the next charge, let me know!" He paused, taking a deep breath, before continuing:

"If they do—tell me the moment they start their charge!"

Bouzes waved back, acknowledging. The chiliarch spoke a few words to Felix and disappeared. The Syrian soldier remained in the doorway. His stance was erect and alert. Even from the distance, Belisarius could see the stern expression on the man's face. A young face, it was—almost a boy's face. But it was also the face of a man determined to do his duty, come what may.

Belisarius smiled. "You're in for a promotion, lad," he whispered. "As soon as the battle's over, I think."

The general now concentrated on listening. The sounds of battle had died away, in the last few minutes. Clearly enough, the Malwa had been beaten back and were regrouping.

He decided he had enough time to make his own preparations.

Again, he made his way back through the rear building and onto the western grounds. Agathius was waiting, not twenty feet from the doorway. The Constantinople cataphract was already mounted on his horse.

Quickly, Belisarius explained the signal relay. Then:

"It'll be a few minutes. Get me a horse, will you? I won't be relaying the message. I'll just come straight back and join you."

He pointed to the doorway.

"As soon as you see me coming through that door, have the cornicens order the sally. That'll give me just enough time to mount up."

Agathius nodded. Then, with a frown:

"Where are your bodyguards?"

Belisarius shrugged, smiling whimsically.

"We got separated, it seems. They must be lost in the crowd."

The Greek chiliarch's frown deepened.

"I'm not sure I like that, general. The idea of you leading a sally without your bodyguards, I mean."

Belisarius scowled.

"I assure you, Agathius, I was taking care of myself long before—"

"*Still*—"

"Enough."

Agathius opened his mouth, closed it. "Yes, sir. It'll be as you say."

Belisarius nodded and strode back toward the gardens. This time, as he made his way through the building, he ordered the men inside to clear a lane for him.

"I'll be coming through here, soon enough, running as fast as I can. I warn you, boys—I'll trample right over the man standing in my way. And I'm wearing spurs, I hope you notice."

The soldiers grinned, pressed aside, cheered. *Belisarius! Belisarius!*

His only acknowledgement:

That sorry bastard will be fucked.

✧   ✧   ✧

Ten minutes later, Felix called out the news across the gardens. *"The Kushans are lining up! They'll be leading the attack!"*

Five minutes after he shouted, *"They're coming!"*

Then:

"Now! Now! Now!"

For a man wearing full cataphract armor, Belisarius thought he did quite well, racing—so to speak—through the building. The men who formed the flesh-and-steel walls on both sides certainly thought so, judging from their encouragement.

Belisarius! Belisarius!

Go, general! Go! Go!

And, one enthusiast:

"Goddam, that man can waddle!"

As soon as he burst out of the doorway onto the grounds, the cornicens started blowing. From the corner of his eye, Belisarius caught the red and green bursts of the signal rockets. But the sole focus of his eyes was the saddled and readied horse ahead of him.

Belisarius almost stumbled, then, from sheer surprise. Standing by the horse, ready to hoist the general aboard, was Anastasius. The giant's own charger was not far away, with a mounting stool at its side.

"How'd you get here?" demanded the general.

"Don't ask," grunted Anastasius, heaving Belisarius onto the horse by sheer brute strength. The huge cataphract headed for his own horse.

Belisarius gathered up the reins. He could see the mass of Greek cataphracts and Syrian light cavalry starting their sally. The horsemen were already dividing into columns, splitting around the villa, heading for the portals in the opposite walls.

A part of his mind noticed that their formations were good—reasonably orderly, and, best of all, well

organized. The rest of his mind, briefly, wrestled with
a mystery.

"How did you get here?" he asked again. This time,
to the man already mounted and ready at his side.

"Don't ask," hissed Valentinian. The cataphract gave
Anastasius a weasel glare. "*His* doing. 'Impossible,'
I told him. 'Even Moses couldn't part that mob.' "

Anastasius, trotting up on his horse, caught the last
words. A grin split his rock-hewn face.

"Moses wasn't as big as I am," he said. He
extended his enormous hand, like an usher.

"After you, sir. Victory is waiting."

"So it is!" cried Belisarius. "So it is!"

He spurred his mount into a gallop. He was not
worried about exhausting his horse, now. They didn't
have far to go. He was only concerned with getting
to the front of the charge, and leading it to victory.

By the time he pounded around the villa, and saw
the nearest portal, he had achieved that immediate
goal. The Syrian infantrymen who were hastily opening the gates—tossing aside the splintered wreckage
of the gates, more precisely—barely had time to
dodge aside before Belisarius drove past. Valentinian
and Anastasius came right behind, followed by droves
of cataphracts.

The infantrymen were cheering wildly; the cataphracts were bellowing their battle cries. But
Belisarius only had ears for an expected mutter.

It never came. He glanced over his shoulder,
cocking a quizzical eye.

A weasel's glare met his gaze. A weasel's hiss:

"Ah, what's the fucking use?"

Chapter 20

The general's first thought, as he came around the villa onto its eastern grounds, was to make a quick assessment of the tactical situation. He had seen nothing of the battle directly, since his return to the villa after the first cavalry charge.

That urgent purpose almost led him to an immediate and humiliating downfall.

Downfall, in the literal sense. Dead, dying and badly wounded Malwa soldiers were scattered all across the grounds in front of the villa. In places, the bodies were piled two and three deep. Belisarius was concentrating so intently on the live Malwa troops that he was oblivious to the obstacles posed by the dead ones. His mount stumbled on a corpse and almost spilled his rider. Only the superhuman reflexes which Aide gave him enabled Belisarius to keep himself in the saddle and his horse on its feet.

First things first! he snarled at himself. For the next few seconds, until he was through the carnage on the villa's eastern grounds, he ignored everything but leading his horse forward. Only a cold, distant, and detached part of his mind took note of the terrible losses the enemy had suffered in their first assault. Arrow wounds, in the main, although a number of the Malwa casualties had apparently been caused by their own grenades, bouncing off the screens.

Finally, he was through the mounded bodies and could concentrate on the active enemy.

His first concern was with the katyushas. He could already hear the hissing shriek of the rockets—unmistakably different from the sound produced by Malwa rockets. The Roman missiles, following Belisarius' instructions, had been fitted with machined bronze venturi. The evenly-distributed thrust provided by those exhaust nozzles made his katyusha rockets far more accurate than their Malwa counterparts. They also made a distinctively different noise.

He could not see the rocket-chariots themselves. The katyushas would be charging at the Malwa from their hiding place in the northeast woods, followed by the Thracian and Illyrian cataphracts. A screen of trees blocked Belisarius' view in that direction. But he could see the rockets themselves. The first volley was even now impacting on the enemy. He watched a line of explosions stitching its way across the Malwa army's right flank, knocking cavalrymen out of saddles and their horses to the ground.

He held his breath. That first volley had come perilously close to landing in the very center of the enemy formation, where the Mahaveda priests were perched atop the gunpowder wagons. It was no part of his plan to have that ammunition—

His held-in breath exploded. The second and third volleys *did* land in the center of the enemy—several of them right among the wagons. Many of the priests standing on those wagons were swept off as if by a broom. One of the wagons was tipped over by a rocket exploding almost directly beneath it. The ammunition cart teetered on two wheels. Teetered, teetered, before finally slamming back down. One of the wheels collapsed under the shock.

Belisarius hunched low, waiting for the whole

ammunition supply to blow up. He turned his head and began yelling at the men behind him to brace themselves for the eruption.

Then, abruptly, stopped. There had been no explosion.

Astonished, he turned his head back and saw that, for all the destruction strewn by the katyushas, the Malwa ammunition had not caught fire.

An arrow sailing past his head reminded him that there were other dangers. The first ranks of dismounted Malwa regulars were less than a hundred and fifty yards away. The enemy soldiers were obviously confused by the sudden and unexpected attack on their flank. But many of them still had enough presence of mind to fire arrows at the Romans sallying from the villa.

Their arrows were neither well-aimed nor fired in coordination, however. Belisarius was about to congratulate himself for surprising his enemy—again—when another flight of arrows erased all sense of self-satisfaction.

Those arrows were well-aimed, and had been fired in a coordinated volley from a hundred yards away. The volley looked like a flight of homing pigeons, coming toward him unerringly from his right front. The general raised his shield, crouching in the saddle as best he could.

No less than three glanced off his shield; another, off the armor guarding his mount's withers; and a fifth, painfully, on his heavily armored right arm. Fortunately, the bow which had launched that arrow lacked the power of a cataphract bow. The arrowhead failed to penetrate the scale armor, although Belisarius was quite sure he would be sporting a bad bruise by morning.

The rest of the volley landed amidst the cataphracts following him. From the cries of pain and surprise, he knew that many had hit their targets.

When the general peeked over the rim of his shield, looking forward and to his right, he saw what he expected to see. The Kushans were already forming a square—shields interlocked, spears bristling, with a line of archers standing right behind the shield wall. The Kushan commander had instantly assessed the new situation and was doing the best thing he could under the circumstances—hunker down, snarl, and bristle like a porcupine surrounded by wolves.

Smart wolves hunt easier prey. So did Belisarius. He angled his horse to the left, guiding his men away from the Kushan formation. He would ride in a shallow arc around the Kushans and fall on the disorganized mass of Malwa regulars who had been following the Kushan vanguard.

His cataphracts—no fools themselves—immediately followed his lead. None of them, in Belisarius' column, even fired back at the Kushans. The general had led the sally erupting from the northern portals and gates of the villa. The Kushans, therefore, were to their right as they galloped past—the worst location for a mounted archer to fire at without exposing his whole body.

So Belisarius and his men simply grit their teeth, sheltered as best they could behind angled shields, and endured the Kushans' raking fire.

The *other* Roman sally, on the other hand—the one which Agathius was leading from the southern portals—was in the ideal position for mounted archers. As they came charging out, the Kushans were on their left front. Every one of those thousand cataphracts who pounded past the Kushan hedgehog, fired at least one arrow into the enemy mass. At a range of fifty yards, full-drawn cataphract bows could send arrows through any kind of armor—even through iron-reinforced laminated wood shields, unless the shields were properly angled.

The Kushan shield wall crumpled under that

withering missile fire. Belisarius and his men on the opposite side were the immediate beneficiaries. The Kushans on the north left off their raking fire and hastened to shore up their bleeding ranks on the south.

Now, the Kushan vanguard was behind the Roman cavalry sally. Belisarius and his cataphracts were within fifty yards of the Malwa regulars who had been advancing behind the Kushans.

Those troops—thousands of dismounted cavalrymen—suddenly broke into headlong flight. Caught between a completely unexpected flank attack and the mass sally of the Romans in the villa, their nerve collapsed. The still-mounted Ye-tai security squads tried to rally the fleeing soldiers—viciously sabring dozens of them as they ran past—but to no avail.

Belisarius gave a quick glance over his shoulder. The Syrian cavalry, following the heavily-armored Greeks, were already spreading wide and beginning to pull ahead of the slower cataphracts. They were staying well away from the Kushans. Their purpose was to ravage the flanks of the rapidly-disintegrating main force of the enemy. Behind them, trotting out of the villa and taking up positions, came the Syrian infantry. They were concentrating in front of the villa itself and to the north—leaving the now-isolated Kushans with a clear line of retreat toward the corrals.

Satisfied, the general turned back. The Malwa soldier nearest to him, racing away, stumbled and fell. Belisarius did not waste a lance thrust. He simply trampled the man under and kept going.

A Ye-tai horsemen came charging, his own lance held high. Belisarius braced in the stirrups and swept the Ye-tai off his saddle with a lance thrust which spilled open his intestines.

Another Malwa regular ran away, his feet flashing like an antelope's. The general's lance took him between the shoulder blades.

Belisarius killed three more soldiers in the same manner before he lost his lance, stuck in a Malwa spine. He drew his long cavalry sword and continued the slaughter.

The front ranks of the enemy were completely routed, now. Even the Ye-tai had given up their efforts to rally the troops. The barbarians, still mounted, were outpacing all others in the retreat.

The Malwa regulars had no thought in their minds but to outrun the Roman cavalry. They were not the first men, in a battle, to be seized by that panicky, hopeless notion. And they were not the first to suffer the penalty.

The general never ceased from his ruthless work, leaving a trail of slashed corpses behind him. But the inner man almost flinched away from the horror, until he found refuge—as he had so often before—in the cold workings of his intellect.

It's the worst mistake infantry ever makes, he thought. *If they stood their ground against a cavalry charge, like the Kushans did, they'd have a chance. Now—nothing. Nothing.*

A sudden line of explosions nearby—almost directly to his left—broke through his grim thoughts. He saw, out of the corner of an eye, one of his cataphracts clutch his face with both hands and fall off his saddle. Another cataphract's horse tumbled, spilling his rider.

Those were katyusha rockets! God damn it, hold your fire!

No luck. Belisarius could see another volley of rockets sailing toward them.

The rockets, of course, had been intended for the Malwa—part of the plan to cave in the enemy's right flank. That was little comfort, when several of those rockets overshot the enemy and wreaked havoc in his own ranks. Loudly and profanely, the general cursed Maurice for a fool—and Basil, the katyusha commander, for a moron sired by an imbecile.

But—

Belisarius himself had instructed Maurice to lead the charge with katyushas. Knowing full well that even Roman rockets were not very accurate, the general had given the orders nonetheless. He had simply not expected the Malwa to cave in so quickly. He had assumed that the rocket volleys would be over and done with by the time the cataphracts arrived.

So he cursed himself, for an idiot.

Rockets are an area-effect weapon, you fucking jackass! Don't ever do this again!

He pushed self-recrimination aside. He had almost reached the center of the Malwa army. Ahead of him, he could see kshatriya and priests frantically trying to turn the wagons around. The mules hauling those wagons, true to their stubborn nature, were obeying their masters' shrieking commands with mute recalcitrance.

The sight almost made him laugh. What did the priests hope to accomplish? Mule-drawn wagons had no more chance of escaping a cavalry pursuit than did men on foot.

One of the Mahaveda standing atop the nearest wagon apparently reached the same conclusion. Belisarius was only twenty yards away when he saw the priest's face stiffen with resolve. The man stooped, seized a small barrel of gunpowder, and spilled its contents over the barrel-stacks.

The priest was just drawing a lighting device out of his tunic when Belisarius' saber cut the legs out from under him. The priest sprawled across the barrels, still holding the striker. Belisarius' next slash removed that hand; his next, the Mahaveda's head.

The general reined in his horse and clambered onto the wagon. From that perch, he began bellowing orders in his thunderous battlefield voice.

The orders were pungent, profane, simple—and quite unnecessary. Anastasius and Valentinian had already secured the two closest wagons. The Greek cataphracts, within ten seconds, had done the same with the rest.

All of the kshatriya still on the wagons—perhaps fifty—tried to surrender, along with the remaining two dozen priests. The cataphracts would have none of it. Many of those men had seen the first priest's suicidal attempt to blow up the ammunition cart. The Greeks slaughtered any Malwa among the wagons without mercy.

Belisarius left off his bellowing. The deed was done. The Malwa wagons, with their great load of gunpowder, were safely in Roman hands.

He clambered onto the highest-placed barrel. From that precarious perch, he strained to see what he could of the battle.

Battle, no longer. The rout was complete.

Maurice's hammer blow had completely shattered the Malwa right. The Ye-tai who had guarded that flank had taken frightful casualties before breaking. Whatever their other characteristics, no one had ever accused Ye-tai of cowardice. So they had stood their ground—almost to a man, Belisarius judged, estimating the mound of corpses.

Their courage had been useless, of course. Not even the best troops, in Belisarius' experience, could put up an effective defense against a surprise mass attack coming on their flank. Not on an open field of battle, at any rate, with no place to shelter and regroup. Such troops could fight—fight bravely—but they would fight as confused individuals against a well-organized, steady and determined attacker. The conclusion was foregone.

It was equally obvious that the Malwa regulars had not come to the assistance of the barbarians. The Malwa regulars clustered with the main force had still been mounted, unlike their luckless comrades who had been advancing on foot behind the Kushan attack.

They had seen no reason to abandon that good fortune, and had immediately taken flight away from the Roman flank attack.

Good fortune—fleeting fortune. In their natural desire to make the quickest escape from that frightening mass of oncoming Thracians, Illyrians and Persians—heavy cavalry, all of them, shaking the very earth in their charge out of the northeast woods— the Malwa regulars had broken to the south.

A mass rout, thousands of horsemen galloping frantically around the edge of the forest—into the Euphrates. As soon as they realized their error, of course, the fleeing Malwa began racing east down the riverbank, toward the far-distant refuge of the Malwa forces besieging Babylon.

Few of those men would ever find that refuge, two hundred miles away. Very few.

The men pursuing them were veterans, led by experienced and capable commanders. Maurice and Kurush, seeing the direction of the Malwa retreat, had sent their cataphracts and dehgans angling southeast. They would cut off the Malwa escape, trap them against the river.

Belisarius watched his katyusha rocket-chariots wheel into a line, some three hundred yards away. A small figure—their commander Basil, he assumed, although he could not recognize any faces at the distance—was prancing back and forth on his horse issuing commands. A moment later, a volley of hissing rockets sailed toward the Euphrates.

Belisarius watched their flight. It was his first opportunity to observe the rockets without the distraction of immediate battle. The missiles flew in a shallow trajectory, with little of the erratic serpentine motion of Malwa rockets. Seconds later, the general saw the warheads erupt, scattering shrapnel through the milling mob of Malwa packed on the riverbank.

The carnage was impressive. Belisarius had seen

to it that Roman rockets carried well-designed shrapnel in their warheads. Lead drop-shot, rather than the pebbles and other odds-and-ends which Malwa rockets used.

Belisarius now looked toward the villa. Here too, he saw, the situation was progressing nicely. Those Malwa infantrymen who had managed to escape the sally were also pouring toward the river. The Syrian cavalry had peeled off from the captured powder wagons and were driving the Malwa toward the north bank of the Euphrates.

Behind them, the Syrian infantry had taken formations opposite the Kushans. The Kushans were already withdrawing toward the corrals. The Syrians followed, at a respectful distance, content to let them go.

He heard Agathius' voice, raised in a cheerful hail. Turning, Belisarius saw Agathius and several of his cataphracts trotting toward him. "I sent most of my men to help the Syrians," he announced, "after I saw you doing the same."

Belisarius had not actually given that order. There had been no need, since Cyril had done so without any prompting, and the general had wanted to concentrate his attention on watching Maurice's half of the battle. But now, looking around, he saw that there were only a hundred or so cataphracts left, guarding the wagons.

Belisarius was immensely pleased. *Immensely*. There were few things the general treasured more than quick-thinking and self-reliant subordinates. He was firmly convinced that at least half his success as a commander was due to his ability to gather such men around him. Men like Maurice, Ashot, Hermogenes, John of Rhodes—even Bouzes and Coutzes, once he'd knocked the crap out of them.

And now, men like Agathius and Cyril.

Something of his delight must have shown. A

moment later, he and his two new Greek officers were beaming at each other. There was nothing at all crooked in the general's grin, now; and not a trace of veteran sardonicism, in those of Agathius and Cyril.

"Jesus, general," exclaimed Agathius, "this is the sweetest damn battle I ever saw!"

"Beautiful, beautiful," agreed Cyril. "Only fuck-up was that one rocket volley."

Belisarius grimaced. "My fault, that. I should have remembered the damn things still aren't that accurate. And I wasn't expecting we'd get so close this quickly."

Cyril did not seem in the slightest aggrieved, even though it was his men who had suffered from that friendly fire. The Greek cataphract simply shrugged and pronounced the oldest of all veteran wisdom:

"Shit happens."

Agathius nodded his agreement. "Live and learn, that's all you can do. Besides—" He twisted in his saddle, studying the effect of the current rocket volleys on the Malwa massed by the river.

"—they're doing fine work now. Save a lot of Roman boys, the katyushas will, by the time they're done. Those Malwa shits'll be like stunned sheep."

Belisarius heard another hail. Turning, he saw that Maurice was approaching from the north. The chiliarch was accompanied by one of his hecantontarchs, Gregory, and a half-dozen cataphracts.

When Maurice drew up alongside the wagon, his first words were to Cyril and Agathius.

"Sorry about the rockets," he stated. His voice was firm and level. Very courteous in tone, although the expression on his face seemed more one of embarassment than remorse.

Maurice now looked to Belisarius.

"Don't even bother asking," he growled. "The answer's no. My boys'd probably be willing enough, even if those raggedy-ass Malwa fucks couldn't come up with two solidus ransom amongst them. But the Persians are completely berserk and there's no way to stop them without—"

Belisarius shook his head. "I know. I can hear their battle cries."

He cocked his ear, listening. Even at the distance, the Persian voices were quite distinct.

Charax! Charax!
Death to Malwa!
No quarter!

Seeing the look of confusion on the faces of Agathius and Cyril, Maurice chuckled.

"The young general here"—he pointed a thumb at Belisarius—"has a soft and tender heart. Likes to avoid atrocities, when he can."

The two Greek officers eyed the general uncertainly, much as men gaze upon someone pronounced to be a living saint. Possible, possible—but, more likely, just a babbling madman.

Then, remembering his savage punishment of the eight cataphracts at Callinicum, uncertainty fled.

Agathius winced. "Mother of God, general, Maurice is right. There's no way—"

Again, Belisarius shook his head, smiling crookedly. "I'm not asking, Agathius. The Persians won't be stopped, not after Charax. I'm quite aware of that."

The smile faded, replaced by a look of scrutiny. "But I'll ask you to remember this day, in the future. The very near future, in fact. When the Persians demand the heads of two thousand Kushans, and I refuse."

He pointed toward the river.

"Atrocities produce this kind of massacre. That's one of the reasons I try to avoid them. You might be on the other end, the next time. Pleading for mercy, and not getting it, because you showed none yourself."

"Wouldn't get it from the Malwa, anyway," pointed

out Maurice. He spoke mildly—as usual, when he was contradicting Belisarius in public—but firmly.

"From Malwa, no," replied the general. "But what *is* Malwa, Maurice?"

He nodded toward the river. "You think those men are all Malwa? Or Ye-tai? Precious few of them, in truth. The priests and kshatriyas, most of the officers. Perhaps a thousand of the regulars. The rest? Biharis, Bengalis, Orissans—every subject nation of India is spilling its life blood into that river."

He transferred his scrutiny to Agathius and Cyril. "In the end," Belisarius told them, his voice as hard as steel, "we will not defeat Malwa on a great field of battle, somewhere here in Persia. Or in Anatolia, or Bactria, or the Indus plain. We will shatter them in the heart of India itself, when their subjects finally throw off the yoke."

Uncertainty returned to the faces of the two Greeks. Now, however, it was not the bemused skepticism of men regarding a proclaimed saint. It was the simple doubt—the veteran questioning—of fighting men who were beginning to wonder if their commander might, after all, be that rarest of generals. A supreme strategist, as well as a wizard on the battlefield.

"I would spare all of them who tried to surrender, if I could," mused Belisarius. "All, at least, except the Mahaveda priests. For the sake of the future, if nothing else."

He shrugged heavily. "But—I can't risk an idiot brawl with the Persians. Not today, when their blood's a-boil."

He clambered off the barrel. A moment later, he was back astride his horse. "Today, I can only deal with the Kushans."

He pointed to the river. "Agathius—Cyril—I want you to give full support to the Persians. Back them to the hilt. As maddened as they are, they won't be thinking clearly. There are still thousands of live and armed enemy troops packed against the river. They'll fight like cornered rats, once they realize surrender's not being offered. The Persians are likely to wade into them without thinking, get surrounded."

Agathius and Cyril nodded.

"Take all your men," Belisarius added, "except a hundred or so to guard over the wagons. Have those men bring the wagons back to the villa. But be careful—in fact, better wait until you have some of the katyusha men to help. They're more familiar with handling gunpowder."

The two Greek officers nodded again. They turned their horses and trotted off, shouting commands. Within a few seconds, two thousand Constantinople cataphracts were thundering toward the river, preparing to throw their weight into the butchery on the Euphrates.

Belisarius turned to Maurice and Gregory.

"You do the same, Maurice, with the Thracians and the Illyrians. Gregory, I want you to find Coutzes—and Abbu," he added, chuckling—"if he managed to find a new horse. Get the Arab skirmishers and half the light cavalry across the river. Leave me the other half, to keep the Kushans cornered."

"They'll have to use the ford we found a few miles upstream," remarked Gregory. "That'll lose us several hours."

"Yes, I know. It doesn't matter. They'll still be in time to harry whatever Malwa make their way across the Euphrates."

His face and voice were cold, grim, ruthless.

"*Harry them, Gregory.* I want them pursued without mercy. For days, if that's what it takes. *I want this Malwa army destroyed.* Not more than a handful of survivors, trickling back to their lines in Babylon. Let the enemy know he can't hope to go around Emperor Khusrau."

Gregory's face twisted into his own crooked smile. "Might not even be a handful, general. Those few that get away from us will still have two hundred miles to go. With the desert on one side, and on the other—every peasant in the flood plain ready to hack them down. Whole villages will turn out, to join the pursuit. They've heard about Charax, too, you can bet on it."

Belisarius nodded. Gregory spurred his horse, heading south. A moment later, going in the opposite direction, Maurice did the same.

Only Valentinian and Anastasius were left, in the immediate vicinity.

"What now, general?" asked Anastasius.

Belisarius clucked his horse into motion, trotting back toward the villa. "We'll make sure the Kushans are completely boxed in. After that—" He looked up, gauging the sun. "That'll probably take the rest of the day. Till late afternoon, for sure. The Kushans may try to break out. We've probably still got some fighting ahead of us."

"Not much," rumbled Anastasius. "The Kushans are no fools. They won't waste much effort trying to find an escape route. Not on foot, knowing we've got cavalry." The giant sighed. "Not Kushans. They'll be working like beavers, instead, doing what they can to turn the barns and corrals into a fortress. Ready to bleed us when we come in after them tomorrow."

"I hope to avoid that problem," said Belisarius.

"You think you can talk them into surrendering?" asked Valentinian skeptically. "After they'll have spent half a day listening to the rest of their army being massacred?"

"That's my plan." Oddly, the general's voice lost none of its confident good cheer.

Neither did Valentinian's its skepticism. "Be like walking into a lion's den, trying to talk them out of their meat."

"Not so hard, that," replied Belisarius. "Not, at least, if you can speak lion."

He eyed Valentinian. Smiled crookedly. "I speak Kushan fluently, you know."

The smile grew *very* crooked. Anastasius scowled. Valentinian hissed.

"Now that I think about it, both of you speak Kushan too. Not as well as I do, perhaps. But—well enough. Well enough."

He cocked his ear toward Valentinian.

"What? No muttering?"

The cataphract eyed Belisarius with a weasel's glare.

"Words fail me," he muttered.

That evening, just as the sun was setting on the horizon, Belisarius approached the forted Kushans for a parley. He was unarmed, accompanied only by Valentinian and Anastasius.

Anastasius, also, was unarmed.

Valentinian—well, he swore the same. Swore it on all the saints and his mother's grave. Belisarius didn't believe him, not for a minute, but he didn't push the matter. Whatever weapons Valentinian carried would be well-hidden. And besides—

He'd rather try to talk lions into surrendering than talk a weasel out of its teeth. An entirely safer proposition.

In the end, talking the Kushan lions out of their determination to fight to the last man proved to be one of the easiest things the general had ever done. And the doing of it brought him great satisfaction.

Once again, a reputation proved worth its weight in gold.

Not a reputation for mercy, this time. Kushans had seen precious little of mercy, in their harsh lives, and would have disbelieved any such tales of a foreign general.

But, as it turned out, they were quite familiar with

the name of Belisarius. It was a name of honor, their commander had been told, by one of the few men not of Kushan blood that he trusted.

"Rana Sanga told me himself," the man stated. He drew himself up proudly. "I visited Rajputana's greatest king in his palace, at his own invitation, before he left with Lord Damodara for the Hindu Kush."

The man leaned over, pouring a small libation into Belisarius' drinking cup before doing the same in the one before him. The vessels were plain, utilitarian pieces of pottery, like the bottle from which the wine was poured. After Belisarius had taken his seat, sitting cross-legged like his Kushan counterpart on a thin layer of straw spread in a corner of the stable, the Kushan soldiers gathered around had produced the jug and two cups out of a field kit.

Belisarius took advantage of the momentary pause to study the Kushan commander more closely. The man's name, he had already learned, was Vasudeva.

In appearance, Vasudeva was much like any other Kushan soldier. Short, stocky, thick-chested. Sturdy legs and shoulders. His complexion had a yellowish Asiatic cast, as did his flat nose and narrow eyes. Like most Kushans, the man's hair was drawn up into a topknot. His beard was more in the way of a goatee than the thicker cut favored by Romans or Persians.

And, like most Kushans, his face seemed carved from stone. His expression, almost impossible to read. The Kushan Belisarius knew best—the former Malwa vassal named Kungas, who was now commander of Empress Shakuntala's personal bodyguard—had had a face so hard it had been like a mask.

An iron mask—but a mask, nonetheless, disguising a very different soul.

Remembering Kungas, Belisarius felt his confidence growing.

"And how was Rana Sanga, when you saw him?" he asked politely.

The Kushan shrugged. "Who is to know what that man feels? His wife, perhaps his children. No others."

"Do you know why he asked you to visit him?"

Vasudeva gave Belisarius a long, lingering look. A cold look, at first. Then—

The look did not warm, so much as it grew merry. In a wintry sort of way.

"Yes. We had met before, during the war against Andhra. Worked well together. When he heard that I had been selected one of the Kushan commanders for the Mesopotamian campaign, he called me to visit before his own departure." The Kushan barked a laugh. "He wanted to warn me about a Roman general named Belisarius!"

Vasudeva's eyes lost their focus for a moment, as he remembered the conversation.

" 'Persians you know, of course,' Lord Sanga told me. 'But you have never encountered Romans. Certainly not such a Roman as Belisarius.' "

The Kushan commander's eyes refocussed, fixed on Belisarius.

"He told me you were as tricky and quick as a mongoose." Another barking laugh. " 'Expect only the unexpected, from that man,' he said. 'He adores feints and traps. If he makes an obvious threat, look for the blow to come from elsewhere. If he seems weak, be sure he is strong. Most of all—remember the fate of the arrogant cobra, faced with a mongoose.' "

He laughed again. All the Kushan soldiers standing around shared in that bitter laugh.

"I tried to tell Lord Kumara, when I realized we were facing Roman troops. I was almost sure you would be in command. Lord Kumara is—*was*—the commander of this expedition."

"Lord Fishbait, now," snarled one of the other Kushans. "And good riddance."

Vasudeva scowled. "Of course, he refused to listen. Fell right into the trap."

Belisarius took a sip from his cup. "And what else did Rana Sanga say about me?"

Again, Vasudeva gave Belisarius that long, lingering look. Still cold. Gauging, assessing. "He said that one thing only is predictable about the man Belisarius. He will be a man of honor. He, too, knows the meaning of vows."

Belisarius waited. Vasudeva tugged the point of his goatee with his fingers. Looked away.

"It's difficult, difficult," he murmured.

Belisarius waited.

Vasudeva sighed. "We will not be broken up, sold as slaves to whichever bidder. We must be kept together."

Belisarius nodded. "Agreed."

"Any labor will be acceptable, except the work of menials. Kushan soldiers are not domestic dogs."

Belisarius nodded. "Agreed."

"No whippings. No beatings of any kind. Execution will be acceptable, in cases of disobedience. But it must be by the sword, or the ax. We are not criminals, to be hung or impaled."

Belisarius nodded. "Agreed."

"Decent food. A bit of wine, now and again."

Belisarius shook his head. "That I cannot promise. I am on campaign, myself, and will be using you for a labor force. My own men may eat poorly, at times, and go without wine. I can only promise that you will eat no worse than they do. And enjoy some wine, if there is any to spare."

From the little murmur which came from the surrounding soldiers, the general knew that his forthright answer had pleased them. He suspected, although he was not sure, that the last question had been Vasudeva's own little trap. The Kushan commander was obviously a seasoned veteran. He would

have known, full well, that any other answer would
be either a lie or the words of a cocksure and fool-
hardy man.

"Agreed," said Vasudeva.

Belisarius waited.

Finally, the word came: "Swear."

Belisarius gave his oath. Gave it twice, in fact. Once
in the name of his own Christian god. And then, to
the Kushans' great surprise, on the name of the
Buddha to whom they swore in private, when there
were no Mahaveda priests to hear the heresy.

That evening, late at night, Belisarius began his
negotiations with the Persians—seated, now, amidst
the splendid wreckage of what had once been an
emperor's favorite hunting villa.

Here, too, he found the task much easier than
anticipated.

Kurush, in the event, was not baying for Kushan
blood. After the young sahrdaran heard what Belisarius
had to say, he simply poured himself some wine. A
noble vintage, this, poured from a sahrdaran's jug into
a sahrdaran's gorgeous goblet.

He drank half the goblet in one gulp. Then said,
"All right."

Belisarius eyed him. Kurush scowled.

"I'm not saying I like it," he grumbled, "but you
gave your word. We Aryans, you know, understand
the meaning of vows."

He emptied the goblet in another single gulp.
Then, he gestured toward his blood-soaked garments
and armor. "Charax has been well enough avenged,
for one day."

Growl: "I suppose."

Belisarius let it be. He saw no reason to press
Kurush for anything beyond his grudging acceptance.

He did cast a questioning glance at Baresmanas.
The older sahrdaran had said nothing, thus far, and

it was obvious that he intended to maintain his silence. He simply returned Belisarius' gaze with his own fair imitation of a mask.

No, Baresmanas would say nothing. But Belisarius suspected that the Persian nobleman had already had his say—earlier, to his young and vigorous nephew. Reminding him of a Roman general's mercy at a place called Mindouos. And teaching him—or trying, at least—that mercy can have its own sharp point. Keener than any lance or blade, and even deadlier to the foe.

Chapter 21

THE MALABAR COAST
Summer, 531 A.D.

The refugee camps in Muziris swarmed like ant-hills. Families gathered up their few belongings and awaited the voyage to the island of Tamraparni. Maratha cavalrymen and Kushan soldiers readied their gear. The great fleet of ships assembling in the harbor cleared their holds. Keralan officials presented chests full of gold and silver, to fund the migration. An empress and her advisers schemed.

And old friends arrived.

In midafternoon of a sunny day—a rarity, that, in southwest India during the monsoon season—five Axumite warships entered the harbor at Muziris.

They were not hailed by Keralan guard vessels. There was no pretense, any longer, that the port of Muziris was under anyone's control but Shakuntala's. The Ethiopian vessels were met by a warship "requisitioned" from Kerala but manned by Maratha sailors.

Once their identity was established, the Ethiopians

were immediately escorted into the presence of the Empress. There were four hundred of the Axumite soldiers, along with four other men. Shakuntala, forewarned, greeted them with a full imperial ceremony before the great mansion she had taken for her palace.

The three Ethiopians who led that march were deeply impressed by what they saw—as were the four men walking with them who were not African. The seven men at the front were familiar with India, and with Shakuntala's situation. They had been expecting something patchwork and ragged. A rebel empress— a hunted young girl—hiding in a precarious refuge, with nothing but the handful of Kushan soldiers who had spirited her out of the Malwa empire.

Instead—

The street down which they were escorted, by hundreds of Maratha cavalrymen, was lined with thousands of cheering people. Most were refugees, from Andhra and other Malwa-conquered lands of India. But there were many dark-skinned Keralans among that crowd, as well. Her own grandfather might have disowned her, and Malwa provocateurs might have stirred up much animosity toward the refugees who had poured into the kingdom, but many of her mother's people had not forgotten that Shakuntala was a daughter of Kerala herself. So they too cheered, and loudly, at this further evidence that the Empress-in-exile of Andhra was a force to be reckoned with. Allies—from far off Africa! And such splendid-looking soldiers!

Which, indeed, they were. The sarwen rose to the occasion, abandoning their usual Axumite informality. In stiff lines they marched, their great spears held high, ostrich-plume headdresses bobbing proudly.

As they approached the Empress' palace, kettledrums began beating. At the steps leading up to the palace doors, the march halted. The doors swung wide, and dozens—then hundreds—of Kushan soldiers trotted out and took positions on the palace steps. The last Kushans to emerge were Shakuntala's personal bodyguard, the small band of men who had been with her since she inherited her throne. Since the very day, in fact. For these were the men who had taken her out of her father's palace in Amaravati, on the day her family was slaughtered, as a Malwa captive. And then, months later, had spit in Malwa's face and taken her to freedom.

Finally, Shakuntala herself emerged, with Dadaji Holkar at her side. Four imperial ladies-in-waiting came behind them.

She stepped—say better, pranced—down the stairs to greet her visitors.

For all the pomp and splendor, the dignity of the occasion was threadbare. Genuine joy has a way of undermining formality.

Among the Ethiopians who stood before the palace were four Kushans—the squad, led by Kujulo, who had assisted Prince Eon in his escape from India the year before. As soon as Shakuntala's bodyguard spotted their long-lost brethren, their discipline frayed considerably. They did not break formation, of course. But the grins on their faces went poorly with the solemnity of the occasion.

It hardly mattered, since their own Empress was grinning just as widely. Partly, at the sight of Kujulo and his men. Mostly, at the familiar faces of the three Ethiopians at the front.

Garmat, Ezana and Wahsi. Three of that small band of men who had rescued her from Malwa captivity.

Seeing an absent face, her grin faded.

Garmat shook his head.

"No, Shakuntala, he did not come with us. The negusa nagast sent Eon on a different mission. But the Prince asked me to convey his greetings and his best wishes."

Shakuntala nodded. "We will speak of it later. For the moment, let me thank you for returning my Kushan bodyguards."

Smiling, she turned and beckoned one of her ladies-in-waiting forward.

"And I have no doubt you will want to take Tarabai back with you. As I promised Eon."

The Maratha woman stepped forward. Although she was trying to maintain her composure, Tarabai's expression was a jumbled combination of happiness and anxiety. Happiness, at the prospect of being reunited with her Prince. Anxiety, that he might have lost interest in her after their long separation. During the course of Prince Eon's adventures in India the year before, he and Tarabai had become almost inseparable. Before they went their separate ways in escaping the Malwa, Eon had asked her to become his concubine, and she had accepted. But—that was then, and princes are notoriously fickle and short of memory.

Garmat immediately allayed her anxiety.

"Eon may not be in Axum upon your arrival, Tarabai. He is occupied elsewhere, at the moment. But he hopes you have not changed your mind."

The old half-Arab smiled.

"Actually, he does more than hope. He is already adding a wing to his palace. Your quarters, when you arrive—as well as those of your children, when *they* arrive. As I'm sure they will, soon enough."

Tarabai blushed. Beamed.

That business done, Garmat's gaze returned to the Empress. His smile faded. "So much is pleasure, Your Majesty. Now, for the rest—"

He straightened. Then, in a loud voice:

"I bring you an official offer of alliance from the negusa nagast of Axum. A full alliance against the Malwa."

A buzz of whispered conversation filled the air at this announcement.

"We heard, upon our arrival, that you plan to transport your people to the island of Ceylon. Let me make clear that, if you desire, you and your people may seek refuge in Ethiopia instead."

Shakuntala would have sworn that her expression never changed. But she had forgotten Garmat's uncanny shrewdness.

"Ah," he murmured. His voice was soft, and pitched low. So low that only she and Dadaji could now hear him. "I had wondered. Exile to a distant land did not really seem in your nature. So. I have five ships, Your Majesty. On board those ships came half of the Dakuen sarwe—four hundred soldiers, under the command of Ezana and Wahsi. One of those ships must convey Tarabai and myself back to Ethiopia. The rest—including all of the sarwen—are at your disposal."

Shakuntala nodded. She, too, spoke softly. "Warships, I believe?"

Garmat's smile returned. "*Axumite* warships, Empress." He coughed modestly. "Rather superior, don't you know, to those Malwa tubs? And I dare say our sarwen could handle three times their number of Malwa's so-called marines."

"Yes, I know," she replied. "As it happens, I can use them. The ships and the sarwen both. Have you heard the news of Deogiri?"

Garmat nodded. His smile widened.

She leaned forward.

"As it happens—"

Three days later, in a pouring rain, the fleet left Muziris. The Matisachiva Ganapati and the city's viceroy stood watching from the docks. All day they remained there, sheltered from the downpour under a small pavilion, until they were certain that every single one of the cursed "Empress-in-exile's" followers had quit Keralan soil.

Not until the last ship disappeared into the rain did they summon their howdah.

"Thank the gods," muttered the viceroy.

Ganapati's expression was sour.

"For what?" he demanded. "The damage may already have been done. A courier arrived this morning from Vanji. The Malwa have been issuing the most pointed and severe threats. They are demanding that the King arrest Shakuntala and return her to captivity."

The viceroy shook his head.

"They can hardly expect the King to do that. She *is* his granddaughter, after all."

"Probably not," agreed Ganapati. He shrugged. "Hopefully, they will be satisfied with the fact that we have expelled her—and her followers—from Keralan soil. I will immediately dispatch a courier with the news."

The elephant bearing their howdah loomed up in the rain. Hurriedly, the two Keralan officials scrambled aboard the great beast. Despite their haste, they were soaked through by the time they reached the shelter of the howdah.

Ganapati's expression was still sour.

"Cursed monsoon," he muttered.

A sudden, freakish gust blew aside a curtain and drenched his companion.

"Cursed monsoon!" cried the viceroy.

"Blessed monsoon," stated Kungas cheerfully. The commander of Shakuntala's bodyguard leaned over the rail of the ship and admired the view. He did not seem in the slightest aggrieved by the fact that he was soaking wet. Or that there was no view to be admired.

Neither did the man standing next to him.

"Blessed monsoon," agreed Dadaji Holkar. "No-one will be able to see which direction we take. Let's just hope that the rain keeps up."

"This time of year?" demanded Kungas, chuckling. "Be serious, Dadaji! Look!"

He pointed eastward. Their ship was not more than two miles from the shore, but the coast of Malabar was completely invisible.

"Can't see a thing," he pronounced. "It'll be that way nine days out of ten, for at least another month. More than long enough for us to reach Suppara, even with this slow fleet."

Dadaji began to stroke his beard, but quickly left off the familiar gesture. It was a bit too much like wringing a sponge.

"True," he murmured. "And there is this additional advantage, as well—the refugees won't know where we're going either. Most of them will continue to think we're heading for Tamraparni until the very day we sail into Suppara."

Kungas cast him a sidelong glance.

"Might be a bit of trouble, then."

Dadaji shook his head.

"I don't think so. I had many spies in the camps, and they all reported that the great majority of the refugees are devoted to the Empress. I believe they will accept her decision. Besides, she intends to offer those who don't want to return to Majarashtra the alternative of Tamraparni. Whichever so choose, she will provide them with the necessary ships to make the voyage. After we've seized Suppara, of course."

A thin smile cracked Kungas' face.

"Not much of an alternative, that. The King of Tamraparni is not going to be pleased when he hears how Shakuntala used his name in vain. His own son in marriage, no less!"

Holkar made no reply. For a few minutes, the two men simply stared out at nothing. Nothing but beautiful, blinding, concealing, sheets of rain.

Eventually, Kungas cleared his throat.

"Speaking of marriage," he stated.

Holkar grimaced. "She refuses to even discuss it," he said softly. "Believe me, my friend, I have tried to broach the subject on many occasions. Each time, she says the question is premature."

Kungas twitched his shoulders. "That's not the point. For her to marry anyone now *would* be premature. She has nothing to offer, at the moment, in exchange for an alliance with real forces. But *after* we take Suppara—*after* we demonstrate to India, and all the world, that Andhra intends to hold southern Majarashtra—*then* the question of a dynastic marriage will pose itself. She must start thinking about it, Dadaji. Or else she will be paralyzed when the time comes."

The Empress' adviser sighed. "You know the problem, my friend."

Kungas stared out to sea. Nodded once, twice. "She is in love with Rao."

Holkar blew out his cheeks. "Please," he growled. "It is the infatuation of a young girl with a man she knew only as a child. She has not seen him—hardly at all—in two years."

"She has seen him for a few hours only, during that time," agreed Kungas. His voice rumbled like stones: "After he gutted the Vile One's palace in order to rescue her. Quite a reunion, that must have been."

Holkar said nothing. Kungas turned his head away, as if something had caught his eye.

In truth, he simply didn't want Holkar to see his face. Not even Kungas, at that moment, could keep from smiling.

Excellent. The thought was full of satisfaction. *Excellent—"child"! Poor Holkar. Even he—even he— is blind on this point.*

For a moment, as he had many times before, Kungas found himself bemused by that peculiarly Indian obsession with purity and pollution. Even his friend Dadaji could not entirely escape its clutches.

So blind, these Indians. When the truth is so obvious.

He turned away from the rail.

"Enough rain," he announced. "I'm going below. The action's going to start soon, anyway. I have to get ready, in case I'm needed."

As he walked across the deck toward the hatch, Kungas' face was invisible to anyone. Now, finally, he allowed his grin to emerge.

Stay stubborn, Shakuntala. Dig in your heels, girl, refuse to discuss it. When the question of marriage is finally posed, you will know what to do. Then, you will know.

He shook his head, slightly.

So obvious!

An hour later, the fleet changed its course. The change was slow—erratic, confused, haphazard. Part of that fumbling was due to the simple fact that the troop commanders on every ship had a different estimate of the right moment to give the command. The only time-keeping devices available to them were hour-glasses and sundials. Sundials were useless in the pouring monsoon. Hourglasses, under these circumstances, just as much so. It would have been impossible to provide each commander with an identical hourglass, much less have them turned over simultaneously.

So, each commander simply gave the order when he thought the time was right.

Most of the confusion, however, was due to the fact that the crews and captains of the merchant ships were bitterly opposed to the change of course. They had been hired to transport the Empress and her people to Tamraparni. They were not, to put it mildly, pleased to hear that the destination had been changed—*especially* when they discovered the new one.

Suppara? Are you mad? The Malwa hold Suppara!

But the captains of the ships were not the *commanders*. The commanders were a very different breed altogether. Kushans and Maratha cavalrymen, in the main, who cheerfully accepted the berating abuse of the Keralan ship captains.

For about one minute. Then the steel was drawn.

Thereafter, Keralan captains and seamen scurried about their new-found task. Grumbling, to be sure. But they had no illusions that they could overpower the squads of soldiers placed on each ship. Not *those* soldiers.

One crew tried. Led by a particularly belligerent captain, the Keralan seamen dug out their own weapons and launched a mutiny. They outnumbered the soldiers two-to-one, after all. Perhaps they thought their numbers would make the difference.

They were sadly mistaken. Within two minutes, the four surviving seamen were huddled in the bow, nursing their wounds and casting fearful glances at the Kushan soldiers standing guard over them. Not one of those Kushans had even been scratched in the "melee."

Then, to add to their misery, they saw the prow of a ship looming out of the downpour. Within seconds, the ship had drawn alongside. The Keralan seamen recognized the craft. One of those swift, fearsome Ethiopian warships.

An Axumite officer leaned over the rail.

"Is problem?" he called out. "We hear noise of— of—" He faltered, having reached the limit of his skill with Hindi.

The Kushan commander glared.

"Yes, there's a problem!" he grated, pointing an accusing finger at the four captives. The Keralan seamen hunched lower.

"There's only four of the bastards left. Not enough to run the ship."

Another Ethiopian came to the rail. The Kushan

commander immediately recognized him—Ezana, one of the Axumite soldiers' top leaders.

Ezana gave the situation a quick scrutiny. He was familiar with Kushans, and knew that they were not a sea-going folk. No hope they could run the ship themselves.

He turned his head and barked out a quick string of names. Within a minute, six Ethiopian soldiers were standing next to him. While they were mustering, Ezana took the opportunity to close with the merchant vessel. It was the work of but seconds for the Ethiopians to tie up alongside.

Lightly, Ezana sprang across onto the Keralan ship. He strode toward the bow where the Kushan commander was waiting, along with his men and the captives.

Once there, Ezana made a little gesture at the six Axumites who were making their own way across.

"These men will stay with you for the duration of the trip," he explained, speaking in heavily accented but quite good Hindi. "Along with the four surviving mutineers, that should be enough."

He gave the ship a quick examination. Judging from his expression, he was not pleased with what he saw.

"Indian tub," he sneered. "Can run a good Axumite trader with six men. Five—even four—in an emergency."

He transferred the sarcastic expression onto the four Keralan survivors. The seamen hunched lower still, dropping their heads. Doing everything in their power to fade out of sight.

No use. Ezana squatted down next to them.

"Look at me," he commanded. Reluctantly, they raised their heads.

Ezana grinned.

"Don't look so unhappy, lads. Consider your good fortune! My men hate running crappy ships like this.

I'd have my own mutiny if I pitched you overboard and appointed four replacements."

Hearing this happy news, the expression on the faces of the Keralans brightened.

A bit, no more—and that little bit immediately vanished under Ezana's ensuing scowl.

"But they don't hate it as much as they hate mutineers," he rumbled. "I'd be on my best behavior from now on, if I were you."

Four Keralan heads bobbed frantic agreement.

Ezana's scowl deepened. "You're seamen. So I assume you're familiar with the Ethiopian treatment for mutineers?"

Four Keralan heads bobbed horrified agreement.

"Good," he grunted.

He rose and turned to the Kushan commander.

"You won't have any more trouble," he pronounced. As he made his way back to the rail, the Kushan accompanied him.

"What *is* the Ethiopian way with mutineers?" he asked.

Ezana climbed onto the rail. Just before making his leap, he bestowed a cheerful grin onto the Kushan commander.

"It involves fishing."

He sprang across. Turned and called back.

"We're partial to shark meat!"

Two days later, Ezana came aboard the Empress' flagship. A council had been called for all the central leaders of the expedition. He, along with Wahsi and Garmat, were to be the Ethiopian representatives at the meeting.

Garmat was already aboard, waiting for him. As the two men fought their way across the deck in the face of a rain so heavy it seemed almost like a waterfall, Ezana grumbled. "This has *got* to be the worst climate in the world."

Garmat smiled. "Oh, I don't know. At least it's not hot. The temperature's rather pleasant, actually. Whereas the Empty Quarter—"

Ezana shook his head firmly. "No contest. At least you can breathe, in Arabia."

He cast a fierce glower at the heavy sky. "How much *does* it rain here, anyway?"

They were at the small shed which provided an entryway into the large cabin amidship. Both men made an effort to wring out their clothes—mere kilts, fortunately—before entering.

Garmat frowned in thought. "I'm not sure, actually. I think I heard somewhere that southwest India during the monsoon season gets—"

He gave a figure in the Ethiopian way of measuring such things. Ezana's eyes widened. The figure was the equivalent of thirteen feet of water in five months.

"Mother of God!"

Garmat nodded toward the east, toward the invisible coast of India.

"Cheer up. If all goes well, soon enough we'll be crossing the mountains into Majarashtra. It's dry, I hear, on that side of the Western Ghats."

"Can't be soon enough," grumbled Ezana. He led the way into the cabin.

The cabin which served as Shakuntala's "imperial quarters" was a bit grotesque, to Ezana's eyes. He was an Ethiopian, brought up in the Axumite traditions of royal regalia. Those traditions leaned toward a style of ornamentation which was massive, but austere. And always practical. When traveling by sea, an Ethiopian royal—even the negusa nagast himself—would enjoy nothing more than a simple cabin decorated with, at most, a lion skin or ostrich feathers.

The Indian tradition was otherwise. Massive also, at times—Ezana had seen, and been impressed by, the size of the Malwa Emperor's palaces and pavilions. But not austere. Not practical.

Never seen so many gewgaws in my life, he thought sourly.

His eye fell on a ivory carving perched atop a slender table by the entrance. The carving, incredibly ornate and intricate, depicted a half-naked couple entwined in a passionate embrace. Ezana almost winced. It was not the eroticism of the carving which offended him—Axumites were not prudes—but the simple absurdity of the thing.

On a warship?

First storm, that thing's so much ballast.

Garmat pushed him forward into the cabin.

"We're diplomats," he whispered. "Be polite."

Shakuntala was perched on a pile of cushions against the far wall of the cabin. Dadaji Holkar sat to her left, in the position of her chief adviser. Next to him sat the religious leader, Bindusara.

Shakuntala's military commanders were clustered to her right. Kungas was there, along with his two chief Kushan subordinates, Kanishka and Kujulo. The Maratha cavalry leaders Shahji and Kondev were accompanied by three of their own top aides.

Wahsi, also, was there. He had arrived earlier. He was perched on a little wooden stool. Two other stools rested nearby. The Empress had provided them, knowing the Ethiopian preference in seating. All of the Indians were squatting on cushions, in the lotus position.

Once Garmat and Ezana took their seats, Shakuntala spoke.

"The first stage of our strategy has been a resounding success. We have broken free from Kerala and eluded the Malwa. It is well-nigh certain that our enemy believes we are headed for exile in Tamraparni."

She paused, scanning the room for any sign of dissent or disagreement. Seeing none, she continued.

"I believe we can assume that our arrival at

Suppara will come as a complete surprise for the enemy. That being so, it is now possible for us to concentrate our attention on the more distant future. We will surprise the Malwa at Suppara, and we will take the city. The question is—then what?"

Kondev stirred. Shakuntala turned toward him, cocking her head inquiringly. The gesture was an invitation to speak.

For a moment, the Maratha officer hesitated. He was a relatively new member of the Empress' inner circle. Accustomed to Indian traditions—he had been a top officer of Shakuntala's father, whose haughty imperial manner had been legendary—he was still nonplussed by her relaxed and easy manner with her advisers.

Recognizing his uncertainty, Shakuntala prompted him.

"Please, Kondev. Speak up, if you have some doubt."

The cavalry officer tugged at his beard nervously. "I do not have doubts, Your Majesty. Not precisely. But I thought our course of action after seizing Suppara was simply to march on to Deogiri. Join our forces with Rao's." He ducked his head in a quick, apologetic manner. "Perhaps I misunderstood."

"You did not misunderstand, Kondev," replied Shakuntala. "That *was* our plan. But the unexpected arrival of the Axumites, and their offer of an alliance, has led me to reconsider. Or, at least, to think in more ambitious terms."

She turned toward the Ethiopians.

"If we held Suppara—permanently, I mean—could your navy hold off the Malwa fleet?"

The three Ethiopians exchanged quick glances. Wahsi was the first to speak.

"No, Empress," he said firmly. "If the Malwa did not possess their gunpowder weapons, it might be possible. Their navy is much larger than ours, in men and ships, but ours is better. Besides, most of their fleet is tied up in the Persian invasion."

He shrugged.

"The fact is, however, that they *do* possess the demon weapons. That nullifies our advantage of superior skill. We cannot close with them to board. Their rockets are erratic, at long range, but they are fearsome weapons against a nearby enemy."

Shakuntala nodded. She did not seem particularly chagrined, or surprised, by Wahsi's reply. "You could not break a Malwa blockade of Suppara, then?"

Wahsi shook his head. Shakuntala leaned forward.

"Tell me this, Wahsi. If we were able to hold Suppara—keep the Malwa from recapturing the city—could you *run* the blockade?"

All three Axumites burst into laughter.

"Be like stealing chickens from a cripple!" chuckled Ezana.

"A very *strong* cripple," qualified Garmat. "Have to be a *bit* careful. Still—"

Wahsi had stopped laughing.

"Yes, Empress," he stated firmly. "We could run the blockade. Penetrate it like water through a fish net, in fact. Not one or two ships, now and then. We could run a Malwa blockade almost at our pleasure."

He made a little gesture of qualification.

"You understand, I am speaking of a blockade of the entire coast. If they amass enough ships, the Malwa could close off Suppara itself. But I assume there must be other nearby places where we could land a vessel and offload cargo."

"A multitude of them!" exclaimed Bindusara. All eyes turned toward the *sadhu*.

"I am familiar with the Malabar coast," he explained. "With the entire western coast of India, in fact, from Kerala to the Kathiawar."

Bindusara turned his head eastward, as if studying the nearby shore through the walls of the cabin.

"The Western Ghats run parallel to the coast, from the southernmost tip of India all the way north to the Narmada River. They form the western boundary of the Deccan." He fluttered his hands. "The Ghats are not tall mountains. Nothing like the Himalayas! Their average height is less than a thousand yards. Even the greatest of them, Anai Mudi in Kerala, is not three thousand yards high. But they are quite rugged. The combination of their ruggedness and low altitude means that the western shore of India boasts a huge number of small rivers, instead of a few mighty ones like the Ganges and the Brahmaputra, as does the east coast."

"Smugglers' terrain," grunted Ezana.

Bindusara smiled. " 'Terrain'? Say better—smugglers' *paradise*. Don't forget the climate, Ezana. India's west coast is the wettest part of our land. Each one of those rivers enters the sea through forests of teak and palms. There are any number of hidden and secluded coves in which a cargo could be unloaded. And the local population would be quite happy to assist in the process. Poor farmers and fishermen they are, mostly, with a great need for extra money and no love for the Malwa."

Shakuntala, seeing Wahsi nod, stated:

"You could do it, then?"

"Without question, Empress." The Ethiopian officer ran fingers through his mass of thick, kinky hair, eyeing Shakuntala all the while.

"You want to break the siege of Deogiri by controlling all of southern Majarashtra," he speculated. "Using Suppara as your logistics base."

The Empress nodded. "Exactly. I wouldn't think of trying it if the enemy's main army wasn't tied up in Persia. But with only Venandakatra to face, I think it can be done—*provided we get access to gunpowder weapons.*"

"There are cannons in Suppara," said the Maratha officer Shahji. "If we take the city, we will take them also."

"Not enough," grunted Kungas. "Not by themselves."

He looked at Holkar. "You have spies in Suppara. If I'm not mistaken, those cannons are fixed siege guns."

Holkar nodded. "They're huge bombards. Three of them, positioned to defend the city against seaborne attack." He grimaced. "I suppose they *could* be moved, but—"

"Forget it," interrupted Kungas. "We can use those cannons to defend Suppara against the Malwa fleet, but they'll be no use to us in a land war against Venandakatra's army. For that, we need help from the Romans. By now, I'm quite sure Belisarius has developed a Roman capacity to produce gunpowder weapons. If we can establish contact with him, the Ethiopians could smuggle the weapons to us. And keep us supplied with gunpowder."

Everyone in the cabin exchanged glances.

"We need to send a mission to Rome, then," said Bindusara.

"Not to Rome," demurred Dadaji. "To *Belisarius*. To the Roman government, we are simply bizarre outlanders. Only Belisarius knows us well."

The peshwa straightened his posture.

"I will go," he announced. "Our delegation must be led by someone who is both highly placed in the Empress' government and personally known to Belisarius. I am the obvious choice."

"Nonsense!" exclaimed Shakuntala. "The idea is utterly mad. You are my peshwa, Dadaji. I need you to remain here."

Holkar frowned. "But I am the only one who—"

He broke off, casting a startled glance at Kungas. The Kushan commander huffed. Coming from

someone else, the noise would have been interpreted
as humor. Coming from Kungas, it was hard to tell.

"He is the commander of your bodyguard!" protested Dadaji.

Shakuntala waved her hand. "He is not needed in
that capacity, anymore. Kanishka is more than capable
of taking his place. Actually, his talents are being
wasted there."

Everyone in the room was staring at Kungas. The
expression on the faces of most of the Indians was
a mixture of skepticism and hesitation.

Shahji cleared his throat.

"If you will forgive me, Your Majesty, it seems
to me that sending Kungas might be a bad idea.
He is not of noble blood—neither brahmin nor
kshatriya—and I fear the Roman general Belisarius
might be offended if your ambassador were of such
a low—"

The rest of the sentence was lost, buried beneath
an eruption of laughter. Coming from the Ethiopians,
mainly, but the Empress herself was participating and
even Kungas emitted a chuckle or two.

Dadaji simply smiled. Then said, shaking his head,
"You do not understand, Shahji. Romans in general—
and Belisarius in particular—do not look at these things
the way we Indians do. They are punctilious about the
forms of nobility, but, as to its real content—" He
shrugged. "So long as Kungas is the official envoy of
the Empress, and carries with him a sufficiently
resounding title, the Romans will be quite satisfied.
Certainly Belisarius will."

"Excellent point, Dadaji," stated Shakuntala. She
bestowed an imperial nod upon Kungas.

"I hereby appoint you my ambassador to Rome,
and give you the titles of *Mahadandanayaka* and
Bhatasvapati."

Kungas' incipient smile surfaced. Barely.

" 'Great commandant' and 'lord of army and

cavalry,' " he murmured. "My, how I've risen in the world!"

Catching a glimpse of Garmat's face, Shakuntala turned toward him. The Ethiopian adviser's gaiety had quite vanished, replaced by a frown.

"You disagree," she stated. There was no accusation in the words, simply a question.

The old half-Arab stroked his beard.

"Yes, Empress, I do." He made a dismissive gesture with his hand. "Not, of course, for the reasons advanced earlier. Kungas would be quite acceptable as an ambassador, from the Roman point of view. More than acceptable, as far as Belisarius is concerned. The general trusts and admires the man, deeply. I know—he told me so himself."

The Indian officers in the cabin moved their eyes to Kungas. As ever, the Kushan commander's face was impassive, like a mask. But they were reminded, again, that the unprepossessing Kushan—whom they tended, unconsciously, to regard as a lowborn half-barbarian— enjoyed a reputation among the greatest folk of their world which was far beyond their own.

"What is the problem, then?" asked Shakuntala.

Garmat pursed his lips. "The problem, Empress, is three-fold."

He held up a thumb.

"First. You will be sending off your—*one* of your— most capable military commanders on the very eve of a decisive battle. Suppara can be taken, I believe, despite its guns. But doing so, as we've discussed before, will depend on the Kushans seizing the cannons by a surprise assault. Until they do so, you cannot think to land in Suppara itself with your Maratha cavalry. The ships would be destroyed before they reached the docks."

He pointed at Kungas. "If I were you, that is the man I would want leading that attack. No other."

Shakuntala was shaking her head. Garmat held up

a hand, forestalling her words. "No, Empress. You cannot wait until *after* the battle to send Kungas away. There is no time to lose, if you want to get Roman help. I myself must leave this expedition tomorrow, to report back to the negusa nagast. Your ambassador—whoever it is—should accompany me on that ship."

Shakuntala bowed her head, thinking. As always, the young Empress was quick to decide.

"I agree. We *are* pressed for time."

She raised her eyes. "The other reasons?"

Garmat held up a finger alongside his thumb.

"Second. I think Kungas' mission would be futile. *How will he find Belisarius?* In that chaos in Persia?"

The Ethiopian chuckled dryly. "It would be hard enough to find anyone, much less Belisarius. The general told me once that he considered the chaos of war to be his best friend. There is always an advantage to be found, he told me, if you seize it in a willing embrace. Do you understand what that means?"

Shakuntala's Maratha officers were frowning, as was the Empress herself. All of them, it was clear, found the notion of *treasuring* war's confusion bizarre.

But Kungas, understanding, nodded his head.

"Belisarius will be riding the whirlwind," he said. "He will do everything in his power to create chaos, and then take advantage of it."

The Kushan rubbed the topknot on his head. "He not only *could* be anywhere, he will be doing everything he can to make it seem as if he were one place while he is going somewhere else." He grunted, partly with admiration, partly with chagrin. "The intention, of course, is to confuse the enemy. But it will have the same effect on allies trying to find him."

The top-knot rubbing grew vigorous. "It will be difficult. Difficult."

"It will be impossible," countered Garmat. "And, finally, *quite unnecessary*."

He waited for those last words to register, before raising another finger.

"My third reason, Empress, is simple. There is no need to send Kungas as an ambassador to Rome, for the simple reason that I am quite sure Rome—and Belisarius—are sending an ambassador to *you*. That ambassador, I am certain, will be bringing what you need."

Everyone stared at Garmat. The surprise was obvious on all faces—except those of the other Ethiopians.

"You know something," stated Holkar.

"Nothing specific," said Ezana. "Only—"

Garmat cleared his throat.

"The Kingdom of Axum has maintained a small but quite effective espionage service in the Roman Empire. For well over a century, now." He made a small, half-apologetic grimace. "There has been no trouble between us and Rome, mind you. Ever since the Roman Emperor Diocletian set Elephantine as the southern limit of Roman territory in Africa, the border has been quite tranquil. Still—"

He shrugged.

"Rome is a great empire, ours is much smaller. It always behooves a less powerful kingdom to keep an eye on its more powerful neighbor. Regardless of their current intentions or attitudes. You never know. Things might change."

The Indians in the room all nodded. Common sense, that. And they had their own memories of the long and turbulent history of India.

"Most of our attention, naturally, is given to their province of Egypt. There, we have the advantage that most of the population is Monophysite. Our own creed is very similar, and many of the Egyptian Monophysites look upon us as their religious brethren. Any number of Monophysite religious leaders have taken refuge in Ethiopia, over the years, whenever the orthodox persecution became—"

He broke off, seeing the incomprehension in the faces of the Indians. Only Dadaji Holkar, he realized, understood anything of what he was saying.

Garmat had to restrain himself from muttering *"Damned arrogant Indians!"*

"Never mind," he sighed. For all that he genuinely liked and admired many Indians, Garmat was struck again by their peculiar insularity. Even the most broad-minded Indians—with a few exceptions like Holkar—tended to look on the whole vast world beyond their own culture as an undifferentiated mass of semi-barbarians. The divisions within Christianity were quite beyond their ken—or interest.

"The point is this," he drove on. "We discovered some time ago that the Roman Empress is sending a military and political expedition to Egypt. The official purpose of that expedition is to quell an incipient rebellion and reestablish tight imperial control over their richest province. But who did they send to command this force? *Belisarius' own wife, Antonina.*"

He shrugged. "We are speculating, of course. But, knowing Belisarius, I think the speculation is quite sound. Antonina's expedition is real enough on its own terms, of course—the Romans *do* need to keep a firm hand on Egypt. But we are quite sure that there is another purpose hidden within that public objective. We think Belisarius is sending his own wife in order to open a second front against the Malwa. It would be astonishing to us if that strategy did not include providing support for Andhra."

He gave Shakuntala and Holkar a quick, knowing glance. The young Empress and her peshwa, understanding, nodded in reply. In order to maintain her prestige, Shakuntala had never publicly explained where she obtained the large fortune which served as her imperial war chest. Her Maratha officers, who rallied to her after her escape from Malwa, had never even thought to ask. Empresses are rich. Everyone knows that. It's a law of nature.

In reality, the hunted young girl had been given that treasure by Belisarius himself, on the eve of her escape. The vast treasure with which Emperor Skandagupta had tried to bribe Belisarius into treason, the Roman general had turned over to Shakuntala in order to finance a rebellion in Malwa's rear.

"Would *that* man have forgotten you?" asked Garmat quietly. "Would *that* man not have continued to develop his plans?"

Shakuntala's eyes widened, slightly.

"You're right," she whispered. "He is sending someone to us. Belisarius has thought of it already."

Her shoulders slumped, just a bit. From relief, it was obvious. It suddenly dawned on everyone how hard a decision it had been for her, to send Kungas away.

"You will stay, Kungas," she announced. "You will stay here, with me."

The Kushan commander nodded. Then, with a sly little smile, murmured, "How quickly fortune passes."

Shakuntala frowned, fiercely.

"Nonsense! I did not remove your titles—except that of ambassador to Rome. You are still Maha-dandanayaka. Still, my Bhatasvapati."

Her eyes softened, gazing on the man who had once been her captor, and always her protector.

"As you have been since Amaravati," she whispered. "When you saved me from the Ye-tai beasts."

Later, as they filed out of the cabin, the Maratha commander Shahji remarked to Garmat:

"I wonder who the Romans are sending to us? A general of renown, no doubt."

Fighting down a smile, Garmat made no reply. He glanced at Ezana and Wahsi, and saw that his two Ethiopian compatriots were fighting the same battle.

Shahji moved on.

"Poor fellow," murmured Wahsi.

"What a shock, when he discovers," agreed Ezana.

Now, Garmat found himself fighting down an outright laugh. Ezana and Wahsi had accompanied him, three years earlier, in his mission to Rome. *They* knew the realities of the Roman court. *They* knew the Empress Theodora's foibles.

But he said nothing. Not until after the three Ethiopians had clambered into their small skiff and begun the trip back to their own ship. Only then did he burst into laughter. Ezana and Wahsi joined him in that gaiety.

"It's bound to be a woman!" choked out Ezana.

"Theodora wouldn't trust anyone else," gasped Wahsi. "Shahji'll die of horror!"

Garmat shook his head. "That's not fair, actually. He's Maratha, don't forget. They recognize the legitimacy of female rulers. They even have a tradition of women leading armies. Still—"

He fell silent. He was not sure, of course—it was pure speculation. But he thought he could guess who Theodora and Belisarius would send.

Not Antonina. Garmat was quite sure that Belisarius had bigger plans for her. Of the Empress Theodora's inner circle of advisers—*female* advisers— that left only—

Ezana completed the thought aloud.

"They may have those traditions, Garmat," he chuckled. "But not even the Maratha have a tradition of sarcastic, quick-tongued, rapier-witted women who've read more books than they even knew existed."

"Poor Shahji," concluded Wahsi. "He's such a stiff and proper sort. I foresee chagrin in his future. Great discomfiture."

Chapter 22

THE EASTERN MEDITERRANEAN
Summer, 531 A.D.

"Be careful!" hissed Antonina.

"I *am* being careful," growled Irene. "It's the stupid boat that's being careless!"

Hesitantly, gingerly, the spymaster stuck out her foot again, groping for the rail of the little skiff bobbing alongside Antonina's flagship. The sea was not particularly rough, but Irene's experience with climbing down a large ship into a smaller one was exactly nil.

Her foot touched the rail, pressed down, skidded aside. Frantically, she clutched the rope ladder. A stream of vulgar curses ensued. Coarse phrases; unrefined terms. Aimed at the world in general and boats in particular.

Above, Ousanas grinned down.

"Witness, everyone! A miracle! There *is* a book which Irene has never read, after all! I refer, of course, to *On the Transfer of Personnel From Craft to Craft At Sea,* by the famous author Profanites of Dispepsia."

A stream of *really* vulgar curses ensued. Utterly obscene phrases; incredibly gross terms. Aimed exclusively at one particular African.

The African in question grinned even wider.

"May I lend you a hand?" he asked pleasantly.

Irene glared up at him furiously. "Yes!" she snarled. "Get me into this stupid fucking boat!"

"No problem, noble Greek lady," said Ousanas cheerfully. The dawazz leapt onto the rail of Antonina's flagship, gauged the matter for perhaps a micro-second, and sprang directly down into the boat below. He landed lightly on his feet, easily finding his balance. Then, turned to face Irene. The spymaster was swinging against the hull of the larger ship above him. Her face was pale; the knuckles of her hands, clutching the rope ladder, were white as snow.

"Jump," he said.

Irene's eyes widened. She stared down at him, as if ogling a dangerous lunatic.

"Jump," repeated Ousanas. "I will catch you."

"You are completely insane!" she shrieked.

Ousanas glanced up at the flagship above. Antonina and Eon were both leaning over the rail. Antonina's face was filled with deep concern. Eon's, with a struggle to contain his laughter.

"Eon!" shouted Ousanas. "Cut the ladder!"

"Good idea!" boomed Eon. The Prince drew his blade from its baldric. It was a typical Axumite sword, other than being more finely made than most. Which is to say, it was short, square-tipped, and very heavy—more like a huge cleaver than a Roman spatha.

Irene's terrified eyes stared up at the thing. The sword would obviously cut through the thin ropes of the ladder like an axe.

Eon, muscled like a Hercules, raised the blade high.

"*Ooo!*" she screamed. And then, convulsively, let go of the ladder.

She fell no more than four feet. Ousanas caught her easily, easily; then, neatly, set up her upright on the deck of the skiff. An instant later, she collapsed onto a pile of cordage coiled in the bilge.

"You are a foul creature," she hissed, "from a foul land." Gasp, gasp. "Now I know where Homer got the inspiration for the Cyclops."

Ousanas clucked his tongue. "So cruel," he complained. "So vicious!"

From above came Antonina's voice.

"All you all right, Irene?"

The spymaster took a deep shuddering breath. Then, suddenly, burst into a smile.

"I'm quite fine, actually. The first mission is accomplished!"

She transferred the smile onto Ousanas.

"I apologize for my insulting and intemperate remark."

Ousanas winced, awaiting the inevitable.

Hiss.

"I did not mean to slander the memory of an honorable monster of legend."

Above, Antonina and Eon turned to face each other.

"You are certain, Antonina?" asked the Prince. "You have your own difficult task ahead of you. My sarwen would be of help. I have the authority to use them any way I wish. As I told you, my father's offer is for a full alliance."

Antonina shook her head.

"No, Eon. The negusa nagast's offer we accept, certainly. Theodora gave me the authority to seek out that alliance myself, in fact. But if I can't establish my authority in Egypt with the Roman troops at my disposal, another four hundred Axumite soldiers won't make the difference."

She cast a quick glance toward the Ethiopian warship. The craft was rolling gently in the waves just a hundred yards away. The rail was lined with soldiers of the Dakuen sarwe. There were, she estimated, about fifty of them. The rest of Eon's troops were waiting for him at the small port of Pelusium, at the far eastern end of the Nile Delta.

"Besides," she added, "the presence of Axumite sarwen would create political problems. I want to quell the ultra-Chalcedonian fanatics in Egypt without alienating the majority of orthodox Greeks. You know they'll look on Ethiopians as allies of the Monophysites. Foreign heretics, used by the empire against them."

Thoughtfully, Eon nodded. Antonina laid a friendly hand on his arm.

"So, I must decline your offer. Though I *do* thank you for it. Please pass those thanks on to your father."

"I will."

"Pass on to him also Rome's agreement to the proposed alliance. When she gets to Axum, Irene can negotiate the details with the negusa nagast. She is fully authorized to do so, and you may tell your father that she carries Empress Theodora's complete confidence. Providing an escort for her is the best use of your sarwen, at the moment."

She broke into her own smile.

"And I'm happier this way. I hate sending Irene into that maelstrom in India. But at least I'll have the comfort of knowing she has you, and Ousanas, and four hundred Dakuen to protect her."

Her shoulders shuddered, just slightly. "For that matter, I'll be happier knowing she doesn't have to face Red Sea pirates without—"

"*Pirates*," growled Eon. He barked a laugh.

Behind him stood three officers of the Dakuen sarwe. Leaders of the Prince's own royal regiment, they considered themselves—quite rightly—as elite soldiers. And seamen, for that matter. They matched the Prince's growl with their own glares, Eon's barking laugh with their own sneers of derision.

"*Pirates*," they murmured. So might a pride of lions, if they could, mutter the word, *hyenas*. Or, for that matter, *elands. Impalas*.

Meat.

Antonina grinned. She gave the Prince a warm embrace. He returned it, somewhat gingerly, in the way that a courteous and well-bred young royal returns the embrace of a respected, admired—and very voluptuous—older woman.

"Be off," she whispered. "Take care of Irene for me, and for Theodora. And take care of yourself."

A moment later, Eon and his officers made their own easy and effortless descent into the skiff. Once they were aboard, the line was cast off and the boat began pulling away. The officers did their own rowing. In the Axumite tradition, they had all risen from the ranks. They were accustomed to the task, and did it with familiar expertise. Quickly, the skiff pulled toward the waiting Ethiopian warship.

Antonina and Irene stared at each other, for a time, during that short voyage. Close friends—best friends— they had become, during the past three years of joint work and struggle against the Malwa menace. Each of them, now, was taking her own route into the maw of the beast. In all likelihood, they would never see each other again.

Antonina fought back her tears.

"God, I'll miss you," she whispered. "So much."

Thirty yards away, she saw Irene turn her head aside. She did not miss the slight sheen in those distant eyes. Irene, she knew, was fighting back her own tears.

Antonina tore her gaze from the figure of her friend

and stared at Eon. The Prince was sitting in the stern-sheet of the skiff. Antonina could see his head slowly turning, as he scanned the surface of the waves.

Already, she realized, Eon was fulfilling his promise to protect Irene from any danger.

Then, seeing the arrogant ferocity lurking in Eon's huge shoulders, she could not help smiling. She found great comfort in those shoulders.

Sharks, of course, do not have shoulders. But if they did, so might a great shark confront the monsters of the sea.

Tuna. Squid. Devil-rays.

Meat.

By the time the skiff bearing Irene reached its destination, other skiffs were making their own way to the Axumite warship from other Roman craft, bearing their own cargoes.

Three of those skiffs carried barrels of gunpowder. Two hauled cannons—brass three-pounders, one in each skiff. And two more carried the small band of Syrian grenadiers, and their wives and children, who had volunteered to accompany Irene to India. Trainers, if all went well, for whatever forces the Empress Shakuntala might have succeeded in gathering around her. Trainers, and their gear, for the future gunpowder-armed rebellion of south India.

Antonina's little hands gripped the rail. Her husband Belisarius, while he was in India, had done everything in his power to help create that rebellion. He was not a man to forget or abandon those he had sent in harm's way.

Not my husband, she thought, proudly, possessively.

She did not know the future. But Antonina would not have been surprised to learn that in humanity's future—*any* of those possible futures—the name of Belisarius would always be remembered for two things, if nothing else.

Military brilliance.

Loyalty.

She cast a last glance at the small and distant figure of her friend Irene and turned away from the rail. Then, walked—marched, rather—to the bow of her own ship and stared across the waters of the Mediterranean.

Stared to the southwest, now. Toward Alexandria.

She gripped the rail again, and even more tightly.

Silently, she made her vows. If Irene reached India safely, she would not be stranded. If Belisarius' determination to support the Andhra rebellion was thwarted, it would not be because Antonina failed her share of that task.

She would take Alexandria, and Egypt, and reestablish the Empire's rule. She would harness the skills and resources of that great province and turn it into the armory of Rome's war against Malwa.

That armory, among other things, would be used to support Shakuntala and her rebels. Many of those guns would go south. Guns, cannons, rockets, gunpowder—and the men and women needed to use them and train others in their use.

South, to Axum. Then, across the Erythrean Sea to Majarashtra. Somehow, someway, those weapons would find their way into the hands of the young Empress whom Belisarius had freed from captivity.

She clutched the rail, glaring at the still-unseen people who would resist her will. The same people— the same type of people, at least—who had sneered at her all her life.

Had a shark, in that moment, caught sight of the small woman at the prow of the Roman warship, it would have recognized her. It would not have recognized the body, of course—Antonina's shapely form did not evenly remotely resemble that of a fish—nor would its primitive brain have understood her intellect.

But it would have known. Oh, yes. Its own instincts would have recognized a kindred spirit. *Hungry. Want meat.*

Chapter 23

MESOPOTAMIA
Summer, 531 A.D.

At Peroz-Shapur, Belisarius ordered the first real break in the march since they had left Constantinople, three months earlier. The army would rest in Peroz-Shapur for seven days, he announced. All the soldiers were given leave to enjoy the pleasures of the city, save only those assigned—by all units, on a rotating basis—to serve as a military police force.

After announcing this happy news, before the assembled ranks of the army, Belisarius departed for his tent as quickly as possible. (Ten minutes, in the event, which was the time the troops spent cheering his name.) He left it to Maurice to make the savage, bloodcurdling and grisly warnings regarding the fate of any miscreant who transgressed the proper bounds of Persian hospitality.

The army was not taken aback by Maurice's slavering. His sadistic little monologue was even cheered. Though not, admittedly, for ten minutes. The grinning soldiers had no doubt that the threats would be made good. It was simply that the warnings were quite superfluous.

Those soldiers were in a *very* good mood. As well they should be.

First, there was the prospect of a week with no marching.

Second, there was the prospect of spending that week in a large and well-populated city. The Persians had already arranged billeting. *Beds*—well, pallets at least.

Finally—O rapturous joy!—there was the *delightful* prospect of spending those days in a large and well-populated city when every single man in the army had money to burn.

More money that most of them had ever seen in their lives, in fact. Between the Persian Emperor's involuntary largesse—there might have been three ounces of gold left in the villa when the army departed; probably not—and the considerable booty of the destroyed Malwa army, Belisarius' little army was as flush as any army in history.

They knew it—and the Persians in Peroz-Shapur knew it too. The Roman soldiers would have been popular, anyway, even if they had been penniless. Belisarius and his men had just scored the only great defeat for the Malwa since they began their invasion of Persia. And while Kurush and his seven hundred lancers received their fair share of the glory, most of it went to the arms of Rome.

The citizens of Peroz-Shapur had just been relieved of any immediate prospect of a siege, and the men who had eliminated that threat were also in position— literally overnight—to produce a massive infusion of cash into the city's coffers.

Hail the conquering heroes!

As the Romans marched into Peroz-Shapur, the streets were lined with cheering Persians. Many of

those were simply there to applaud. Others—
merchants, tavern-keepers, prostitutes, jewelers—had
additional motives. Simple, uncomplicated motives,
which suited the simple and uncomplicated Roman
troops to perfection.

So, as he retired to his tent, Belisarius was not
concerned that there would be any unfortunate
incidents during the army's stay in Peroz-Shapur.
Which was good, because the general needed some
time for himself, free of distraction.

He wanted to think. And examine a possibility.

Baresmanas visited him in his tent, in midafternoon
of the third day.

"Why are you not staying in the city?" he asked,
after being invited within. The sahrdaran glanced
around at the austere living quarters which Belisarius
always maintained on campaign. Other than an
amphora of wine, and the cooling breeze which blew
in through the opened flaps, the general's tent showed
no signs of a man enjoying a well-deserved rest.

Belisarius looked up from the pallet where he was
sitting, half-reclined against a cushion propped next
to the chest which contained his personal goods.
Smiling, he closed the book in his hand and gestured
toward the chair at his little writing desk. The chair
and the desk were the only items of furniture in the
tent.

"Have a seat, Baresmanas. You looked exhausted."

The Persian nobleman, half-collapsing on the chair,
heaved a sigh.

"I *am* exhausted. The city is a madhouse! People
are carousing at every hour of the day and night!"

"Shamelessly and with wild abandon, I should
imagine." The general grinned. "You can't get any
sleep. You can't hear yourself think. To your astonishment, you find yourself remembering your tent
with fond memories."

Baresmanas chuckled. "You anticipated this, I see."

"I have no experience with Persian troops enjoying a celebration. Perhaps they're a subdued lot—"

"Ha!"

"No?" Belisarius grinned. "But I *do* know what Roman soldiers are like. They'd drive the demons of the Pit to mad distraction, just from the noise alone."

The general cocked his head. "There have been no serious problems, I trust?"

Baresmanas shook his head.

"No, no. A slew of complaints from indignant matrons, of course, outraged at the conduct of their wanton daughters. But even they seem more concerned with the unfortunate consequences nine months from now than with the impropriety of the moment. We Aryans frown on bastardy, you know."

Belisarius smiled. "Every folk I know frowns on bastardy—and then, somehow, manages to cope with it."

He scratched his chin. "A donation from the army, do you think? Discreet sort of thing, left in the proper hands after we depart. City notables, perhaps?"

Baresmanas considered the question.

"Better the priesthood, I think." Then, shrugging: "The problem may not be a major one, in any event. The matrons are more confused than angry. It seems any number of marriage proposals have been advanced—within a day of the army's arrival, in some cases!—and they don't know how to deal with them. As you may be aware, our customs in that respect are more involved than yours."

As it happened, Belisarius was quite familiar with Persian marital traditions. Unlike the simple monogamy of Roman Christians, Persians recognized several different forms of marriage. The fundamental type—what they called *patixsayih*—corresponded quite closely to the Christian marriage, except that polygamy was permissible. But other marriages were also given legal status in Persia, including one which was "for a definite period only."

Belisarius smiled. He was quite certain that his Syrian troops, with their long acquaintance with Medes, had passed on this happy knowledge to the other soldiers.

His smile, after a moment, faded to a more thoughtful expression.

"It occurs to me, Baresmanas—"

The sarhadaran interrupted. His own face bore a pensive little smile.

"Roman troops will be campaigning in Mesopotamia for quite some time. Years, possibly. Peroz-Shapur, because of its location, will be a central base—*the* central base, in all likelihood—for that military presence. Soldiers are men, not beasts. They will suffer from loneliness, many of them—a want in the heart, as much as a lust in the body."

Belisarius was struck again, as he had been many times before, by the uncanny similarity between the workings of his mind and that of the man sitting across from him in the tent. He was reminded of the odd friendship which had developed between him and Rana Sanga, while he had been in India. There, also, differences in birth and breeding had been no barrier—even though Sanga was his sworn enemy.

For a moment, he wondered how the Rajput King was faring in his campaign in Bactria.

All too well, I suspect, came the rueful thought. *Yet I cannot help wishing the man good fortune—in his life, at least, if not his purpose.*

He brought his thoughts back to the matter at hand.

"I think we can make a suitable arrangement, Baresmanas. Talk to your priesthood, would you? If they are willing to be cooperative, I will encourage my soldiers to approach their romantic liaisons with a more—ah, what shall I call it . . . ?"

The sahrdaran grinned.

"Long-term approach," he suggested. "Or, for those who are incorrigibly low-minded, guaranteed recreation."

Baresmanas stroked his beard. The gesture positively exuded satisfaction. A well-groomed man by temperament, he had taken advantage of the stay in Peroz-Shapur to have the beard properly trimmed and shaped. But some of his pleasure, obviously, stemmed from the prospective solution of a problem. A minor problem, now—but small tensions, uncorrected, have a way of festering.

"Yes, yes," he mused. "I foresee no problems from the Mazda priests. Even less from the matrons! It is in every Persian's interest to avoid the shame of illegitimacy, after all. The absence of a legal father is a small thing to explain—especially if there is a subsidy for the child."

He eyed the general, a bit skeptically.

Understanding the look, Belisarius shrugged.

"The subsidy is not a problem. The army is rich. Well over half of that booty is in my personal possession. Much of it is my personal share. The rest is in my trust as a fund for the disabled, along with widows and orphans. Between the two, there's plenty to go around."

"And your soldiers?"

"I can't promise you that all of them will act responsibly, Baresmanas. I do not share the commonly-held opinion that soldiers have the morals of street cats, mind you. But I'm hardly about to hold them up as models of rectitude, either. Many of my troops won't care in the slightest what bastards they leave behind them—even leaving aside the ones who like to boast about it. But I will spread the word. If my commanders support me—which they will—"

He paused for an instant, savoring the words.

Which they will. Oh, yes, I have my army now.

"—then the soldiers will begin to develop their own customs. Armies tend to be conservative. If taking a Persian wife while on campaign in Mesopotamia—a wife of convenience, perhaps, but a wife nonetheless—becomes ingrained in their habits, they'll frown on their less reputable comrades. Bad thing, being frowned on by your mates."

He gave Baresmanas his own skeptical eye.

"You understand, of course, that many of those soldiers will already have a wife back home. And that any Persian wife will not be recognized under Roman law?"

Baresmanas laughed. "Please, Belisarius!" He waved his hand in a grand gesture of dismissal. "What do we pure-blood Aryans care about the superstitious rituals of foreign barbarians, practiced in their far-off and distant lands?"

A thought came from Aide.

"Thou hast committed fornication!"

"But that was in another country, and besides, the wench is not *patixsayih*."

It's from a future poet. A bit hesitantly: **It's appropriate, though, isn't it?**

Belisarius was astonished. He had never seen Aide exhibit such a subtle grasp of the intricacies of human relationships.

The "jewel" exuded quiet pride. Belisarius began to send a congratulatory thought, when his attention was drawn away by Baresmanas' next words:

"What are you reading?"

Belisarius glanced down at the book in his lap. For a moment he was confused, caught between his interrupted dialogue with Aide and Baresmanas' idle query. But his attention, almost immediately, focussed on the question. To Baresmanas, the matter had been simply one of polite curiosity. To Belisarius, it was not.

"As a matter of fact, I was meaning to speak to

you about it." He held up the volume. "It's by a
Roman historian named Ammianus Marcellinus. This
volume contains books XX through XXV of his *Rerum
Gestarum*."

"I am not familiar with the man. One of the
ancients? A contemporary of Livy or Polybius?"

Belisarius shook his head. "Much more recent
than that. Ammianus was a soldier, actually. He
accompanied Emperor Julian on his expedition into
Persia, two centuries ago." He tapped the book on
his lap. "This volume contains his memoirs of the
episode."

"Ah." The sahrdaran's face exhibited an odd combination of emotions—shame, satisfaction.

"The thing began badly for us, true," he murmured.
"Most of the towns we just marched through—Anatha,
for instance—were destroyed by Julian. So was Peroz-
Shapur, now that I think about it. Burnt to a shell. In
the end, however—"

Satisfaction reigned supreme. Belisarius chuckled.

"In the end, that damned fool Julian burned his
boats in one of those histrionic gestures you'll never
see *me* doing."

He snorted. A professional deriding the flamboy-
ant excesses of an—admittedly talented—amateur.

"The man won practically every battle he fought,
and every siege he undertook. And then—God save
us from theatrical commanders!—stranded his army
without a supply line. Marched them to surrender
from starvation, after losing his own life."

He shook his head. "Talk about snatching defeat
from the jaws of victory. Yes, it ended well for you
Persians. You got Nisibis and five other provinces in
ransom, for allowing the Romans to march out of
Mesopotamia."

The satisfaction on Baresmanas' face ebbed.

"Not so well as all that, my friend. The towns were
still destroyed, and the countryside ravaged." He

rubbed his scarred shoulder, pensively. "In the end, it was just another of the endless wars which Aryans and Greeks seem obsessed with fighting. How many times has Nisibis changed hands, over the centuries? You have sacked Ctesiphon, and we, Antioch. Is either Empire the better for it?"

Belisarius shook his head. "No, Baresmanas. I, for one, would like to see an end to the thing." A crooked smile. "Mind you, I suppose I could be accused of unworthy motives. Ending a millennium-long conflict with a victory at Mindouos, I mean."

Still rubbing his shoulder, Baresmanas smiled.

"I will allow you that personal triumph, Belisarius. Quite cheerfully. I hope never to meet Romans on a field of battle again."

Belisarius laughed. "I, too! You Persians are just too damned tough."

He eyed the sahrdaran slyly. "That was Justinian's main argument for accepting your proposals, you know. He said that making a hundred years' peace would cement the Roman army's allegiance to the dynasty. Anything to avoid another clash with those damned Persian dehgans!"

Baresmanas, for all his scholarly nature, was too much of a dehgan himself not to be pleased. But he did not linger over the gratification. He pointed at the book.

"Why are you reading it, then?"

Belisarius scratched his chin.

"I brought it with me—borrowed it from a bibliophile friend named Irene—just on speculation. I thought it might contain some useful material. As it happens, I think it does. Quite useful, in fact."

He gave Baresmanas an amused look.

"Have you had enough rest and relaxation in Peroz-Shapur? Does the thought of two days' travel in the countryside appeal to you? It'll be scorching hot, of course. On the other hand, there will be certain subtle pleasures. You know, things like quiet, solitude, serenity—"

"Enough!" laughed Baresmanas. "Anything to get away from this insane revelry! The bleakest desert in the world sounds like paradise to me, at the moment."

"It won't be all that bad, actually. I just want to retrace our route. Go back up the river to the old canal we passed by on our way here."

Baresmanas frowned. "The Nehar Malka? The Royal Canal?"

Belisarius nodded. The sahrdaran's puzzlement deepened.

"Whatever for? That canal's as dry as a bone. It hasn't been used since—" He stopped. Belisarius completed the thought:

"Since you Persians blocked it off, two centuries ago. After the Roman Emperor Julian used it to float his ships from the Euphrates to the Tigris, in order to besiege Ctesiphon."

Baresmanas blew out his cheeks. "Yes, yes. That little episode—*not* so little, actually. Julian failed to take Ctesiphon, but it was a close thing. Anyway, after that we decided the irrigation and trading value of the canal was not worth the risk of providing Romans with a perfect logistics route to attack our capital."

He cocked his head quizzically. "But still—I ask again? Why are you interested in a canal which is empty of water?"

"That's precisely the reason I *am* interested in it, Baresmanas."

He held up his hand, forestalling further questions.

"Please! At the moment, I am simply engaged in idle speculation brought on by reading an old book. Before I say anything else, I need to look at the thing. I was not able to examine it closely on our way into Peroz-Shapur."

Baresmanas rose. "As you will. When do you wish to depart?"

"Tomorrow morning, as early as possible." A little frown appeared on his brow. "I hate to drag any of my troops away from their celebration, but we'll need an escort. Some of my bucellarii will just have to—"

"No, Belisarius! Leave the lads to their pleasures. My household troops have been awaiting me here for almost a month. We can take our escort from among their ranks. I insist!"

To Belisarius' surprise, the expedition which set out the next morning turned out to be quite a major affair. A full two thousand of Baresmanas' household troops showed up outside his tent, at the crack of dawn. Even if he hadn't already been awake, the sound of those horses would have tumbled him from his pallet. Half-expecting a surprise cavalry raid, the general emerged from his tent with sword in hand.

After dismounting, Baresmanas grinned at the Roman general's wide-eyed stare.

"It seems I am not the only one who seeks a bit of peace and quiet," he remarked. "Almost all of my household troops clamored to join the expedition, once the word got out. But I didn't think we needed six thousand men."

"*Six* thousand?" asked Belisarius.

The sahrdaran's cheerful grin widened.

"Amazing, isn't it? I was expecting three thousand, at the most. It seems the news of our great victory at the battle of Anatha has caused dehgans to spring up from the very soil, desperately seeking to share in the glory. Truth is, I think it was the faint hope that we might encounter another party of Malwa raiders that inspired this great outpouring of enthusiasm for our little expedition."

One of the general's servants approached, leading his horse. As he took the reins, Belisarius remarked:

"They are not all troops from your household, then?"

The sahrdaran gave his shoulders a little inscoucient shake.

"Who is to say? The majority are from my province of Garamig. The rest? Who knows? Most of them, I suspect, are from Ormazd's own province of Arbayistan."

Belisarius nodded, and mounted his horse. As they began to ride off, he mulled over Baresmanas' last words.

For all their similarities, there were some important differences in the way the Roman and Persian Empires were organized. One of those differences—a key difference—was in their military structure. The Roman army was a professional army supplemented by mercenary auxiliaries, usually (though not always) drawn from barbarian tribes. The Persian army, on the other hand, was a much more complicated phenomenon.

Feudalism is always complicated, came Aide's interjection. **Most convoluted system you—*we* humans have ever come up with. And we're a convoluted folk. Especially you protoplasmic types.**

"So it is," murmured Belisarius. He did not inquire as to the meaning of "protoplasmic." He suspected he didn't want to know.

Each nobleman of sahrdaran and vurzurgan rank maintained a private army, made up of soldiers from their province or district. Some of those—the "household troops"—were financially supported by their lord. The rest were dehgans, whose obligation to provide military service was a more nebulous affair.

The dehgans were village and small town knights, essentially. The lowest rank in the aristocracy, but still part of what Aryans called the azadan. Though they were officially under the command of the higher nobility, the dehgans were economically independent and not, as a class, given to subservience. When it came to rallying the support of "his" dehgans, a high lord's prestige counted for more than formal obligation.

For their part, each dehgan maintained a small body of retainers who would accompany him on campaign. Not more than a handful, usually. Well-respected men of their village or town—prosperous farmers and blacksmiths, in the main—who had not only the strength, fitness and skill to serve as armored archers but could afford the horse and gear as well.

The Persian Emperor himself, beyond his own household troops, directly commanded nothing but his personal bodyguard—a regiment of men who still bore the ancient title of the Immortals. For the rest, the Shahanshah depended on the support of the great nobility. Who, in turn, depended on the support of the dehgans.

In theory, it was all very neatly pyramidal. In practice—

Aide summed it up nicely: **Victory has a multitude of fathers. Defeat is an orphan. Or, in this case: victory has a multitude of would-be sons.**

Belisarius smiled.

And defeat is childless.

He twisted in his saddle, passing the smile onto Baresmanas.

"You think Ormazd's joints are aching, then?"

The sahrdaran chuckled.

"I suspect that Ormazd, right now, is feeling very much like a victim of arthritis. Each morning, when he wakes up, he finds his army has shrunk a bit more. While faithless dehgans disappear, seeking fame and fortune in more likely quarters."

Belisarius studied the huge "escort" which surrounded them. The Persians were marching in good order, although, to a Roman general's eye, the formation seemed a bit odd. After a moment, he realized that the peculiar "lumpiness" was due to the

formation's social order. Rather than marching in
Roman ranks and files, the Persians tended to cluster in small groups. Retainers accompanying their
dehgans, he realized. Where the basic unit of the
Roman army was a squad, that of the Persian force
was a village band. Men who had grown up together,
and known each other all their lives.

After a minute or so, Belisarius found himself
deep in a rumination over the most effective way
to combine Roman and Persian forces, given each
people's habits and characteristics. He shook off the
thoughts, for now. He had something more immediate to attend to.

"We need to make a stop at the prisoners' camp,"
he announced.

Baresmanas raised a questioning eyebrow, but made
no protest. He simply called out a name.

Immediately, one of the Persians riding nearby
trotted his horse over to the sahrdaran and the Roman
general. As soon as he arrived, Baresmanas made a
little sweeping gesture with his hand.

"I would like to introduce the commander of my
household troops, General Belisarius. Merena is his
name, from a fine azadan family affiliated to the
Suren."

Belisarius nodded politely. The Persian commander returned the nod, very stiffly. Examining
him, Belisarius was not sure if the stiffness was
inherent in the man himself, or was due to the
specific circumstances.

A bit of both, he decided. As a rule, in his experience, Persians tended toward a certain athletic slen-
derness. Merena, on the other hand, was a large man,
almost as heavyset as Belisarius' friend Sittas. But
where Sittas handled his weight and girth with a certain sprawling ease, Merena seemed to prefer a far
more immobile method. For all the man's obvious
horsemanship, he sat his saddle almost like a statue.

Baresmanas passed on the command to visit the prisoners' camp on the way north. Merena nodded—again, very stiffly—and trotted away to give the orders.

"Not the most informal sort of fellow," remarked Belisarius.

Baresmanas' lips twisted.

"Normally, he is not so rigid and proper. But I think he is unsure of how to manage the current situation. This is not, actually, the first time you and he were introduced. In a manner of speaking."

Belisarius pursed his lips.

"He, too, was at Mindouos." It was a statement more than a question.

"Oh, yes. Right by my side, during Firuz' mad charge. He tried to come to my aid, after a lance spilled me from my horse. But he was disabled himself, by a plumbata right through the thigh."

Belasarius winced. The plumbata was the weapon which modern Roman infantrymen used in place of the pilum, the javelin favored in the earlier days of the Empire. The plumbata was a much shorter weapon—more like a dart than a throwing spear. But what it lost in range it gained in penetrating power, due to the heavy lead weight fitted to the shaft below the spearpoint. At close range, hurled with the underarm motion of an expert, it could penetrate even the armor of cataphracts or dehgans. The wounds it produced were notoriously brutal.

"Pinned him right to the saddle," continued Baresmanas. "Then, when his horse was hamstrung and gutted, the beast rolled over on top of him. Almost took off his leg. Would have, I'm sure, if he were a smaller man. He still walks with a terrible limp."

The general's wince turned into a grimace. Seeing the expression, Baresmanas shrugged.

"He does not bear you any ill-will, Belisarius. Ill-will over that battle, of course, he has in plenty—but all of it is directed toward Firuz. Still, he does not exactly count you among his bosom companions."

"I imagine not!" The general hesitated, for a moment. Then, deciding that politeness was overridden by necessity:

"I must know, however—please do not take offense—if he will be able to serve properly. Being forced in such close—"

"Have no fear on that score," interrupted Baresmanas. "Whatever his attitude may be toward you, there is not the slightest doubt of his feelings for me, and my family."

Belisarius' face must have exhibited a certain skepticism, for the sahrdaran immediately added:

"It is not simply a matter of duty and tradition. Merena's family is noted—even famed—for its military accomplishments. But they are not rich. He would still be in captivity had I not paid his ransom out of my own funds."

Belisarius nodded. He and Baresmanas rode together in silence, for a minute. Then the sahrdaran remarked, almost idly:

"I have noted that you yourself are quite generous to your bucellarii. I was told that you dispense a full half of your battle-gained treasure to them, in fact. Most munificent, indeed."

Belisarius smiled crookedly. "That's quite true. My retainers are sworn to my service anyway, of course. But I'm a practical man. Men are not tools, mind you. Still, a blacksmith takes good care of the implements of his trade. Keeps them clean, sharp—and well-oiled."

Silence fell upon them again, as they neared the prisoners' camp. A very companionable silence, between two men who understood each other quite well.

It was Belisarius' first visit to the camp, since the army had reached Peroz-Shapur. He was pleased to see that his bucellarii had carried out his instructions to the letter.

Merena was riding alongside Baresmanas as they entered. His eyebrows lifted.

"This is a *prisoners'* camp?" he asked.

To all outward appearances, the place looked like any other Roman field encampment. The tents—the multitude of tents; no crowding men like hogs in a pen here—were arranged in neat rows and files. Latrines had been dug to the proper depth and at the proper distance from the tents themselves. The campfires were large and well-supplied, both with fuel and with cooking implements.

By the time they arrived, all two thousand Kushans were standing in the open ground between the tents. They had heard the horses coming, naturally. And while the sound of those hooves hadn't been those of an attacking force, still—

Why two thousand cavalrymen?

Seeing the alert and ready stance of those unarmed men, Merena grunted his approval.

"Good, good! Staunch fellows. Be a massacre, of course, but at least they wouldn't die from back wounds."

At the entrance to the camp, they were greeted by a small contingent of Roman soldiers. A mixed unit, this, made up of men from all the forces under Belisarius' command, serving their assigned rotation in the duty of guarding the prisoners. The very unwanted duty, needless to say, while their comrades were cavorting in Peroz-Shapur. But Belisarius could detect no signs of resentment or bitterness. The men knew that the rotation would be faithfully followed. In a day or so, they too would be enjoying the fleshpots while others took their appointed turn.

Fairly apportioned, in Belisarius' army—the duties as well as the rewards. Of that, his men were by now quite satisfied.

To the general's surprise—and sheer delight—the commander of that detachment proved to be Basil, the man who led his contingent of katyusha rocket chariots. Before leaving on the expedition, Belisarius had toyed with the idea of summoning Basil to go along. But he had dropped the notion, assuming that the man would be well-nigh impossible to find in the saturnalia at Peroz-Shapur.

Yet here he was. One of the two men—three or four, perhaps—that he most wanted to accompany him.

"You'll be going with me, Basil," he announced. "We're taking a little surveying party to that old canal we passed on our way in."

He glanced over his shoulder at the huge mass of Persian cavalrymen waiting outside the camp.

"Well, not all that little. But I need your expertise. You've had more practical experience handling gunpowder than I have."

Basil did not seem sulky at the news, even though it would mean that the hecatontarch would have to forego his own turn at the pleasures of Peroz-Shapur.

Belisarius was not surprised. He had personally selected Basil for his new post, after going over every possibility with Maurice at great length. Both of them had settled on Basil. Partly, for the man's apparent comfort around gunpowder—which was not typical of most of the Thracian cataphracts. Even more, however, for his reliability.

"Yes, sir. When do we leave?"

"Within minutes, I hope. As soon as I can collect a Kushan or two. Where's Vasu—never mind. I see him."

The commander of the Kushans was trotting toward them, accompanied by a handful of his top subordinates. Once he reached the general, Vasudeva gazed up at the man on horseback. There was no expression on his face at all.

"Is there a problem, General?"

Belisarius smiled cordially, shaking his head.

"Not in the least, Vasudeva. I am simply on my way to investigate a nearby ruin. Less than a day's ride away, as it happens. I came here because I would like one or two Kushans to come along."

No expression.

"Me, I assume."

Still, no expression.

Belisarius, on the other hand, grinned from ear to ear.

"Of course not, Vasudeva! That would look terrible, I think—taking the prisoners' commander off on a mysterious trip. From which—judging from all too many sad histories—he might never return. No, no. What I want is the Kushan soldier—or soldiers, if there's more than one—who is most familiar with—"

He groped for the word. There was no equivalent in Kushan, so far as he knew, for the Roman term "engineering."

He settled on an awkward makeshift.

"Field architecture. Watermoving works. Ah—"

Vasudeva nodded. "You want an expert in siegecraft."

"Yes! Well put."

For the first time, Vasudeva's mask slipped a bit. A hint of bitterness came into his face.

"For that, general, you could pick almost any Kushan at random. We are all experts. The Malwa are fond of using us for siegework. Up until the victory, of course. Then we are allowed to bind our wounds, while the Ye-tai and the kshatriyas enjoy the plunder."

The mask returned. "However—" Vasudeva turned his head, looking toward one of the men by his side.

"Vima, you go. You're probably the best."

The Kushan named Vima nodded. He began to move toward one of the saddled but riderless horses which Belisarius had brought with him into the camp. Then, apparently struck by a thought, he paused.

"A question, General Belisarius. You said 'water-moving works.' Is this—whatever we are going to see—is it connected with irrigation?"

Belisarius nodded. Vima glanced at the three extra horses.

"Two more all right?" he asked. Again, Belisarius nodded.

Vima scanned the large crowd of Kushans who, by now, were gathered about.

"Kadphises!" he called out. "You come. And where's Huvishka?"

A man shouldered his way to the front.

"Here," he announced.

Vima gestured. "You also."

Once Belisarius and his party emerged from the prisoners' camp and began heading up the road north from Peroz-Shapur, Vima issued a little sigh.

"Nice to ride a horse again," he commented. Then, eyeing Belisarius:

"I don't suppose this is an omen of things to come?"

Belisarius shook his head, a bit apologetically.

"No, Vima. If we find what I hope to find, I'm afraid you Kushans are in for a long stint of very hard labor in one of the hottest places in the world."

Vima grunted. So did the two Kushans riding beside him.

"Could be worse," mused the one called Huvishka.

"Much worse," agreed Kadphises.

Vima grunted. Curious, Belisarius inquired:

"You are not displeased at the prospect?"

All three Kushans grunted in unison. The sound, oddly, was one of amusement.

"We Kushans tend to approach things from the bottom up, general," remarked Vima. "A *long* stint—of whatever kind of labor—sounds distinctly better than many alternative prospects."

Kadphises grunted. Huvishka interpreted:

"Being executed, for instance, can be viewed as a very short stint of very easy labor. Bow your head, that's about it—*chop!*—it's over. Executioner's the only one working up a sweat."

When Belisarius interpreted the exchange, Baresmanas immediately broke into laughter.

Merena did not. He simply grunted himself.

"Good, good. Staunch fellows, as I said."

Chapter 24

Within an hour of their arrival at the Nehar Malka, Belisarius had settled on his plan. The next two hours he spent with Basil and—separately—the Kushans, making sure that the project was technically feasible.

The rest of the day, that evening, and the entire day following, he spent with Baresmanas. Just the two of them, alone in a tent, discussing the real heart of the plan—which was not technical, but moral.

"You are asking a great deal of us, Belisarius."

"We will do all of the work, and provide most of the material resources needed—"

Baresmanas waved those issues aside.

"That's not the problem, and you know it perfectly well." He gave the Roman general a fish-eyed look.

"An *Aryan*, examining your plan, cannot help but notice that you propose to recreate the very conditions which enabled Emperor Julian to strike so deeply into Mesopotamia, two centuries ago."

The little smile which followed took some of the sting out of the statement. Some.

Belisarius shrugged. "Not exactly, Baresmanas. If my scheme works as I hope, the situation will revert back—"

Again, Baresmanas waved his words aside. "Yes, yes—*if* it works as you hope. Not to mention the

315

fact that a *skeptical and untrusting* Aryan cannot help but notice that you Romans will be in control of that part of the plan which would, as you put it, 'revert back' the situation. What if you decide otherwise?"

Belisarius returned the hard stare calmly. "And *are* you a 'skeptical and untrusting Persian,' Baresmanas?"

The sahrdaran looked away, tugging his beard thoughtfully.

"No," came the reply. "I am not, myself. But others will be, especially once they realize that no Aryan commander will have authority over the final implementation of the complete plan."

Belisarius began to shrug, but stopped the gesture before it started. This matter could not be shrugged off. It had to be faced squarely.

"There is no other way, sahrdaran. In order for it to work, my plan requires complete security—*especially* the final part. You know as well as I do that Persian forces, by now, will have been penetrated by Malwa agents."

"And yours haven't?" snapped Baresmanas.

"It is not likely. Not the troops who will be playing the key role, at least. Keep in mind that the Malwa spy network has been active in Persia longer than it was in Rome—*and* that we smashed the center of that network half a year ago."

Baresmanas scowled. "That's another thing I don't like! Your scheme *presupposes* treachery on the part of Aryans!"

Belisarius said nothing. He simply gave the sahrdaran his own fish-eyed look.

After a moment, Baresmanas sighed. He even chuckled.

"I admit, I think your assessment is accurate. Much as I hate to admit it."

Belisarius chuckled himself. "Don't be so downcast about it. Treachery is probably more of a Roman than an Aryan vice. It's not as if we didn't find our own highest circles riddled with traitors, after all. At least Emperor Khusrau still has his eyes, which is more than Justinian can say."

"Very good eyes," grunted Baresmanas. The sahrdaran straightened in his chair.

"The matter must be put before the Emperor himself, Belisarius. Only he can make this decision. I cannot possibly make it in his stead."

"I do not expect you to," came the immediate response. "I know full well that only Khusrau Anushirvan has that authority. But he will ask you what you think. And the question boils down to this: *Can we trust this man Belisarius?*"

The two men in the tent stared at each other.

"I will give my oath, of course," added Belisarius.

For the last time that day, Baresmanas waved the matter aside.

"An oath is only as good as the man who gives it. Your oath will not be necessary."

Suddenly, Baresmanas laughed. "It occurs to me that Valentinian will be most gratified! His job just got much easier!"

Belisarius' brows knit with puzzlement.

"But it's obvious! Khusrau will only agree if he decides that *the man Belisarius* can be trusted. He will certainly not put his trust in *any* Roman general."

Still frowning. Again, the sahdaran laughed.

"So blind! It's so obvious! You will have to promise the Emperor that you will be *alive*—when the time comes to give the final order."

Belisarius' eyes widened.

"Oh, yes," murmured Baresmanas. "Your days of leading cavalry charges are over, my friend. For quite some time."

"I hadn't thought of that," admitted the general.

Aide spoke in his mind:

I did. Then, with great satisfaction:

**And Valentinian isn't the only one who will
be most gratified. So will I.**
So will I. Very much.

Upon his return to Peroz-Shapur, Belisarius sent
couriers into the city, summoning his top commanders
to a conference. It took several hours for all of those
men to be tracked down. Many—most—were found
in the obvious locales. Dens of iniquity, so to speak.
Two or three were nabbed in more reputable spots.
And one—the last to be found—in a very odd sort
of place. For a man of his type.

"Sorry I'm late," said Agathius, as he came into the
command tent. Looking around, he winced a bit. He
was the last one to enter.

"No matter, chiliarch," said Belisarius pleasantly.
"I realize this meeting was called with no warning.
Please—take a chair."

As he waited for the commander of the Constantinople troopers to settle in, Belisarius found himself
a bit puzzled by the man's behavior—and by those of
his subordinates, for that matter. Agathius seemed
distracted, as if his mind were elsewhere. That was
quite unlike the man. Agathius was only twenty-eight
years old, which was quite young for a soldier risen
from the ranks to have become a hecatontarch, much
less a chiliarch. Yet, despite the man's youth and his
outward appearance as a muscular bruiser, Belisarius
had found Agathius to be not only intelligent but pos-
sessed of an almost ferocious capacity for concentration.

Odd, that air of distraction, mused Belisarius. *And
why are his subordinates giving him such peculiar
sidelong glances? You'd almost think they were
smirking.*

He pushed the matter out of his mind. To business.

In the three hours which followed, Belisarius
presented his commanders with two matters for their
consideration.

The first—which took up two of those hours—was
an outline of the stratagem he was developing for using
the Nehar Malka in their next campaign against the
Malwa. Many aspects of his plans he left unspoken—
partly, for security reasons, partly, because they were
still half-formed. But he said enough to allow the
commanders to join in a discussion of the allotment of
Roman troops to the different tasks involved.

Interestingly enough, he noted, Agathius' distraction seemed to vanish during that discussion. Indeed,
the Greek chiliarch played a leading role in it.

"It's essential that Abbu remain behind," insisted
Agathius, "—*with* most of his skirmishers—"

The Constantinople man beat down the protests
coming from other commanders.

"Quit whining!" he snapped. "The rest of us are
just going on a march to Babylon, by way of
Ctesiphon. Right in the heart of Persian territory,
for the sake of God! We already crushed the only
Malwa raiding force anybody knows of—so what do
we need scouts for?"

He jabbed a thumb at Basil, then nodded toward
the Syrian infantry leaders.

"Whereas these boys are going to be left alone up
here. With two thousand Kushans to keep an eye on,
and the desert not ten miles away. They'll be sitting
ducks, if the Lakhmids come on them unawares."

Belisarius sat back, more than satisfied to let the
Greek handle the problem.

Having squelched that little protest, Agathius rolled
over the next.

"And as for this crap about the Callinicum
garrison"—here he glowered at his own Constantinople subordinates, who had been the most
vocal in their protests—"I don't want to hear it!
They did well enough—*damn well*, all things
considered—in the fight at the villa. Sure, they're
not up to the standards of the Syrian lads—not yet,

anyway—but that's all the more reason not to leave them behind. The katyusha-men and the Syrians have got enough on their plate already, without having to train inexperienced men in the kind of heavy engineering work they'll be doing."

Another glare. "So they're coming with us, just as the general proposed. *And* there'll be no grousing about it."

The other Greeks in the tent—who had been doing most of the grousing about "Callinicum crybabies"—lowered their heads. It was all Belisarius could do to keep from grinning. He already knew that Agathius had the easy, relaxed confidence of his subordinates. Now, when needed, the man had shown that he could also break them to his will.

So much met with Belisarius' silent approval. The next, with his admiration.

Agathius' hard eyes left the Greeks, and settled on Celsus, the commander of the Callinicum garrison troops. Celsus was sitting, hunched, on a stool in a corner of the tent. He was a small man, rather elderly for a soldier, and diffident by nature. As usual during command conferences, he had been silent throughout the entire discussion. A silence which had grown purely abject as the qualities of his men had been subjected to the beratement of other, younger, more assertive, more confident—and certainly louder—officers.

Agathius gave the man a little nod, lingering over the gesture just long enough to make his approval clear to everyone. Celsus nodded back, his eyes shining with thanks. For a moment, his skinny shoulders even lost their habitual stoop.

As Agathius resumed his seat, Belisarius sent a quick thought to Aide.

Absolutely marvelous! Did you see that, Aide?— and do you understand why it is so important?

Hesitantly: **I am not sure. I think—**

Hesitation faded. **Yes. It is how humans—your kind of humans—facet each other. Strength grows from building other strength, not from trampling on weakness.**

Exactly.

The officers in the tent were, once again, focussed on Belisarius. The general rose, preparing to speak on another subject. But, before he did so, he took the time for a private moment.

I am so proud of you—grandchild.

You are my old man.

In the next hour, Belisarius broached with his officers the delicate matter which he had discussed with Baresmanas.

"So," he concluded, "I'm not telling anyone what to do. But I repeat: *this war is not going to be settled in one battle.* Not even in one campaign. We're going to be locked against the Malwa for years, probably. Hopefully—eventually—we'll be fighting the Malwa on their own soil. But for now, and probably for quite some time, we'll be fighting here in Persia. Better that, when it comes down to it, than fighting on Roman territory."

He took a little breath.

"I've said this before, many times, but I'll say it again. *We have to stay on good terms with the Persians.* If they start feeling that their Roman allies aren't much better than the Malwa, there'll be the risk that they'll try to back out of the way. Get out of Mesopotamia, retreat to the plateau, and let the Romans fight it out alone."

He gave the gathered men a stern gaze.

"As I said, I'm not telling anyone what to do. But I ask you to try and set an example, at least, for your men. I don't care what any Roman soldier does in taverns and whorehouses, as long as there's no roughhousing. But if you or your men want to cast your net a little wider, so to speak—" he waited for the little chuckle to die down "—keep in mind that Persians have their own customs."

He stopped speaking. Studied his officers, as they sat there staring at him.

Silent themselves, as he had expected. Though he noted, carefully—and with considerable amusement— their differing reactions.

The Syrian officers (as well as Celsus, the Callinicum commander) had little smiles on their faces. Long familiar with Persian customs—*sharing* many of those customs—the Syrians and Arabs obviously found the confusion elsewhere in the room quite entertaining.

His own Thracian bucellarii were also smiling, just a bit—even the dour Maurice. Not with quite the same smirk as the Syrians, true. The Thracians were familiar with Persians, but it could hardly be said that they shared any particular empathy for the haughty Aryans. No, their amusement came from elsewhere. They were *very* familiar with Belisarius. And so they found it entertaining to see neophytes scrambling to catch up with their general's often odd way of looking at the world.

The Illyrian officers were examining Belisarius as if he were one of the fabled two-headed creatures reputed to live somewhere south of Nubia. Illyrians were even more rustic than Thracians, and their experience with "other folks" was restricted almost entirely to barbarians. They understood those barbarians, true. Barbarian blood flowed in their own veins, come down to it. But the idea of *catering* to the so-called "customs" of—of—of—

Belisarius looked away, to keep from laughing. His eyes settled on the Greeks.

They were the key, he knew. The Roman Empire was a Greek Empire, in all but name. A Thracian-Egyptian dynasty might sit on the throne, Egypt might be the richest and most populous province, and Thracians and Syrians might play a disproportionate role in the leadership of the army, but it was the Greeks who were the Empire's heart and soul. Their language was the common language. Their nobility was the axis of the imperial elite. Their traders and merchants commanded the sinews of commerce.

And their soldiers, and officers, were the core of Roman strength.

Here, for the first time, Belisarius found a reaction he had not expected. Agathius' distraction was back, with a vengeance. For all that Belisarius could determine, the man seemed lost in another world. The attitude of his subordinates was equally puzzling. Belisarius had expected the Greeks to react much as the Illyrians. With more sophistication, of course— but, still, he had expected them to be staring at him as if he were at least half-crazed.

Greeks—worry about what a bunch of sorry Persians think?

Instead, they weren't looking at Belisarius at all. They were casting quick, veiled glances at their own commander, with their lips pressed tightly together. As if fighting—very hard—to keep from smirking themselves.

Odd. Very odd.

Belisarius left off his study of the Greeks and glanced at the rest of his subordinates. It was obvious that none of the officers in the tent were prepared to speak on this rather unusual subject. He had expected as much. So, after another minute's silence, he thanked them politely for attending the conference and gave them leave to depart.

Which they did. Agathius led the way, at first, almost charging for the entrance. Then, stopping suddenly, he formed a broad-shouldered stumbling block for the officers who squeezed past him. The man seemed to dance back and forth on his feet, as if torn between two directions. At one point, he began to turn around, as if to re-enter the command tent. Stopped, turned back; turned back again; stopped. Danced back and forth.

Except for Belisarius and Maurice, Agathius was the only one left in the tent. For just a moment, the Constantinople commander's eyes met those of the general. A strange look he had, in his face. Half-pleading; half—angry?

No, decided Belisarius. It was not anger, so much as a deeply buried resentment.

Of what? he wondered.

Suddenly, Agathius was gone. Belisarius cocked an eye at Maurice.

"Do you know something I don't?"

Maurice snorted.

"What do you want? I'm Thracian, for the love of God. Bad enough you want to tax my simple mind with outlandish Persian ways. Am I supposed to understand Greeks, too?"

Two nights later, early in the evening, Agathius showed up at Belisarius' tent.

After being invited within, the man stood rigidly before the general.

"I need to ask you a question, sir," he said. His voice seemed a bit harsh.

Belisarius nodded. Agathius cleared his throat.

"Well. It's this way, sir. I know it's often done—well."

Again, he cleared his throat. The harshness vanished, replaced by a sort of youthful uncertainty. Embarassment, perhaps.

The words came out in a rush.

"I know it's often done that troop commanders—of chiliarch rank, I mean—after a successful campaign—or even sometimes a single battle, if it was a big victory—well—they get taken into the aristocracy. Official rank, I mean."

His mouth clamped shut.

Belisarius scratched his chin.

"Yes," he said, nodding. "It's happened. More than once. Myself, for instance. I was born into the *clarissimate*—as low as it gets in the nobility, outside of equestrians. After Justinian promoted me into his bodyguard, he— Never mind. It's a long story. Today, of course—since my stepson was acclaimed Emperor—I'm ranked at the very top of the senatorial *illustres*." He smiled crookedly. "A *gloriosissimi* I am now, no less."

Agathius did not return the smile. Belisarius realized that he was treading on very sensitive soil. "And yourself, Agathius? I've never asked." A little, dismissive gesture. "I don't care about such things, mind you, in my officers. Only their ability. But tell me—what is your own class origin?"

Agathius stared at the general.

"My father was a baker," he replied. His voice was very soft; but his tone, hard as a rock.

Belisarius nodded, understanding.

In the eastern Roman Empire, unlike the western, men had never been forced by law to remain in their father's trades. Still, the trades tended to be hereditary. All tradesmen were organized into guilds, and were considered freemen. Yet, while some of those trades carried genuine prestige—metalworkers, for instance—none of them were acceptable occupations for members of the nobility.

And *certainly* not bakers, who were considered among the lowest of men, outside of those in outright slavery or servitude.

So. Agathius, like many before him, had sought escape from his father's wretched status through the principal avenue in the Roman Empire which was, relatively speaking, democratic and open to talent: the army.

Yet—Belisarius was still puzzled. He had encountered

men—any number of them—who were obsessed with their official class ranking. But Agathius had never seemed to care, one way or another.

The general thrust speculation aside. Whatever might be the man's motives or past state of mind, the question seemed to be of importance to him now.

"This matters to you?" he asked.

Agathius nodded. "Yes, sir. It does. It didn't used to, but—" His lips tightened. "It does now," he finished, softly. Almost through clenched teeth.

Belisarius abandoned his relaxed stance. He sat up straight in his chair.

"You understand that any rank I give you must be confirmed by the Emperor? And by the Senate, in the case of a senatorial rank?"

Agathius nodded. Finally, his rigid countenance seemed to break, just a bit.

"I don't need to be in any senatorial class, sir. Just—something."

Belisarius nodded.

"In that case, I see no problem." His crooked smile appeared. "Certainly not with the Emperor!"

Agathius managed a little smile himself, now.

Belisarius scratched his chin. "Let's keep it military, then, if the Senate doesn't matter to you. It is well within my authority to give you the rank of *comes*. How is that—Count Agathius?"

Agathius bowed his head stiffly.

"Thank you, sir." Then, after a moment's hesitation, he asked, "How does that compare to a Persian dehgan?"

"Depends how you look at it. Formally speaking, a Roman count is actually a higher rank than a dehgan. Equivalent"—he wobbled his hand back and forth—"to one of the lower grades of their vurzurgan class, more or less."

Belisarius shrugged.

"But that's the way we Romans look at it. *Officially,*

the Persians will accept the equivalence. In practice—
in private—?" Again, he shrugged.

"They view our habit of connecting rank in the
nobility with official position rather dimly. Bloodlines
are far more important, to their way of thinking."

Suddenly, to the general's surprise, Agathius' stiffness disappeared. The burly officer actually grinned.

"Not a problem, that. Not with—"

He fell silent. The grin faded. Agathius squared his
shoulders.

"I thank you again, sir. It means much to me. But
I would like to impose on you again, if I might."

"Yes?"

"Would you do me the honor of joining me tomorrow afternoon? On a social occasion?"

Belisarius' eyes widened, just a bit. To the best of
his knowledge, Agathius' idea of a "social occasion"
was a cheerful drinking session at a tavern. But he
did not think—

Agathius rushed on.

"Lord Baresmanas will escort you, sir. I've already
spoken to him and he agreed. The occasion is taking place at the governor's palace in the city."

By now, Belisarius was quite bewildered. What in
the world did Baresmanas have to do with—?

Enough, he told himself firmly. *This is important
to the man, whatever it is.*

"I will be there, Agathius."

The Greek officer nodded again, thanked him
again, and left.

Odd. Very odd.

Baresmanas arrived early in the afternoon of the
next day. Kurush was with him, as were all of the top
commanders of his household troops with the exception of Merena.

None of the men wore armor, and only two were
even carrying swords. Seeing the finery of their

raiment, Belisarius congratulated himself for having decided to wear his own best clothing. Like the Persians, he was unarmored, carrying no weapon beyond a dagger.

On the ride into the city, the general tried to pry information out of Baresmanas regarding the mysterious "social occasion." But the sahrdaran gave no response beyond an enigmatic little smile.

When they arrived at the governor's palace, Belisarius took a moment to admire the structure. The outer walls were massive, due to the ancient Mesopotamian tradition of using rubble and gypsum mortar for heavy construction. The intrinsic crudity of the material was concealed by an outer layer of stucco painted in a variety of vivid designs. Most of the motifs, ironically, were borrowed from Graeco-Roman civilization—dentils, acanthus, leaf scrolls, even the Greek key. Still, the effect was quite distinct, as Persians had their own approach to color, in which brilliant black, red and yellow hues predominated.

The edifice was forty yards wide and approximately twice that in length. A complex pattern of recesses and projected mouldings added to the intricacy of the palace's outer walls. The palace was three stories tall, judging from its height. But Belisarius was familiar enough with Persian architecture to realize that most of the palace's interior would be made up of very tall one-story rooms. Only in the rear portions of the palace, given over to the governor's private residence, would there actually be chambers on the upper stories.

The front of the palace was dominated by a great *aivan*—the combined entrance hall/audience chamber which was unique to Persian architecture. In the case of this palace, the aivan was located on the narrower southern wall. Almost half of the wall's forty yards were taken up by a huge arch, which led into the barrel-vaulted aivan itself. The aivan was open to the elements, a feature which, in the Mesopotamian climate, was not only practical but pleasant. It was forty feet high, measuring from the marbled floor to the top of the arch, and its walls were decorated both with Roman-style mosaics as well as the traditional Mesopotamian stucco bas-reliefs.

Belisarius had assumed that, whatever the nature of the social occasion, it would be held in the aivan itself. But, after dismounting and following Baresmanas within, he discovered that the aivan was almost empty. The only people present were Agathius and a small group of his subordinates—Cyril, as well as the other three tribunes of the Constantinople unit.

The five Greek officers were standing in the much smaller arch at the rear of the aivan. Past that arch, Belisarius could see a short hallway—also barrel-vaulted—which opened into a room beyond. That room, from what little he could see of it, seemed to be packed with people.

As they walked through the aivan, Belisarius leaned over to Baresmanas. "I thought—"

Baresmanas shook his head. The enigmatic smile was still on his face, but it was no longer quite so little. "Ridiculous!" he proclaimed. "The aivan is for public gatherings. Given the nature of this event, the governor naturally saw fit to offer the use of his own quarters. His private audience chamber, that is to say."

The sahrdaran gestured ahead. "As you can see, it is just beyond."

Agathius stepped forward to meet them. His expression was very stiff and formal, but Belisarius thought he detected a sense of relief in the man's eyes.

"Thank you for coming, sir," he said softly. He turned on his heel and led the way through the arched corridor.

The room beyond was a large chamber, approximately sixty feet in width and length. The walls rose up thirty feet, decorated with frescoes depicting heroic deeds from the various epics of the Aryans. A great dome surmounted the chamber, rising another twenty feet or so.

There were a multitude of people already present, all of them Persians. Belisarius recognized the district governor, standing against the north wall, surrounded by a little coterie of his high officials. The larger body of men—perhaps a dozen—who stood behind them were obviously scribes.

In the western side of the chamber stood an even larger group of men. Mazda priests, Belisarius realized. He was interested to note, judging from their distinctive garb, that both branches of the Zoroastrian clergy were present. The Persians called their priests either *mobads* or *herbads*. When Belisarius first encountered that distinction, years earlier, he had thought it to be roughly parallel to the distinction which Christians made between priests and monks. Further acquaintance with Persian society had undermined that neat assumption. The differences between mobads and herbads were of a subtler nature, which he had never been able to pinpoint precisely—other than observing that mobads seemed to embody the juridical power of the clergy, where the herbads functioned more like teachers or "wise men."

What was significant, however, was that both were represented. That was a bit unusual. There was considerable, if subdued, rivalry between the two branches of the clergy. As a rule, Belisarius had found, mobads and herbads avoided each other's company.

Now he examined the final, and largest, group of Persians in the room. These men were clustered toward the eastern wall, and they seemed to be made up almost entirely of dehgans. Merena, the commander of Baresmanas' household troops, was standing in the midst of them. As he studied the dehgans,

Belisarius suddenly realized that many of them bore a certain resemblance to each other.

Baresmanas' whisper confirmed his guess.

"That's Merena's clan—those of them who were present in the city, at least."

The sahrdaran's enigmatic smile was now almost a grin. He shook his head.

"You still don't understand? Odd, really, for a man who is normally so acutely perceptive. I would have thought—"

A small commotion was taking place. The little mob of dehgans along the eastern wall was stepping aside, clearing a space for a small party advancing into the chamber through an archway in the eastern wall.

Four women appeared—the first women Belisarius had seen since he entered the palace.

Aide's voice—smug, smug:

I figured it out yesterday.

The woman in front was middle-aged. The three walking behind her were quite young. Her daughters, obviously.

Belisarius felt his jaw sag.

What a dummy.

The girl in the center, the oldest, was perhaps sixteen years of age.

It's the first signs of senility, that's what it is.

She was dressed in an elaborate costume. Her sisters, flanking her, wore clothing which was generically similar but not quite as ostentatious.

Don't worry, grandpa.

Her face was covered with a veil, except for her eyes. Dark brown eyes, they were. Gleaming with excitement. Beautiful eyes. Belisarius had no doubt that the rest of the girl was just as beautiful.

I'll take care of you.

Belisarius was not able to follow most of the ritual—the long ritual—which followed. Just the obvious highlights. Partly, because he was caught off-guard. Partly, because it was the ceremony of a foreign religion. Mostly, though, because Aide kept interrupting his train of thought.

The lighting of the sacred fire—

You'll have to stick with porridge from now on.

The presentation by the chief scribe of the intricate property rights and obligations which were a central feature of *patixsayih* marriages—

Can't risk you eating meat. Cut yourself, for sure, forgetting which end of the dagger to use.

The stiff presentations, by Agathius and Merena, of their respective noble rankings—

We'll get rid of your horse, of course.

The learned counsel of the herbads, added to the judgement of the mobads, weighed by the district governor and his assembled advisers—

Find you a donkey to ride.

—who agreed, after lengthy consultation, that the marriage maintained the necessary purity of the Aryan nobility.

A small donkey. So you won't get hurt, all the times you'll fall off.

After the ceremony was over, during the feast which followed, Merena approached Belisarius.

"I have a question," he asked. Stiff as ever.

Politely, Belisarius inclined his head in invitation.

"Was Agathius at Mindouos? I did not wish to ask him, before. And now that he is my son-in-law, I cannot."

"No, Merena. He wasn't."

The dehgan grunted. "Good, good." Merena rubbed his thigh. "That would have been—difficult," he murmured. Then, moved away, limping very badly.

Walking out of the palace, Belisarius glanced at Baresmanas. The smile was still there. Not enigmatic, however. Simply smug.

"And how did you find out about it?" growled the general.

"I didn't 'find out about it,' my friend. I am the one who—ah, what is that word you Romans are so fond of? Yes, yes—I *engineered* the whole thing."

Belisarius' eyes widened. Baresmanas chuckled.

"Oh, yes. *I* am the one who introduced the gallant young officer to Merena and his family—*after* conspiring with his wife to make sure that Sudaba would be present, looking her very—beautiful! beautiful!—best. *I* am the one—"

"Stop bragging," grumbled Belisarius. "I will fully admit that it was a masterstroke, insofar as the problem we discussed—"

"You think I did it because of *that*?" The sahrdaran snorted. "I had a much more immediate problem to solve, my friend. As I told you, Merena is a famous warrior and an absolute paragon of Aryan propriety. He is also, by dehgan standards, poor. So—the man had a daughter of marriageable age and no respectable dowry to give her. Think of the shame! The disgrace! No suitable Persian nobleman would accept a bride with no dowry."

Belisarius smiled crookedly.

"Whereas a vigorous, ambitious young Roman officer risen from the ranks—and newly rich from the booty of Anatha—would be far more concerned with increasing his status than his wealth."

"Precisely."

Belisarius shook his head sadly. "I am a lamb among wolves. An innocent babe surrounded by schemers."

Don't worry, old man. I'll take care of you. Oh—be careful! There's a step coming up!

Chapter 25

BABYLON
Autumn, 531 A.D.

Khusrau Anushirvan sprang lightly onto the low wall which surmounted the highest level of Esagila, the ancient ruin which had once been the great temple of the god Marduk. From that vantage point, the Emperor of Persia could gaze south at the huge Malwa army encamped before Babylon.

An instant later, Belisarius joined him. The general took a moment to make sure his footing was good. The wall—almost a battlement—was at least a yard wide, but there was nothing to stop someone who overbalanced from plunging to their death on the stone rubble sixty feet below.

Khusrau smiled.

"Does altitude bother you?" he asked. The question was polite, not scornful.

The Roman general shook his head. "Not particularly. Still, I wouldn't want to dance up here."

"Lucky man! I myself am petrified by heights. Anything above the level of horseback."

Belisarius glanced at the Persian Emperor. In truth, Khusrau's face seemed a bit pinched, as if he were controlling himself by sheer force of will.

He was impressed, again, by the Emperor's self-discipline. Since his arrival in Babylon three days before, Belisarius had been struck by the way Khusrau kept his obviously exuberant and dynamic personality under a tight rein. That same self-control was being manifested now, in the Persian ruler's ability to remain standing on a perch which would have sent most men to their knees seeking safety.

For ten minutes or so, the two men said nothing. They simply stood side by side, studying the battle being waged below them.

Belisarius' attention was immediately drawn by the roar of siege guns. A cloud of gunsmoke, well over a mile distant, indicated the presence of a battery of the huge cannons. After the wind blew the cloud away, he could spot the actual guns themselves. Eight of them, sheltered behind a berm. He recognized the pattern from his previous experience at the siege of Ranapur. His eyes ranged north and south, quickly spotting two more batteries. Another roar, another cloud of gunsmoke, and one of those batteries was also hidden from view.

Belisarius shifted his gaze to the walls of the besieged city. His eyes widened.

The defenses of Babylon were gigantic. The outer ring was so massive that it was impossible, almost, to think of it as anything other than a low ridge. The fortifications were not particularly tall—perhaps twenty feet, no more—but they spanned perhaps forty yards in thickness.

Studying it more closely, Belisarius saw that the outer defenses were actually a triple wall—or, at least, had been so once. The inner wall, some twenty feet wide, was constructed of sun-dried mud brick. Squat towers spaced at regular intervals projected another twenty feet above the wall itself, topped with sheltered platforms for Persian soldiers manning scorpions and other artillery engines. A rubble-strewn space fifty feet wide separated this inner wall from the middle wall. The middle wall was a bit thicker than the inner wall, with no towers. Unlike the inner wall, this wall was made of harder and more durable oven-baked brick.

That same type of brick was used in the third, outermost wall. No space separated this outermost wall from the midwall. The third wall, originally ten feet in thickness, served both as a bulwark for the midwall as well as the escarpment for the huge moat beyond it.

There was not much left of that third wall, however. Over the centuries, peasants had plucked away the good bricks for their own use. Today, the moat which lapped at the crumbled edge of the wall seemed more like a natural river than a man-made artifact. The size of the moat, of course, was partly responsible for producing that impression—Belisarius estimated that it was at least a hundred yards wide.

Belisarius watched a cannonball slam into the outer wall. A little avalanche of broken bricks slid into the moat, leaving a ripple in their wake. Other than that, the siege gun seemed to have made no impact whatsoever.

"At that rate," he mused, "they'll fill the moat with rubble and cannonballs before they ever finish breaking down the wall."

Khusrau snorted.

"We were terrified—myself also, I will admit it— when they first began firing with those incredible machines. 'Siege guns,' as you call them. But after a few days—then weeks, and now months—we have little fear of them. It's ironic, actually. Most of my advisers urged me to make a stand at Ctesiphon, taking advantage of its tall, stone walls. But I think if I had done so—"

"You would have been defeated by now," concluded Belisarius. "I have seen these guns in use before, and I have seen the walls of Ctesiphon. Those walls would have been brought down within two months."

He pointed to Babylon's outer fortifications. "Whereas this wall—this wide, soft, low wall—is actually more of a berm. Exactly the best kind of defenses against siege guns."

Both men watched as another cannonball struck the wall—the inner wall, this time. The cannonball buried itself in the crumbly mudbrick, without so much as shaking the tower thirty yards away from the impact.

"The wall just got stronger, I think," chuckled Khusrau.

"How many assaults have they mounted?" asked Belisarius.

"Seven. The last one was a month ago. No—almost six weeks now."

The Persian Emperor turned and pointed to his right, toward the Euphrates.

"That one they attempted with barges, loaded with soldiers. It was a massacre. As you can see, the western walls of the city are still standing, almost as they were built by Nebuchadrezzar a thousand years ago. Stonework. Very tall. We poured burning naphtha on them, and sank many of the barges with catapults."

He elevated his finger, still pointing to the west.

"If they could position their siege guns to the west, they could probably break down those stone walls. But I ordered the dikes and levees broken."

Belisarius gazed toward the river. It was now late in the afternoon, and the sun's rays were reflected off a vast spread of water. Khusrau, following a Mesopotamian military tradition which went back to the ancient Sumerians, had ordered the flooding of the low ground. Unchecked by manmade obstructions, the Euphrates had turned the entire area west of Babylon into a swamp. Impossible terrain even for an infantry assault, much less the positioning of artillery.

The area east of Babylon had been protected in the same manner. The ancient city was almost an island now, surrounded by water and marshes to the west, east and northeast. The Malwa army held the southern ground. Persian forces still retained control of the narrow causeway which led from the Ishtar Gate on Babylon's northwest side to the northern regions of Mesopotamia. Even after all these months, the Malwa had not been able to surround and isolate the besieged city.

Khusrau looked back to the south.

"The first six assaults were made here. The Malwa suffered great losses in all of them, with no success at all except, temporarily, during the third assault. In that attack, some of their troops—those excellent ones with the strange hair style—"

"Kushans."

"Yes. About a thousand of them got past the outer fortifications, in three different places. But—"

He shrugged. Belisarius, gazing down, could not help wincing.

"Must have been a slaughter."

"Yes," agreed Khusrau. The Emperor pointed at the inner fortifications, which consisted of a second ring of walls positioned about two hundred yards inside the outer ring.

"That is a double wall. The outer wall is twenty feet thick; the inner, fifteen. These fortifications were also built by Nebuchadrezzar. Very clever, he was—or his engineers and architects, at least. You can see that the two walls are separated by a space of twenty feet. The area between is a built-up road, perfect for military traffic. Then, beyond the outer wall, is a low berm. You can't see it from here. But you can see the moat which butts up against that berm. It's fifty yards wide."

Belisarius shook his head. "A pure killing ground. If the enemy manages to cross the first moat and fight their way over the outer defenses, they find themselves trapped in the open—with another moat to cross, and still more fortifications to be scaled."

"That, too, was slaughter. I had the road packed with dehgans and their retainers. It is quite solid and wide enough for horsemen. They were able to fire their bows from the saddle, sheltered by the outer wall, and rush to whatever spot looked most in danger. I don't think we lost more than two hundred men. And that's about how many of the Kushans finally made it back across the outer fortifications alive."

He began to add something else, but his attention was distracted by the sight of a rocket arching up from the Malwa lines. Khusrau and Belisarius followed the rocket's erratic trajectory, until it plunged harmlessly into the open area between Babylon's two rings of defenses.

"The rockets actually have been more of a problem," commented the Emperor. "They do almost no damage to the walls, and many of them miss the city entirely. But those which do fly straight have a longer range than the siege guns, and they have caused casualties. It is the unpredictability of the cursed things which bothers my soldiers the most."

Belisarius nodded, but said nothing in reply. He was now preoccupied with studying the enemy's field fortifications.

That study was brief. He had seen their equivalent at Ranapur and, again, was not overly impressed. A Roman army, this many months into a siege, would have constructed much better and more solid fieldworks.

Now his eyes were drawn to a further distance, and toward the river. Several miles away, he could see the crude piers which the Malwa had constructed on the left bank of the Euphrates. Crudely made, but very capacious. He estimated that there were at least forty ships tied up to those docks, each of which had a capacity of several hundred tons. Another half dozen or so could be seen coming up the river, their oar banks flashing in the sun as they fought their way against the sluggish current.

Remembering Ranapur, he scanned the river more closely. As he expected, the Malwa were providing security for their supply fleet with a small armada of swift war galleys.

"It's incredible, isn't it?" asked Khusrau. "Not even the ancient legends speak of a logistics effort on this scale."

He fell silent, tight-lipped.

Belisarius eyed the Emperor covertly. Khusrau's face was expressionless, but the general realized that the man's fear of heights was taking a toll on him.

"I've seen enough," he announced. He made a little motion, as if to depart.

Still, no expression crossed Khusrau's face.

"You are certain?" he asked.

Belisarius nodded. Now—possibly—a little look of relief came to the Emperor. Quickly, he turned away and leapt down to the temple roof four feet below.

Belisarius copied that leap, although he landed more heavily than the Persian.

Partly that was because Belisarius was a much bigger man. Khusrau was young and athletic, but his was the build of a gymnast—on the short side, and wiry. Mostly, however, Belisarius' thudding arrival on the roof was due to the half-armor he was wearing. The Emperor, in contrast, was clothed in nothing but the simple tunic and trousers of a Persian nobleman taking his ease.

As he landed, the general staggered slightly. Khusrau steadied him with a helping hand.

"It must be dreadful," he remarked with a smile, "to have to wear that stuff all the time."

Belisarius grimaced. "Especially in this heat! But—there it is. Can't have a general prancing around a siege, while all of the soldiers are sweating rivers."

Khusrau shook his head in sympathy. "Wouldn't do at all," he agreed. His smile became an outright grin. "Whereas an Emperor—"

Belisarius laughed. "I heard all about it, even before we arrived, from your admiring troops. How the fearless Khusrau Anushirvan faces the Malwa with a bared breast."

The Emperor glanced down at his tunic. A simple tunic, in its design. But, of course, not the garment of a simple man.

"Hardly that," he murmured. He fingered the sleeve.

"It's cotton, you know, not linen. Very valuable. Almost as valuable as silk—"

He broke off. Belisarius chuckled.

"More valuable, now. Cotton only comes from India. There won't be more of it for some time."

The two men stared at each other.

Enemies, once. Khusrau had not been at Mindouos, three years earlier. He had been in the capital at Ctesiphon, like all his brothers and half-brothers, plotting to seize the throne after the death of the ailing Emperor Kavad. But it had been his father's army which Belisarius shattered there.

Allies, now.

"Better this way," murmured the Emperor. He took Belisarius by the arm and began leading him toward the small ziggurat at the center of the roof. There was an entrance there, leading to the stairs which descended into Esagila's immense interior.

"Much better," agreed Belisarius.

Much better, chimed in Aide. **The greatest Persian Emperor in a millennium makes for a bad enemy.**

Idly, Belisarius wondered how things might have turned out, had the Malwa never been raised to power by the creature called Link. The thing—half-human, half-computer—which Aide called a cyborg. A cybernetic organism, sent back in time by the "new gods" of the future.

Aide answered. **In that future, you will also defeat the Persians. At a battle near Daras, not far from Mindouos.**

And then?

And then, ten years later, Khusrau will sack Antioch.

They were at the entrance to the ziggurat. Khusrau led the way into the interior. It was much cooler. Belisarius heaved a little sigh of relief.

Much better this way.

Khusrau leaned back in his chair and spread his arms in a gesture which encompassed their entire surroundings.

"I forget, Belisarius—you are a Christian. This must be a marvel for you!"

A little crease of puzzlement came to the general's brow. He paused from raising his wine goblet.

Khusrau laughed.

"Don't tell me you don't know! You're sitting right on top of the Tower of Babel!"

Belisarius' eyes widened. He stared down between his feet. Then, gazed all around him.

He and Khusrau were sitting under a canopy which had been erected at the summit of a large hill right in the middle of what had once been Babylon. The Persian Emperor's great pavilion was located not far to the north, just over the crest of the hill. The two men were alone, except for a handful of servants standing ten yards off.

The hill was the highest point in Babylon, and provided a magnificent view of the entire city. But there was not much left of that city, now, other than its outer fortifications.

Esagila, Marduk's temple, was still largely intact. That huge structure was just to their south. To the west, separated from the foot of the hill by a tall stone wall, the Euphrates carved its way through the soft soil of Mesopotamia. To the north, Belisarius could see the ruins of the ancient royal palaces. Next to them—still standing, almost intact—was the famous Ishtar Gate.

Other than that—

The huge eastern portion of Babylon—almost three-quarters of its entire area—was now farmland, dotted here and there with orchards and livestock pens. And the hill which they sat upon had been the site of a thriving village. On their way up its slopes, they had passed the huts where peasants had succeeded, centuries later, to the former thrones of ancient monarchs.

The peasants were gone from the village, now. The huts had been sequestered for their use by Khusrau's bodyguard. But the farmland was still in use. Belisarius could see men and women at work in those fields, surrounded by Babylon's walls. He noted, with some interest, that none of those people even bothered to look up at the sound of the Malwa cannons. The siege had gone on for months now, and they had grown accustomed to it.

His attention came back to the hill itself. Perhaps half a mile in circumference, several hundred feet high—it was the most elevated spot in Babylon, which was why Khusrau had chosen to pitch his pavilion here—it seemed, to all outward appearances, a hill like many others.

Except—

"It's quite regular, now that I think about it," he mused. "The circumference is almost a perfect circle."

"Not quite," demurred Khusrau. The Emperor leaned forward and pointed quickly to the southwestern and southeastern portions of the hill base.

"If you study it very closely, you can still find traces of the original four corners. The same is true on the northeast and northwest side." Here he gestured with his head, flicking it back over his shoulders in either direction. "I had my architects examine the hill at great length. They even dug a tunnel deep into it from the north. Thirty yards in, they began encountering the baked brick walls of what seems to have been a gigantic ziggurat."

He leaned back, exuding satisfaction. "It's the Tower of Babel of ancient legend. I'm quite sure of it. Crumbling slowly, century after century. Covered with wind-blown soil, century after century. Until it is as you see today. This is not uncommon, by the way. There are many hills like this in Mesopotamia, which are all that's left of ancient ruins."

Belisarius eyed the Emperor with respect. "That must have been a lot of work."

Khusrau laughed.

"Not for me!"

The gaiety vanished. "I was curious, true. But I also needed projects to keep my men occupied. Once it became clear that the Malwa could not break the walls without long effort, and that we would not face starvation, tedium became our worst enemy. You know from experience, I'm sure, how dangerous it can be to have a garrison fretting away their time in idleness."

Belisarius nodded.

"Besides, I was making plans for the future. We are digging out great tunnels and rooms inside this hill. For food storage, and, I hope, ammunition. The food will not spoil quickly—the interior of the hill is much cooler than it is outside. And even if the Malwa eventually breach the outer fortifications, and can move their guns close enough to bombard Babylon's interior, a direct hit on the hill would pose no danger to gunpowder stored deep within its depths."

The Persian Emperor fell silent here, fixing Belisarius with his intense, intelligent eyes.

The Roman general met that gaze squarely. The moment had come, and it could be postponed no further.

"I have already argued in favor of giving gunpowder weapons to the Aryans, Emperor Khusrau. I have gone further, in fact. I have argued that we should give Persians the secret of their manufacture. But—"

"The Empress does not agree," finished Khusrau.

Belisarius fluttered his right hand, indicating that the matter was not quite so simple. "Yes—and no. She agrees that it would aid the war against Malwa. Aid it immensely, in fact. But she fears the repercussions in the future."

Khusrau nodded, calmly. The Emperor of Persia had no difficulty understanding the quandary which faced Rome's ruler. Someday, hopefully, Malwa would be gone. Rome and Persia, on the other hand—those two great Empires had clashed for centuries.

Aide's voice spoke. Belisarius could sense the agitation of the facets.

Stupid woman! She is so unreasonable about this!

The general had to physically restrain himself from making an actual calming gesture. Fortunately, from long experience, he had learned to keep his interchanges with Aide unnoticeable to the people around him. Still, it was distracting, and—

This is not the time for that, Aide!

The facets subsided, grudgingly. Belisarius brought his attention back to the Emperor. Khusrau was speaking.

"I understand her suspicions," he mused. "And, unfortunately, there is nothing I can say or do that would alleviate them. We can swear to a Hundred Years' Peace—we can swear to a *Thousand* Years' Peace, for that matter. But Rome and Persia will still be there, long after Theodora and I are gone. Who is to know if that peace would be kept? Or if Persian and Roman armies would not clash again, on the field of battle, armed this time with cannons and rockets?"

Aide could not control his frustration.

So what? The problem is now—with Malwa! If that problem is not solved, Rome and Persia *won't* be there a century from now to be worrying about this. And besides—

Be quiet! commanded Belisarius. It was one of the few times he had ever been abrupt with Aide. The facets immediately skittered in retreat.

Belisarius could sense the hurt feelings emanating from Aide. He was not concerned. They weren't hurt much. Aide reminded him, in that moment, of a child obeying an adult's command. Sulking, pouting; thinking dark thoughts about cosmic injustice.

But he needed to concentrate on the problem before him. And he already knew Aide's opinion. During the days at Constantinople when this very question had been thrashed out by Theodora and her advisers, Aide had practically overwhelmed him with visions drawn from the human future.

A thousand visions, it had seemed. The ones he remembered best had been the portraits of the British Raj's conquest of India. "Conquest" was not, even, the right term. The establishment of British rule would be a long and complex process which, in the end, would not primarily be decided by military factors. True, the British would have guns. But so, soon enough, would the Indian rajahs who opposed them. Yet those Indian monarchs would never match the superior political, social and economic organization of the British.

For the same reason, Aide had argued, giving the secret of gunpowder to Persia posed no long term threat to Rome. It was not weapons technology, by itself, which ever determined the balance of power between empires and nations. It was the entirety of the societies themselves.

Rome was a cosmopolitan empire, rich in traders, merchants and manufacturers. And, for all the elaborate pomp of its official aristocracy, it was a society open to talent. To a degree, at least.

Persia was none of those things. The Empire of the Aryans was a thoroughly feudal society. It had nothing like the population of Rome, and was positively dwarfed in terms of industry and manufacture. The military equality which Persia had been able to maintain vis-a-vis its western rival was entirely due to the ferocious skill of its heavy cavalry.

Introduce gunpowder into that mix, and the result would be the exact opposite of Theodora's worst fears. Within half a century, Aide had predicted, Persia would be no match for Rome at all.

Belisarius had agreed with Aide, then, and had argued that very case. Along with the more pressing point that the defeat of Malwa overrode all other concerns.

But Theodora—

He shook his head. "She is a suspicious woman, I'm afraid."

Khusrau chuckled. "Nonsense, Belisarius. *All* emperors are suspicious. Trust me on this point. I speak from experience. Even your own brothers—"

He bit off the sentence. "We will discuss that problem later. For now, I must officially request that the Roman Empire provide us with a gunpowder capability."

The Emperor gestured to the south. "As you can see, we have been able to hold them off so far with traditional weapons. But I must do more, Belisarius." He clenched his fist. "I must *break* this siege."

He sighed. "We made one attempt at a sally, early on. It was a foolish gesture. I cursed myself for it, then, and damn myself for it to this day. Our soldiers were butchered. As soon as they came within range, the Malwa fired on us with those great siege guns. Loaded, this time, not with great stone balls but a multitude of pebbles and pieces of iron."

"Cannister," said Belisarius.

"They stood no chance at all. The slaughter was horrible, even in the short time before I ordered the retreat."

He wiped his face, in a gesture combining sorrow with self-reproach. But Khusrau was not deflected from his purpose.

"I *must* break the siege—within a year, no more. And for that I need my own cannons. The Malwa siegeworks are not as strong as the walls of Babylon, of course, but they are still strong enough to repel a sally. Only cannons in the hands of my own troops could shatter them enough for a successful counter-attack."

Belisarius frowned.

"Why are you so certain that you *must* break the siege—within a year?"

He turned a bit in his chair, staring to the south.

"I do not think the Malwa will break into Babylon. Not unless they bring twice the force to bear. And as powerful as they are, the Malwa are not *that* powerful."

His eyes now scanned the flooded lowlands to the west. "It's true that you will begin suffering from disease, soon enough, especially with the marshes. But disease usually strikes the besieger worse than the besieged."

He turned back, glancing to the east—to the

enormous spread of agricultural land within the walls of Babylon—before adding, "They will have to starve you out. And I think that would take many years. Even if you can't grow everything you need right here in Babylon, you can import the rest. The city is not surrounded, after all. We marched in from the north with no opposition. I'm quite sure you can bring barges down the river."

Khusrau waved his hand.

"I'm not worried about *Babylon*, general. I will hold Babylon, of that I have no doubt. But what good will that do me if I lose the rest of Persia?"

Again, he sighed. "They have me penned here, along with most of my army. While they send out raiding parties to ravage Mesopotamia—"

He broke off, for a moment, barking a laugh.

"One less, now—thanks to you! But, still, there are others, destroying everything they can. And what is worse—" He half-rose from his throne, stretching his arm and pointing to the northeast. "They have that damned army marching into eastern Persia. Defeating every force I send against them!"

Belisarius cocked his eyebrow. Khusrau fell back in his throne, nodding bitterly.

"Oh, yes. They win every battle we fight."

For a moment, he scowled. The expression was more one of puzzlement than anger.

"Odd, really. I can't say I've been very impressed by the *quality* of the Malwa army. Not here in Mesopotamia, that's for sure. Immense numbers and gunpowder are what make them powerful. It's certainly not the skill of their commanders. But in the east, where they have little in the way of gunpowder weapons, their forces fight supremely well."

"I'm not surprised, Emperor. Those forces are mainly Rajput, under the command of Rana Sanga. I know him personally. The Rajputs are among the world's finest cavalry—Rana Sanga is certainly among the world's finest generals. And the Malwa who is in overall command of that army, Lord Damodara, is also said to be their best."

"Said? By whom?"

Belisarius smiled crookedly.

"By Rana Sanga, as it happens."

"Ah." The Persian Emperor gripped the armrests tightly. He took a deep breath.

"That explains much. It also illustrates my quandary. I can hold the Malwa here at Babylon, but only at the expense of giving up my freedom to maneuver. If I retreat from Babylon, there is nowhere else I can make a stand to prevent the Malwa from seizing all of Mesopotamia. But if I stay—"

"The Malwa will gut everything around you. And, eventually, take Fars and the entire plateau from the east."

Khusrau nodded. Then, noticing that the goblet which Belisarius was toying with in his hands was empty, began to gesture toward the servants standing a few yards away. But Belisarius waved down the offer.

"No more, please." He set the goblet down firmly on the small table next to his chair.

"I will send instructions to Rome, ordering that cannons be brought to Babylon. Along with a large supply of gunpowder. That much is in my authority. I will also—" here he blew out his cheeks "—strongly urge the Empress to give me permission to train your soldiers in their use."

Khusrau stroked his beard.

"Do you think she will agree?"

"Possibly. She will insist, of course, that the cannons and gunpowder remain under the control of Roman troops. Still, they will be here. And then—"

Khusrau's lips curled into a faint smile. "Under the control of Roman troops," he murmured. "Yes, yes. That has a nice—ah, *secure*—sound to it."

For a moment, a Persian Emperor and a Roman general stared at each other, in silent conspiracy.

Belisarius broke the silence with a little laugh. "She is not naive, Emperor. Far from it! She will understand the inevitable results, once lonely young Roman troops—" He broke off, gazing into the distance. "It's amazing," he mused, "how many beautiful women you Aryans seem to produce."

Khusrau grinned. "We are a comely folk. It cannot be denied." The grin faded. "But you think the Empress Regent will still agree?"

Belisarius nodded. "It will be enough, I think, if Theodora can tell her suspicions that she didn't actually *give* the secrets outright. At least the damned Persians had to sweat for them."

"In a manner of speaking," chuckled Khusrau. He planted his hands on his knees and rose to his feet. As always, the movement was quick and energetic.

"Speaking of beautiful Persian girls," he said, "I have ordered a reception tonight in my pavilion. In honor of Merena's daughter, now married to one of your top commanders. She accompanied him here, I understand."

Belisarius rose, nodding. "Yes, she did. She insisted on it, apparently, much to Agathius' surprise."

The Persian Emperor began leading the way toward the pavilion. He cocked his head.

"Was he angry? Did he really believe all those tales about obedient Persian wives?"

Belisarius laughed. "Actually, he was quite pleased. He's very taken by the girl, I think. It was not simply a marriage of ambition."

Khusrau smiled. "Good. That bodes well for the future. Most auspicious, that wedding—I would like to see more of them."

"So would I," agreed Belisarius.

As they walked slowly toward the pavilion, Khusrau's smile turned a bit sly. "That's part of the reason, of course—well, actually, it is *the* reason—that I commanded this little reception. Once my haughty nobles see the favor which their Emperor bestows on such marriages, they'll find a daughter or two to marry off to some promising Roman officer. Oh, be sure of it—be sure of it! We Aryans like to talk about the purity of our bloodlines, but we are by no means immune to ambition ourselves."

He paused for a moment, struck by the sunset. Belisarius joined him in that admiration.

"It is a beautiful world, in truth, for all the evil in it. Let us never lose sight of that, Belisarius, however dark the future may seem."

The Emperor shook his head, glancing at the pavilion. "Speaking of dark futures—and a near one, at that—my brother Ormazd will be at the reception." He scowled fiercely. "I will have to be polite to him, of course. In the end, he did not—quite!—disobey me."

Belisarius snorted. "It was amazing, actually, how quickly he made his decision. Once Baresmanas and I showed up at his camp outside Ctesiphon, with almost twenty thousand troops *and* the aura of our victory at Anatha. He did not even dawdle, during the march here."

"I should think not," snarled the Emperor. "He had a lot of face-saving to do."

The Roman general's smile faded. Belisarius turned to face Khusrau, his gaze intent. He said nothing. There was no need to explain—not with *this* emperor.

Khusrau sighed.

"Yes, Belisarius. I agree. You have my permission to implement your plan."

Belisarius hesitated. "Do you understand—did Baresmanas explain it to you *fully?* At the end—"

Khusrau made a short, chopping gesture with his hand. "Yes, I understand. I will have to trust you."

"I will give you my oath, if you so desire."

The Emperor laughed, now, quite cheerfully.

"Nonsense! I don't want *your* oath. I want—those two bodyguards of yours? That is their permanent duty?"

Belisarius nodded.

Khusrau took the general by the arm and resumed their progress toward the pavilion. His stride was no longer the leisurely amble of a man enjoying the sunset. It was the determined pace of a decisive man, who had made up his mind.

"Good," he announced. "They will be at the reception, then. I will want to meet with them privately."

Belisarius' eyes widened.

"Privately? With Valentinian and Anastasius? Whatever for?"

"I want *their* oath. To keep you safe and alive, at all costs."

He eyed the general. "Even if that means binding you with ropes and hitting you over the head, to keep you from any more of the cavalry charges for which you have become quite famous. Among my dehgans, no less!"

The Emperor shook his head. "Any general who can impress *dehgans* with his heroism and disregard for personal safety needs close supervision. *Strict* supervision."

They were almost at the pavilion, now.

"That Anastasius fellow? Is he the gigantic one?"

Belisarius nodded. Khusrau stopped at the pavilion's entrance, eyeing the general up and down, much like a man estimating livestock.

"Yes, yes," he murmured. "He should have no difficulty. Even if it comes to shackling you."

He turned and strode within. And called over his shoulder:

"I will have *his* oath on it!"

Anastasius kept a straight face. Valentinian didn't even try.

"—in the name of God and his son Jesus Christ," they concluded simultaneously.

The solemnity of the occasion was undermined, of course, by the fact that Valentinian was grinning from ear to ear. But Khusrau did not seem dissatisfied with the result, judging from his own smiling face.

"Excellent," he pronounced.

Anastasius and Valentinian took that as their cue. A moment later, bowing respectfully, they backed through the silk curtains which separated Khusrau's private quarters from the main area of the imperial pavilion.

A little frown came to the Emperor's brow. He cocked his head toward Belisarius. "What did he say? The smaller one—he muttered something on the way out."

Belisarius smiled. "I think he said: 'God bless wise emperors.' But, perhaps I misunderstood. Perhaps he said—"

"Nonsense!" exclaimed Khusrau. "I'm quite sure that's what he said."

He took Belisarius by the arm and began leading him out. "Excellent fellow! Marvelous, marvelous! Even if he does look like a vicious weasel."

Belisarius kept his own counsel. Aide did not.

I agree. Excellent fellow. And Anastasius! Try to be philosophical about the whole thing, Belisarius. Perhaps you could ask Anastasius to quote some appropriate words from Marcus Aurelius, or—

What was that? You muttered something in your mind.

Chapter 26

THE EUPHRATES

"And the charges are laid?" asked Belisarius. "*All* of them?"

Seeing the hesitation on Basil's face, the general sighed.

"Don't tell me. You laid as many as you could, using the captured Malwa gunpowder. *But you didn't use any of our own.*"

Basil nodded. His eyes avoided the general's.

Belisarius restrained his angry outburst. He reminded himself, firmly, that he had chosen Basil to command the katyusha rocket force because the man was one of the few Thracian cataphracts who had a liking and affinity for the new weapons. It was hardly surprising, therefore, that he would be unwilling to dismantle them.

"Finish the job, Basil," he rasped. "I don't care if you have to use every single pound of gunpowder in our supply train—even if that includes emptying the katyusha rockets themselves. *Finish the job.*"

Basil opened his mouth; closed it.

"Yes, sir," he said glumly.

Belisarius resumed his study of the work which Basil had overseen in his absence. After a minute or so, he found that his ill-temper with the man had quite vanished. In truth—except for his understandable reluctance to disarm his cherished rockets—Basil had done an excellent job.

There was not much left, now, of the great dam which had formerly sealed off the Nehar Malka from the Euphrates. With the exception of a thin wall barely strong enough to withstand the river's pressure, the vast pile of stones had been removed and mounded up on the north bank of the canal. Already, a thin trickle of water was seeping through, creating a small creek in what had been the dry bed of the former Royal Canal.

Back-breaking work, that must have been, he thought. *Most of it, of course, was done by the Kushan captives.*

He cocked his head at Basil.

"Did they complain? The Kushans, I mean."

Basil shook his head. "Never the once. They didn't even try to shirk the work. Not much, anyway—no more than our own boys did."

Belisarius grunted with satisfaction. Here, at least, Basil had apparently followed his instructions to the letter.

"What rotation did you use? Three and one?"

"For the first week," was Basil's reply. "After that I went to one and one."

Belisarius' eyes widened.

"Wasn't that a bit—"

"Risky? I don't think so, general."

The katyusha commander glanced at Belisarius, gauging his temper, before adding:

"I thought about the way you handled their surrender, sir. Then, after the first week, I talked to Vasudeva. He gave me his oath that the Kushans would not try an uprising." The cataphract smiled. "Actually, it was he who insisted that we maintain half our troops on guard duty while the other half pitched into the work. After he gave me his oath, I was going to just keep a token force on patrol. But Vasudeva—"

Belisarius laughed, and clapped his hands. "He said it would be too insulting!"

Basil nodded.

Belisarius' usual good humor had completely returned. He placed an approving hand on the cataphract's shoulder. "Nice work, Basil."

Again, Basil eyed the general, gauging his mood. He opened his mouth to speak, but Belisarius cut him off with a shake of the head. Not an angry headshake; but a firm one, nonetheless.

"No, Basil. I won't reconsider. It may well be that the Malwa gunpowder alone would do the trick, but I'm not going to take the chance. I want that dam to rupture instantly—and completely."

He turned to face his subordinate squarely.

"Think it through, Basil. If the charges are insufficient, and we wind up with a half-demolished dam— what then? You know as well as I do that it would be a nightmare to set new charges, with half the river pouring through. Take days, probably—not to mention the lives it would cost. In the meantime, the Malwa down at Babylon would have those same days to try and salvage their fleet. If the Euphrates drops slowly, they could probably get most of their ships downriver to safety before they ground. They could certainly get the ships far enough from Babylon that Khusrau couldn't strike at them."

He didn't raise his voice, not in the least, but his tone was like iron:

"*I want that fleet grounded instantly, Basil.* I want the Euphrates to drop so fast that the Malwa are caught completely off-guard."

Basil took a deep breath. Nodded.

Again, Belisarius clapped him on the shoulder.

"Besides, man—cheer up. We should be getting a new supply of gunpowder and rockets from Callinicum. Good Roman powder and rockets, too, not that Malwa crap. A *big* supply. I sent orders calling for every pound of gunpowder available. We've got more demolition work ahead of us. Lots more."

Basil grimaced.

Belisarius, understanding that grimace, made a little mental wince of his own.

I hope. If the usual screw-ups with logistics aren't worse than normal.

But there was no point in brooding on that matter, so he changed the subject.

"What's your opinion on security?" he asked.

Basil's face cleared up instantly.

"It's beautiful, sir. Between Abbu and our scouts, and Kurush and his Persians, I don't think a lizard could get within ten miles of here without being spotted."

From their vantage point on top of what remained of the ancient dam, the cataphract pointed down at the Nehar Malka. "The Malwa have no idea what we're doing here. I'm sure of it. The one thing I was worried about was that the Kushans might try to sneak out a few of their men to warn the Malwa down at Babylon. No way to do that in the daytime, of course, but I had Abbu maintain full patrols at night and he swears—*swears*—that no Kushan ever tried to—"

"No," interrupted Belisarius, shaking his head firmly. "That wouldn't—how can I say it?—that wouldn't be something the Kushans would do."

Basil's brow creased in a frown. "Why not? Vasudeva's oath was that they wouldn't try a *rebellion*— or a mass breakout. He never swore that he wouldn't send a few men to report back."

Belisarius looked away. It was his turn to hesitate, now. He was as certain of his understanding of the Kushans as he was of anything in the world, but to explain it to Basil would require—

Aide broke through the quandary.

Tell him.

Belisarius almost started.

You are sure of this, Aide?

Tell him. As much, at least, as you need to. It will not matter, Belisarius. Even if he talks, so what? By now, Link will have deduced my presence in this world. At the very least, it will do so very soon. Much sooner than any loose talk among Roman troops could ever find its way to the ears of Malwa spies. Secrecy about me is not so important, anymore. Not as important, certainly, as the trust of your subordinate officers.

Belisarius sighed—with immense relief. He had always believed that his success as a general, as much as anything, rested on his ability to build a team around him. The need to keep Aide's presence a secret had cut across his most basic nature and instincts as a leader.

He was glad to be done with it.

Of course, came the firm thought, **that doesn't mean you have to turn into a babbling babe.**

Belisarius, smiling, turned back to the cataphract standing next to him. "I am—sometimes—blessed with visions of the future, Basil."

The Thracian soldier's eyes widened. But not much, Belisarius noted.

"You are not surprised?"

Basil shrugged. "No, sir. Not really. Nobody talks, mind you. But I'm not stupid. I've noticed how Maurice—and Valentinian and Anastasius, for that matter—get very close-mouthed about certain things. Like exactly how you got the secret of gunpowder from the Malwa—and somehow managed to get it to

Antonina in time for her to build a whole secret little
army in Syria before you even got back. And exactly
what happened—or didn't happen—in India. And
exactly how it was that you were so sure that the Malwa
would be our enemy, when nobody else ever gave India
more than two thoughts. And why did Michael of
Macedonia—*Michael of Macedonia?*—wind up such a
close friend of a general? And just exactly—"

Belisarius held up his hand, laughing. "Enough!"

He glanced around. He and Basil were quite
alone on top of the dam. The nearest Roman soldiers were the small cavalry escort waiting patiently
at its base. No Persians could be seen in the
vicinity—and there was nowhere to hide, anyway,
except in the reeds which lined the Euphrates. The
nearest clump of such reeds was thirty yards away.
Much too distant for any eyes to see the small thing
which Belisarius drew out of a pouch handing from
his neck.

He cupped Aide in his hands, sheltered from sight.
Basil leaned over, awestruck.

"Michael of Macedonia brought this to me," said
Belisarius softly. "Over three years ago, now. He calls
it the Talisman of God."

"It is so beautiful," whispered Basil. "I've never
seen anything so wondrous."

"It is a marvel. It is a messenger from the future,
who came to warn us of the Malwa danger. It did
so by giving me a vision of the future which Malwa
would bring to the world."

He paused, letting Basil absorb the shimmering
glory of the facets. "Later, I will tell you all of what
I saw, in that future. Indeed—"

He hesitated. Aide spoke.

Yes. It is time.

"I will tell all of you. All of the army commanders. It is time, now. But, for the moment—"

He spoke gently, then, for a few minutes. Telling

the cataphract Basil of the vision he had received, once, of a princess held in captivity by the Malwa. Held for them, by a Kushan vassal named Kungas. And he told how, in that future, the Kushan named Kungas had held his tongue when a Malwa lord had entered his chamber to take possession of his new concubine. Had not warned the great lord that his new concubine was an assassin. And how that lord had died, in that future, because a Kushan had his own harsh concept of honor.

And then he told of how, in the future which Belisarius had created, that same Kushan had held his tongue, once again. Held it, and said nothing to his Malwa masters, when he realized that the Romans were smuggling the girl out of captivity.

"And where is he today, this Kungas?" asked Basil.

Belisarius slipped Aide back into his pouch.

"Today, the Kushan named Kungas—along with all of his men—are the personal bodyguard of the *Empress* Shakuntala. The heir of Satavahana. Rightful ruler of great Andhra."

Basil looked up, startled. His eyes flashed south, looking toward the distant encampment of the Kushan captives.

"You think—?"

Belisarius shrugged.

"Who knows? Kungas is an unusual man. But in some things, I believe all Kushans are much alike. They have their own notions of loyalty, and duty. They are Malwa vassals, and have served them faithfully. But I do not think they bear any great love for their masters. None at all, in fact."

He turned away, and began climbing down the dam.

"Most of all," he added, over his shoulder, "they have their own peculiar sense of humor. Very wry. Rather on the grim side, too. But they cherish it quite deeply."

At the bottom of the slope, he waited for Basil to join him. Once he had done so, Belisarius grinned.

"I'm counting on that sense of humor, you see. The Kushans wouldn't warn the Malwa of what we're doing. God, no—it would spoil a great joke."

That night, in the gloom of his little tent, Vasudeva leaned over and filled Belisarius' cup.

"Good wine," he said. "Not enough, of course. The Persians are stingy. But—good. Good."

He and Belisarius drained their cups. Vasudeva smiled.

"We like to gamble, you know. So we have a great bet going. All the Kushans have taken sides." He shrugged modestly. "We have not much to wager, of course, being war captives. But it is always the spirit of a wager which is exciting, not the stakes."

He refilled Belisarius' cup. Again, he and the general drained their wine. When they lowered their cups, Belisarius stated:

"You are wagering over whether I will succeed. In my plan to drain the Euphrates dry and leave the Malwa stranded at Babylon without supplies."

Vasudeva sneered. Waved his hand in a curt, dismissive little gesture. "Bah! What Kushan would be so stupid as to bet on *that*?"

He refilled the cups, again. Brought his own to his lips; but, before, drinking, added with a little smile: "No, no, Belisarius. We are betting on what you will do *afterward*."

Belisarius managed to drain his cup without choking. Vasudeva's smile became a grin.

"Oh, yes," murmured the Kushan commander. "*That's* the real question."

He drained his own cup.

Vasudeva held up the amphora, in a questioning gesture. Belisarius shook his head, placing his hand over his cup.

"No, thank you. I've had enough. Tomorrow will be a busy day."

As he stoppered the wine jug, Vasudeva grimaced. "Please! We will be doing most of the busy-ness. And in that miserable sun!"

Belisarius rose, stooping in the low shelter provided by the simple tent. Vasudeva rose with him. Much shorter, he did not need to stoop.

The Kushan's little smile returned. "Still—that's the way it is. Really good jokes always take a lot of work."

Outside the tent, in the quiet air of the Kushan encampment, Valentinian and Anastasius were waiting with the horses. Quickly, Belisarius mounted.

Vasudeva had come out of his tent to see the Roman general off. From other tents nearby, Belisarius could see other Kushans watching. For a moment, he and the Kushan commander stared at each other.

"Why did you come tonight, Belisarius?" asked Vasudeva suddenly. "You asked me nothing."

The general smiled, very crookedly. "There was no need, Vasudeva. I simply wanted to know if Kushans still had their sense of humor."

Vasudeva did not match that smile with one of his own. In the moonlit darkness, his hard face grew harder still.

"It is all that is left to us, Roman. When men have little, they keep what they have in a tight fist."

Belisarius nodded. He clucked his horse into motion. Valentinian and Anastasius followed on their own mounts, trailing a few yards behind.

"Yes, they do," he murmured softly to himself. "Yes, they do. Until finally, when they have nothing left, they realize—" His words trailed into a mutter.

"What did he say?" whispered Anastasius, leaning over his saddle.

Valentinian's face was sour. "He said that damned stupid business about only the soul mattering, in the end."

"Quite right," said Anastasius approvingly. Then, spotting Valentinian's expression, the giant added:

"You know, if you ever get tired of being a soldier, I'm sure you could make a good living as a miracle worker. Turning wine into vinegar."

Valentinian began muttering, now, but Anastasius ignored him blithely.

"I thought it was a good joke," he said.

Mutter, mutter, mutter.

"A sense of humor's very important, Valentinian."

Mutter, mutter, mutter.

"Wine into vinegar. Yes, yes. And then—! The possibilities are endless! Turn fresh milk sour. Make puppies grim. Kittens, indolent. Oh, yes! Valentinian of Thrace, they'll be calling you. The miracle worker! Everybody'll avoid you like the plague, of course. Probably be entire villages chasing you with stones, even. But you'll be famous! I'll be able to say: 'I knew him when he was just a simple nasty ill-tempered disgruntled soldier.' Oh, yes! I'll be able—"

Mutter, mutter, mutter.

Early the next morning, construction began on the second phase of Belisarius' plan. The Roman soldiers played more of a role, now, than they had earlier. Undermining the old canal, except for the work of laying the charges, had been simple and uncomplicated work. Brutal work, of course—hauling an enormous quantity of stones out of a canal bed. But simple.

This new project was not.

Belisarius oversaw the work from a tower which his troops erected on the left bank of the Euphrates, just below the place where the Nehar Malka branched off to the east. The tower was sturdy, but otherwise crude—nothing more than a twenty-foot-high wooden framework, which supported a small platform at the top. The platform was six feet square, surrounded by a low railing, and sheltered from the sun by a canopy. Access to it was by means of a ladder built directly onto the framework.

There was only room on that platform to fit three or four men comfortably. Belisarius and Baresmanas, who occupied the platform alone that first day, had ample room.

The Roman general drew the sahrdaran's attention to the work below.

"They're about to place the first pontoon."

Baresmanas leaned over the rail. Below, he could see Roman soldiers guiding a small barge down the Euphrates. The barge was the standard type of rivercraft used in Mesopotamia and throughout the region—what Egyptians called a *skaphe*. It was fifty feet long by sixteen feet wide, with a prow so blunt it was almost shaped like the stern. The craft could be either rowed or sailed. The only thing unusual about this barge was that the mast had been braced and the sails were made of wicker—useless for catching the wind, but excellent for securing the baskets of stones which would eventually be laid against them.

A squad of soldiers were on the barge itself, shouting orders to the mass of soldiers who were doing the actual work of placing the barge. Many of those soldiers were on the riverbank, holding onto the barge by means of long ropes. Others were on the two barges which were serving as tugs—one directly behind, helping to hold the barge against the sluggish current; the other in mid-river, counteracting with its own ropes the pull of the soldiers on land.

Surprisingly quickly, the barge was brought into location about thirty yards from the riverbank. The barge was facing upstream, its bow heading into the current. The craft was riding very low in the water. From their vantage point, Belisarius and Baresmanas could see the stones in the hull which weighted down the craft to the point where it was almost already submerged.

The soldier in charge looked up at Belisarius. The general waved his hand, indicating that he was satisfied with the positioning. Immediately, two of the soldiers on the barge clambered down into the hull. Belisarius and Baresmanas could hear the hammering sounds as the soldiers knocked loose the scuttling pins.

A minute or so later the soldiers reappeared. The entire squad, except for their commander, clambered aboard a small boat tied alongside the barge. They attached the boat to a rope from the tub directly astern, and then released the rest of the ropes coming from that tug. The barge was now settling below the river's surface.

The squad commander quickly climbed up a ladder to the top of the barge's mast. There he remained, watching carefully as the barge sank into the river, ready to issue commands if the current moved it out of location. Not until the water was lapping at his feet did the squad commander climb into the small boat alongside. A moment later, the only thing visible was the upper three feet of the mast. The barge was securely grounded on the riverbed.

"That's the first one," announced Belisarius. "Well done, that was."

Already, another barge was being jockeyed into position next to the first. Baresmanas, watching, was struck by the speed with which the Romans scuttled that craft next to the first, further into the river's main course. And the next. And the next.

The sahrdaran said nothing, but he was deeply impressed. Persians had often matched Roman armies on the battlefield—outmatched them, as often as not. But no people on the face of the earth had that uncanny Roman skill with field fortifications and combat engineering.

"Will you have enough barges?" he asked, toward the end of the day. By then, eleven pontoons had been sunk.

Belisarius shrugged.

"I think so. The supplies are coming from Callinicum steadily now. Since there's nothing to send back on those barges, I can use almost all of them for pontoons."

He smiled, remembering the look of relief on Basil's face when the supply barges which had arrived the day before proved to be carrying an ample supply of gunpowder to refurbish his rocket force. Refurbish it—and more. New stocks of rockets had also arrived, along with three more katyushas and the crews to man them.

Belisarius glanced toward the west. The sun was almost touching the horizon. He decided there wouldn't be enough daylight to position another pontoon, and he didn't want to risk his men's lives in a night operation unless it was critical. For all the relaxed ease with which his soldiers went about their task, it was dangerous work.

So he leaned over the rail and shouted the order to quit for the day. His squad commanders, familiar with their general's attitudes, were obviously anticipating the order. The oncoming barge was gently grounded on the riverbank, where it could be easily pushed off the next morning.

On the third day, Belisarius shifted his operations to the other side of the river, where a similar command tower had been erected. While Maurice oversaw the work on the left bank, Belisarius started the process of extending a line of pontoons from the west.

By the fifth day, the operation was in full swing. The Euphrates, at that point, was a shallow but very broad river—almost a mile wide. Sinking twenty to twenty-five pontoons a day, the Roman engineers were building their dam at the rate which would, theoretically, bridge the river within a fortnight.

Of course, the rate at which the pontoons were sunk began slowing. As the dam took shape, the current became faster. And, what was worse, turbulent.

Two men were killed on the eighth day. After knocking loose the scuttling pins, they failed to emerge from the hold quickly enough. What happened? No-one knew, or ever would. Probably one of them had slipped, and the other had gone to his aid. But there was no time, now, for anything but haste. The river which poured into the settling hull was not the sluggish stream it had been. The water hammered into the barge and drove it down like a pile driver. Days later, one of the bodies floated loose and was salvaged downstream.

By the end of the second week, the Euphrates was a snarling beast. As the Roman engineers extended the two lines of pontoons closer and closer to each other, the center of the river became a thundering torrent of water. The rest was not much better. As the water level rose behind the dam, the entire Euphrates became a cataract, pouring over the line of pontoons all across its width.

Casualties were now occurring daily—a matter of broken limbs and crushed fingers, for the most part, but there were fatalities also. On the twelfth day, the entire crew of a pontoon perished when they lost control of the barge just at the point when they were preparing to scuttle it. The heavily weighted craft was swept into the narrow channel in the center of the river. Before it was halfway through, the barge disintegrated, spilling its men into the torrent. Most of them were dead by the time their bodies were recovered. One man survived for half a day, his skull shattered and pulpy, before he finally expired.

The Roman troops had the worst of it, since they

were doing the most dangerous part of the job, but those were not happy days for the Kushans either. Behind the Roman engineers extending the pontoons, the Kushans were set to work building the dam higher. Using their own barges, the captives hauled baskets full of stones and dropped them onto the submerged pontoons. The current piled the heavy baskets up against the wicker "sails." The strain on those sunken masts and spars would probably have broken some of them, except that the Romans had lashed the masts together as they extended the line of pontoons.

Most of the Kushans, however, were engaged elsewhere. The stones used to bolster the dam had to be hauled out of the surrounding landscape. Fortunately, there were many stones to be found within a mile of the river. Mesopotamia had been farmed for millennia, but the topsoil was constantly being blown away and annual plowing brought up another layer of stones. These stones, as the centuries passed, were piled at the center or edges of fields. So there was no lack of stones, and none of them had to be dug up out of the soil. But it was still hard work for the Kushans, loading sledges and dragging them to the river.

At first, the Kushans were disgruntled.

Crazy Roman!

Why doesn't the stupid bastard use the stones we already dug out of the Nehar Malka? Look! There's a giant pile of the things—not three hundred yards away!

Who ever made this idiot a general, anyway?

As the days passed, however, the Kushans began to realize that the cretin Roman general apparently had other plans for those stones. What those plans were, the Kushans did not know. They were no longer permitted in the vicinity of the Nehar Malka. But, from a distance, they could catch glimpses of Roman engineers working around the enormous mound of rocks which the Kushans had piled on the north bank of the Nehar Malka. Digging tunnels, so it appeared. And they noted that the men involved in that work were the same Romans who manned the rocket chariots. Gunpowder experts.

The betting among the Kushan captives intensified.

Kurush and his Persian soldiers were not involved in any of this work. Theirs was the task of ensuring the work-site's security. Every day, Kurush and his ten thousand Persian cavalrymen patrolled the region, extending their skirmishers to a distance of thirty miles in every direction. Abbu and the Arab scouts accompanied them in this work, as did a small number of the Roman troops. On a rotating basis, two battalions of Belisarius' soldiers—one cavalry, one infantry—were assigned each day to assist the Persians. In truth, the assignment was more in the way of a relief than anything else. After the back-breaking and risky work of building the dam, every Roman soldier looked forward to a day spent in a leisurely march.

Finally, on the nineteenth day, the last pontoon was maneuvered into place and scuttled. The Romans took four days well-deserved rest, while the Kushans finished the job of bolstering the pontoons with baskets of stones.

It was done. Twenty-three days' work had turned that strip of the Euphrates into a waterfall. A low waterfall, to be sure. But it was impressive, nonetheless.

The Roman troops and the Kushan captives spent the twenty-fourth day in a cheerful celebration, lining the banks and getting drunk while they admired the raging cataract which they had built. At Belisarius' order, the wine ration was very generous—as much for the Kushans as the Romans. A Malwa officer, had there been one present to notice, would have been outraged at the free and easy fraternization between captives and captors.

Belisarius and his top officers, however, did not join in the revelry. They spent that entire day in the general's command tent. The first two hours of that day were taken up with Belisarius' immediate plans.

The rest was given to awe, and mystery, and wonder.

As he had promised Basil, Belisarius brought his entire command into the secret. He told them the secret, first, using his own words. Then, when he was done, brought forth the Talisman of God.

Aide was prepared. The coruscating colors which filled the command tent were so dazzling that they caused the leather walls to glow.

Roman soldiers who saw, from outside the tent, whispered among themselves. *Witchcraft*, muttered a few. But most simply shrugged the thing off. Belisarius was—unique. A blessed man. Hadn't Michael of Macedonia himself said so?

So why shouldn't his tent glow in daylight?

Kushans also noticed, and discussed the matter. Here, the opinion was unanimous.

Sorcery. The Roman general was a witch. It was obvious. Obvious.

The wagering became feverish.

When evening fell, Belisarius' officers filed quietly out of his tent. None of them said a word, except Agathias. As the commander of the Greek cataphracts passed by Belisarius, he whispered: "We will not fail you, general. This I swear."

Belisarius inclined his head. A moment later, only Maurice was left in the tent.

"When?" asked the Thracian chiliarch.

"How soon can you reach Babylon? A week?"

"Be serious," growled Maurice. "Do I look like a pewling babe?"

Belisarius smiled.

"Four days," grunted Maurice. "Three to get there, and a day for Khusrau to make ready."

"Five days," countered Belisarius. "Khusrau should be ready, but an extra day may help. Besides, you never know—you might fall off your horse."

Maurice disdained any reply.

Early the next morning, Maurice left. He was accompanied by a hundred of his Thracian cataphracts as well as a squad of Arab scouts.

At the same time, one of Kurush's top officers—Merena himself, in fact—led a similar expedition to Ctesiphon. Their purpose was to bring warning to the residents of the capital.

The next four days, Belisarius spent overseeing the final preparations at the Nehar Malka. None of the Roman troops except Basil and his men were engaged in this work, however, so they spent those days resting.

By late afternoon of the fifth day, the entire allied force was thronging the banks of the Euphrates. Over twenty thousand men—Romans, Persians, Kushan captives—were jostling each other for a vantage point. Belisarius had to use his bucellarii to keep the onlookers from piling too close to the Nehar Malka.

The general himself was standing atop the command tower. He was joined there by Baresmanas and Kurush.

"You should not have made the announcement," fretted Kurush. "It was impossible to keep the security patrols out beyond noon."

Belisarius shrugged.

"And so? By the time a spy reaches the Malwa with the news, they will know already."

He leaned over the rail. Below him, standing at

the base of the tower, Basil looked up. The katyusha commander held a burning slowmatch in his hand.

Belisarius began to give the order to light the fuse. Then, hesitated.

"New times," he murmured. "New times need new traditions. 'Light the fuse' just won't do."

He sent a thought inward.

Aide?

The reply came instantly.

Fire in the hole.

Belisarius grinned. Leaned over.

"Fire in the hole!"

Basil needed no translation. A moment later, the fuse was burning. As it hissed its furious way toward the last barrier across the Nehar Malka, Basil began capering like a child.

"I like that! I like that!" he cried. *"Fire in the hole!"*

The cry was taken up by others. Within three minutes, the entire army was chanting the words. Even the Kushans, in their newly-learned and broken Greek.

"FIRE IN THE HOLE! FIRE IN THE HOLE!"

The fuse reached its destination.

There was fire in the hole.

Chapter 27

The demolition had been well-planned. So much was immediately obvious. Guided by Aide, Belisarius and Basil had emplaced the charges in the optimum locations to do the job.

Across most of its width, the lower bank of the dam blew sidewise, clearing an instant path for the pent-up energy of the Euphrates. The great river, now released, literally burst into the new channel opened for it. Raging like a bull, the torrent charged down the long-dry Nehar Malka, scouring it deeper and wider as it went.

But Belisarius was unable to appreciate the sight. As so often happens in life, practice subverted theory. The charges had been perfectly placed, true. And then, doubled beyond Aide's instructions; and then, doubled again.

Aide had complained, of course. Had warned, cautioned, chastened, chastised; been driven, in fact, into its own crystalline version of a gibbering fit.

To no avail. With the simple logic of men whose familiarity with gunpowder was still primitive, Belisarius and Basil had both insisted that more was vastly preferable than enough. Better to make sure the job was done, after all, than to risk a feeble half-result through cringing niggardliness.

Applied to the task of splitting a log with an axe, such logic simply results in unnecessary exertion. Applied to the task of demolishing a dam with gunpowder, however—

I told you so, groused Aide, as Belisarius watched the *top* layers of the dam sailing into the sky. Hundreds upon hundreds of rocks and boulders—tons and tons of stony projectiles—soaring every which way.

Not all of those missiles, of course, were heading for the tower where Belisarius stood. It just seemed that way.

Baresmanas and Kurush scrambled down the ladder first. The Roman general was halfway down—

Stupid humans.

—when the first rocks began pelting into the tower. By the time he was three-fourths down—

Protoplasmic idiots.

—covered, now, with wood splinters—

Glorified monkeys.

—the tower collapsed completely.

That probably saved his life, as well as those of Baresmanas and Kurush—and Basil, who had also instinctively sought shelter beneath the tower. The half-shattered platform hammered Belisarius and the other three men into the ground, battering them almost senseless. Thereafter, however, it acted as a sort of huge shield, sheltering them—in a manner of speaking—from the hail of rocks which would otherwise have turned two Roman officers and two Persian noblemen into so much undifferentiated pulp.

At the time, Belisarius found little comfort in the fact. The platform lying on him did not deflect the blows, in the manner of a true shield, so much as it simply spread the shock across his entire body. He was not pulped, therefore. Amazingly, none of his bones were even broken. But he did undergo a version of being pounded into flatcake, except that flatcakes do not suffer the added indignity of being lectured throughout the experience.

Crazy fucking Thracian.

Whoever made you a general, anyway?

It's amazing you even made it out of the womb, as stupid as you are. I'm surprised you didn't insist on finding your own way out. God forbid you should listen to your mother.

Crazy fucking Thracian.

Whoever—

And so on, and so forth.

It took his soldiers an hour to dig Belisarius and the others out, after the rocks stopped falling. The digging itself, actually, took only a few minutes. The delay was caused by the fact that his men had fled a full half mile away after the barrage started.

His first, semiconscious, croaking words:

"Did it work? I couldn't see."

His ensuing croaks, after being assured of full success in the project:

"Next time. Smaller charges."

"Much smaller," croaked Basil.

"Crazy fucking Romans," croaked Baresmanas.

"Whoever put him in charge?" croaked Kurush.

Others, also, failed to heed warnings. When Merena arrived at Ctesiphon to warn the governor of the oncoming tidal wave, the man responded with derision. Partly, that was due to his personality. Arrogant by nature, his recent naming to the post of *shahrab* of the Persian Empire's capital city had swelled his head even further. In the main, however, his attitude was determined by politics. The shahrab of Ctesiphon—Shiroe was his name—was allied with Ormazd's faction. The appearance before him of an officer of Emperor Khusrau's most ferociously-loyal follower, Baresmanas, seemed to him a perfect opportunity to score a political point. So, Shiroe responded to Merena's warning with jocular remarks on lunacy, embellished with denunciations of Romans and those Persians besotted with them, and concluding with a not-so-veiled thrust on the subject of miscegenation.

Merena's men had to restrain him.

After the unfortunate session, once Merena had calmed down enough to think clearly, he ordered his men to take informal and unofficial warnings to the boatmen plying their trade on the Tigris. As best they could, given their relatively small numbers, his soldiers tried to warn the city's fishermen and boat captains.

Approximately half of the men they were able to speak to heeded their warnings. The other half—as well as all the men they were unable to reach in time—did not.

When the tidal wave arrived, two days later, the destruction of property was immense. Few lives were lost, however. By the time the newly-released waters of the Euphrates reached Ctesiphon, they took the form of a sudden five-foot high surge in elevation rather than an actual wall of water. Most of the men caught in the river had time to scramble or swim to safety. But their boats, as well as a multitude of shore-lining structures, were pounded into splinters.

Shiroe's prestige plummeted, and, with it, the allegiance of most of his military retainers. The huge mob of enraged and impoverished boatmen whom Merena and his soldiers led to the shahrab's palace poured over the few guards still willing to defend their lord. Shiroe was dragged out, weighted down with chains, and pitched into the newly-risen Tigris. In those changed and raging waters, he vanished without a trace.

❖   ❖   ❖

In Babylon, on the other hand, everything went smoothly and according to plan. Khusrau had been preparing for this moment for weeks. The two days' warning which Maurice gave him were almost unnecessary.

Belisarius had deliberately blown the dam in the late afternoon, calculating that the effects of the river's diversion would thereby strike Babylon the following morning. That would give Emperor Khusrau a full day in which to take advantage of the new situation.

His calculations, of course, were extremely crude— simply an estimate of the river's current divided into an estimate of the distance between the Nehar Malka and Babylon. In the event, Belisarius' guess was off by several hours. He had failed to make sufficient allowance for the fact that the current would ebb once the built-up pressure of the backwater dropped. So it was not until noon of the next day that the effects of his work made themselves felt.

The difference was moot. The Persian Emperor's confidence in the Roman general was so great that he had decided to launch the attack at daybreak, whether or not the river level had dropped. It was a wise decision. As always, getting a major assault underway took more time than planned. Much more time, in this instance. The Persian troops, lacking the Roman expertise in engineering fieldcraft, required several hours to bring into position and ready the improvised pontoons which they would use to cross the Euphrates.

By then, alerted by the slowly-unfolding work of Khusrau's engineers, the Malwa had realized that the Persians were planning a sally across the Euphrates. But the foreknowledge did them no good at all.

Quite the contrary. Lord Jivita, the Malwa high commander, thought the Persian project was absurd.

"What is the point of this?" he demanded, watching the Persian preparations from his own command tower.

None of the half-dozen officers standing there with him made any reply. The question was clearly rhetorical—as were most of Jivita's queries. The high commander's aides had long since learned that Jivita did not look kindly upon subordinates who provided their own answers to his questions.

Jivita pointed to the Persian troops massing on the left bank of the river, just below the great western wall of Babylon.

"Madness," he decreed. "Even if they succeed in crossing, what is there for them to do? On the *western* side of the Euphrates?"

He swept his arm. The gesture was simultaneously grandiose and dismissive.

"There is nothing on that side, except marshes and desert."

He slapped his hands together.

"No matter! They will not cross in any event. I see the opportunity here for a great victory."

He turned to one of his officers, the subordinate encharged with the Malwa's fleet of war galleys.

"Jayanaga! Send the entire flotilla forward! We will butcher the Persians as they try to cross!"

With a fierce glower: "Make sure your galleys do not fire their rockets until the enemy's lead elements are almost across. I want to make sure we catch as many of them as possible on their pitiful pontoons. Do you understand?"

Jayanaga nodded, and immediately left.

Lord Jivita turned back to his examination of the enemy. Again, he clapped his hands with satisfaction.

"We will butcher them! Butcher them!"

The Malwa flotilla—forty-two galleys, in all—was almost within rocket range of the pontoon bridge

when the captain of the lead ship realized that
something was wrong.

His first assumption, however, was far off the mark.
He turned to the oarmaster.

"Why have you slowed the tempo?" he demanded.

The oarmaster immediately shook his head, pointing to the two men pounding on kettledrums.

"I didn't! Listen! They're beating the right
tempo!"

The captain's scowl deepened. Before the oarmaster had even finished speaking, the captain
realized that he was right. Still—

The ship was slowing.

No! It was going backward!

"Look!" cried one of the other officers, pointing
to the near bank. "The river's dropping!"

"*What?* Impossible! Not that fast!"

The captain leaned over the railing, studying the
shore. Within seconds, his face paled.

"They've diverted the river upstream," he whispered. "It must be. Nothing else could—"

He broke off, his attention drawn by the sound of
hooves pounding on wooden planks. *Lots* of hooves.
Upstream, he could see Persian cavalry racing across
the pontoon bridge. Dozens—hundreds—*thousands*—
of Persian lancers and armored archers were stream-
ing over to the west bank of the Euphrates.

Like his commander, Lord Jivita, the galley captain had been puzzled by the Persian sally. There had
seemed no purpose for the enemy to cross the
Euphrates, especially when the crossing itself would
expose the Persians to withering rocket fire from the
Malwa galleys. Who was there to fight, on that side
of the river? The great mass of the Malwa army was
concentrated on the east bank, south of Babylon's
fortifications.

Now he understood. The captain was a quick-
thinking man.

"They knew about it ahead of time," he hissed. "They're going to burn the supply ships."

He twisted, staring back at the huge mass of supply barges some half mile south. Already, he could see the unwieldy craft yawing out of control, driven by the rapidly ebbing waters of the river. Within a minute, he knew, they would start grounding. Helpless targets.

Especially helpless when there would be no war galleys to protect them. His own flotilla would be grounded also—not as quickly, for they had a much shallower draft—unless—

"Row toward the center of the river!" he roared. "Signal the other ships to do likewise!"

Immediately, the drums began beating a new rhythm. The Malwa had no sophisticated signaling system for controlling their fleet. But the captain of the lead galley also served as the commodore of the flotilla. The message of the drums was simple:

Do as I do.

But it was already too late. The drums had barely begun beating when the flotilla commander saw the first of his warships ground. There was no dramatic splintering of wood—the bed of the Euphrates was mud, not rock—just the sudden halting of the galley's motion, a slight tilt as it adjusted to the angle of the riverbed.

Nothing dramatic, nothing spectacular. But the result was still deadly.

Helpless targets.

The captain felt his own galley lurch, heard the slight hissing of mud and sand against the wooden hull. His craft jerked loose. Another hiss, another lurch. Jerked loose. *Stopped.*

A quick-thinking man. He wasted no time trying to pry the vessel out. The muddy soil of the river-bed would hold the hull like glue. Instead, he turned his attention to preparing his defenses.

"Move the rocket troughs around!" he bellowed. "Set them to repel boarders!"

His rocket handlers scurried to obey. One of them cried out, clutching his arm. An arrow was suddenly protruding from his elbow. The cry was cut short by another arrow penetrating his throat.

The captain spun around. To his despair, he saw that the enemy charging down the west bank had drawn parallel to his craft. Already, the first Persian lancers were guiding their mounts into the riverbed. Their pace was slow, due to the thick mud and reeds, but the powerful Persian warhorses were still driving forward relentlessly. They would cover the distance quickly enough.

There would be no time to bring the rockets to bear, he knew. And there was no chance—*no chance*—that his lightly armored sailors could withstand Persian dehgans in hand-to-hand combat.

A quick-thinking man. He began to shout his surrender. But fell instantly silent, hearing the warcry of the oncoming Persians.

Charax! Charax! Charax!

He understood at once that there would be no surrender. *No chance.*

He died eight seconds later, struck down by an arrow which tore through his heart. He made no attempt to evade the missile. There would have been no point. The enemy arrows were like a flock of geese. Instead, he simply stood there, silent, unmoving, presenting his chest to the enemy.

When all was said and done, the quick-thinking man was kshatriya. He would die so.

The Persians who saw were impressed. Hours later, they retrieved his body—the charred remnants of it— from the burned hulk of his galley. They carried the corpse back into Babylon, and gave it an honored resting place along with their own dead. Perched, in the Aryan way, atop a stone tower called a *dakhma*.

There, exposed to carrion eaters, the unclean flesh would be stripped away, leaving the soul pure and intact.

But that act of grace was yet to come. For now, the Persian cavalrymen thought only of slaughter and destruction. The dehgans and their archers rampaged down the west bank of the river for miles, destroying every ship within their reach. The huge Malwa army on the opposite shore could only watch in helpless fury.

Malwa officers drove many of their soldiers into the riverbed in an attempt to rescue the stranded ships. But the mud and reeds impeded those troops at least as much as they had the Persian lancers on the west bank—and the Malwa were far more distant. By the time the soldiers struggling through the muck could reach them, the ships would be nothing but burning wreckage.

The Persians were not able to destroy the entire fleet, of course. Many of the Malwa galleys and supply ships—whether through their own effort, or good luck, or both—wound up stranded on the east bank of the river. Those ships, protected by the nearby Malwa troops, were quite safe. They did not even suffer much damage from the grounding itself, due to the soft nature of the riverbed.

But all of the ships which grounded within bow range of the Persians were doomed. Those close enough for the Persians to storm were burned by hand, after their crews were massacred. Those too far into the center of the river to be stormed were simply burned with fire-arrows. Those sailors who could swim survived. Those who could not, died.

At sunset, the Persians broke off their sally and retreated back into Babylon. By the time the last dehgan trotted back across the pontoon bridge, almost a third of the Malwa fleet had been destroyed, along with most of the sailors who had manned those ships.

Those sailors were only the least of the casualties which the Malwa suffered, that day. An hour into the Persian sally, Lord Jivita ordered a mass assault against the walls of Babylon. The assault began almost immediately—his officers were terrified by his temper—and was carried on throughout the rest of the afternoon.

It is possible that Lord Jivita ordered the assault because he thought the Persian sally had emptied Babylon of most of its defenders. Possible, but unlikely. The Malwa espionage service had kept Jivita well-informed of the enemy's strength throughout the siege. A simple count of the Persians across the river should have led the Malwa commander to the conclusion that Emperor Khusrau had kept the big majority of his troops behind the city's walls.

No, Lord Jivita's action was almost certainly the product of nothing more sophisticated than blind fury. The petulant, squawling rage of a thwarted child. A very spoiled child.

The price was paid by his troops. Khusrau had read his opponent's mentality quite accurately. The Emperor had expected just such a mindless attack, and had prepared his defenses accordingly. The Malwa soldiers crossing the no-man's land were ravaged by his catapults and his archers, stymied by the moats and walls, butchered at the walls themselves by heavily armored dehgans for whom they were no match in close-quarter combat. The casualties were horrendous, especially among the Kushans who spearheaded most of the assaults. By the end of day, when the attack was finally called off, six thousand Malwa soldiers lay dead or dying on the field of battle. Thirteen thousand had suffered injuries—from which, within a week, another five thousand would die.

In all, in that one day, the Malwa suffered over twenty thousand casualties. Any other army in the world would have been broken by such losses. And even the Malwa army reeled.

Lord Jivita himself did not reel. His fury grew and grew as the hours passed. By sundown, his despairing officers realized, Jivita was still determined to press the attack through the night.

The abyss of total disaster yawned before them. They were pulled back from that pit by an old woman.

When Great Lady Holi clambered painfully up the ladder onto the command tower, silence immediately fell over the small crowd of top officers packed there. Even Lord Jivita broke off his bellowing.

The Great Lady cast only a glance at Jivita.

"You are relieved," she announced. Her empty eyes moved to a figure standing next to Jivita.

"Lord Achyuta, you are now in command of the army."

Jivita's eyes bulged. "You can't do that!" he screeched. "Only the Emperor has the authority—"

"Kill him," said Great Lady Holi.

The two guards stationed on the platform stiffened. Hesitated, their eyes flashing back and forth between Holi and Jivita. *He* was their commander, after all. She was—*officially*—nothing but—

Nothing—*but*. They had heard tales. All Malwa soldiers had heard tales.

The Great Lady's eyes were now utterly barren. When she spoke again, her voice was inhuman. Empty of all life.

"KILL HIM."

The guards had only heard tales. But the officers on that platform were all members of the Malwa dynastic clan. They knew the truth behind the tales.

Lord Achyuta's sword was the first to slice into

Jivita's belly, but only because he was standing the closest. Before Jivita slumped to the ground, five other swords had cut and sliced the life from his body.

The two guards were still standing stiff and rigid. Great Lady Holi's vacant eyes fell upon them. If she hesitated at all, it was for less than a second.

"KILL THEM ALSO. THERE MUST BE NO TALES."

Pudgy, middle-aged generals fell upon vigorous young soldiers. If the two guards had not been mentally paralyzed, they would undoubtedly have held their own against those unathletic officers. As it was, they were butchered within seconds.

Great Lady Holi lowered herself into Jivita's chair. She ignored the three bodies and the pools of blood spreading across the platform.

"CALL OFF THIS INSANE ATTACK," she commanded.

"At once, Great Lady Holi!" cried Achyuta. He glanced at one of his subordinates. An instant later, the man was scrambling down the ladder.

Reluctantly, Achyuta came to stand before the old woman. Reluctantly, for he knew that the aged figure hunched on that chair was only an old woman in form. Within that crone's body dwelt the spirit called *Link*. He feared that spirit as much as he was awed by it.

"DESCRIBE THE DAMAGE."

Achyuta did not even try to calculate the casualty figures. Link, he knew, would be utterly indifferent. Instead, he went straight to the heart of the problem.

"Without the supply fleet, we cannot take Babylon."

He glanced toward the Euphrates. The sunset was almost gone, but the river was still well-illuminated by the multitude of burning ships.

"Under the best of circumstances, we have been set back—"

He hesitated, quailing, before summoning his courage. Link, he knew, would punish dishonesty faster than anything. In this, at least, the divine spirit was utterly unlike Jivita. Mindless rages were not Link's way. Simply—cold, cold, cold.

He cleared his throat.

"Until next year," he concluded.

A human would have cocked an eye, or—something. Link simply stared at Achyuta through those empty, old woman's eyes.

"SO LONG?"

Again, he cleared his throat.

"Yes, Great Lady Holi. Until we can replace the destroyed ships, we will only have sufficient supplies to maintain the siege. There will be no chance of pressing home any attacks. And we have—"

He waved his hand helplessly, gesturing toward the invisible barrenness of the region.

"—we have no way to build ships here. They will have to be built in India, and brought here during the monsoon next year."

Great Lady Holi—*Link*—was silent. The old woman's eyes were still empty, but Achyuta could sense the lightning-quick calculations behind those orbs.

"YES. YOU ARE CORRECT. BUT THAT IS NOT THE WORST OF IT."

The last sentence had something of the sense of a question about it. Achyuta nodded vigorously.

"No, Great Lady Holi, it isn't. There will be no point in bringing a new fleet of supply ships if the river—"

Again, that helpless gesture. Great Lady Holi filled the silence.

"WE MUST RESTORE THE RIVER. THEY HAVE DAMMED IT UPSTREAM. AN EXPEDITION MUST BE SENT—AT ONCE—TO DESTROY THE DAM AND THE FORCE WHICH BUILT IT."

"At once!" agreed Achyuta. "I will assemble the force tomorrow! I will lead it myself!"

Great Lady Holi levered herself upright.

"NO, LORD ACHYUTA, YOU WILL NOT LEAD IT. YOU WILL REMAIN HERE, IN CHARGE OF THE SIEGE. APPOINT ONE OF YOUR SUBORDINATES TO COMMAND THE EXPEDITION."

Achyuta did not even think to argue the matter. He nodded his head vigorously. Asked, in a tone which was almost fawning:

"Which one, Great Lady Holi? Do you have a preference?"

The divine spirit glanced around the platform, estimating the officers standing there rigidly. It was a quick, quick glance.

"IT DOES NOT MATTER. I WILL ACCOMPANY THE EXPEDITION PERSONALLY. WHOEVER IT IS WILL OBEY ME."

Achyuta's eyes widened.

"You? *You yourself?* But—"

He fell silent under the inhuman stare.

"I CAN TRUST NO ONE ELSE, ACHYUTA. THIS WAS BELISARIUS' WORK. HIS—AND THE ONE WHO GOES WITH HIM."

She turned away.

"I KNOW MY ENEMY NOW. I WILL DESTROY IT MYSELF."

Moments later, assisted by the hands of several officers, the figure of the old woman disappeared down the ladder. Achyuta was relieved to see her go. So relieved, in fact, that he did not wonder for more than an instant why Great Lady Holi had referred to the man Belisarius as "it."

Personal peeve, he assumed. Not thinking that the divine spirit named Link was never motivated by such petty concerns.

❖   ❖   ❖

The next morning, from his perch atop the hill which had once been the Tower of Babel, Emperor Khusrau watched the Malwa expeditionary force begin their march to Peroz-Shapur and the Nehar Malka.

The sight was impressive. There were at least sixty thousand soldiers in that army across the Euphrates. At the moment, from what he could see, Khusrau thought the enemy force was infantry-heavy. But he had no doubt that they would be joined along the march by the mounted raiding parties which the Malwa had kept in the field, ravaging Mesopotamia. By the time that army reached its destination, he estimated, its numbers would have swelled by at least another ten thousand.

Most of the Malwa army's supplies were being carried on camelback, but the expedition was also accompanied by small oared warships which were being laboriously portaged past Babylon. Those vessels would have a shallow enough draft to negotiate the Euphrates upstream. The water level of the river had dropped drastically, but it was still a respectable stream.

He could see no siege guns. He would have been surprised to have done so. Weeks earlier, Belisarius had explained to him that heavy guns, even sectioned, require carts—or better, barges—for transport. Barges would be too heavy for the shrunken river, and, as for carts—how to haul them? Camels make poor draft animals, and horses could not manage a long and heavy-loaded march through the desert. There was no way to haul carts alongside the river itself, of course. The terrain directly adjoining the Euphrates was much too marshy—even more so now that the water level had dropped.

No, he thought with satisfaction, *it is just as Belisarius predicted. They will be restricted to rockets and grenades—weapons which they can carry on camelback.*

Without taking his eyes from the Malwa army, the

Persian Emperor cocked his head toward the man standing at his side.

"You are certain, Maurice? It is still not too late. I can order a sally against that force."

Maurice shook his head.

"That would be unwise, Your Majesty." With only the slightest trace of apology: "If you forgive me saying so."

Maurice pointed to the south. Even at the distance, it was obvious that the main force of the enemy was mobilized and ready.

"They're hoping for that. They'll be prepared, today. They've erected their own pontoon bridges across the river. If you make another sally, they'll overwhelm you."

Khusrau did not pursue the matter further. In truth, he agreed with Maurice. He had made the offer simply out of a sense of obligation. He owed much to the Romans, and he was a man who detested being in debt.

Inwardly, he sighed. He would not be able to repay that debt for some time. If ever. Once again, circumstances forced him to allow his allies to fight for him. The great Malwa expeditionary force would have no Persians to contend with, other than Kurush's ten thousand men. And those troops would be needed to defend Peroz-Shapur, which the Malwa expedition would bypass on its way to the Nehar Malka. Kurush and his men would tie up at least their own number of enemy troops, true. But they would be unavailable to help in the defense of the dam itself.

Once again, Belisarius would fight for him. Almost unaided.

A sour thought came.

Except, of course, for the aid of a traitor.

Khusrau squared his shoulders. The foul deed needed to be done. He would not postpone it.

He turned to one of his aides. "Send for Ormazd," he commanded.

As the officer trotted away, Khusrau grimaced. Then, seeing the slight smile on Maurice's face, he grimaced even more.

"And *this*, Maurice? Are you also certain of *this*?"

The Roman chiliarch shrugged. "If you want my personal opinion, Your Majesty—no. I am not certain. I suspect that Belisarius is being too clever for his own good." Scowl. "*As usual.*"

The scowl faded.

"But—I have thought so before. And, though I'd never admit it to his face, been proven wrong before." Again, he shrugged. "So—best to stick to his plan. Maybe he'll be right again."

Khusrau nodded. For the next few minutes, as they waited for Ormazd to make his appearance, the Persian Emperor and the Roman officer stood together in silence.

Maurice spent the time in a careful study of the enemy's expeditionary army. He would be leaving himself, the next day, to rejoin the Roman army awaiting the Malwa onslaught at the Nehar Malka. Belisarius would want a full and detailed description of his opponent's forces.

Khusrau, on the other hand, spent the time in a careful study—of Maurice.

Not of the man, so much as what he represented. It might be better to say, what the man Maurice told him of the general he followed. Told the Persian Emperor, not by any words he spoke, but by his very nature.

Belisarius.

Khusrau had spent many hours thinking about Belisarius, in the past weeks.

Belisarius, the ally of the present.

Belisarius, the possible enemy of the future.

Khusrau was himself a great leader. He knew that

already, despite his youth. Part of that greatness was due to his capacity to examine reality objectively, unswayed by self-esteem and personal grandiosity. No small feat, that, for an Emperor of Iran and non-Iran. And so Khusrau knew that one of the qualities of a great leader was his ability to gather around him other men of talent.

He had never seen such a collection of capable men as Belisarius had cemented together in his army's leadership. He admired that team, envied Belisarius for it, and feared it at the same time.

Crude men, true. Low born, almost to a man. Men like Maurice himself, for instance, whom Khusrau knew had been born a peasant.

But the Persian Emperor was a great emperor, and so he was not blinded by his own class prejudices. Pure-blood empires had been brought down before, by lowborn men. The day could come, in the future, when the peasant-bred Maurice might stand again on that very hilltop. Not as an ally, but a conqueror. On that hill in Babylon; on the walls of Ctesiphon; on the horse-pastures of the heartland plateau.

So, while they waited for Ormazd, and Maurice gave thought to the near future, the Emperor of Iran and non-Iran gave thought to the more distant future. By the time his treacherous half-brother finally made his appearance, Khusrau had decided on a course of action.

He would outrage Aryan opinion. But he shrugged that problem off. With Ormazd removed, Khusrau did not fear the squawks of Aryan nobility. He trusted Belisarius to remove Ormazd for him, and he would entrust the future of his empire to an alliance with that same man.

Ormazd's progress up the slope of the hill was stately—as much due to his horde of sycophants as to his own majestic pace. So Khusrau had time to lean over and whisper to Maurice, "Tonight. I wish to see you in my pavilion."

Maurice nodded.

When Ormazd was finally standing before the Emperor, Khusrau pointed to the Malwa expedition making its own slow way across the river.

"Tomorrow, brother, you will take your army and join the allied forces at the Nehar Malka. You will give Baresmanas and Belisarius all the assistance you can provide, in their coming battle against that enemy force."

Ormazd scowled.

"I will not take orders from a Roman!" he snapped. "Nor from Baresmanas, for that matter. I am higher-born than—"

Khusrau waved him down.

"Of course not, brother. But it is *I*, not they, who is commanding you in this. I leave it to your judgement how best to assist Belisarius, once you arrive. You will be in full command of your own troops. But you *will* assist them."

His half-brother's scowl deepened. Khusrau's own expression grew fierce.

"You *will* obey your Emperor," he hissed.

Ormazd said nothing. Put *that* way, there was nothing he could say unless he was prepared to rise in open rebellion that very moment. Which he most certainly wasn't—not in the middle of Khusrau's main army. Not after his own prestige had suffered such a battering during the past two months.

After a moment, grudgingly, Ormazd nodded. He muttered a few phrases which, charitably, could be taken for words of obedience, and quickly made his exit.

Later that night, when Maurice arrived at the Emperor's pavilion, he was ushered into Khusrau's private chamber. As he entered, Khusrau was sitting at a small table, occupied with writing a letter. The

Emperor glanced up, smiled, and gestured toward a nearby cushion.

"Please sit, Maurice. I'm almost finished."

After Maurice took his seat, a servant appeared through a curtain and presented him with a goblet of wine. Before Maurice could even take a sip, Khusrau rose from the table and embossed the letter with the seal ring which was one of the Persian Emperor's insignia of office. With no apparent signal being given, a man immediately appeared in the chamber and took the missive from the Emperor. A moment later, he was gone.

Maurice, watching, was impressed but not surprised. Persia had always been famous for the efficiency of its royal postal system. The man who took the letter to its destination was known as a *parvanak*, and it was one of the most prestigious positions in the imperial Persian hierarchy. In contrast, the Roman equivalent—the *agentes in rebus*—were more in the way of spies than postal officials.

Which might be good for imperial control, thought Maurice sourly, *but it makes for piss-poor delivery of the mail.*

As soon as they were alone in the room, Khusrau took a seat on his own resplendent cushion.

"Tell me about the Emperor Photius," he commanded. "Belisarius' son."

Maurice was puzzled by the question, but he let no sign of it show. "He's not really his son, Your Majesty. His stepson."

Khusrau smiled. "His *son,* I think."

Maurice stared at the Emperor for a moment, then nodded. It was a deep nod. Almost a bow, in fact.

"Yes, Your Majesty. His *son.*"

"Tell me about him."

Maurice studied the Persian, still puzzled. Understanding, Khusrau smiled again.

"Perhaps I should give my question more of a focus."

He rose and strode over to one side of his chamber. Drawing aside the curtain, he called out a name. A moment later, moving with stiff and shy uncertainty, a young girl entered the chamber.

Maurice estimated her age at thirteen, perhaps fourteen. The daughter of a high Persian nobleman, obviously. And very beautiful.

"This is Tahmina," said Khusrau. "She is the oldest daughter of Baresmanas, the noblest man of the noble Suren."

With a gesture, Khusrau invited the girl to sit on a nearby cushion. Tahmina did so, quickly and with a surprising grace for one so young.

"My own children are very young," said Khusrau. Then, with a little laugh: "Besides, they are all boys."

The Emperor turned and bestowed an odd look on Maurice. Maurice, at least, thought the look was odd. He was now utterly bewildered as to the Emperor's purpose.

"Baresmanas cherishes his daughter," said Khusrau sternly. Then, even more sternly: "As do I myself, for that matter. Baresmanas placed her in my care when he left for Constantinople with his wife. She is an absolutely delightful child, and I have enjoyed her company immensely. It has made me look forward to having daughters of my own, some day."

The Emperor began pacing back and forth.

"She is of good temper, and intelligent. She is also, as you can see for yourself, very beautiful."

He stopped abruptly. "So. Tell me about the Roman Emperor Photius."

Maurice's eyes widened. His jaw almost dropped. "He's only eight years old," he choked.

The gesture which Khusrau made in response to that statement could only have been made by an emperor: *August dismissal of an utterly trivial matter.*

"He will age," pronounced the Emperor. "Soon enough, he will need a wife."

Again, the stern look. "*So*. Tell me about the Emperor Photius. I do not ask for anything but your personal opinion of the boy himself, Maurice. You will say he is a child. And I will respond that the child is father to the man. Tell me about the *man* Photius."

For just a moment, Khusrau's imperial manner faltered. "The girl is very dear to me, you see. I would not wish to see her abused."

Maurice groped for words. Hesitated; vacillated; jittered back and forth in his mind. He was floundering in waters much too deep for him. *Imperial* waters, for the sake of Christ!

Then, as his eyes roamed about, they happened to meet those of Tahmina. Shy eyes. Uncertain eyes.

Fearful eyes.

That, Maurice understood.

He took a deep breath. When he spoke, his voice had more in it than usual of the Thracian accent of his peasant upbringing. "A good lad, he is, Your Majesty. A sweet-tempered boy. Not nasty-spirited in the least. Bright, too, I think. It's a bit early to tell yet, of course. Precocious lads—which he is—sometimes fritter it all away as they get too sure of themselves. But Photius—no, I think not." He stopped, bringing himself up short. "I really shouldn't say anything more," he announced. "It's not my place."

Khusrau's eyes bore into him. "Damn all that!" he snapped. "I only want the answer to a simple question. Would you marry *your* daughter to him?"

Maurice started to protest that he *had* no daughter—not that he knew of, at least—but the sight of Tahmina's eyes stilled the words.

That, he understood. *That*, he could answer.

"Oh, yes," he whispered. "Oh, yes."

Chapter 28

ALEXANDRIA
Autumn, 531 A.D.

As her ships approached the Great Harbor of Alexandria, Antonina began to worry that her entire fleet might capsize. It seemed to her, at a glance, that the soldiers on every one of her ships were crowding the starboard rails, eager for a look at the world-famous Pharos.

The great lighthouse was perched on a small island, also called Pharos, which was connected to the mainland by an artificial causeway known as the Heptastadium. The causeway, in addition to providing access to the lighthouse, also served to divide the Great Harbor from the Eunostus Harbor on the west.

Built in three huge "stories," the Pharos towered almost four hundred feet high. The lowest section was square in design, the second octagonal, and the third cylindrical. At the very top of the cylindrical structure was a room in which a great fire was kept burning at all hours of the day and night. The light

Eric Flint & David Drake

produced by that fire was magnified and projected
to seaward by a reflecting device. At night, the light
could be seen for a tremendous distance.

She and her troops had seen that light only a few
hours earlier, as her fleet approached Alexandria in
the early hours of the morning. Now, two hours after
dawn, the beam seemed pallid. But in the darkness,
the light of the Pharos had truly lived up to its
reputation. And now that they could see it clearly,
so did the lighthouse itself.

Her soldiers were absolutely *packing* the starboard
rails. Antonina was on the verge of issuing orders—
futile ones, probably—when a cry from the lookout
in the bow drew her attention.

"*Ships approaching!*" he bellowed. "*Dromons! Eight
dromons!*"

She scrambled down the ladder from the poop
deck and hurried along the starboard catwalk to the
bow. Within a minute, she was standing alongside the
lookout, peering at the small fleet which was emerging
from the Great Harbor.

Eight dromons, just as he had said. Five of them
were full-size, the other three somewhat smaller. In
all, she estimated that there were at least one and
a half thousand soldiers manning those dromons. Most
of them were oarsmen, but, after a quick count, she
decided there were well over four hundred marines
aboard as well.

Armed and armored. And the oarsmen would also
have weapons ready to hand, in the event of a boarding action.

As she watched, seven of the dromons spread out,
forming a barrier across the entrance to the Great
Harbor. The eighth, one of the smaller ones, began
rowing toward her.

She felt someone at her elbow. Turning her head,
she saw that Hermogenes had joined her, along with
two of his tribunes and the captain of her flagship.

"What are your orders?" asked the captain.

"Stop the ship," she said. "And signal the rest of the fleet to do likewise."

A pained look came on the captain's face, but he obeyed instantly.

"What did I say wrong *this* time?" grumbled Antonina.

Hermogenes chuckled. "Don't know. I'm not a seaman either. But I'm sure you don't just 'stop' a ship. Much less a whole fleet! That's way too logical and straightforward. Probably something like: 'belay all forward progress' and 'relay the signal for all ships to emulate execution.'"

Smiling, Antonina resumed her study of the approaching dromon. The warship was two hundred yards away, now.

"I assume that dromon is bearing envoys."

"From whom?" he asked. Antonina shrugged.

"We'll find out soon enough."

She pushed herself away from the rail. "When they arrive, usher them into my cabin. I'll wait for them there."

Hermogenes nodded. "Good idea. It'll make you seem more imperial than if you met them on deck."

"The hell with that," muttered Antonina. "It'll make me seem *taller*. I had that chair in my cabin specially designed for it." Ruefully, she looked down at her body. "As short as I am, I can't intimidate anybody standing up."

As she hurried down the catwalk toward her cabin, Antonina noted that the appearance of the eight dromons had at least had the salutory effect of eliminating the danger of capsizing her ships. The soldiers of her fleet had left off their sight-seeing and were taking up battle positions.

She stopped for a moment, steadying herself against a stay. Now that Antonina's fleet had come to a halt, the flagship was wallowing in the waves, drifting slowly before the wind. The sea was calm that morning, however, and the wind not much more than a light breeze. The ship's motion was gentle.

Searching the sea for John's gunship, Antonina spotted the *Theodora* within seconds. To her satisfaction, she saw that John was already tacking to the northwest. In the event of a conflict, the gunship would be in perfect position to sail downwind toward the dromons blocking the harbor.

Ashot came to meet her.

"There'll be several envoys from that ship"—she pointed to the dromon—"coming aboard. Hermogenes will usher them into my cabin. I want you and—" She broke off, studying the officers in the oncoming warship. Taking a count, to be precise. "—and four of your cataphracts to be there with me," she concluded.

Ashot smiled, rather grimly. "Any in particular?"

Antonina's returning smile was just as grim. "Yes. The four biggest, meanest, toughest ones you've got."

Ashot nodded. Before Antonina had taken three paces toward her cabin, the Armenian officer was already bellowing his commands.

"*Synesius! Matthew! Leo! Zenophilus! Front and center!*"

The first thing the visiting officers did, after Hermogenes ushered them in, was to study the four cataphracts standing in each corner of Antonina's large cabin. A careful study, lasting for at least half a minute.

Antonina fought down a grin. The visiting officers reminded her of nothing so much as four sinners in the antechamber of Hell, examining the denizens of the Pit.

Four devils, one in each corner. Counting arms and armor, Antonina estimated their collective gross weight at twelve hundred pounds. Two of the cataphracts were so tall their helmets were almost brushing the ceiling of the cabin. One of them was so wide he looked positively deformed. And the last one, Leo, was considered by all of Belisarius' bucellarii to be the ugliest man alive.

Not "cute" ugly. Not pug-nosed bulldog "ugly." *Ugly* ugly. Rabid vicious slavering monster ugly. Ogre ugly; troll ugly—even when Leo wasn't scowling, which, at the moment, he most certainly was. A gut-wrenching, spine-freezing, bowel-loosening *Moloch* kind of scowl.

Antonina cleared her throat. Demurely. Ladylike.

"What can I do for you, gentlemen?" she asked.

The officer in the forefront tore his eyes away from Leo and stared at her. He was a middle-aged man, with greying hair and a beard streaked with white. He was actually a bit on the tall side, Antonina thought, but he looked like a midget in the same room with Ashot's four cataphracts.

For a moment, the man's stare was simply blank. Then, as recognition came to him, his eyes narrowed.

"You are the woman Antonina?" he demanded. "The wife of Belisarius?"

She nodded. The officer's lips tightened.

"We have been told—that is to say, it is our understanding that you have been appointed in charge of this—uh—fleet."

She nodded. The officer's lips grew thinner still, as if he had just tasted the world's sourest lemon.

"The situation here in Alexandria is very complicated," the officer stated forcefully. "You must understand that. It will do no one any good if you simply charge into—"

"The situation in Egypt is *not* complicated," interrupted Antonina. "The situation is very simple. The *former* civil, ecclesiastical and military authorities have lost the confidence of the Emperor and the Empress

Regent. For that reason, I have been sent here to
oversee their replacement by people who enjoy the
imperial trust. On board this fleet are the newly-
designated Praetorian Prefect, Patriarch, *and* the
merarch of the Army of Egypt."

She pointed a finger at Hermogenes. The young
merarch was leaning his shoulder into a nearby wall,
the very figure of casual relaxation.

"Him, as it happens. May I introduce you?"

The four naval officers were goggling at her.
Antonina smiled sweetly and added:

"I will also be glad to introduce you to the new
Praetorian Prefect and Patriarch, as soon as possible.
But I'm afraid they are not on this ship."

One of the younger officers in the rear suddenly
exploded.

"This is absurd! You can't—"

"I most certainly can. I most certainly will."

The same officer began to speak again, but the
older officer in the forefront hushed him with an
urgent wave of the hand.

"We agreed that I would do the talking!" he hissed,
turning his head a bit.

When he looked back at Antonina, his lips had
disappeared entirely. The lemon had been swallowed
whole.

"I can see you are not open to reason," he snapped.
"So I will speak plainly. The naval authorities in
Alexandria—of which we are the representatives—will
take no sides in the disputes which are roiling the
city. But we must insist that those disputes be settled
by the city itself. We cannot agree—we *will* not
agree—to the imposition of a forcible solution by
outsiders. Therefore—"

"Arrest them," said Antonina. "All four." She spoke
softly, calmly, easily.

The officers gaped. One of them reached for his
sword. But before he could begin to draw the blade

from its scabbard, a hand clamped around his wrist like a vise. Zenophilus' hand, that was about the size of a bear's paw. The other huge hand seized the officer by the back of the neck. The officer began to shout.

Zenophilus *squeezed*. The man stopped shouting instantly. Began to turn blue, in fact.

The other three officers were likewise pinioned, wrist and neck, by the rest of Ashot's cataphracts.

"You can't do this!" shrieked the one in Matthew's grip.

Matthew was one of the cataphracts who almost had to stoop to clear the cabin's ceiling. He grinned cheerfully and *squeezed*.

Silence.

"Why not?" asked Antonina, smiling like a seraph. She made a little gesture at Matthew. The cataphract eased up the pressure on his captive's throat.

The man coughed explosively. Then, gasping: "Those dromons have orders! If we don't return within an hour, they're to assume that hostilities have commenced!"

" 'Hostilities have commenced,' " mused Hermogenes. "My, that sounds ominous."

He glanced at Ashot, leaning against the opposite wall in an identical pose.

" 'Hostilities have commenced,' " echoed the Armenian cataphract. "Dire words."

With a little thrust of his shoulder, Ashot stood erect. He and Hermogenes exchanged a smile.

"Dreadful words," said Ashot. "I believe I may defecate."

The officer who had issued the threat snarled.

"Make light of it if you will! But I remind you that those are eight *warships*. What do you have, besides those grain ships and that horde of corbitas? Two dromons—that's it!"

"Not quite," murmured Ashot. He swiveled his head, looking at Antonina.

She nodded. Ashot walked out of the cabin. Seconds later, his voice was heard:

"Send a signal to the Theodora! *The blue-and-white flag! Followed by the red!"*

A moment later, he ambled back inside the cabin.

"That means 'hostilities have commenced,'" he explained to the four arrested officers. Then, grinning:

"In a manner of speaking."

The captives were so busy staring at Ashot that they never heard Antonina's little murmur:

"'Cross the T,' to be precise. And 'fire broadside.'"

Aboard the *Theodora*, John of Rhodes and Eusebius were standing on the poop deck. Seeing the blue-and-white pennant, followed by the red, John whooped.

"Yes! *At last!* Now we'll see what this beautiful bitch can do!"

"Wouldn't let the Empress hear you say that, if I were you," muttered Eusebius. The artificer was standing next to John, clutching the rail. His face was drawn and pale. The *Theodora's* tacking against the wind had awakened Eusebius' always-latent seasickness.

"Why not?" demanded John cheerfully. "The ship's named after her, isn't it? Isn't the Empress a beauty? And isn't she just the world's meanest bitch?" Gaily, he slapped Eusebius on the shoulder. "But she's *our* bitch, boy! *Ours!*"

John pointed to the ladder leading to the deck below. "Get on down, now, Eusebius. I want you keeping a close eye on those overenthusiastic gunners."

Making his way gingerly down the ladder, Eusebius heard John bellowing to his sailors and steersman:

"Head for that fleet of dromons across the harbor! I want to sail right across their bows!"

When Eusebius reached the gundeck, he headed to the starboard side of the ship. On the *Theodora's* new heading, northwest to southeast, she would be bringing the five cannons on that side to bear on the enemy.

Soon enough, Eusebius forgot his seasickness. He was utterly preoccupied with the task of preparing the cannons for a broadside. He scampered up and down the gundeck, fretting over every detail of the work.

For once, the Syrian gunners and their wives did not curse him for a fussbudget and mock him for an impractical philosopher. This was not an exercise. This was the real thing. They would not be firing at empty barrels tossed overboard. They would be firing at front-line warships—which would be attacking *them*.

True, those warships had no cannons. But the word *dromon* meant "racer," and the sleek naval craft positioned at the entrance to the Great Harbour lived up to the term. Beautifully designed—elegant, in fact, as no tubby sailing ship ever was—they reminded the Syrian gunners of so many gigantic wasps, ready to strike in an instant.

Long, narrow—deadly.

By the time the *Theodora* was halfway to the dromons, the gunners had the cannons loaded and ready to fire. They were very familiar with the process, now, due to the relentless training exercises which Eusebius had insisted upon during the weeks of their voyage.

They had resented those exercises, at the time. The *Theodora's* gunners were all volunteers from the Theodoran Cohort. When the posts had been opened, the bidding had been fierce. Most of the Syrian grenadiers had wanted those prestigious jobs. Prestigious and, they had all assumed, *easy*— certainly compared to the work of toting grenades and handcannons under the hot sun of Egypt. Lounging about on a ship, never walking more than a few steps—what could be better?

They had soon learned otherwise. Within a week of setting sail from Rhodes, they had become the butt of the Cohort's jokes. The rest of the grenadiers had lolled against the rails of their transports, watching while the gunners were put through their drills. Watching and grinning, day after day, as the gunners sweated under the Mediterranean sun. Not as hot as Egypt's, that sun, but it was hot enough. Especially for men and women who practiced hauling brass cannons to the gunports, lugging ammunition and shot forward from the hold, loading the guns, firing them—and, then, doing it all over again. Time after time, hour after hour, day after day. All of it under the watchful eye of a man who, by temperament, would have made an excellent monk. The kind of monk who vigilantly oversees the work of other monks, copying page after page of manuscript, alert for every misstroke of the quill, every errant drop of ink.

A fussy man. A prim man, for all his youth. A nag, a scold, a worrywart. Just the sort of man to drive peasant borderers half-insane.

Now, as they stood by their guns, the Syrian gunners gave silent thanks for Eusebius. And took comfort from his presence. The young twit was a pain in the ass, sure—but he was *their* pain in the ass.

"Knows his shit, Eusebius does," announced one.

"Best cannon-man alive," agreed another.

Suddenly, one of the wives laughed and cried out, "Let's hear it for Eusebius! Come on! Let's hear it!"

Her call was taken up. An instant later, the entire contingent of gunners was shouting: "EUSEBIUS! EUSEBIUS! EUSEBIUS!"

Startled by the cheers, Eusebius stiffened. He knew

that a commanding officer was supposed to give a speech on such occasions. A ringing peroration.

Eusebius was no more capable of ringing perorations than a mouse was of flying. So, after a moment, he simply waved his hand and smiled. Quite shyly, like the awkward young misfit he had been all his life.

The smile was answered by grins on the faces of the Syrians. They were not disappointed by his silence. They knew the man well.

Their overseer. *Their* pain in the ass.

Above, on the poop deck, John of Rhodes smiled also.

Not a shy, awkward smile, this. No, not at all. John of Rhodes was neither shy nor awkward nor a misfit. True, his former naval career had been shipwrecked by his incorrigible womanizing. But he had been universally recognized by his fellow officers—except, perhaps, those whose wives he had seduced—as the Roman navy's finest ship captain.

He knew a fighting crew when he saw one. And now, understanding that Eusebius would give no ringing peroration—*could* give none—John made good the lack.

In his own way, of course. Pericles would have been aghast.

"Gunners! Valiant men and women of the Theodoran Cohort!"

He leaned over the rail, pointing dramatically at the seven dromons some three hundred yards distant. *"Those sorry bastards are fucked! Fucked!"*

A loud and boisterous cheer went up from the gunners and their wives. Then, coming from far off, John heard a faint echo. Puzzled, he turned and stared at the causeway leading to the Pharos.

The causeway was now lined with people. He could see more and more running down the Heptastadium, coming from Alexandria. Residents of the city, he realized. The news had spread, and Alexandria's people were pouring out to watch the show.

Alexandria's *poor* people, to be precise. Even at the distance, John could see that the men, women and children on the causeway were dressed in simple clothing. Alexandria's busy harbor area was surrounded by slums. It was the occupants of those tenement buildings who had first gotten the word and were packing the Heptastadium and, he could now see, every other vantage point overlooking the Great Harbor and the sea.

He grinned. "*Our* people, those."

Aboard her flagship, Antonina came to the same conclusion. She had come out of her cabin as soon as the four captured officers had been securely bound and gagged. Hearing the distant cheers, she studied the crowd lining the Heptastadium. Then, walked over to the starboard rail and stared at the dromon rolling in the waves not far from her ship. After disembarking the four envoys, the dromon had withdrawn some thirty yards and positioned itself facing her flagship. The oar banks were poised and ready for action. At the moment, they were simply being used to keep the dromon in position. But it was obvious to Antonina that the dromon would be able to ram her on an instant's notice.

She would not give them that instant.

She turned her head and called out for Euphronius. The commander of the Theodoran Cohort immediately trotted over.

Antonina gestured toward the nearby dromon with her head. "I want that ship obliterated. Can you do it?"

The young Syrian officer eyed the dromon. A quick glance, no more. "At that range? Easily. Won't even need to use slings."

"Do it," she commanded. As Euphronius began to turn away, she restrained him with a hand.

"I want a hammer blow, Euphronius. Not just a few grenades. If that dromon can get up to ramming speed, it'll punch a hole right through the side of this ship."

Euphronius nodded. A moment later, using gestures and a hissing whisper, he was assembling his grenadiers amidships. The grenadiers, Antonina saw, would be invisible to the seamen manning the low-lying dromon until they appeared at the rail itself, tossing their grenades.

Hermogenes came out of the cabin. Seeing the activity amidships, he hurried to her side.

"You're not going to give them any warning?" he asked. "Call on them to surrender?"

Antonina shook her head.

"I don't dare. That dromon's too close. If they have a warning, they might be able to ram us before the grenades do their work. And if they get close enough, the grenades'll pose a danger to *us*."

Thoughtfully, Hermogenes nodded. "Good point." He stared out at the nearby warship. He could see several officers standing in the bow of the dromon. They were close enough for their expressions to be quite visible.

Frowns. They were worried. Wondering what had happened to their envoys. Beginning to get suspicious.

"Fuck 'em, then," growled Hermogenes.

Antonina heard a low hiss. Turning, she saw that Euphronius had his grenadiers ready. At least three dozen of them were poised, grenades in hand. Their wives stood immediately behind them, ready to light the fuses. The fuses had been cut *very* short.

Casually, she gestured with her hand held waist-high, waving the grenadiers forward.

Do it.

The wives lit the fuses. The Syrians charged for the rail, shouting their battle slogan.

"For the Empire! The Empire!"

The officers on the dromon stiffened, hearing the sudden outcry. One of them opened his mouth. To shout an order, presumably. But his jaw simply dropped when he saw the mob of grenadiers appearing at the rail of the taller ship.

He never said a word. Simply watched, agape, while the volley of grenades soared into the air. Then, along with all his fellow officers, crouched down and ducked.

He must have thought the objects coming his way were stones. He never learned the truth. The six grenades which landed in the bow blew him into fragments, along with the bow itself.

Grenade explosions savaged the dromon down its entire length. The warship's orientation—faced toward Antonina's flagship, with its ram forward—was the worst possible position in which to avoid a grenade volley. Some of the grenades missed the ship entirely, falling into the water on either side. But in most cases the grenadiers' aim was true. And if one grenadier threw farther than another, it simply spread the havoc. The dromon stretched almost a hundred feet from bow to stern. Most of the grenadiers were easily capable of throwing a grenade across the hundred feet of water which separated Antonina's ship from the target. Many of them could reach halfway down the length of the craft, and some could heave their grenades all the way into the dromon's stern.

The grenades landed almost simultaneously, and exploded within three seconds of each other. Dozens of bodies were hurled overboard. Precious few of the men who remained in the ship survived, and they, primarily in the stern. The middle of the warship, where at least a dozen grenades had landed in the midst of two hundred men, was a mass of blood and shredded pieces of flesh.

The warship's hull had been breached, badly— outright holes, or simply planks driven apart. The sea poured in, pulling the dromon under the waves. Some of the surviving sailors began diving off the stern. Others, not knowing how to swim, simply watched their death approach, too stunned to even cry out in despair.

Without turning her head, Antonina spoke to Hermogenes.

"Rescue the ones you can," she commanded. "Put them under guard in the hold."

Antonina's eyes searched for the other dromons in the mouth of the harbor. The warships were stirring into motion. Already she could see the oar banks begin to flash. But, after a moment, she realized that only four of the dromons were heading toward her. The other three were moving to intercept the *Theodora*, bearing down on them from the northwest.

Trying to intercept the *Theodora*, that is to say. Even to Antonina's inexperienced eye, it was obvious that the gunship would pass across their bows with at least a hundred yards of searoom.

"I'm counting on you, John," she murmured. "Smash up some of those dromons for me."

On the *Theodora*, John was issuing new orders.

"Ignore those three heading for us, Eusebius!" he bellowed. "Concentrate your fire on the ones heading for Antonina!"

Eusebius did not bother to look up. Preoccupied with helping a guncrew lay their cannon, he simply waved a hand in acknowledgement.

Finally, satisfied with the work, he looked up at the enemy. Already they were crossing the bows of the three warships who had peeled off to intercept

them. The nearest of those ships was two hundred
yards away—much too far to be able to get into
ramming position, even given the greater speed of the
dromons.

Eusebius turned his attention to the other four
ships. The nearest of those was still three hundred
yards distant. Estimating the combined speed,
Eusebius decided they would be within firing range
in less than two minutes.

"Fire on my command!" As always, Eusebius tried
to copy John of Rhodes' commanding bellow. As
always, the result was more of a screech. But he had
been heard by all the gunners, nonetheless.

Again, he screeched:

"No broadside! Fire each cannon as it bears! On
my command!"

He scurried forward to the lead cannon. For a
moment, he almost pushed the chief gunner aside.
Then, restraining himself, he took a position looking
over his shoulder. Sighting, with the chief gunner,
down the barrel of the cannon.

Two hundred and fifty yards, now.

Two hundred.

They would cross the nearest dromon's bow with
a hundred yards to spare. Good range.

Eusebius blocked everything from his mind but
the dromon looming ahead. As near-sighted as he
was, the ship was not much more than a blur. But
it didn't matter. His decision would be based on
relative motion, not acute perception.

He and the chief gunner moved aside, so as not
to get caught by the cannon's recoil. The effort did
not distract Eusebius' attention in the least.

The moment came. He tapped the chief gunner
lightly on top of his leather helmet.

"Fire," he said, quite softly.

The cannon roared. Bucked; recoiled. A cloud of
gunsmoke hid the target.

But Eusebius wasn't looking at the target, anyway. He was scampering down the line to the next cannon. By the time he got there, the chief gunner had already stepped aside, clearing a space for the cannon's recoil.

He gave a quick, myopic look. Again, all he saw was a blur. Relative motion, relative motion—all that mattered.

He tapped the chief gunner's helmet. "Fire."

Down the line; next cannon.

Blur. Relative motion; relative motion. Tap. *Fire.*

Down the line; next cannon.

Blur. Relative motion; relative motion. Tap. *Fire.*

Down the line; next cannon.

Blur.

Blur.

No motion.

He looked up, squinting. Suddenly, the noise around him registered. Cheers. Syrian gunners cheering. Syrian wives shrieking triumph. And then, above it all, John of Rhodes' powerful bellow.

"Oh, beautiful! Great work, Eusebius! She's nothing but a pile of kindling!"

The chief gunner of the last cannon in line was grinning up at him. "That dromon is still floating," he said. "You want I should smash it up?"

Eusebius shook his head. "No, save it. There's more of them."

He squinted. Everything was a blur. He thought he could make out two ships clustered together, but—

Years later, the young artificer would look back on that moment and decide that was when he finally grew up. All his life he had been sensitive about his terrible eyesight. Yet, too proud—too shy, also—to ask for help.

Finally, he did.

"I can't see very well, chief gunner," he admitted. "Am I right? Are the next two ships lying alongside each other?"

The Syrian's grin widened. "That they are, sir. Bastards almost collided, shying away from the gunfire. They *did* get their oars tangled."

Eusebius nodded. Then, straightened up and screeched: "Gunners! Are the cannons re-loaded?"

Within seconds, a chorus of affirmative answers came.

Screech: "Prepare for a broadside! Aim for those two ships! *Fire on my command!*"

He leaned over, whispering, "Help me out, chief gunner. Tell me when you think—"

"Be just a bit, sir. Captain John's bringing the ship around to bear. Just a bit, just a bit."

The Syrian studied the enemy. Two dromons, a hundred yards away, just now getting their oars untangled. A fat, juicy target.

He tapped Eusebius on the knee. "Do it now, sir," he murmured.

Immediately Eusebius screeched:

"Fire! All cannons fire! All cannons—"

The rest was lost in the broadside's roar.

When the smoke cleared away, a new round of cheers went up. True, the broadside had not inflicted as much damage as the earlier single-gun fire had done to the first dromon. It hardly mattered. The rams of war galleys were braced and buttressed, but the hulls of the ships themselves were made of thin planking for the sake of speed. Those hulls had never been designed to resist the impact of five-inch diameter marble cannonballs.

One of the warships had been holed in the bow. Not enough to sink it, but more than enough to send it scuttling painfully back to shore.

As for the other—

The bow was badly battered, though not holed. But one cannonball, by sheer good luck, must have caught the portside bank of oars just as they were lifting from the water. Many of those oars were shattered. What was worse, the impact had sent the oarbutts flailing about in the interior of the galley, hammering dozens of rowers like so many giant mallets. Objectively speaking, the warship was still combat-capable. But its crew had had more than enough of these terrible weird weapons. That dromon, too, began heading for the Great Harbor, yawing badly with only half a bank of oars on one side.

On the poop deck, John was bellowing new commands. The four ships which had been heading for Antonina's flagship were effectively destroyed—one sinking, two fleeing, and the last floundering about with indecision. Antonina could handle that one on her own. John had his own problem, now.

The Rhodian brought the ship around to face the three dromons which had tried to intercept him earlier. The war galleys had chased after him and, with their superior speed, were rapidly approaching.

Not rapidly enough. By the time they got within range, John had brought the ship's port side to bear—with its five unfired cannons and fresh guncrews.

Eusebius was already there, prepared. John was a bit puzzled to see that the artificer had brought one of the chief gunners from the starboard battery along with him. He saw Eusebius and the man confer, briefly. Then, Eusebius' unmistakeable screech:

"Broadside! On my command!"

John smiled. As he often had before, he found the young artificer's boyish voice comical. But, this time, there was not a trace of condescension in that smile.

Comical, yes. Pathetic, no.

Again, he saw Eusebius and the chief gunner's heads bobbing in urgent discourse. The three dromons were two hundred yards away, their oarbanks flashing, their deadly rams aimed directly at the *Theodora.*

Again, the screech: *"Fire! All cannons fire! All—"*

Lost in the roar. A cloud of smoke, obscuring the enemy.

Screech: *"Reload! Reload! Quick! Quick!"*

John watched the guncrews racing through the drill. He gave silent thanks for the endless hours of practice that Eusebius had forced through over the Syrians' bitter complaints.

They weren't complaining, now. Oh, no, not at all. Just racing through the drill. Shouting their slogan:

"For the Empire! The Empire!"

The smoke cleared enough for John to see the enemy. The three dromons were only fifty yards away, now. He flinched. No way to stop them from ramming.

Except—

Their forward motion had stopped, he realized. None of the ships were sinking, true. Only one of them, judging from appearance, had even suffered significant hull damage. Still, the shock had been enough to throw the rowers off their stroke. The men on those galleys were completely unprepared for the sound and fury of a cannon broadside. Instead of driving forward in the terrifying concentration of a war galley's ramming maneuver, the dromons were simply drifting.

Again, the screech: *"Fire! All cannons—"*

Lost in the roar. Cloud of smoke. Enemy invisible. John leaned over the rail, ready to order—

No need. Eusebius was already doing it.

Screech: *"Cannister! Cannister! Load with cannister!"*

The smoke cleared. Enough, at least, for John to see.

One dromon was sinking. Another had been battered badly. It was still afloat, but totally out of control. Yawing aside, now, its deadly ram aiming at nothing but the empty Mediterranean.

But the third ship was still coming in. Not driving

for a ram, however, so much as clawing forward with broken oars and wounded rowers. Desperately seeking to grapple. Anything to get away from that horrible hail of destruction.

No use. John could see Eusebius at the middle cannon, fussing over the guncrew. The dromon was only ten yards away—close enough for the artificer's myopic eyes.

John saw Eusebius tap the gunner on his helmet. He saw his lips move, but couldn't hear the words.

An instant later, the cannon belched smoke. Cannister swept the length of the dromon like a scythe.

John of Rhodes was, in no sense, a squeamish man. But he could not help flinching at the sheer brutality which that round of cannister inflicted on the dromon's crew. Firing at point-blank range at a mass of men seated side-by-side on oarbanks—one oarbank lined up after another—

He shuddered. Saw Eusebius scamper down to the next cannon in line. Aim. Tap the gunner's helmet.

Another roar. Another round of cannister savaged the dromon. Blood everywhere.

Eusebius scampering. Aim. Tap. *Fire*.

It was sheer murder, now. Pure slaughter.

Eusebius scampering.

John leaned over, bellowing: *"Enough, Eusebius! Enough!"*

The artificer, his hand raised just above the next gunner's helmet, ready to tap, looked up. Squinted near-sightedly at the poop deck.

"Enough!" bellowed John.

Slowly, Eusebius straightened. Slowly, he walked to the rail and leaned over. Looked down into the hull of the dromon, which was now bumping gently against the *Theodora's* side. Studying—for the first time, really—his handiwork.

Under other circumstances, at another time, the artificer's Syrian gunners—country rubes, the lot of them, coarse fellows—would have derided him then. Mocked and jeered, ridiculed and sneered, at the sight of their commander Eusebius puking his guts into the sea.

But not that day. Not then. Instead, Syrian gunners and their wives slowly gathered around him, the gunners patting him awkwardly on the shoulder as he vomited. And then, after he straightened, a plump Syrian wife held the sobbing young man in a warm embrace, ignoring the tears which soaked her homespun country garments.

Above, on the poop deck, John sighed.

"Welcome to the club, lad. Murderers' row."

He raised his head, scanning the sea.

Victory. Total. Four ships and their crews destroyed. Three battered into a pulp. The only unscathed dromon racing away.

He looked toward Antonina's flagship.

"She's all yours, girl. Alexandria's yours for the taking."

Aboard her flagship, Antonina studied the situation. Studied the pulverized enemy fleet, first, with satisfaction. Studied the wildly cheering mob on the Heptastadium, next, with equal satisfaction.

Then, all satisfaction gone, she studied the city itself. Beyond the harbor, looming in the distance above the tenements and warehouses, she could see Pompey's Pillar. And, not far away, the enormous Church of St. Michael. The Caesareum, that edifice had been called, once—the temple of Caesar. Its two great obelisks still stood before it. But the huge pagan structure, with its famous girdle of silver-and-gold pictures and statues, was now given over to the worship of Christ.

And, of course, to the power of Christ's official spokesmen. The Patriarchs of Alexandria resided there, as they had for two hundred years. A hundred years after they took up residence, in the very street before the Church, a brilliant female teacher of philosophy named Hypatia had been stripped naked and beaten to death by a mob of religious fanatics.

"*Fuck Alexandria*," she hissed.

Chapter 29

SUPPARA
Autumn, 531 A.D.

By the end of the first hour, Kujulo was complaining.

"What a muck! Gives me fond memories of Venandakatra's palace. Dry. Clean."

Ahead of him, picking his way through the dense, water-soaked forest, Kungas snorted.

"We were there for six months. As I recall, you started complaining the first day. Too dull, you said. Boring. You didn't quit until we got pitched out of the palace to make room for the Empress' new guards."

Another Kushan, forcing his own way forward nearby, sneered:

"Then he started complaining about the new quarters. Too cramped, he said. Too drafty."

Kujulo grinned. "I'm just more discriminating than you peasants, that's all. Cattle, cattle. Munch their lives away, swiping flies with their tails. What—"

He broke off, muttering a curse, swiping at his own fly.

Ahead, Kungas saw the small party of guides come to a halt at a fork in the trail. The three young Maratha woodcutters conferred with each other quickly. Then one of them trotted back toward the column of Kushan soldiers slogging through the forest.

Watching, Kungas was impressed by the light and easy manner in which the woodcutter moved through the dense growth. The "trail" they had been following was nothing more than a convoluted, serpentine series of relatively-clear patches in the forest. The soil was soggy from weeks of heavy rain. The Kushans, encumbered with armor and gear, had made heavy going of the march.

When the woodcutter reached Kungas, he pointed back up the trail and said, "That is it. Just the other side of that line of trees begins the hill leading to the fortress. You can go either right or left. There are trails."

He stopped, staring at the strange-looking soldier standing in front of him. It was obvious that the woodcutter was more than a little afraid of Kungas.

Some of that fear was due to Kungas' appearance. The Maratha fishermen and woodcutters who inhabited the dense forest along the coast were isolated, for the most part, from the rest of India. Kushans, with their topknots and flat, steppe-harsh features, were quite unknown to them.

But most of the young man's apprehension was due to more rational considerations. The woodcutter had good reason to be wary. Poor people in India—poor people in most lands, for that matter—had long memories of the way soldiers generally treated such folk as they.

The woodcutters had agreed to guide the Kushans to the fortress for two reasons only.

First, money. *Lots* of money. A small fortune, by their standards.

Second, the magic name of the Empress Shakuntala. Even here, in the remote coastal forest, the word had spread.

Andhra lived, still. Still, the Satavahana dynasty survived.

For the woodcutter, Andhra was a misty, even semi-mythical notion. The Satavahanas, a name of legend rather than real life. Like most of India's poor, the woodcutter did not consider politics part of his daily existence. Certainly not imperial politics.

Yet—

The new Malwa rulers were beasts. Cruel and rapacious. Everyone knew it.

In truth, the woodcutter himself had no experience with the Malwa. Preoccupied with subjugating the Deccan, the Malwa had not bothered to send forces to the coast, except for seizing the port of Suppara. Isolated by the Western Ghats, the sea-lying forests were of little interest to the Malwa.

But the coast-dwellers were Maratha, and the tales had spread. Tales of Malwa savagery. Tales of Malwa greed and plunder. And, growing ever more legendary with the passing of time, tales of the serene and kindly rule of the Satavahanas.

In actual fact, the woodcutter—for that matter, the oldest great-grandfather of his village—had no personal memory of the methods of Satavahana sovereignty. The Satavahana dynasty had left the poor folk of the coast to their own devices. Which was exactly the way those fishermen and woodcutters liked their rulers. Far off, and absent-minded. Heard of, but never seen.

So, after much hesitation and haggling, the young woodcutters had agreed to guide Kungas and his men to the fortress. They had not inquired as to Kungas' purpose in seeking that fearsome place.

Their work was done. Now, the woodcutter waited apprehensively. Would he be paid the amount still owing, or—

Kungas was a hard, hard man. Hard as stone, in most ways. But he was in no sense cruel. So he was not even tempted to cheat the woodcutter, or toy with the man's fears. He simply dipped into his purse and handed over three small coins.

A huge smile lit up the woodcutter's face. He turned and waved at his two fellows, showing them the money.

Kungas almost smiled himself, then. The other two woodcutters, still waiting twenty yards up the trail, had obviously been ready to bolt into the forest at the first sign of treachery. Now, they trotted eagerly forward.

"And that's another thing," grumbled Kujulo. "I miss the trusting atmosphere of the Vile One's palace."

The Kushans who were close enough to hear him burst into laughter. Even Kungas grinned.

The noise startled the woodcutters. But then, seeing that the jest was not aimed at them, they relaxed.

Not much, of course. Within seconds, they were scampering down the trail toward their village ten miles away. Being very careful to skirt the five hundred Kushan soldiers coming up that trail.

Kungas strode forward.

"Let's take a look at this mighty fortress, shall we?"

Twenty minutes later, Kujulo was complaining again.

"I don't believe this shit. *Those* are guards? *That's* a fortress?"

Kungas and the five other Kushan troop leaders who were gathered alongside him, examining the fortress from a screen of trees, grunted their own contempt.

They were situated southeast of the fortress. The structure was perched on top of a small hill just before them. Two hundred feet tall, that hill, no more. On the other side of the hill, still invisible to the Kushans concealed within the trees, stretched the huge reaches of the ocean.

The forest which blanketed the coast was thinner on the hill. But not much. Some trees—mature, full-grown ones—were growing at the base of the fortress' walls. The branches of one particularly large tree even spread over part of the battlements.

"What kind of idiots don't clear the trees around a fortress?" demanded Kujulo.

"My *favorite* kind of idiots," replied Kungas softly. "Really, really, really idiotic idiots."

Kungas turned to face his subordinates. For once, he was actually smiling. A real, genuine smile, too. Not the crack in his iron face that usually passed for such.

"What do you think? Can we do it?"

Five sarcastic grunts came in reply. Kujulo pointed a finger at the fortress' entrance. The heavy wooden gates on the fortress' south side were wide open. In front of them, in the shelter provided by a makeshift canopy, eight Malwa soldiers lounged at their ease. Only one of them was even bothering to stand. The rest were sprawled on the ground. Two were apparently sleeping. The other five seemed to be engaged in a game of chance.

"Fuck the scaling equipment," growled Kujulo. "Don't need it. I can get my men within ten yards of those pigs without being seen. A quick rush and we've got the gate."

"How long could you hold it, do you think?" asked Kungas. The Kushan commander studied the trees growing on the hill. "You can get your men up there without being seen. But I don't think I can get more than three other squads close before they're spotted.

The rest of us will have to wait here until you start the attack."

He glanced up, gauging the weather. The sky was overcast, but Kungas did not think it would rain anytime soon. Not for several hours, at least. He lowered his gaze and examined the hill itself. Estimating the distance and the condition of the terrain.

"Five hundred feet. Muddy. Steep climb. It'll take us two minutes."

Kujulo sneered.

"Two minutes? You think I can't hold a big gate like that against *those* sorry shits? With the help of three other squads? *For a lousy two minutes?*"

Kungas was amused. Kujulo's complaint, this time, was filled with genuine aggrievement.

"Do it, then. Pick whichever other squads you want for immediate support. While you're working your way up the hill, I'll get the rest of the men ready for the main charge."

Kujulo began to rise. Kungas stayed him with a hand on the shoulder.

"Remember, Kujulo. *Prisoners.* As many as we can get—especially the ones who're manning the cannons. We'll need them later."

Kujulo nodded. An instant later, he was gone.

The other troop leaders did not wait for Kungas' orders to start organizing the small army for an assault. Kungas did not bother to oversee their work. He had hand-picked the officers for this expedition and had complete confidence in them. He simply spent the time studying the fortress. Trying to determine, as best he could, the most likely internal layout of the structure.

Despite the slackness of its guards, the fortress itself was impressive. A simple square in design, the walls were thick, well-cut stone, rising thirty feet from the hilltop. The corners were protected by round towers rising another ten feet above the battlements. Two similar round towers anchored the gatehouse guarding the entrance. Along with the usual merlons and embrasures, the battlements also sported machicolations—enclosed stone shelves jutting a few feet out from the walls, with slots through which projectiles or boiling water could be dropped on besiegers below. The open embrasures were further strengthened by the addition of wooden shutters, which could be closed to shield against missiles.

Those battlements would have posed a tremendous challenge—if the walls had been manned by alert guards. As it was, during the minutes that he watched, Kungas saw only four soldiers appear atop the fortress. From their position, it was obvious that they were moving along an allure, or rampart walk, which served as the fighting platform for the battlements. But the Malwa were simply ambling along, preoccupied with their own business. Not one of those soldiers cast so much as a glance at the surrounding forest.

He tried to spot the location of the three siege guns, but couldn't see them. He knew they were there. Days earlier, from fishermen brought aboard Shakuntala's flagship, Kungas had heard good descriptions of the fortress' seaward appearance. There was some kind of heavy stone platform on the fortress' northwest corner. Atop that platform rested the siege guns. From that vantage point, the huge cannons could cover the harbor of Suppara less than half a mile to the north.

But they were on the opposite side of the fortress from where Kungas lay waiting in the trees.

Inwardly, he shrugged. He was not concerned about the cannons, for the moment. The Maratha fishermen had no idea how those cannons worked, or were positioned. Kungas himself, for that matter, had only a vague notion. Despite the many years he had served the Malwa, he had never gotten a close look at their siege guns. The Malwa were always careful to keep their Kushan and Rajput vassals from knowing too much about the "Veda weapons." But he knew enough, both from his own knowledge and the information imparted by the Ethiopians, to know that such enormous cannons could only be moved with great difficulty. There would be absolutely no way the Malwa in the fortress could reposition them in time to repel the coming assault.

Speaking of which—

He thought that Kujulo was probably in position, by now. No way to tell for sure, of course. Kungas had selected Kujulo to lead the attack because of the man's uncanny stealth. Not even Kungas, knowing what to look for, had caught more than a glimpse or two of Kujulo's men as they worked their way carefully up the hill. He was quite sure the Malwa guards had seen nothing.

He swiveled his head slowly, scanning right and left. He was pleased, though not surprised, to see that his entire army was in position, waiting for the signal.

Satisfied, Kungas turned his eyes back to the fortress. As if that little head motion had been the signal, Kujulo launched his attack.

Kungas could not see all the details of that sudden assault. Partly, because of the distance. Mostly, because of Kujulo.

That was the other reason Kungas had picked the man. Quick, quick, he was. He and the men whom he had trained. Quick, quick. Merciless.

He saw Kujulo's ten men lunging out of the trees. They had gotten within ten yards of the guard canopy without being spotted.

Three seconds later, the killing began. Eight seconds later, the killing ended. Most of that time had been spent spearing the five Malwa gamblers, whose squawling, writhing, squirming huddle had presented a peculiar obstacle to the Kushan soldiers. Almost like spearing a school of fish.

Kungas watched none of it, however. As soon as he saw Kujulo's men lunge out of the trees, he gave the order for the general assault. Five hundred Kushans—less the forty already charging the gate— began storming up the hill.

It was a veteran kind of "storm." The Kushans paced themselves carefully. There was no point in arriving at the fortress too exhausted to fight. Kujulo and his men would just have to hold on as best they could.

That task proved much less difficult than it should have been. Before the alarm was sounded within the fortress, Kujulo and his squad had not only killed the eight guards outside the gates, but had managed to penetrate the gatehouse itself. The tunnel through the gatehouse was occupied by two other men, neither of whom was any more alert than the eight soldiers lounging outside the gate.

Kujulo himself killed the two Malwa soldiers in the gatehouse. That done, he immediately tried to find the murder holes. But, searching the ceiling which arched over the entryway, he could see none.

One of his soldiers trotted up to him. Like Kujulo, the man's eyes were examining the stone-work above, looking for the holes through which enemies could thrust spears or drop stones and boiling water.

"Don't see 'em," he muttered.

Kujulo shook his head.

"Aren't any." He spit on the stone floor, then made for the far entrance. His squad followed. Five seconds later, soldiers from the three squads serving as their immediate backup began pouring into the entryway.

The entryway—in effect, a stone tunnel running straight through the gatehouse—was thirty feet long

and about half as wide. The arched ceiling, at its
summit, was not more than twelve feet high. The
inner gate, opening into the fortress' main ground,
was standing wide open. When Kujulo reached it, he
saw that there were no Malwa troops standing guard.

"Fucking idiots," he sneered. He could hear
shouts coming from somewhere inside the fortress.
The alarm had finally been given. Either someone
had heard the sound of fighting or a guard standing atop the battlements had seen the attack.

After passing through the inner gate, Kujulo took
three steps forward before stopping to study the
situation. The inside of the fortress was designed like
a hollow square. The walls on the north, east and
south of the structure were simply fortifications.
Outside of the horse pens and corrals nestled up
against the northeast corner, there were no rooms
built into the walls themselves.

The western end of the fortress was a different
proposition altogether. There, massive brick buildings
abutted directly against the outer wall. Above those
buildings, resting on a stone platform reinforced with
heavy timbers, Kujulo could see the fortress' three
great cannons.

Those buildings would be the quarters for the
garrison. Already, Kujulo could see Malwa soldiers
spilling out from the many doors set into the brickwork. The soldiers fumbled with spears and swords.
Many of them were still putting on their armor.
Flimsy, leather armor. Kujulo almost laughed, seeing
one of the Malwa stumble and flop on his belly.

But Kujulo could see no grenades, and, what was
better—

"Look at that, will you!" exclaimed one of his men.
"They can't have more than two hundred men guarding this place!"

Kujulo nodded. His squad member had immediately spotted the most important thing about the

fortress. The first thing Kujulo himself had noticed.

No tents.

The flat, empty ground which formed most of the fortress' interior should have been *covered* with tents. There was not enough room in the brick buildings for more than a small garrison. Kujulo thought his squad member's estimate of two hundred was over-generous. The garrison's officers, for one thing, would have undoubtedly taken the largest rooms for themselves. For another, Kujulo could see no sign of any cookfires on the open ground. That meant a kitchen, taking up even more of the brick buildings' space.

"A hundred and fifty, tops," he pronounced. He studied the Malwa soldiers advancing toward them from the west—if the term "advancing" can be used to describe a mode of progress that was as skittish as a kitten's. Studied the soldiers, and, more closely, their leather armor.

"Shit." He spit on the ground. "Those aren't soldiers. Not proper ones. Those are nothing but fucking *gunners*. Cannon handlers."

His squad was now ranged on both sides of him. Behind, he could hear the thirty men from the next three squads moving up.

All of his men grinned. Like wolves eyeing a herd of caribou.

"I do believe you're right," said one.

Another laughed. "Think we can hold this gate against them? For the minute it'll take Kungas to get here."

Again, Kujulo spit on the ground.

"Fuck that," he snarled. "I intend to *defeat* those bastards. *Follow me*."

He stalked toward the Malwa gunners. By now, all four squads had taken position in a line stretching a third of the way across the inner grounds.

Forty Kushans, wearing good scale armor, hefting their swords and spears with practiced ease, began marching on the Malwa.

The gunners stopped. Stared.

Kujulo broke into an easy trot. Forty Kushans matched his pace.

The gunners stared. Edged back.

Kujulo raised his sword and bellowed the order to charge. Shrieking like madmen, forty Kushans charged the hundred or so Malwa some thirty yards away.

The gunners turned and raced for the brick buildings. Half of them dropped their weapons along the way.

By the time Kungas arrived, a minute or so later, Kujulo was already organizing a siege. And complaining, bitterly, that he would have to go into the fucking forest and cut down a fucking tree since the fucking Malwa didn't have any fucking timber big enough to ram through the fucking doors.

Cutting down a tree proved unnecessary. The "siege" was perhaps the shortest in history. As soon as the Malwa gunners forted up in the brick buildings saw Kungas' five hundred men storming into the fortress, they immediately began negotiating a surrender.

The biggest obstacle in those negotiations were the five Mahaveda priests holed up with the gunners. The priests, bound by holy oaths to safeguard the secret of the Veda weapons, demanded a fight to the death. They denounced all talk of surrender as impious treason.

Kungas, hearing the priests' shouting voices, called out his own offer to the Malwa gunners.

Cut the priests' throats. Pitch their bodies out. You'll be given good treatment.

The first corpse sailed through one of the doors not fifteen seconds later. Within a minute, the lifeless

bodies of all five priests were sprawled in the dirt
of the fortress grounds.

Kungas cocked his head at Kujulo. "What's your
opinion? Think those gunners'll spill their secrets?"

Kujulo spit on the ground. "Imagine so. Especially
after I reason with them."

"We're family men," complained the garrison
commander. He was squatting in the middle of the
fortress' gun platform, where Kungas had chosen to
interrogate him. Kungas himself was standing by one
of the great siege guns, five feet away. Near him,
Kujulo sat on a pile of stone cannonballs.

"They told us this was just garrison work," whined
the captured officer. "A formality, sort of."

Kungas studied the man quivering with fear in
front of him. It was obvious that the garrison was not
one of the Malwa's elite kshatriya units. Technically,
true, many of the gunners were kshatriya. But, just
as there are dogs and dogs—poodles and pit bulls—
so also are there kshatriya and kshatriya.

Kungas realized that Rao's savage guerrilla war had
stretched Venandakatra's resources badly. The Goptri
of the Deccan didn't have enough front-line troops
to detail for every task. So he had assigned one of
his sorriest units to garrison Suppara's fortress.

And why not? he mused. *Suppara's on the coast side
of the Western Ghats. Too far away for Venandakatra
to worry about. Too far away for Rao to strike at, even
if he wanted to.*

But none of his good cheer showed on his face.
Kungas eyed the captive stonily.

The garrison commander flinched from that pitiless gaze.

"We're fathers and husbands," he wailed. "Way too
old for this kind of thing. You won't hurt our families, will you? We brought them with us to Suppara."

Kujulo sat erect, his eyes widening. With a little

sideways lurch, he slid off the pile of cannonballs and strode over to the Malwa commander. Then, leaning over the frightened officer, he barked, "Brought your families, did you? *Women, too? Wives and daughters?*"

The garrison commander stared up at Kujulo's leering countenance. The Kushan's expression was venery and lust personified. Gleaming eyes, loose lips—even a hint of slobber.

Now completely terrified, the officer looked appealingly toward the Kushan commander.

"Depends," growled Kungas. Face like an iron mask.

"On what?" squeaked the officer.

Kungas made a little gesture, ordering the man to rise. The Malwa sprang to his feet.

Another gesture. *Follow me.*

Kungas walked over to the edge of the gun platform. A low stone wall, two feet high, was all that stood between him and a vertical drop of about a hundred feet. The western wall of the fortress, atop which the gun platform was situated, rose straight up from a stone escarpment. To the northwest, the town and harbor of Suppara were completely within view. View—and cannon range.

Gingerly, the Malwa officer joined Kungas at the wall. Kungas pointed at the harbor below. To the three war galleys moored in that harbor, more precisely.

"It depends on whether—"

He broke off, seeing that the Malwa officer was not listening to him. Instead, the garrison commander was staring to the southwest.

Kungas followed his eyes. On the horizon, barely visible, were the sails of a fleet. A vast fleet, judging from their number.

"Ah," he grunted. "Just in time."

He bestowed his crack-in-the-iron version of a smile on the Malwa officer. "Such a pleasure, you know, when things happen when they're supposed to. Don't you think?"

The garrison commander transferred his stare from the distant fleet to Kungas. Again, Kungas pointed to the three galleys in the harbor below.

"*Depends*," he growled. The Malwa's eyes bulged.

"You can't be serious!" he exclaimed.

Kungas flicked his eyes toward Kujulo. The Malwa's eyes followed. Kujulo, standing fifteen feet away, grinned savagely and grabbed his crotch.

The Malwa recoiled, pallid-faced.

"*Depends*," growled Kungas. "*Depends*—on whether you and your men destroy those three ships for us. *Depends*—also—on whether you show us how to use the cannons."

Silence followed, for a minute. The garrison commander stared at the galleys below. At Kujulo.

Listened, again, to the growl:

"*Depends*."

The first cannon fired when Shakuntala's flagship, in the van of the fleet, was not more than three miles from the entrance to the harbor. The Empress and her peshwa, standing in the bow, saw the cloud of gunsmoke; moments later, heard the roar.

Another cannon fired. Then, a third.

"Are they firing at us?" queried Holkar. Ruefully: "I'm afraid my eyes aren't as good as they used to be."

The Empress of Andhra had young eyes, and good ones.

"No, Dadaji. They are firing at something in the harbor. Malwa warships, I assume."

Holkar sighed. "Kungas has done it, then. He has taken the fortress."

Young eyes, good eyes, suddenly filled with tears.

"My *Mahadandanayaka*," she whispered. "*Bhatas-vapati*."

She clutched Holkar's arm, and pressed her face against his shoulder. For all the world, like a girl seeking shelter and security from her father.

"And you, my peshwa."

As the huge fleet sailed toward the harbor of Suppara, Dadaji Holkar held his small Empress in his arms. Thin arms, they were, attached to the slender shoulders of a middle-aged scholar. But, in that moment, they held all the comfort which the girl needed.

If an Empress found shelter there, the man himself found a greater comfort in the sheltering. His own family was lost to him, perhaps forever, but he had found another to give him comfort in his search. A child, here. A brother, there on the fortress above.

A bigger, tougher kind of brother. The kind every bookish man wishes he had.

"Mine, too," he murmured, staring at the clouds of gunsmoke wafting over the distant harbor. "My *Mahadandanayaka*. My *Bhatasvapati*."

Chapter 30

THE EUPHRATES
Autumn, 531 A.D.

"Tell me again," said Belisarius.

Standing next to the general on top of the giant pile of rocks which the Kushans had hauled out of the Nehar Malka, Maurice decided to misunderstand the question.

"Fifteen thousand cavalry they've got now," he gruffed. He pointed a stubby, thick finger at the cloud of dust rising out of the desert some ten miles to the southeast. "Five thousand of them, by my estimate, are Lakhmid Arabs. They're riding camels, the most, and—"

Belisarius smiled crookedly.

"Tell me again, Maurice."

The chiliarch puffed out his cheeks. Sighed. "This is not my province, general. I don't have any business mucking around in—"

"I'm not asking you to *muck around,*" growled Belisarius. "And spare me the protestations of humble modesty. Just tell me what you *think.*"

436

Again, Maurice puffed out his cheeks. Then, exhaled noisily.

"What I think, general, is that the Emperor of Persia is offering the Roman Empire a dynastic marriage. Between Photius and the eldest daughter of his noblest sahrdaran."

Maurice glanced down at Baresmanas. The father of the daughter in question was perched sixty feet away on a large boulder further down the man-made hill. Out of hearing range. Maurice continued:

"He'd offer one of his own daughters in marriage—Khusrau made that clear enough—but he doesn't have any. So Baresmanas' daughter is the best alternative, other than choosing from one of his brothers' or half-brothers' various girls."

Belisarius shook his head. "That's the last thing he'd do. Khusrau's trying to bridle that crowd of ambitious brothers. And, if I'm reading him right, trying to cement the most trustworthy layers of the nobility to his rule."

The general scratched his chin, idly staring at the cloud of dust in the desert. His eyes were not really focussed on the sight, however. From experience, he knew that the Malwa army advancing on him would not be in position to attack until the following day. In the meantime—

"Khusrau's canny," he said. "Part of our conversations in Babylon consisted of his questions regarding the Roman methods of organizing our Empire. I think he's planning—groping, is maybe a better way to put it—to break Persia from its inveterate—"

He paused. The word "feudalism" would mean nothing to Maurice. It had meant nothing to Belisarius, either, until Aide explained it to him.

"—traditions," he concluded, waving his hand vaguely.

"Think he can do it?" asked Maurice. "Persians are set in their ways."

Belisarius pondered the question. Aide had given him, once, a vision of the Persia which Khusrau Anushirvan had created, in the future which would have been if the "new gods" hadn't intervened in human history. The greatest Emperor of the Sassanid dynasty had tried to impose centralized, imperial authority over the unruly Aryan nobility, inspired by Rome's example, to some degree; guided by his own keen intelligence, for the rest.

In many ways, Khusrau would succeed. He would break the military power of the great aristocracy. He would win the allegiance of the dehgans, transform them into the social base for a professional army paid and equipped by the Emperor, and place them under the authority of his own generals—*spahbads*, he would call them. Never again would ambitious sahrdarans or vurzurgans pose a threat to the throne.

Khusrau would succeed elsewhere, too. His greatest reform—the one for which history would call him "Khusrau the Just"—would be his drastic overhaul of taxation. Khusrau would institute a system of taxation which was not only far less burdensome to the common folk but which also stabilized the imperial treasury.

Yet—

If there was one thing which Aide had shown Belisarius, it was that human history never moved in simple, clear channels. Khusrau's dynasty—the Sassanid dynasty—would vanish into history, as all dynasties did. But his tax system would remain. The Arab conquerors of Persia would be so impressed by it that they would use it as the model for the tax system of the great Moslem Caliphates.

Belisarius' mind was now wandering very far from the moment. He knew of the Moslem Caliphates of the future that would have been. Aide had shown him. Just as Aide had shown him the fall of the Roman Empire, almost a thousand years in the future. The sack of Constantinople at the hands of the so-called Fourth Crusade. The final conquest of Byzantium, a quarter of a millennium later, by a new people called the Turks.

Belisarius wondered, now, as he often had before, what he thought of all that Aide had shown him. He was a general in the service of the Roman Empire. Indeed, one of the greatest generals which Rome ever produced. He knew that for a simple fact. And knew, also, that he was the only general in the long history of that great Empire who fought for it while understanding, all along, that the Empire was doomed.

He hoped to saved Rome, and the world, from the Malwa tyranny. But he would not save Rome itself. Rome would fall—someday, somehow. If not by the hand of Sultan Mehmet and his Janissaries, by the hand of someone else. All human creations fell, or collapsed, or simply decayed. Someday, somehow, somewhere.

Mentally, Belisarius shrugged. His was not the task of creating a perfect human future. His was the task of making sure that people had a future they could create. Create badly, perhaps—but *create*. Not be forced into a mold created for them.

Maurice was still waiting patiently for an answer. Belisarius smiled, and gave him the simple one.

"Yes, he can do it. He *will* do it."

Maurice grunted. The grunt carried a great deal of satisfaction—which was odd, really, for a Roman soldier. But Maurice had met Khusrau Anushirvan, and, like many people, even that crusty veteran had come under the spell of the Persian Emperor's powerful personality.

"What do *you* think?" he now asked. "About the proposal for a dynastic marriage, I mean?"

Belisarius smiled again. "I think it's a great idea. Theodora'll be twitchy about it, of course. But Justinian will seize on it with both hands."

Maurice frowned. "Why?"

"Because Justinian always has his—'mind's eye,' let's call it—on the position of the dynasty. *His* dynasty, for all that Photius isn't his own son. And he knows that there'd be nothing that would cement the army's allegiance more than a dynastic marriage with a Persian Princess."

Maurice tugged his beard thoughtfully. "True enough," he agreed. "Anything that would prevent another bloody brawl with those tough fucking dehgans. Bad for your retirement prospects, that is."

A thought came to him. His eyes widened, slightly. "Now that I think about it— When was the last time a Roman Emperor married a Persian noblewoman?"

Belisarius chuckled. "It's *never* happened, Maurice. The Persians consider us Roman mongrels unfit for their blood."

"That's what I thought," mused Maurice. "God, the army'll be tickled pink. They already think of Photius as one of their own, you know. If he marries a Persian sahrdaran's daughter—"

The chiliarch broke off, eyeing the figure of Baresmanas below. "Does *he* know about it, d'you think? It's his daughter we're talking about, after all. Maybe *he* won't like the idea."

Belisarius laughed, clapping the chiliarch on the shoulder.

"Unless I'm badly mistaken, Maurice, the whole thing was Baresmanas' idea in the first place."

As if he had been cued, Baresmanas chose that moment to turn his head and look up at the two Roman officers standing on the very top of the rock-pile. For a moment, he and Belisarius stared at each other. Then, Baresmanas hopped off the rock—his shoulder might be half-crippled, but he was still quite spry for a middle-aged man—and began climbing toward them.

As soon as he reached the hill-top, Baresmanas asked, "So—what do you think?"

For a moment, the Roman general was startled. How could Baresmanas have overheard—?

Then, realizing that the sahrdaran was talking about their military situation, Belisarius grimaced.

"We're not going to be able to surprise them with another flank attack, that's for sure."

Baresmanas nodded. Neither he nor Belisarius had really thought that option would be available. Having been shattered at Anatha, the Malwa would not make the mistake of overconfidence again. The army approaching them from the southeast was much larger than the force they had faced at the hunting park. Still, the commander of those oncoming Malwa was keeping a massive guard on his flanks. *Well* out on his flanks, using his best troops for the job. On his left, in the desert, the Malwa commander was using Lakhmids on camelback. On his right, in the fertile terrain on the other side of the almost-dry Euphrates, he was using Kushan cavalry. Four thousand of them, according to Kurush's scouts, maintaining an excellent marching order, with a large contingent of skirmishers guarding their own flank.

There would be no way to surprise the Malwa with any clever maneuver with concealed troops. Not this time.

"We will have to rely on your main plan, then," said Baresmanas. The sahrdaran heaved a sigh. "Casualties will be high."

Belisarius tightened his lips. "Yes, they will. But I don't see any other option."

Baresmanas turned his head, staring to the west. Across the river, he could see the huge camp where Ormazd's twenty thousand lancers and archers had taken position, after arriving the week before. Even at the distance, he could see Ormazd's own pavilion, towering over the much-less-elaborate tents of his soldiers.

"If he does not—"

"He will," said Belisarius confidently. His crooked smile came, in full force.

"You will have noticed, I'm sure, that Ormazd pitched his camp *there*—instead of further down the river."

Baresmanas nodded, scowling. "The swine," he growled. "Upstream of the dam, where he pitched his camp, there is no way he can cross the Euphrates in time to give you help, should you need it. He should have taken position several miles further down, where the riverbed is almost empty."

Belisarius shook his head.

"Not a chance, Baresmanas. His troops would take the brunt of the assault, then. Whereas now—"

"They are obviously out of the action," concluded the sahrdaran. "The Malwa will recognize that immediately, and concentrate most of their forces here. They will only need to keep a screen against the chance of Ormazd attacking their left."

Belisarius chuckled, making clear his opinion on the likelihood of Ormazd ordering any massive sally. The Persian Emperor's half-brother, it was clear, intended to sit on his hands while the Romans and the Malwa army slugged it out on the other side of the Euphrates.

"How did he explain it?" demanded Baresmanas angrily.

Belisarius shrugged. "In all truth, he didn't have much explaining to do. I didn't press him on the matter, Baresmanas. I *want* him where he is."

Baresmanas' scowl deepened. Intellectually, the sahrdaran understood Belisarius' stratagem. Emotionally, however, the Aryan nobleman still choked at the idea of actually *using* another Aryan's expected treachery. A *Sassanid*, no less.

Baresmanas eyed the Roman general. "I forget, sometimes, just how incredibly cold-blooded you can be," he muttered. "I cannot think of another man who would develop a battle plan based on his expectation that an ally would betray him. Take such a possibility into account, certainly—any sane commander does that, when fighting with foreign allies. But to *plan* on it— No, more! To actually engineer it, to maneuver for it!—"

Baresmanas fell silent, shaking his head. Belisarius, for his part, said nothing. There was nothing to say, really. Despite the many ways in which he and Baresmanas were much alike, there were other ways in which they were as different as two men could be.

For all his sophistication and scholarship, Baresmanas was still, at bottom, the same man who had spent his boyhood admiring Persian lancers and archers. Spent hours of that boyhood watching dehgans on the training fields of his father's vast estate, demonstrating their superb skill as mounted archers.

Whereas Belisarius, for all his own sophistication and subtleties, was still—at bottom—the same man who had spent his boyhood admiring Thracian blacksmiths. Spent hours of that boyhood watching the blacksmiths on his father's modest estate, demonstrating their own more humble but—when all is said and done—much more powerful craft. Men die by the dehgan's steel. People *live* by the blacksmith's iron.

Even as a boy, however, Belisarius had had a subtle mind. So, where other boys admired the strength of the blacksmith, and gasped with awe at the mighty strokes of hammer on anvil, Belisarius had seen the truth. A blacksmith was a strong man, of necessity. But a *good* blacksmith did everything he could to husband that strength. Time after time, watching, the boy Belisarius had seen how cunningly the blacksmith positioned the glowing metal, and with what a precise angle he wielded the hammer.

So, he said nothing to Baresmanas. There was nothing to say.

❖   ❖   ❖

A few minutes later, called down by one of his tribunes with a problem, Maurice left the artificial hilltop. Belisarius and Baresmanas remained there alone, studying the huge Malwa force advancing toward them.

They did not speak, other than to exchange an occasional professional assessment of the enemy's disposition of its forces. On that subject, not surprisingly, they were always in agreement. If Baresmanas did not have his Roman ally's sheer military genius, he was still an experienced and competent general in his own right.

Underlying that agreement, however, and for all their genuine friendship, two very different souls readied for the coming battle.

The one, an Aryan sahrdaran—noblest man of the noblest line of the world's noblest race—sought strength and courage from that very nobility. Sought for it, found it, and awaited the battle with a calm certitude in his own valor and honor.

The other, a Thracian born into the lower ranks of Rome's parvenu aristocracy, never even thought of nobility. Thought, not once, of honor or of valor. He simply waited for the oncoming enemy, patiently, like a blacksmith waits for iron to heat in the furnace.

A craftsman at his trade. Nothing more.

And nothing less.

Chapter 31

ALEXANDRIA
Autumn, 531 A.D.

"This is madness!" shouted one of the gymnasiarchs. The portly notable was standing in the forefront of a small crowd packed into the audience chamber. All of them were men, all of them were finely dressed, and most were as fat as he was.

Alexandria's city council.

"Madness!" echoed another member of the council.

"Lunacy!" cried a third.

Antonina was not certain which particular titles those men enjoyed. Gymnasiarchs also, perhaps, or possibly *exegetai*.

She did not care. The specific titles were meaningless—hoary traditions from the early centuries of the Empire, when the city council actually exercised power. In modern Alexandria, membership in the council was purely a matter of social prestige. The real authority was in the hands of the Praetorian

445

Prefect, the commander of the Army of Egypt, and—above all—the Patriarch.

After disembarking her troops, Antonina had immediately seized a palace in the vicinity of the Great Harbor. She was not even sure whose palace it was. The owner had fled before she and her soldiers occupied the building, along with most of his servants.

Each of the many monarchs who had ruled Egypt in the eight hundred and sixty-two years since the founding of Alexandria had built their own palaces. The city was dotted with the splendiferous things. Over the centuries, most of those royal palaces had become the private residences of the city's high Greek nobility.

No sooner had she established her temporary headquarters than the entire city council appeared outside the palace, demanding the right to present their petitions and their grievances. She had invited them in—well over a hundred of the self-important folk—simply in order to gauge the attitude of Alexandria's upper crust.

Within ten minutes after they surged into the audience chamber, they had made their sentiments clear. As follows:

One. The Empire was ruled by a madwoman.

Two. The mad Empress had sent another madwoman to spread the madness to Alexandria.

Three. They, on the other hand, were not mad.

Four. Nor would they tolerate madness.

Five. Not that they themselves, of course, would think of raising their hands in violence against the Empress and her representative—perish the thought, perish the thought—even if they *were* nothing but a couple of deranged females. But—

Six. The dreaded mob of Alexandria, always prone to erupt at the slightest provocation, was even now coming to a furious boil. Any moment now, madness would be unleashed in the streets. Which—

Seven. Was the inevitable fate for madwomen.

Eight. Who were, they reiterated, utterly mad. Insanity personified. Completely out of their wits. Bereft of all sense and reason. Raving—

Antonina had had enough. "Arrest them," she said. Demurely. Ladylike. "The whole lot."

A little flip of the hand. "Stow them in the hold of one of the grain ships, for now. We'll figure out what to do with them later."

As Ashot and his cataphracts carried out her order, Antonina ignored the squawls of outrage issued by the city's notables as they were hog-tied and frog-marched out of the palace. She had other problems to deal with.

Some of those problems were simple and straight-forward.

Representatives from the very large Jewish popu-lation of the city inquired as to their likely welfare. Antonina assured them that the Jews would be unmolested, both in their civil and religious affairs, so long as they accepted her authority. Five minutes later, the Jewish representatives were ushered out. On their way, Antonina heard one of them mutter to another, "Let the damned Christians fight it out, then. No business of ours."

Good enough.

Next problem:

Representatives of the city's powerful guilds demanded to know what the Empire's attitude would be toward their ancient prerogatives.

Complicated, but not difficult.

Antonina assured them that neither she, nor Emperor Photius, nor the Empress Regent, had any desire to trample on the guilds' legitimate interests. Other than, in the case of the shipbuilding and metalworking guilds, providing them with a lot of work. Oh, yes, and work for the huge linenmakers guild also. Sails would be needed for all the new

ships they'd be building. And no doubt there'd be
some imperial money tossed at the glassworkers
guild. The Empress Regent—as everyone knew—was
exceedingly fond of fine glasswork.

The papyrus-makers, of course, were sitting pretty.
The influx of imperial officials would naturally
increase the demand for paper. As for the jewelers,
well, what with the enormous booty that'd soon be
rolling in from the Malwa, writhing in defeat and
humiliation, all of the soldiers—the many, many,
many soldiers—who would be arriving to strengthen
Egypt's garrison would naturally want to convert their
bulky loot into items which were both portable and
readily liquifiable, of which—O happy coincidence—
fine jewelry took pride of place, especially the jewelry produced in Alexandria, which city was famed
throughout the Empire—O happy coincidence—for
the unexcelled craft of its gold- and silversmiths.

Now, as to the matter of grain-shipping guilds, well,
soldiers are strapping lads. Need to eat a lot. So—

Two hours later, the representatives of the city's
commercial and manufacturing guilds tottered out of
the palace, reeling dizzily at the thought of their
newfound wealth.

Other problems, of course, were hard as nails. But
those, at least, Antonina did not have to spend hour
after hour sitting on a chair to deal with. Those
problems could only be dealt with in the streets.

Hermogenes stalked into the audience chamber
just as the last guild representatives were leaving.
He strode directly to Antonina's chair, leaned over,
and whispered, "It's starting. Paul just finished a
sermon at the Church of St. Michael, calling on
the city's faithful to reject the Whore of Babylon."

"Which one?" asked Antonina whimsically. "Me?
Or Theodora?"

Hermogenes shrugged. "From what our spies

report, the Patriarch wasn't specific. The former Patriarch, I should say."

Antonina shook her head. "He's *still* the Patriarch, Hermogenes. In fact, if not in name. Theodosius may have the title, but it means nothing until we can install him in the Church of St. Michael and keep him there."

She cast a glance at the man in question. Theodosius was standing twenty feet away, conferring with two of the deacons who served as his ecclesiastical aides. Zeno, the commander of the Knights Hospitaler, was standing next to him, along with two of his own subordinates.

Antonina was pleased to note that Theodosius seemed neither agitated nor apprehensive.

I don't know about his theology, but the man's got good nerves. He'll need them.

She looked back at Hermogenes. "What about Ambrose?"

Hermogenes scowled. "The bastard's holed up at the army camp in Nicopolis. *With* all of his troops."

Ashot and Euphronius arrived just in time to hear the last words.

"Only thing he can do, for the moment," said Ashot. "He's a general in the army, subject to the Empire's stringent rules governing mutiny. Whereas"— the Armenian cataphract sneered—"the Patriarch can give sermons, and claim afterward that he was just preaching to his flock. No fault of his if he was misunderstood when he denounced the Whore of Babylon. *He* was just cautioning men against sin. *He* certainly didn't intend for a huge mob to assault the Empress' representative. He is shocked and distressed to learn that the unfortunate woman was torn limb from limb."

By this time, Theodosius and Zeno had joined the little circle around Antonina. "It's happened before," commented the Knights Hospitaler. "The prefect Petronius was stoned by the mob, during Augustus' reign. And one of the Ptolemies was dragged out into the streets and assassinated. Alexander II, I think it was."

Antonina pursed her lips. "How long do you think Ambrose will sit on the sidelines, Ashot?"

The commander of her Thracian bucellarii shrugged. "Depends on his troops, mostly. Ambrose only has three options." He held up his thumb. "One—accept his dismissal."

"Not a chance," interjected Hermogenes. "I know the man. Sittas was being polite when he called him a stinking bastard. Ambitious, he is."

Ashot nodded. "Rule out that option, then. That only leaves him two." He held up his other thumb. "Mutiny. But—"

Hermogenes started shaking his head.

"—that'd be insane," continued Ashot. "Every one of his soldiers knows the penalty for mutiny in the Roman army. The risk isn't worth it unless—" He held up his forefinger alongside his thumb.

"Option two. Ambrose declares himself the new Emperor. His soldiers hail him, start a civil war, and hope to enjoy the bounty if they win."

Hermogenes nodded vigorously. "He's right. A Patriarch can play games with street violence. A general can't. For him, it's all or nothing."

Antonina looked back and forth between the two officers. "You still haven't told me how long I've got before he decides."

"A day, at the very least," said Ashot immediately. "He's *got* to have the support of his soldiers. Most of them, anyway. That'll take time."

"Speeches," amplified Hermogenes. "Perorations to the assembled troops. Negotiations with his top officers. Promises to make to everybody."

"For sure he'll promise a huge *annona* if he takes the throne," added Ashot immediately. All the officers nodded, their faces grim. The annona was the pay bonus which Roman emperors traditionally granted their troops upon assuming the throne. During the chaotic civil wars three centuries earlier, when Rome often had two or three simultaneous emperors—few of whom survived more than a year or two—the claimants for the throne had bid for the loyalty of the armies by promising absurd bonuses.

"Pay increases," elaborated Hermogenes, "after he's been made Emperor. Better retirement pensions. Anything else he can think of."

"He'll be talking nonstop for hours," concluded Ashot. "All through the day and halfway through the night."

Antonina rose. "Right. The gist of it is that I've got a day to deal with the Patriarch's mob, without interference from the Army of Egypt."

Ashot and Hermogenes nodded.

"Let's get to it, then. How big is that mob?"

Ashot spread his hands. "Hard to know, exactly. Thousands from the crowd packing St. Michael's. Most will be his fanatic adherents, but there'll be a lot of orthodox sympathizers mixed in with them. Then—"

He turned to Theodosius.

"How many hardcore Chalcedonian monks are there, residing in the city?"

The Patriarch grimaced. "At least two thousand."

"Five thousand," added Zeno, "if you include the ones living in monasteries within a day's march of Alexandria."

Ashot turned back to Antonina. "Every last one of those monks will be in with the mob, stirring them up."

"Leading the charge, more like," snarled Hermogenes.

Ashot barked an angry little laugh. "*And* you can bet that the Hippodrome factions will join the fray.

The Blues, for sure. They'll be interested in looting, for the most part. But they'll throw their weight in on Paul's side, if for no other reason than to get his blessing for their crimes."

"They'll head for Delta quarter, right off," added Zeno.

Antonina nodded thoughtfully. Alexandria was divided into five quarters, designated by the first five letters of the Greek alphabet. Delta quarter, for centuries, had been the city's Jewish area.

She moved her eyes to Euphronius. Throughout the preceding discussion—as was usual in these command meetings—the commander of the Theodoran Cohort had said nothing. The young Syrian grenadier was too shy to do more than listen.

"How do you feel about Jews?" she asked him abruptly.

Euphronius was startled by the question.

"Jews?" He frowned. "Never thought much about it, to be honest. Can't say I like them, but—"

He fell silent, groping for words.

Antonina was satisfied. Anti-Jewish sentiment was endemic throughout the Roman Empire, but only in Alexandria did it reach rabid proportions. That had been true for centuries. Syrians, on the other hand, had managed to co-exist with Jews without much in the way of trouble.

"I want you and the Cohort to march to the Jewish quarter. It'll be your job to defend it against the Hippodrome thugs. Take one of Hermogenes' infantry cohorts for support."

It was Ashot and Hermogenes' turn to be startled, now.

"What for, Antonina?" asked Hermogenes. "The Jews can take care of themselves. Won't be the first time they've fought it out with Blues and Greens."

Antonina shook her head. "That's exactly what I'm afraid of. I intend to"—she clenched her fist—

"*suppress* this street violence. The last thing I want is for it to spread."

"I agree with Antonina," interjected Theodosius. "If the Jews get involved in street fighting, Paul will use that to further incite the mob."

"*Whereas*," said Antonina, "if the mob is stopped before it can even start the pogrom—*by the Empress' own Cohort*—it'll send a very different signal."

She straightened, back stiff. "I promised their representatives that Alexandria's Jews would be unmolested if they remained loyal to the Empire. I intend to keep that promise."

She began moving toward the great set of double doors leading out of the audience chamber, issuing commands as she went.

"Hermogenes, detail one of your cohorts to back up the grenadiers in the Delta Quarter. Find one with officers who are familiar with Alexandria. The Syrians'll get lost in this city without guides."

"Take Triphiodoros and his boys, Euphronius," said Hermogenes. "He's from Alexandria."

"He's a damned good tribune, too," agreed the Syrian grenadier, nodding with approval.

Antonina stopped abruptly. She turned to face the commander of the Theodoran Cohort. Her expression was stern, almost fierce.

"Good tribune or not, Euphronius—*you're in charge*. The infantry's there to back you up, nothing more."

Euphronius started to make some protest, but Antonina drove over it.

"You've always been subordinate to someone else. Not today. Today, you're leading an independent command. You're ready for it—and so are the grenadiers. *I expect you to shine*."

The young Syrian commander straightened. "We will, Antonina. We will not fail."

Antonina turned to Ashot and Hermogenes.

"Get your troops ready. I want all of them in full armor. That includes the cataphracts' horses. *Full armor*—nothing less. Make sure of it. In this heat, a lot of the men will try to slide through with half-armor."

"Full armor?" Ashot winced. "Be like an oven. Antonina, we're not dealing with Persian dehgans here, for the sake of Christ. Just a pack of scruffy—"

Antonina shook her head firmly. "That's overkill, I know, against a street mob. But your troops won't be in the middle of the action, anyway, and I want them to look as intimidating as possible."

Ashot's eyes widened. So did Hermogenes'.

"Not in the middle of it?" asked the Armenian cataphract.

Antonina smiled. Then, turned to face Zeno.

"I believe it's time for the Knights Hospitaler to take center stage."

Zeno nodded solemnly. "So do I, Antonina. And this is the perfect opportunity."

"I'm not so sure about that," muttered Hermogenes. He gave Zeno a half-apologetic, half-skeptical glance. "Meaning no offense, but your monks have only had a small amount of training. This is one hell of a messy situation to throw them into."

Antonina started to intervene. But then, seeing the confident expression on Zeno's face, decided to let the Knight Hospitaler handle the matter.

"We have trained much more than you realize, Hermogenes," said Zeno. "Not"—he waved his hand—"with your kind of full armor and weapons in a field battle situation, of course. But we took advantage of the very long voyage here to train on board the grain ships. With quarterstaffs."

Hermogenes stared at the Knights Hospitaler as if the man had just announced that he was armed with bread sticks. Ashot was positively goggling.

"*Quarterstaffs?*" choked the Armenian cataphract.

Now, Antonina did intervene. "That was my husband's idea," she stated. "He said it was the perfect weapon for riot duty."

Hearing the authority of Belisarius invoked, Ashot and Hermogenes reined in their disdain. A bit.

Zeno spoke up again. "I do not think you fully understand the situation here, Hermogenes. Ashot." He cleared his throat. "I am Egyptian myself, you know. I wasn't born in Alexandria—I come from Naucratis, in the Delta—but I am familiar with the place. And its religious politics."

He pointed through the open doors. "We must be very careful. We do not want to create martyrs. And—especially—we don't want to infuriate the great masses of orthodox Greeks who make up a third of Alexandria's populace."

He nodded approvingly at Antonina. "You saw how well Antonina handled the guilds, earlier. But you musn't forget that almost all of those men are Greeks, and orthodox. They completely dominate the city's commerce and manufacture. They are the same men we will be relying on—tomorrow, and for years to come—to forge the Roman arsenal against the Malwa. For doctrinal reasons, most of those people are inclined to support Paul and his diehards. But they are also uneasy about their fanaticism, and their thuggery. Bad for business, if nothing else."

Antonina pitched in. "It's essential that we drive a wedge between Paul's fanatics and the majority of the orthodox population. If we have a massacre, the city's Greeks will be driven into open opposition. And you know as well as I do—*better* than I do—how the cataphracts and the regular infantry will hammer into that mob if they're in the forefront."

She stared at Ashot and Hermogenes. The two officers looked away.

"You know!" she snapped. "Those men are trained to do one thing, and one thing only. *Slaughter people.*

Do you really want to unleash a volley of cataphract arrows against a crowd? This is not the Nika revolt, God damn it! There, we were dealing with Malwa kshatriya and thousands of professional thugs armed to the teeth. Here—"

She blew out her breath. "Christ! Half of that crowd will be there more out of excitement and curiosity than anything else. Many of them will be women and children. You may be crazy, but I'm not. Theodora sent me here to stabilize imperial rule in Egypt. To *stop* a civil war, not start one."

Ashot and Hermogenes were looking hangdog, now. But Antonina was relentless.

"That's the way it's going to be. *I* have complete confidence that the Knights Hospitaler can handle the situation. I simply want you there—*in the background, but fully armed and armored*—to add a little spice to the meal. Just to let the crowd know, after Paul's goons have been beaten into a pulp and routed, that it could have been one hell of a lot worse."

She chuckled, very coldly. "You may sneer at quarterstaffs, but my husband doesn't. And I think, by the end of the day, you won't be sneering either."

She straightened, assuming as tall a stance as she could. Which wasn't much, but quite enough.

"You have your orders. *Follow them.*"

Hermogenes and Ashot left then, very hastily. An unkind observer might have said they scurried. An instant later, Zeno followed. His pace, however, was slower. Very proud, that stride was.

Euphronius, also, began to leave. But after taking three steps, he stopped. He fidgeted, then turned around.

"Yes?" asked Antonina.

The Syrian cleared his throat. "My grenadiers are also not trained to do anything other than—uh, slaughter people. And grenades are even more indiscriminate than arrows. I don't understand how you expect me to—"

Antonina laughed. "Euphronius! Relax!"

She walked over, smiling, and placed a reassuring hand on his arm.

"First of all, you're not going to be dealing with a crowd. You're going to be dealing with *gangs*. There won't be any innocent onlookers in *that* mob, believe me. Hippodrome thugs, they'll be, looking to pillage the Jews. Robbers, rapists, murderers—nothing else."

The smile vanished. Her next words were almost snarled.

"Kill as many of them as you can, Euphronius. *The more, the better*. And then have Triphiodoros and his infantry hang whatever prisoners you take. On the spot. No mercy. *None*. If you wind up draping the outskirts of the Delta Quarter with intestines, blood, brains, and corpses, you'll make me a very happy woman."

Euphronius gave out a little sigh of relief. "Oh," he said. Then, with a sudden, savage grin:

"We can do that. No problem."

Now he, too, was hurrying out of the room. Antonina was left alone with Theodosius.

For a moment, she and the new Patriarch stared at each other. Theodosius had said nothing, during the preceding discussion. But his anxiety had been obvious to Antonina. The anxiety was gone, now. But she was uncertain what emotion had replaced it. Theodosius was giving her a very odd look.

"Is something troubling you, Patriarch?"

"Not at all," replied Theodosius, shaking his head. "I was just—how can I explain?"

He smiled, fluttering his hands. "I suppose you could say I was contemplating God's irony. It's an aspect of the Supreme Being which most theologians miss entirely, in my experience."

Antonina frowned. "I'm afraid I don't—"

Again, the fluttering hands. "When the fanatic Paul calls you the Whore of Babylon, he demonstrates his ignorance. His stupidity, actually. The essence of Christ is his mercy, Antonina. And who, in this chaos called Alexandria, could find that mercy—other than a woman who understands the difference between sin and evil?"

Antonina was still frowning. Theodosius sighed.

"I am not explaining myself well. Let me just say that I am very glad that you are here, and not some-one else. Someone full of their own self-righteousness. I will leave it at that."

Her frown faded, replaced by a half-rueful little smile. "I suppose I've adopted my husband's crooked way of looking at things."

"Crooked? Perhaps." The Patriarch turned to go. "But I would remind you, Antonina, that a grapevine is also crooked. Yet it bears the world's most trea-sured fruit."

When she was finally alone, Antonina walked slowly back to her chair and took a seat. She would not be able to enjoy that rest for long, for she intended to take her place with the cataphracts backing the Knights Templar. Within minutes, she would have to don her own armor. And wear it, throughout the day, under the hammering sun of Egypt. She grimaced, thinking of the sweltering heat that armor would bring.

But she needed that moment, alone. To remem-ber the crooked mind—and the straight soul—of her absent husband.

"Be safe, love," she whispered. "Oh, please—be safe."

Chapter 32

THE EUPHRATES
Autumn, 531 A.D.

"This is ridiculous!" snarled Belisarius. "This isn't *'safe'*—it's absurd!"

"We gave our oath, general," said Anastasius solemnly.

"To the Persian Emperor himself," added Valentinian, trying—and failing quite miserably—to look suitably lugubrious.

Belisarius glared at both of them. Then, transferred the glare onto the enemy, some distance away.

Quite some distance away. Belisarius, along with Anastasius and Valentinian, were standing on top of the huge pile of stones which the Kushans had dug out of the Nehar Malka. The Syrian infantrymen who defended that man-made hill had constructed an observation platform from which Belisarius could watch the progress of the battle. They had also built a narrow, winding road—more

459

of a path, really—which led up to the summit from
the protected northern side of the rockpile.

As a vantage point from which to observe the
battle, Belisarius could find no fault with the thing.
Even without his telescope, the rock-hill's elevation
gave him an excellent view of the enemy's dispositions on the south side of the Euphrates and the
Nehar Malka. The telescope enabled him to pick out
even small details of the enemy's formations.

But—

"God damn it," he growled, "I'm too far away. By
the time a courier gets up here and back again—no
way to ride a horse up that so-called road—I might
as well have given orders for yesterday's breakfast."

It's safe, insisted Aide.

Before Belisarius could make a reply, one of the
Malwa rockets fired at the Roman troops defending
the dam below veered wildly off course. For a
moment, it seemed as if the missile was heading
directly for the rockpile. Close enough, at least, that
Valentinian and Anastasius began to take cover behind
the low wall surrounding the platform.

Growling with satisfaction, Belisarius stood as erect
as possible.

Get down! Get down!

Belisarius, sarcastically:

"Safe," remember? *"Safe,"* you said.

And, in truth, safe it was. With typical unpredictability, the rocket suddenly swerved to the east.
A few seconds later, it exploded harmlessly over the
middle of the Nehar Malka.

Wisely, Aide refrained from comment.

Belisarius took a deep breath, controlling his temper. There was no point in trying to force the issue,
at the moment. Valentinian and Anastasius were
obviously ready and willing to enforce a strict com-
pliance with their vow to Emperor Khusrau. For that
matter, *all* of Belisarius' officers had made clear their

own agreement with Khusrau's position. Belisarius had
been shocked, actually, when he realized how adamant his commanders were that he stay out of the
direct line of fire in the coming battle.

"There's no need for you in the front line, sir,"
Agathius had argued, at the command meeting on the
eve of the battle. "No need—and a lot to be lost if
you're killed or injured. This is just going to be a
slugging match, at least in the beginning."

On that point, Agathius had been correct.

It was late afternoon, and the battle had been
raging for hours. The Malwa had made their first
probes at dawn, on both sides of the Euphrates.
Encountering the large body of Persians guarding
Ormazd's camp on the south bank, the Malwa had
early on decided to take a purely defensive stance
there. They were obviously more than happy to let
Ormazd and his twenty thousand heavy cavalry sit on
the sidelines while they concentrated their attack on
the Roman forces.

Those Roman forces would have been their principal target, in any event. It was the Romans, not
Ormazd's Persians, who were forted up on the dam
across the Euphrates. It was the Romans, also, who
were positioned to guard the dam from any attack
coming up the Nehar Malka.

A slugging match, the first day—with the Romans
in position to outslug the Malwa.

The defensive position of Belisarius' army was
excellent. With the desert to the west and Ormazd's
twenty thousand lancers encamped on the south bank
of the Euphrates, the Malwa had no choice but to
advance up the riverbed and along the narrow strip
of land between the Euphrates and the Nehar Malka.
As that strip of land approached the point where the
Royal Canal branched directly east from the east-by-
southeast-flowing Euphrates, it narrowed down to a
mere spit. The tip of that triangle was guarded by

well-built Roman fieldworks—complete with timber brought all the way down the Euphrates by barges. Buttressed with rocks and tamped earth, the walls of that palisade were guarded by Syrian dragoons. When needed, the dragoons were backed up by all of the Constantinople cataphracts, ready to sally at a moment's notice. Which they had, over and again, as the day wore on, waiting until the Syrians had worn out another Malwa assault before driving them back in defeat.

Nor could the enemy outflank the fieldworks to the east. To do so would require crossing the rapid flow of the Nehar Malka, in the face of another Roman barrier. The giant pile of rocks on the north bank of the Royal Canal which the Kushans had excavated had been turned into an impromptu fortress, anchoring the Roman left flank. More Syrian troops were stationed on that rockpile, under the command of Coutzes, along with the Callinicum garrison. So far, those soldiers had had an easy day. The Malwa had not yet made any attempt to cross the Nehar Malka and attack the dam from the north bank of the Royal Canal. They had concentrated their efforts on the dam itself, especially its eastern anchor, trying to hammer their way to victory.

Yes, on *that* point, Belisarius could not argue. The first day was a slugging match, nothing else, just as Agathius had predicted. And, it was true, the general would have been able to play no particularly useful role on those front lines.

But Belisarius knew that would not last. The Romans were not facing the normal run of Malwa generals here. He had seen, with his telescope, the arrival of a howdah-bearing elephant with the enemy's army. A small mob of servants had been splashing that howdah with pails of water drawn from the river—a crude but effective way of cooling the howdah's interior.

Link itself was here. He was as certain of it as he was of his own name.

I must get closer, he thought to himself. *Soon enough, this simple slugging match of Agathius' is going to start unraveling.*

I must be closer.

Suddenly, hearing a change in the distant shouts of the enemy's forces, Belisarius cocked his head. The battle was so far away that he found himself forced to rely on his hearing as much as his eyesight.

"We're beating off the attack," he said.

Anastasius and Valentinian copied his stance. Listening with the trained ear of veterans.

"I think you're right," agreed Valentinian.

Anastasius nodded. Then asked: "What's that make? Five assaults?"

"Four," replied Belisarius. "That first one, just after dawn, was more in the way of a reconnaissance. There've only been four mass charges."

"Crazy bastards," sneered Valentinian. "Do they really think they can hammer their way onto that dam—without siege guns? Jesus, that must be a slaughter down there. The onagers and scorpions would be bad enough, backed up by Bouzes and his dragoons. But they've got to face Maurice and the Illyrians, too."

He gave his general an approving glance. "That was a great idea, that road you had the Kushans build."

Belisarius smiled crookedly. "I can't take credit for it, I'm afraid. I stole the idea from Nebuchadrezzar."

Inspired by the design of Babylon's fortifications, Belisarius had ordered a road built just behind the crest of the dam. A stone wall had then been hastily erected on the very crest. The road and the wall were jury-rigged, to be sure. The road was just wide enough and sturdy enough to allow the Thracian and Illyrian cataphracts to rush to any part of the dam which was under heavy attack. The wall was just thick enough, and just high enough, to shelter them from most missile fire. At the same time, it allowed the mounted archers to shoot their own bows over the wall at the Malwa soldiers trying to slog their way forward.

Combined with the torsion artillery mounted all along the dam, and the dismounted Syrians' archery and grenades, the result had been murderous. Most of the enemy troops had been forced to charge the dam up the riverbed of the Euphrates. Not only did that muddy terrain slow them down, but it also broke up the cohesion of their formations. The Euphrates had not dried up completely. The dam had diverted most of its water into the Nehar Malka, but there was still enough seeping through to produce a network of small streams and pools. Eventually, those streams converged and produced a small river—but not for several miles. Below the dam itself, the riverbed was an attacker's nightmare—mud, reeds, sinkholes, pools, creeks.

As far as possible, the Malwa had concentrated their efforts against the eastern end of the dam. There, the enemy troops could advance along the dry land which had once been the left bank of the Euphrates. But Belisarius had expected that, which was why he'd positioned the Constantinople troops on that end of the dam, backed up by the katyusha rockets. He had spent the night before the battle with Agathius and his men, exhorting them to stand fast. The Greeks, he explained, were the anchor of the entire defensive line. They would take the heaviest blows, but—so long as they held—the enemy could not prevail. When Belisarius finished, they gave him a cheer and vowed to hold the line.

Hold it they had, through four savage assaults. But they had driven back each charge, and added their own heavy charges onto the enemy's butcher bill.

The sounds of battle were fading rapidly now. It

was obvious that the Malwa were retreating. Within a minute, Belisarius could see streams of enemy soldiers retreating from the dam. They were bearing large numbers of wounded with them, chased on their way by rocket volleys fired from the katyushas.

Belisarius glanced up at the sky. The sun was beginning to set.

"There'll be a night attack," he predicted. "A mass assault all across the line." He pointed to the eastern anchor. "The crunch will come there. Count on it."

"Agathius'll hold them," said Anastasius confidently. "Come what may, Agathius will hold."

Valentinian grunted his agreement.

Belisarius glared at the distant enemy. Then, glared at his bodyguards. If he could have turned his eyes inside out, he would have glared at Aide.

"I'm too far away!" he roared.

The attack began two hours after dusk, and it lasted halfway through the night. The worst of it, as Belisarius had predicted, came on the eastern anchor of the dam.

Hour after hour, the general spent, perched on his cursed observation platform. Leaning over the wall, straining to hear what he could.

Cursing Khusrau. Cursing Valentinian and Anastasius. Cursing Aide.

He got a little sleep in the early hours of the dawn, after the enemy assault had been clearly beaten off. At daybreak, Valentinian awakened him.

"A courier's coming," announced the cataphract.

Belisarius scrambled to his feet and went over to the side of the platform where the path came up from below. Peering down, he could see an armored man making his laborious way up that narrow, twisting trail through the rocks.

"I think that's Maurice," said Anastasius.

Startled, Belisarius looked closer. He had been expecting one of the young cataphracts whom Maurice had been using to keep the general informed of the battle's progress—not the chiliarch himself.

But it was Maurice, sure enough. Belisarius stiffened, feeling a chill in his heart.

Valentinian verbalized his thought. "Bad news," he announced. "Sure as taxes. Only reason Maurice would come himself."

As soon as Maurice made his way to the crest, Belisarius reached down and hauled him over the wall.

"What's wrong?" he asked immediately. "From the sound, I thought they'd been beaten off again."

"They were," grunted Maurice. He took off his heavy helmet and heaved a sigh of relief.

"God, it's like being in a furnace. Forgotten what fresh air tastes like."

"God damn it, Maurice! *What's wrong?*"

The chiliarch's gray eyes met Belisarius' brown ones. Squarely, unflinchingly. Sternly.

"The same thing that's usually wrong in a battle, whether it's going well or not. We're hammering the bloody shit out of them, sure, but they get to hammer back. We've taken heavy casualties—especially the Greeks."

Maurice drew in a long, deep breath.

"Timasius is dead. He led the Illyrians in a charge against some Malwa—Kushans, worse luck—who made it over the wall. Horse got hamstrung and gutted, and—" Maurice shrugged, not bothering to elaborate. There were few things in a battle as certain as the fate of an armored cavalryman brought down by infantry. Timasius wouldn't have survived ten seconds after hitting the ground.

"Liberius?" asked Belisarius.

"He's taken command of the Illyrians," replied Maurice. "He's doing a good job, too. He organized the counter-attack that drove the Kushans back down the dam."

Belisarius studied Maurice's grim face. He felt his chill deepen. Maurice hadn't climbed all the way up that hill just to tell him that a dull, dimwitted commander had been succeeded by a more capable subordinate.

"I'm sorry about Timasius," he said softly. "He was a reliable man, if nothing else. His family'll get his full pension—I'll see to it. But that's not what you came here to tell me. So spit it out."

The grizzled Thracian wiped his face wearily. "It's Agathius."

"*Damn,*" hissed Belisarius. There was a real anguish in that hiss, and the three cataphracts who heard it understood that it was the pain of a man losing a treasured friend, not a general losing an excellent officer.

"Damn," he repeated, very softly.

Maurice shook his head. "He's not dead, general." Grimacing: "Not quite, anyway. But he's lost one leg, for sure, and I don't know as how he'll still be alive tomorrow."

"What happened?"

Maurice swiveled, staring back at the dam. "They really pushed hard this time, especially at the eastern anchor. Solid Ye-tai, that was—fighting on their own, not just chivvying Malwa regulars."

Still looking to the southwest, the chiliarch muttered an incoherent curse. "They're mean, tough, gutsy bastards—I'll give 'em that. I don't even want to think how many casualties they took before they finally broke through."

He turned back to Belisarius. "The Syrian dragoons couldn't hold them, so Agathius led a lance charge. In pitch dark, can you believe it? Man's got brass balls, I swear he does. That broke the Ye-tai—crushed 'em—but he got hit by a grenade blast. Took off his right leg, clean, just above the knee. Mangled his left foot, too. It'll have to be amputated, I think. Beyond that—" He shrugged. "Shrapnel tore him up pretty fierce. He's lost a lot of blood."

"Get him off the dam," commanded Belisarius. He turned and pointed to the small fleet of barges anchored in the middle of the Euphrates about a mile to the north.

"Get him to one of the ambulance barges."

Maurice rubbed his face. "That's not going to be easy. He's still conscious, believe it or not." A half-wondering, half-admiring chuckle. "Still wants to fight, even! When I left the dam, he was yelling at the doctor to tie up the one leg and cut off the fucking useless foot on the other so he could get back on a horse."

Valentinian and Anastasius laughed. Belisarius couldn't help smiling himself.

"Hit him over the head, if you have to, Maurice. But I want him out of there."

Again, he pointed to the barges. "There's better medical care available in the ambulance barges. And his wife's on one of those boats, too. I don't know which one, but I'll find out. She'll probably be more help keeping him alive than anyone else."

Maurice's eyes widened. "His wife? Sudaba's here? What in the world is that young girl doing on a battlefield? That's the craziest—"

He broke off, remembering. Belisarius' own wife, Antonina, had had the habit of accompanying her husband on campaign also. All the way to the battle-field.

Belisarius clasped Maurice's shoulder firmly.

"I want him alive, Maurice. Get him out of there. Now. Put Cyril in command of—"

"Already done it," gruffed Maurice.

Belisarius nodded, took a deep breath. "All right. What else?"

The chiliarch scowled. Strangely, the expression cheered Belisarius up. Maurice—scowling morosely—meant a problem. Which was not the same thing as *bad news*.

"They're going to change tactics," Maurice announced. "Even the Malwa won't keep throwing troops away like this forever."

"They might," countered Belisarius mildly, "if they think they're wearing us down fast enough."

Maurice shook his head. "They're not. We're taking pretty heavy casualties, sure, but we're giving out four or five to every one we take. At that rate, attrition will chew them up before it does us." His scowl darkened. "And I'm sure they know it, too. I'll tell you something, general. Whoever's running the show on their side is no fool. The frontal attacks have been beaten off, but that's because the terrain favors us and we're on the defensive. The attacks themselves have been organized and directed as good as you could ask, given that Godawful riverbed they have to plow through. There's been none of their usual cocksure stupidity, thinking they can roll over everybody just with their numbers. Ye-tai and Kushans have been leading every attack, and the Malwa regulars have been backing them up the way they should."

A thought came instantly from Aide:

Link. Link itself is here.

I know, replied Belisarius.

Maurice was shaking his head again.

"They tried the straight-up tactic, to see if it would work. Pressed it home, hard. But now that we've proven to them that they can't just roll over us, they'll try a flank attack. I'm sure of it."

Belisarius scratched his chin, nodded. "I'm not arguing the point, Maurice. As it happens, I agree with you."

He glanced across the river. Upstream of the dam,

just before the river diverted into the narrower channel of the Nehar Malka, the Euphrates was still a mile wide. But he could see the Persian camp where Ormazd's army had forted up throughout the day's battle.

"Any signs of movement over there?" he asked.

Maurice snorted. "About as much as a crocodile, waiting in the reeds. The only thing moving over there is Ormazd's nostrils, taking in the sweet air of opportunity."

Belisarius smiled. "Well, unless they want to hammer away at twenty thousand dehgans, that only leaves the Malwa one other option."

Maurice grimaced skeptically. He turned and pointed down the slope, to the Nehar Malka. "Do you have any idea how hard it would be for them to get across? The Nehar Malka's no shallow, placid river like the Euphrates was, general. It's narrower and deeper. The water's moving through there fast, and there aren't any fords within four days' march. They'll have to build a pontoon bridge, using those little barges they've got a few miles downriver."

He turned back, shaking his head. "While Coutzes and his boys on this rockpile piss pain all over them, and the katyushas come up to the riverbank and fire rockets at point-blank range, and me and Cyril and Liberius bring up all the cataphracts to hammer whichever poor bastards *do* manage to stagger across a rickety little pontoon bridge."

He jerked his head, pointing with his face at Ormazd's camp. "Personally, I'd rather take on the dehgans. If the Malwa can clear the right bank of the Euphrates, they can move upstream and cross back over damn near anywhere. We'd be trapped here. Have to abandon the dam and race back to Peroz-Shapur. Join forces with Kurush and try to hold out a siege."

Belisarius' smile was very crooked.

Maurice glared at him. "Are you *really* that sure of yourself?" he demanded.

Belisarius made a mollifying gesture with his hands. A gentle little patting motion.

Maurice was not mollified. "What's that?" he demanded. "Soothing the savage beast? Or just petting the dog?"

Belisarius left off the motion. Then, grinning:

"Yes, Maurice—I am that sure of myself. So sure, in fact, that I'm going to predict exactly how this next attack is going to happen."

He pointed down the slope of the rockpile to the Nehar Malka below. "I predict they'll start building their pontoon bridge today, in the late afternoon. The attack will begin after dark. You know why?"

"So they might have a chance of getting across the bridge," snorted Maurice. "Never do it in daylight."

Belisarius shook his head. "No. That's not why."

He gave Maurice a hard stare. "You say they've had Ye-tai and Kushans leading every attack?"

Maurice nodded.

"Not this next one, Maurice. You watch. Malwa regulars is all you'll see crossing that pontoon bridge—or would see, if it weren't dark. The reason they're going to attack at night is so that we can't see that none of their Ye-tai or Kushans are participating in the assault. *Those* troops—"

He turned his head, nodding toward the river.

"—will be crossing over to the right bank of the Euphrates, about a mile downstream from the dam. Out of our sight, especially since we'll be preoccupied with the attack on the Nehar Malka. By dawn, just when we think we've beaten off another assault, the Malwa army's best troops will come at us from behind. Like you said, they can find any number of places to ford the Euphrates upstream."

Maurice's scowl was ferocious, now. "You can't be

positive that Ormazd will pull out and give them that opening," he protested.

Belisarius shrugged.

"Positive, no. But I'll bet long odds on it, Maurice. Ormazd knows that the only loyal Persian troops Khusrau has up here are Baresmanas and Kurush's ten thousand. They're forted up in Peroz-Shapur—"

"I wish they were here," grumbled the chiliarch. "We could use them."

"Don't be stupid! If they were here, Peroz-Shapur would be a pile of ashes. As it is, the Malwa expedition had to skirt the town and leave troops to guard against a sally. Just sitting in Peroz-Shapur, Kurush is a threat to them."

He waved his hand. "But let's not change the subject. To go back to Ormazd—this is his best chance to move against Khusrau. If the Malwa destroy us here, they'll return to Babylon. Keep Khusrau penned up while Ormazd takes over all of northern Mesopotamia. The only thing that kept him from doing that before was our intervention—that, and our victory at Anatha. If we're gone, he's got a clear hand."

"How's he going to explain that to his dehgans?" demanded Maurice.

Belisarius laughed. "How else? Blame it on us. Stupid idiot Romans insisted on a hopeless stand. Fortunately, he was too wise to waste his men's lives defending a canal which was obviously just a Roman scheme to reinvade Persia like they did in Julian's day."

"That's pretty tortuous reasoning," muttered Maurice, shaking his head.

Again, Belisarius barked a laugh. "Of course it is! So what? It'll serve the purpose."

Maurice was still shaking his head. "What if you're wrong?" Maurice growled, "Dammit, I *hate* tricky battle plans."

Belisarius smiled. "If I'm wrong, Maurice—so what? In that case, Ormazd will have to fight the Malwa who cross the Euphrates. They may defeat him, but after fighting twenty thousand dehgans I don't think they'll be in any shape to hit us on the flank. Do you?"

Maurice said nothing. Then, sighed heavily. "All right. We'll see how it goes."

The chiliarch started to turn away. Belisarius restrained him with a hand on his shoulder.

"Wait a moment. I'm coming with you."

Maurice gave him a startled look. Valentinian and Anastasius started to squawk. Aide began to make some mental protest.

Belisarius rode them all down.

"Things have changed!" he announced gaily. "The battle's reaching its turning point. I *have* to be down there, now. Ready—at a moment's notice—to fulfill my vow to Emperor Khusrau."

Maurice smiled. Valentinian and Anastasius choked down their squawks. Aide sulked.

"Safe," sneered Belisarius. He took a moment to don his armor.

"Safe," he sneered again, as he began the long trek down the hill.

Behind him, Maurice said, "Do be a little careful, will you? Going down that miserable path, I mean. Be a bit absurd, it would, you breaking your fool neck climbing down a pile of rocks."

"Safe," sneered Belisarius.

Two eager steps later, he tripped and rolled some fifty feet down the hill. When he finally came to a halt, piling up against a boulder, it took him a minute or so to clear his head.

The first thing he saw, dizzily, was Maurice leaning over him.

"Safe," muttered the gray-bearded veteran morosely. "It's like asking a toad not to hop."

He reached down a hand and hauled Belisarius back onto his feet. "Will you mind your step, from here on?" he asked, very sweetly. "Or must we have Anastasius carry you down like a babe in swaddling clothes?"

"Safe," Belisarius assured one and all. None of whom believed him for a moment.

Chapter 33

ALEXANDRIA
Autumn, 531 A.D.

Alexandria was famous throughout the Mediterranean world for the magnificence of its public thoroughfares. The two greatest of those boulevards, which intersected each other west of the Church of St. Michael, were each thirty yards across. The intersection itself was so large it was almost a plaza, and was marked by a tetrastylon—four monumental pillars standing on each corner.

The buildings which fronted on the intersection were likewise impressive. On the north stood a huge church, measuring a hundred yards square. The edifice was hundreds of years old. Originally built as a temple dedicated to the crocodile god Sobek, it had been converted into a Christian church well over a century earlier. Most of the pagan trappings of the temple had been discarded—the crocodile mummies in the crypts had been unceremoniously pitched into the sea—but the building itself still retained the massive style of ancient Egyptian monumental architecture. It loomed over the intersection like a small mountain.

Across from it, on the south, stood a more modern building: the gymnasium which marked Greek culture everywhere in the world. And, next to it, the public baths which were a hallmark of the Roman way of life. The eastern side of the intersection was taken up by another archetypal public structure, a large theater in which the city's upper crust was entertained by dramatists and musicians. Only on the west were there any private buildings—three stately mansions, as similar as peas in a pod.

Taken as a whole, the entire effect was one of grandeur and magnificence.

But Antonina, studying that intersection from her vantage point atop the steps of her palace, was not impressed. She had grown up in a part of the city which was very different from the Greek aristocracy's downtown splendor. She had been born and raised in the native Egyptians' quarter, which still bore its old name of Rhakotis. There, the streets were neither wide nor well-paved. They were dirt alleys, which doubled as open sewers. The buildings in Rhakotis were ancient only in the sense that the collapsed mudbrick of one house served its successors as a cellar. There were no gymnasiums—no schools of any kind. As for public baths—

She snorted, remembering. The human population density in Rhakotis was bad enough. The animal population was even worse. The quarter teemed with cattle, pigs, donkeys, camels, goats—and, of course, the ubiquitous pigeons. And their pigeon shit.

The snort became an outright laugh. Zeno, standing next to her, eyed her quizzically.

"I was just thinking of the provisions of a typical

Alexandrian rental agreement. For a house or an apartment. You know, the one about—"

Zeno smiled, nodding. "Yes, I know." His voice took on a sing-song cadence: " 'At the end of the term, the tenant shall return the house to the lessor free of dung.' "

He laughed himself, now. "It was so embarrassing for me, the first time I rented an apartment in Constantinople. I was puzzled by the absence of that provision in the contract. When I inquired, the landlord looked at me as if I were crazy. Or a barbarian."

Antonina began to say something, but broke off.

"They're coming!" she heard someone shout. One of the Knights Hospitaler, she assumed.

The entire boulevard in front of her was packed with them. A thousand Knights were arrayed there, in rigid formation. They stood in lines of twenty men, covering the entire width of the boulevard, and fifty lines deep. Each man carried a quarterstaff in his hand, held erect. Their only armor, as such, were leather caps reinforced by an iron strip across the forehead. But thick quilted jerkins and shoulder-pads lay under the white tunics emblazoned with the red cross of their order, providing added protection against blunt weapons. And most of the Knights had wound heavy linen around their forearms, as well.

The majority of the other Knights were positioned in the various side-streets debouching onto the main thoroughfare, but Zeno had crammed hundreds below the street itself. Familiar with Alexandria, the Knights' commander had taken advantage of the labyrinth of cisterns which provided the great city with its water supply. If necessary, those men could either pour out onto the street from the basements of nearby houses, or they could move surreptitiously elsewhere. Zeno had twenty couriers standing nearby, ready to carry his orders when the time came.

All in all, Antonina was more than satisfied with

Zeno's dispositions. It remained to be seen, of course, how well the Knights would do in an actual fray. But Zeno, at least, seemed fully confident of their capabilities.

"There they come!" came another shout.

Peering at the distant intersection, Antonina saw that a huge mob was pouring into it from the east. Within two minutes, the intersection itself was packed with people, and the first contingents of the crowd were advancing down the boulevard toward her palace.

"Ten thousand, I make it," murmured Zeno. "Not counting those who are still out of sight."

As it drew near, the mob began to eddy and swirl. Seeing the stern-looking and disciplined formation of the Knights Hospitaler filling the street—not to mention the much scarier sight of armored cataphracts behind *them*—the faint-hearted members of the crowd began trying to get out of the front line. Pushing their way to the rear, or simply standing in one place uncertainly, they created obstacles to their more fanatical and determined compatriots.

For a minute or so, Antonina even hoped that the mob would grind to a stop and retreat. But that hope vanished. Soon enough, the disparate elements which made up the huge crowd had separated themselves out. Those who were timid, or vacillating, or merely curious, fell to the rear or pressed themselves against the walls of the various shops which lined the boulevard. The diehards surged to the fore.

The great majority of them were monks, thought Antonina. It was impossible to be certain, since the custom of monks wearing distinctive habits was still in the future. The uniform of the Knights Hospitaler was another of Belisarius' innovations. But Antonina knew the breed well. Only fanatic monks, as a rule, were quite as disheveled, shaggy-maned, and just generally dirty-looking as most of the men leading the mob. And the practiced, familiar way in which they handled their clubs and cudgels reinforced her supposition.

Antonina smiled ruefully, remembering Belisarius' description of a vision Aide had once given him of the monastic orders of the future, a time which would be called the Middle Ages. He had described to her the good works and gentle demeanor of the Benedictines and the followers of a man who would be called St. Francis of Assisi.

His Alexandria-born-and-bred wife had goggled at the description. The monks *she* knew from her youth bore as much resemblance to St. Francis as a rabid wolf to a lamb. In the Egypt of her day, the monastic orders (orthodox and Monophysite alike) were as prone to street-fighting as the thugs of the Hippodrome factions—and probably better at it. Certainly more savage.

A particularly beefy monk in the very forefront of the mob caught sight of her, standing on the steps of the palace. He raised his thick club and bellowed, "Death to the Whore of Babylon!"

Whether by predeliberation or simple spontaneous enthusiasm, the call was immediately taken up as the mob's warcry.

"Death to the whore! Death to the whore!"

The front lines of the mob charged the Knights Hospitaler barring the way. There was neither hesitation nor halfheartedness in that ferocious rush. The monks in the van were veteran brawlers. They had no fear whatever of the bizarrely-accoutered Knights, and even less of their quarterstaffs.

What the hell's the use of a six-foot-long club, anyway? No room to swing it in a street fight. Silly buggers!

Knowing what was coming, Antonina held her breath. Quarterstaffs, too, were one of Belisarius' innovations—at least, used in this manner. Shepherd's staffs were known, of course, and had featured in many a village brawl. But no-one had ever placed them in the hands of an organized force, who had been systematically trained in their use.

When the monks were just a few feet away, the captain of the front line called the command. In unison, the twenty Knights flipped their quarterstaffs level and drove them into the oncoming monks like spears. Expecting club-blows to the head, the monks were taken completely by surprise. The iron ferrules of the heavy quarterstaffs crushed into their unguarded chests and bellies.

The damage done was horrendous. Two monks died instantly, their diaphragms ruptured. Another, his sternum split and the bone fragments driven into his heart, died within seconds. The rest collapsed, tripping the ones piling up from behind. Some wailed with pain. Most didn't—broken ribs and severely lacerated bellies produce groans and hisses of agony, not loud shrieks.

Instantly, the spear-thrusts were followed by two quick, swirling, pivoting side-blows all across the line. Iron ferrules slammed into heads and rib cages, breaking both.

The captain cried out the command. Again, the stabbing quarterstaffs. Again, the scythe-like follow-on blows. A dozen more were struck down.

The mob piled higher, pushing forward, floundering on fallen bodies. Some managed to force their way through the first line of Knights, only to be mercilessly dealt with by the line which followed.

Again, the command. Again, the spear thrusts. Some of the mob, this time, knew what to expect. Tried to protect their midsections.

The Knights had expected that. This time, many of the iron-shod quarterstaff butts went into faces and heads. Skulls broke, jaws broke, teeth shattered. One throat was crushed. One neck broken.

The mob staggered. Eddied. Hesitated.

Zeno bellowed an order. Immediately, the front line of the Knights swiveled and stepped back. The second line moved forward.

The captain of that line used the forward momentum to drive through the next thrust savagely. The front of the mob reeled back—but only a few steps. The press from behind was too great. The monks in the very fore were trapped, now. Stumbling on fallen bodies, jammed up, unable to swing their own clubs—which were too short to reach the Knights, anyway—they were simply targets.

Command. *Thrust; strike; strike.* Command. *Thrust; strike; strike.*

Again, Zeno bellowed. The second line of Knights swiveled, moved back. The third line stepped forward.

Command. *Thrust; strike; strike.* Command. *Thrust; strike; strike.*

Zeno bellowed. Third line back. Fourth line up.

Command. *Thrust; strike; strike.* Command. *Thrust; strike; strike.*

Zeno was silent. The machine-like routine was established, automatic. Practiced—over and again—on grain ships. Now, tested and proven in action.

Fifth line. Sixth line. Seventh line.

The boulevard was awash in blood. The monks forced up by the surging mob behind them were like sausages pressed into a meat grinder. Their frenzied club swings could only, at best, deflect a thrusting quarterstaff—into the monk jammed alongside, more often than not. Until the next quarterstaff drove through. Then—downed, or staggering. Dead, often enough; crippled or maimed; or simply stunned or unconscious.

As the eighth line moved forward, the great mob of monks were seized by a sudden frenzy. They had seen enough to understand that their only hope was to surge over the Knights by sheer brute mass, damn the cost.

Shrieking and howling, at least two hundred fanatics lunged forward, trampling right over the bodies of the monks in front of them. They weren't even trying to use their cudgels, now. They were simply trying to close with the Knights and grapple—anything to get through that horrible zone where the quarterstaffs reigned supreme.

The surge hammered the line back. Several Knights were driven down, knocked off their feet. One was seized by the ankles and dragged into the mob, where he was savagely stomped to death. Another was pinioned by two monks while a third crushed his skull with three vicious cudgel blows.

But this, too, had been foreseen. Zeno bellowed a new command. The ninth line immediately sprang forward, bracing the eighth. Both lines locked their quarterstaffs, forming a barricade across the street. The mob slammed into that barricade, pushed it back, slowly, slowly—

The tenth line strode forward, drove their quarterstaffs through the gaps. Head-thrusts, these—there was no room for body blows.

Skulls cracked. Jaws shattered. Noses flattened. Eyes were gouged out. Teeth went flying everywhere.

Thrust. Thrust. Thrust.

Swivel. Step back. Eleventh line forward.

Thrust. Thrust. Thrust.

The lines holding back the mob were tiring now, and suffering casualties. Again, Zeno bellowed. The twelfth and thirteenth lines stepped forward and took their place, forming the barricade.

This maneuver was ragged, uneven. Switching places with a man forming a barricade is awkward, even when the man isn't bleeding and half-dazed— which many of them were. But the mob was in no position to take advantage of the momentary confusion. The monks in the fore of that mob were completely dazed, and a lot bloodier.

Soon enough, the hammering resumed.

Standing next to Antonina, Ashot whispered, "Jesus, Son of God. Mary, Mother of Christ."

Antonina's face was pale, but her stiff, cold expression never wavered.

"I told you," she stated harshly. "I told you."

She took a deep breath, almost a shudder. "Belisarius predicted this. He told me—told Zeno and the Knights' captains, too—that if they learned to use their quarterstaffs in a disciplined and organized way they could shatter any mob in the world. Easily."

Ashot shook his head. "I'm not sure the casualties in that mob are going to be much less than if we did it."

"Doesn't matter, Ashot. People don't look at clubs—which is all a quarterstaff is, technically—the same way they do edged weapons. A sword or a knife is an instrument of murder, pure and simple. Whereas a club—" She smiled wryly, and spread her hands in a half-comical little gesture.

"Tavern brawls, casual mayhem," continued Ashot, nodding. "Not *really* a deadly weapon."

He chuckled, very grimly. "Yeah, you're right. If a thousand monks got sabred, or lanced, they'd be martyrs. But if that same thousand just gets the living shit beaten out of them—even if half of them die from it—people will just shrug it off. What the hell? Fair fight. The monks had clubs too, and they've never been shy about using them. Just too bad if this new bunch of monks is a lot tougher."

Seventeenth line, now. *Thrust. Thrust. Thrust.*

"A *whole* lot tougher."

As the eighteenth line stepped forward, the mob finally broke. More accurately, the monks in the van broke. The crowd itself—the great thousands of them—had already begun edging away from the brutal battle. Edging, edging, walking, striding. Running.

There was room to retreat, now. Once they realized

it, the battered fanatics suddenly lost all their fight. Within seconds, they were running away themselves, driving the onlookers before them.

Instinctively, the Knights Hospitaler began to pursue. But Zeno, without waiting for Antonina's command, bellowed again. The Knights halted immediately. Stopped, leaned on their staffs, drew in deep gasping breaths.

Antonina turned to Ashot.

"I want you and your cataphracts to ride through the city's center. Break up into squads."

She gave him a hard stare. "*Don't attack anybody.* Not unless you're attacked yourselves, at least. I just want you to be seen. Put the fear of God in that crowd. By nightfall, I want everyone who came out on the street today to be huddling in their villas and apartments. Like mice when the cats are out."

Ashot nodded. "I understand." Instantly, he trotted toward his nearby horse.

She turned to Zeno. "Call out all the Knights you had in reserve. Divide half of them into your—" She hesitated, fumbling for the word. "What did you decide to call that? Your two-hundred-man groups?"

"Battalions."

"Yes. That should be big enough for anything you'll face now. Send each battalion marching through the streets. The big thoroughfares, only. Don't go into the side streets. And stay out of the purely residential quarters."

He nodded. "We're doing the same thing as the cataphracts. Scaring everybody."

"Hell, no!" she snarled. "I want *them* to avoid trouble. I want you to *look* for it."

Scowling, she pointed with her chin at the bodies of dead and unconscious monks which littered the boulevard.

"Think you can recognize them? Pick them out from simple residents?"

"Sure," snorted Zeno. "Look for a pack of men who'd put any mangy alley curs to shame."

"Right." She took a breath. "Hunt them down, Zeno. Don't go into any side streets—I don't want to risk any ambushes in narrow quarters. And stay out of the areas where orthodox Greek citizens live. But hunt the monks down in the main thoroughfares. It's open season, today, on Chalcedon fanatics. Hunt 'em down, bring 'em to bay, beat 'em to a pulp."

She fixed him with a hot gaze. "I want it *bloody*, Zeno. I don't want those fucking monks huddling in their cells, tonight. I want them lying in the streets. Dead, bruised, maimed, broken—I don't care. Just so long as they're completely terrorized."

"Be a pleasure," growled Zeno. He cast a cold eye at the bloody street below. Not all of the bodies lying there were those of ultra-orthodox Chalcedon monks. Here and there, he could see a few wearing the white tunic with the red cross. Already, their comrades were picking through the casualties, hoping to find one or two still alive.

There wouldn't be any, Zeno knew. Not many Knights had been pulled into the crowd. But those who had could not possibly have survived.

"Be our *pleasure*," he growled again. Then, calming himself with a breath, asked, "And what of the other half? What do you want those Knights to do?"

"They'll be coming with me," replied Antonina, "along with Hermogenes and his infantry."

"Where are we going?"

"First, to the Delta Quarter. I want to see what happened there. Then—assuming that situation's under control—we'll be heading for Beta Quarter."

She swiveled, facing Theodosius. Throughout the street battle, the new Patriarch had stood quietly a few feet behind her, along with three of his deacons.

His face was very pale, she saw. Wide-eyed, he and his deacons were examining the carnage on the street below. Sensing her gaze, the Patriarch jerked his head away and stared at her.

"What's the name of that monastery?" she demanded. "I know where it is, but I can't remember what the bastards call it."

Theodosius pursed his lips, hesitating.

Antonina's face was as hard as steel. Her green eyes were like agates. *"You know the one, Patriarch."*

He looked away, sighing.

"The House of St. Mark," he murmured. Then, with a look of appeal: "Is that really necessary, Antonina?" He pointed down to the street below. "Surely, you've made your point already."

"I'm not in the business of 'making points,' Theodosius," she hissed. "I'm not a schoolteacher, instructing unruly students."

She took three quick steps, thrusting her face into the Patriarch's beard. For all her short stature, it seemed as if it was the Patriarch looking up, not she.

"I am the rod of authority in Alexandria. I am the axe of the Empire."

She stepped back a pace. Waved toward the city's main intersection. "It's good enough to simply intimidate the average orthodox citizen. That's what Ashot and his cataphracts will be doing, now that the crowd is already broken up. But those—those—those—"

All the pent-up hatred of a woman reviled all her life by self-proclaimed holy men erupted.

"Those *stinking filthy putrid monks* are a different story altogether!"

She ground her teeth. Glared at the bodies lying on the street.

"Whore of Babylon, is it?"

When she turned back, the hot hatred was under control. Ice, now. Ice.

The agate eyes fixed on Zeno.

"The monastery called the House of St. Mark is the largest monastery in Alexandria. It's also the center of the city's most extreme Chalcedonians. Ultra-orthodox down to the cockroaches in the cellars. Before they made him Patriach, Paul was its abbot."

Zeno nodded.

"That monastery is *history*," grated Antonina. "By nightfall, it's nothing but rubble. And any monk who hasn't fled by the time we get there is on his way to Heaven."

The hate flared up anew: "Or wherever eternity calls for him. I have my own opinion."

Zeno moved away, then, rounding up his captains and explaining their new orders. Theodosius, for his part, fell back into silence. Long accustomed to the ferocious debate of a high church council, he recognized a hopeless argument when he saw one. And, even if he hadn't had the benefit of that experience, he could not misunderstand the meaning of the phrases which, now and again in the minutes which followed, came hissing out of Antonina's mouth like steam from a volcano. As she stared at the bloody street below, her face filled with cold fury.

Whore of Babylon, is it?
I'll show you the whore.
Come back to my home town, I have.

And, of course, again and again:

Fuck Alexandria.

When Antonina and her escort of Knights Hospitaler and Syrian infantry reached Delta Quarter, by midafternoon, they were immediately met by Euphronius. The commander of the Theodoran Cohort trotted up to her, along with Triphiodoros, the officer whom Hermogenes had placed in charge of the grenadiers' infantry support.

As he peered up at the woman perched on her saddle, looking a bit like a half-broiled little lobster in her armor, the young Syrian's expression was odd. Half-apologetic, half-accusing.

"I'm sorry," he said, "but—".

He gestured at the surrounding area. Looking up and down the street which marked the boundary of the Jewish quarter, Antonina could see perhaps two dozen bodies lying here and there. Hippodrome thugs. All Blues, from their garments. Killed by gunfire, for the most part, although she could see one storefront which had obviously been caved in by a grenade blast, with three bodies mixed in with the rubble.

Her eyes scanned the roofs. Six of the heavy wooden beams which braced the mudbrick construction were festooned with hanged corpses. No more.

"They ran away," complained Euphronius. "As soon as we fired the first volley." He turned, pointing to the shattered storefront. "Except that bunch. They tried to hole up in there. After we tossed in a couple of grenades, the half-dozen survivors surrendered." A self-explanatory wave at the grisly ornaments on the crossbeams.

Then, apologetically:

"We couldn't catch the rest. They ran too fast."

Then, accusingly:

"You didn't give us any cavalry."

"Can't catch routed men without cavalry," chimed in Triphiodoros. The sage voice of experience: "Men running for their lives always run faster than men who are just wanting to kill them."

Sage voice of experience: "Got to have cavalry, to really whip an enemy."

Antonina laughed. Shook her head, half-regretfully, half-ruefully. "I'll remember that!"

She turned her eyes to the Delta Quarter itself, just across the wide thoroughfare. That side of the street was lined with Jews. Young men, mostly, armed with cudgels, knives and the occasional sword or spear. As Hermogenes had predicted, the Jews had been quite ready to fight it out with the Hippodrome mob. Wouldn't have been the first time.

But, just as obviously, the tension of the moment had passed. Even the young bravos were relaxed, now, exchanging half-amicable words with Syrian grenadiers. And she could see women and children, too, here and there, as well as old folks. The children, filled with eager curiosity. The women, beginning to banter with the Syrian wives. And the old folks, of course—not for them this useless time-wasting—were already setting up their foodcarts and vending stalls. Life comes; life goes. Business is here today.

"Very good," Antonina murmured. "Very good."

Euphronius tried to maintain an officer's dignity, but his quiet relief at her approval was evident.

She smiled down at him. "Leave half your grenadiers here, Hermogenes. Along with Triphiodoros and his infantry. Just in case. Doesn't look as if the Greens showed up today. Maybe that's because they usually side with the Monophysites, but maybe it's because they're just dithering. If they change their minds, I want grenadiers here to change it back."

Euphronius nodded.

"Meanwhile, I want you and the rest to come with me."

She cocked her head, admiring the collapsed storefront. Her smile turned positively feral.

"I need some demolition experts."

By nightfall, the House of St. Mark was a pile of rubble. Buried beneath that mound of wooden beams and sundried brick were the bodies of perhaps a hundred ultra-orthodox monks. Nobody knew the exact number. From the rooftop and the windows, the monks had shrieked their defiance at the surrounding troops. Vowing never to surrender. They had particularly aimed their words at the figure of the small woman in armor sitting on a horse.

We will not yield to the Whore of Babylon!

And other phrases—considerably more vulgar—to that effect.

Antonina had not minded. Not in the least. She would not have accepted their surrender even if it had been offered. So, cheerfully, she waited for several minutes before ordering the grenadiers into action. Establishing, for the public record, that the monks had brought their doom onto themselves.

Murmuring, under her breath, a gay little jingle, as the grenades drove the monks into the interior of the huge monastery:

She's back, she's back!
The whore is back!

Chuckling quietly, as the sappers set the charges:

Alas, Alexandria!
Thy judgement has come!

Chortling aloud, as the walls came tumbling down:

How are the righteous fallen!

Chapter 34

Antonina rose before dawn the next morning, at an hour which normally found her fast asleep. But she was determined to drive through her reestablishment of imperial control without allowing the opposition a moment to regain their equilibrium.

Her servants bustled about, preparing her breakfast and clothing. When the time came to don her armor, Antonina was amused by the way her maid ogled the cuirass.

"The thing's obscene, I'll admit," she chuckled.

She walked over and examined the cuirass lying on an upholstered bench against the far wall of her sleeping chamber. Jutting into the air.

"Especially since my reputation must have grown in the telling, by the time the armorer got around to shaping his mold."

Firmly: "My tits are *not* that big."

The maid eyed her hesitantly, unsure of how to respond. The girl was new to Antonina's service. Antonina's regular maid had become ill at sea, and this girl had been hastily rounded up by her head servant Dubazes from the staff of the palace's former occupant.

There had been few of that staff left, when they arrived. Upon the arrival of Antonina's fleet, and the

destruction of the naval forces which tried to block
her way into the Great Harbor, the former owner had
fled Alexandria. He was a Greek nobleman with close
ties to Paul and Ambrose's faction, and had apparently decided that discretion was the better part of
valor. He would wait out the storm at his estate in
far-off Oxyrhynchos.

Antonina thought about that nobleman, as her maid
helped her into the armor. Not about *him* so much—
she didn't even know the man's name—but about
what he represented. He was not alone in his actions.
A very large part of Alexandria's Greek nobility had
done likewise.

By the time she was buckling on the scabbard
which held her cleaver, a task for which the maid was
no use at all, she had made her decision. Two decisions, actually. Possibly three.

First, there would be no repercussions against the
nobles who had stepped aside and remained neutral
in the battle. Not even those who had fled outright.
She was simply trying to establish firm imperial
control over the city. Many—most—of the orthodox
Greek nobility, especially in Alexandria, would remain
hostile to the dynasty no matter what she did. So long
as that hostility remain muted—a thing of whispers
in the salons, rather than riots in the streets—she
would ignore it.

Second—a lesser decision flowing from the first—
she would instruct Dubazes to make sure the palace
was in pristine condition when she left to take up her
new residence at the Prefect's palace. The new Prefect
had been officially installed the previous evening.
There had been no opposition. His predecessor, along
with the deposed Patriarch Paul, had fled to the
military quarter at Nicopolis to take refuge with
Ambrose and his Army of Egypt.

She snorted quietly. When the nobleman, whoever
he was, eventually crept back into his palace, he

would be surprised to discover it had not been ransacked and vandalized. The discovery would not dispose him any more favorably to the imperial authority, of course. But the calm certitude behind that little act of self-discipline might help strengthen his resolve to keep his head down.

Good enough.

Finally, a small thing, but—

She turned to her maid, and examined the girl. Under that scrutiny, the maid lowered her head timidly.

Egyptian. Not twenty years of age. From the Fayum, I'm willing to bet. Her Greek is good, but that accent is unmistakable.

"What is your name?" she asked.

"Koutina," said the maid.

"You are Monophysite?"

Koutina raised her eyes, startled. Antonina did not miss the fear hidden there.

She waved her hand reassuringly. "It means nothing to me, Koutina. I simply—" *Want to know your loyalties. An Egyptian Monophysite from the Fayum. Yes.*

She switched from Greek to the girl's native tongue. Antonina's own Coptic was still fluent, even if her long residence in Constantinople had given it a bit of an accent.

"I'll be leaving here today, Koutina. My regular maid will not recover from her illness soon. In fact, I will be sending her back to Constantinople to be with her family. So I will need a new maid. Would you like the job?"

Koutina was still staring at her uncertainly. The question about her religious loyalties had obviously unsettled the girl. Paul's persecution had been savage.

"I would *prefer* a Monophysite, Koutina." She smiled, patting the heavy cuirass. "I'm not wearing this grotesque thing for protection from heretics, you know."

Koutina began to return the smile. "You are very famous," she said softly. "I was frightened when you came." Her eyes flitted to the blade buckled to Antonina's waist. "We all heard about the Cleaver, even here in Alexandria."

"It has never been used against any but traitors."

"I know," said Koutina, nodding. "Still—"

Suddenly, all hesitation fled. "I would be delighted." She was beaming now. "It would be so exciting! You are going to fight the Malwa, everyone says so. Can I come there too?"

It was Antonina's turn to be startled. She had only intended to keep the girl in her service during her stay in Alexandria. But now, seeing the eagerness in Koutina's face, she began to reconsider. The young Egyptian was obviously not worried about the risks involved. Boredom, not danger, was the girl's lifelong enemy.

It was an enemy which Antonina herself well remembered, from her own girlhood. The grinding, relentless, tedious labor of a woman born into Egypt's poor masses. Koutina had probably left the Fayum seeking a better life in Alexandria—only to find that she had exchanged the toil of a peasant for the drudgery of a domestic servant.

She could not refuse that eager face. True, the girl might find her death, in Antonina's company. But she would not be—*bored.*

And besides, I need servants whose loyalty I can absolutely trust. Dubazes is not enough. I am certain the Malwa have infiltrated spies into my expedition. I must be certain they don't penetrate my own household.

Koutina, from the Fayum. Yes. I know that breed. The Malwa will have nothing to offer her except money, and I—

She laughed. Belisarius had not turned over *all* of the fortune he garnered in India to finance

Shakuntala's rebellion. Nor had he given more than *half* of his war booty to his cataphracts.

And I am richer than any Malwa spymaster.

She grinned. "Done, Koutina. I will pay you well, too. Much better than your former employer."

Koutina's expression was an odd mixture of emotions. Pleasure at the thought of a sudden increases in wages; anger at the thought of her former employer. The man had been a cheapskate, obviously. And had combined that miserliness, Antonina was quite certain, with frequent solicitations. Koutina was pretty as well as young.

Smiling: "And I won't be rattling your door latch, either, late at night, trying to get into your room."

"That bastard!" hissed Koutina.

It was time to go. Time to crush a military rebellion. But Antonina had long since learned to savor all her victories—small ones, as well as large. So she took the moment to exchange a warm look with her new servant. Binding loyalty with her eyes, far more than her purse.

The maid broke the moment.

"You must go, you must go!" Koutina began bustling Antonina out of the room, fussing over the scabbard which held the cleaver. "Ambrose must be brought to heel!"

Out into the corridor, bustling her mistress along. Fussing, now, with the straps that held the cuirass. "He probably won't fight you, anyway. His soldiers will be blinded by the sun, shining off your brass boobs. You must be a giantess, they're so huge! They'll be terrified and run away!"

The stern-faced officers who awaited her in the entryway to the palace were startled, then. Startled—and mightily heartened. Appearing before them was the leader of their grim and perilous mission—a woman, and small at that—howling with laughter. As gay a laughter as they had ever heard. At any time, much less on the morning of a battle.

They took courage from the thought. Stern faces grew sterner still.

And Antonina kept laughing, and laughing, all the way out to her horse waiting in the courtyard. She wasn't sure what amused her most—the thought of her brass breasts, which made her laugh, or the way her laughter so obviously boosted the morale of her men.

Either way, either way. Doesn't matter. Out of small victories come great ones.

As her army marched through the streets of Alexandria, heading toward the suburb of Nicopolis where the Roman garrison had been stationed since the early days of imperial rule, Antonina took the opportunity to assess the city's mood. The streets were lined with people, watching the procession. Most of them were Egyptians and poor Greeks. Both were cheering—the Egyptians with loud enthusiasm, the Greeks with more restraint.

Word had already spread through the city that Theodosius had been installed as the new Patriarch. That news had been greeted by the Egyptian Monophysites with wild acclaim. Theodosius was one of their own. True, he was an adherent of the Severan school, whose moderate and compromising attitude toward the official Church was out of step with the more dogmatic tradition of Egyptian Monophysitism. But the Egyptian residents of Alexandria did not look on these things the same way as the fanatic Monophysite monks of the desert. They had had enough of street brawls, and persecution. Doctrinal fine points be damned. The Empress Theodora was one of them, and she had placed another in the Church of St. Michael.

Good enough—more than good enough!—to declare a holiday.

The Greek residents who watched Antonina pass—and cheered her on—took less pleasure in the news.

Many of Alexandria's Greek population, of course, had adopted Monophysitism themselves. All of the religious leaders of that dogma were Greek, in fact, even if they found their popular base in the Coptic masses of Egypt. But most Greeks, even poor ones, had remained true to orthodoxy.

Still, they were not nobles. Tailors, bakers, linen-makers, glassblowers, sailors, papyrus workers—almost all the Mediterranean world's paper was made in Alexandria—shopkeepers, merchants, domestic servants, fishermen, grain handlers: the list was well nigh endless. Some were prosperous, some merely scraped by; but none were rich. And all of them, even here in Alexandria, had come to accept the general opinion of the Roman Empire's great masses with regard to the imperial power.

That opinion had crystallized, in Constantinople itself, with the defeat of the Nika insurrection. From there, carried by the sailors and merchants who weaved Roman society into a single cloth, the opinion had spread to every corner of the Empire. From the Danube to Elephantine, from Cyrene to Trebizond, the great millions of Rome's citizens had heard, discussed, quarreled, decided.

The dynasty which ruled the Empire was *their* dynasty.

It never occurred to them, of course, to think of the dynasty as a "people's dynasty." Emperors were emperors; common folk were common folk. The one ruled the other. Law of nature.

But they did think of it as *theirs*. Not because the dynasty came from their own ranks—which it did, and they knew it, and took pleasure in the knowing—so much as they were satisfied that the dynasty understood *them*; and based its power on *their* support; and kept at least one eye open on behalf of *their* needs and interests.

Common folk were common folk, emperors were

emperors, and never the twain shall meet. That still leaves the difference between a good emperor and a bad one—a difference which common folk measure with a very different stick than nobility.

The taxes had been lowered, and made more equitable. The haughtiest nobles and the most corrupt bureaucrats had been humbled, always a popular thing, among those over whom the elite lords it—even *executed*. Wildly popular, that. Stability had been restored, and with it the conditions which those people needed to feed their families.

And, finally, there was Belisarius.

As she marched through the streets, Antonina was struck by how often her husband's name made up the cheer coming from the throats of the Greek residents. The Egyptians, too, chanted his name. But they were as likely to call out her own or the Empress Theodora's.

Among the Greeks, one name only:

Belisarius! Belisarius! Belisarius!

She took no personal umbrage in that chant. If nothing else, it was obvious that the cheer was the Greeks' way of approving her, as well. She was Belisarius' wife, and if the Greek upper crust had often sneered at the general for marrying such a disreputable woman, it was clear as day that the Greek commoners lining the streets of Alexandria were not sneering at him in the least.

The Greeks had found their own way to support the dynasty, she realized. Belisarius might be a Thracian himself, and might have married an Egyptian, and put his half-Egyptian, half-who-knows-what bastard stepson on the throne, but he was still a *Greek*. In the way which mattered most to that proudest of Rome's many proud nations.

Whipped the Persians, didn't he? Just like he'll whip these Malwa dogs. Whoever they are.

Hermogenes leaned over to her, whispering: "The word of Anatha's already spread."

Antonina nodded. She had just gotten the word herself, the day before. The semaphore network was still half-finished, but enough of it had been completed to bring the news to Antioch—and from there, by a swift keles courier ship, to Alexandria.

There had been nothing personal, addressed to her, in the report. But she had recognized her husband's turn of phrase in the wording of it. And had seen his shrewd mind at work, in the way he emphasized the decisive role of Greek cataphracts in winning the great victory over Malwa.

That word, too, had obviously spread. She could read it in the way Greek shopkeepers grinned, as they cheered her army onward, and the way Greek sailors hoisted their drinking cups in salute to the passing soldiers.

Thank you, husband. Your great victory has given me a multitude of small ones.

The fortress at Nicopolis where the Army of Egypt lay waiting was one of the Roman Empire's mightiest. Not surprising. The garrison was critical to the Empire's rule. Egyptian grain fed the Roman world—Constantinople depended upon it almost entirely—and the grain was shipped through Alexandria's port. Since Augustus, every Roman Emperor had seen to it that Egypt was secure. For centuries, now, the fort at Nicopolis had been strengthened, expanded, modified, built up, and strengthened yet again.

"We'll never take it by storm," stated Ashot. "Not with the forces we've got. Even grenades'd be like pebbles, against those walls."

He looked up at the battlements, where a mass of soldiers could be seen standing guard.

"Be pure suicide for sappers, trying to set charges."

Ashot, along with Antonina and Hermogenes and the other top officers of the expedition, was observing the fortress from three hundred yards away. Their vantage point was another of the great intersections which dotted Alexandria itself. Very similar to the one at the city's center, if not quite as large, down to the tetrastylon.

Originally, the fortress had been built outside the city's limits. But Alexandria had spread, over the centuries. Today, the city's population numbered in the hundreds of thousands. The fortress had long since been engulfed within the suburb called Nicopolis.

It was a bit jarring, actually, the way that massive stone structure—so obviously built for war—rose up out of a sea of small shops and mudbrick apartment buildings. Comical, almost. In the way that a majestic lion might seem comical, if it were surrounded by chittering mice.

Except there were no chittering mice *that* day. The shops were boarded up, the apartments vacant. Nicopolis' populace had fled, the moment news came that Antonina was advancing against Ambrose. All morning, a stream of people had poured out of the suburb, bearing what valuables they owned in carts or haversacks.

Antonina turned to Hermogenes. "Do you agree?"

Hermogenes nodded instantly. "Ashot's right. I know that fortress. I was stationed in it for a few months, shortly after I joined the army. You can't believe how thick those stone walls are until you see them."

He twisted in his saddle and looked back at Menander.

"Could you take it with siege guns? You're the only one of us who's observed them in action."

Seeing himself the focus of attention, the shy young cataphract tensed. But there was no faltering or hesitation in his reply.

"Yes, I could, if we had them. But John told me

just yesterday that he doesn't expect to produce any for months. Even then, it'd take weeks to reduce those walls."

Very shyly, now: "I don't know as Antonina can afford to wait that long."

"Absolutely not," she said firmly. "The longer this drags on, the more likely it is that revolt will start brewing in other parts of Alexandria. The rest of Egypt, for that matter. Paul has plenty of supporters in every one of the province's Greek towns, all the way up to Ombos and Syene, just below the First Cataract. Antinoopolis and Oxyrhynchos are hotbeds of disloyalty. Not to mention—"

She fell silent. The top officers surrounding her knew the strategic plan which she and Belisarius had worked out, months earlier, to carry the fight to Malwa's exposed southern flank. But the more junior officers didn't. Antonina had no reason to doubt their loyalty, but there was still the risk of loose talk being picked up by Malwa spies.

So she bit her tongue and finished the thought only in her mind:

Not to mention that I don't have weeks—months!— to waste in Alexandria. I've got to get to the Red Sea, and join forces with the Axumites. By early spring of next year, at the latest.

And the next one, full of anguish: *Or my husband, if he's not already, will be a dead man.*

But nothing of that anguish showed, in her face. Simply calm resolution.

"No, gentlemen, we've got to win this little civil war *quickly*."

Ashot tugged his beard and growled. "I'm telling you, it'll be pure slaughter if we try to storm that place."

Antonina waved him down. "Relax, Ashot. I'm not crazy. I have no intention of wasting lives in a frontal attack. But I don't think it's necessary."

Hermogenes, too, was tugging his beard.

"A siege'll take months. A year, probably, unless we get siege guns. That fortress has enough provisions to last that long, easily. And they've got two wells inside the walls."

Antonina shook her head. "I wasn't thinking of a siege, either."

Seeing the confusion in the faces around her, Antonina had to restrain a sigh.

Generals.

"You're approaching the situation upside down," she stated. "This is not really a military problem. It's *political.*"

To Ashot: "Weren't you the one who was telling me, just yesterday, that the reason Ambrose couldn't intervene while we were suppressing the mob was because he needed the day to win over his troops?"

The commander of her Thracian bucellarii nodded.

She grinned. "Well, he's had a day. Just how solid do you think he's made himself? With his troops?"

Frowning.

Generals.

She pointed at the fortress. "How long have those men—the soldiers, I mean—been stationed here? Hermogenes?"

The young merarch shrugged.

"Years. Most of the garrison—the troops, anyway—spend their entire term of service in Egypt. Even units that get called out for a campaign elsewhere are always rotated back here."

"That's what I thought. Now—another question. Where do those men *live?* Not in the fortress, I'm sure. Years of service, you said. That means wives, children, families. Outside businesses, probably. Half of those soldiers—*at least* half—will have married into local families. They'll have invested their pay in their father-in-laws' shops. Bought interests in grain-shipping."

"The whole bit," grumbled Ashot. "Yeah, you're right. Fucking garritroopers. Always takes weeks to shake 'em down on a campaign. Spend the first month, solid, wailing about their declining property values back home."

The light of understanding came, finally, to her officers.

Or so, at least, she thought.

"You're right, Antonina!" cried Hermogenes excitedly. "That'll work!"

He cast eager eyes about, scanning the immediate environment of the fortress. "Most of 'em probably live right here, right in Nicopolis. We'll start by burning everything to the ground. Then—"

"Find their wives and daughters," chipped in his executive officer, Callixtos. "Track 'em down wherever they are and—"

"Won't need to," countered Ashot. "Any women'll do. At this distance, the garrison won't be able to make out faces anyway. Just women being stripped naked in the street with us waving our dicks around and threatening to—"

Antonina erupted. "*Stupid generals!*"

Startled, her horse twitched. Antonina drew back on the reins savagely. Wisely, the horse froze.

"Cretins! Idiots! Morons—absolute morons—the whole lot! You want me to end a small civil war by starting a big one? What the fuck is wrong with you?"

They shrank from her hot eyes. Antonina turned in her saddle and transferred the glare back to Menander.

"*You!* Maybe you're not too old to have lost all your wits! *Maybe.* How would *you* handle it?"

For a moment, Menander was too stunned to speak. Then, clearing his throat, he said, "Well. Well. Actually, while you were talking I was thinking about how the general—Belisarius, I mean—handled the situation with the Kushans. The *second* situation with the Kushans, I mean—not the first one where he tricked Venandakatra out of using them as guards—but the other one, where he—well, they were guarding us but didn't know the Empress—Shakuntala, I mean, not Theodora—was hidden in—well."

He stopped, floundering. Drew a deep, shaky breath.

"What I mean is, I was struck by it at the time. How the general used honey instead of vinegar."

Antonina sighed. Relaxed, a bit.

"You're promoted," she growled. "*Tribune* Menander, you are."

The eyes which she now turned on her assembled officers were no longer hot.

Oh, but they were very, very cold.

"*Here—is—what—you—will—do*. You *will* find the wives and daughters—and the sons and fathers and mothers and brothers and for that matter the second cousins twice-removed—of those soldiers forted up in that place."

Deep breath. *Icy* cold eyes.

"*More precisely*, you and your cataphracts will *escort* the Knights Hospitaler while *they* do the actual finding. You and your soldiers will stand there looking as sweet and polite as altar boys—or I'll have your guts for breakfast—while the Knights Hospitaler *convince* the soldiers' families that a potentially disastrous situation for their husbands and fathers and sons and brothers—and for that matter third cousins three times removed—would be resolved if the families would come back to their homes and reopen the shops. And—most important—would cook some meals."

"*Cook meals?*" choked Hermogenes.

A wintry smile.

"Yes. *Meals*. Big meals, like the ones I remember from my days here. Spicy meals. The kind of meals you can smell a mile away."

She gazed at the fortress, still smiling.

"Let the soldiers smell those meals, while they're chewing on their garrison biscuits. Let them think about their warm beds—with their wives in them—while they sleep on the battlements in full armor. Let them think about their little shops and their father-in-laws' promises that they'll inherit the business, while Ambrose gives speeches."

"They'll *never* agree to it," squeaked Ashot. "Their wives and daughters, I mean. And their families."

He squared his shoulders, faced Antonina bravely. "They won't come back. Not with us here. Hell, *I* wouldn't, come down to it."

An arctic smile. "That I can believe. Which is why you *won't* be here. Not you, not your cataphracts. Not Hermogenes, nor his infantry regulars. *I'll* be here, as a guarantee. Their own hostage, if they want to think of it that way."

"*What?*" demanded Hermogenes. "*Alone?*"

Suddenly, Antonina's usual warm smile returned. "Alone? Of course not! What a silly idea. My grenadiers will stay here with me. Along with *their* wives, and *their* children."

All the officers now stared at Euphronius. The young Syrian met that gaze with his own squared shoulders. And then, with a grin.

"Great idea. Nobody'll worry about *us* raping anybody." A shudder. "God, my wife'd kill me!"

Ashot turned back to Antonina. The short, muscular Armenian was practically gobbling.

"What if Ambrose sallies?" he demanded. "Do you think your grenadiers—*alone*—can stand up to him?"

Antonina never wavered. "As a matter of fact—*yes*. Here, at least."

She pointed down the thoroughfare to the fortress. "We're not on an open field of battle, Ashot. There's only two ways Ambrose can come at me. He can send his men through all the little crooked side streets—and I will *absolutely* match my grenadiers against him in *that* terrain—"

All the officers were shaking their heads. No cataphract in his right mind would even think of driving armored horses through that rabbit warren.

"—*or*, he can come at me with a massed lance charge down that boulevard. Which is what he'll do, if he does anything. Down that beautiful boulevard—which is just wide enough to tempt a horseman, but not wide enough to maneuver."

She bestowed a very benign, approving smile upon the boulevard in question.

"And *yes*, on *that* terrain, my grenadiers will turn him into sausage."

She drew herself up in the saddle, sitting as tall as she could. Which was not much, of course.

"*Do as I say.*"

Her officers hastened to obey, then, with no further protest.

Possibly, that was due to the iron command in her voice.

But possibly—just possibly—it was because when she drew herself up in the saddle the blazing sun of Egypt reflected off her cuirass at such an angle as to momentarily blind her generals. And make a short woman seem like a giantess.

By noon of the next day, the first families began trickling back into Nicopolis. Antonina was there to greet them, from the pavilion she had set up in the very middle of the boulevard.

The first arrivals approached her timidly. But, finding that the legendary Antonina—*she of the Cleaver*—was, in person, a most charming and sweet-tempered lady, they soon began to relax.

By nightfall, hundreds had returned, and were slowly beginning to mingle with the grenadiers. All of the Syrians could speak Greek now, even if many of them still spoke it badly. So they were able to communicate with the soldiers' families. Coptic was the native language of most of those folk, but, as was universally the case in Alexandria, they were fluent in Greek as well.

By morning of the day after, the soldiers' families were quite at ease with the grenadiers. True, the men were a bit scary, what with their bizarre and much-rumored new weapons. But their wives were a familiar thing, even if they were foreign Syrians, as were their children. And it is difficult—impossible, really—to be petrified by a man who is playing with his child, or being nagged by his wife.

By the end of that second day, half of Nicopolis' residents had returned. Antonina's presence and assurances, combined with worry over their businesses and properties, proved irresistable.

On the morning of the following day, Antonina called for a feast. At her own expense, foodstuffs were purchased from all over the city. The great thoroughfare—not three hundred yards from the fortress—was turned into an impromptu, gigantic, daylong picnic.

As the picnic progressed, some of the wives of the garrison soldiers began to approach the fortress. Calling up to their husbands.

The first negotiations began, in a matter of speaking. Soldiers on the battlements began lowering baskets tied to ropes. Foodstuffs went up, to relieve the tedium of garrison biscuits. With those delicious parcels went wifely words, shouted from below. Scolding words, in some cases. Pleading words, in others. Downright salacious promises, in not a few.

Watching from her pavilion, Antonina counted every basket as a cannonball struck. Every wifely word, as a sapper's mine laid.

She leaned back easily in her couch, surrounded by the small horde of Nicopolis' housewives who had adopted her as their new patron saint, and savored the moment.

Great victories out of small ones.
Generals. Ha!

On the fifth day of the "siege," the first real trouble began. As one of the wives approached the fortress—this had now become a daily occurrence, almost a ritual—a small crowd of officers forced their way through the mob of soldiers standing on the battlements.

Threats were exchanged between officers and men. Then, one of the officers angrily grabbed a soldier's bow and took it upon himself to fire an arrow at the wife standing on the street below.

The arrow missed its mark, badly. The startled, squawking, outraged housewife was actually in much greater danger of being struck by the next missile hurled from the walls.

The officer himself, half-dead before he even hit the ground, fifty feet below.

The shaken housewife squawled, now, as she was spattered by his blood. Shrieked, then, covering her head and racing from the scene, as six more officers were sent on the same fatal plunge.

The rest of the day, and into the night, the crowd standing outside the fortress could hear the sounds of brawling and fighting coming from within. Antonina herself, even from the pavilion's distance, could hear it clearly.

By now, Antonina had relented enough to allow Ashot and Hermogenes to return to Nicopolis. Some of Hermogenes' soldiers had been allowed in, as well—just enough to provide her grenadiers with an infantry bulwark in the event of a battle. But she still kept the cataphracts well out of sight.

She stood in the entry of her pavilion next to her two officers, gauging the sounds.

"It's not a full battle, yet," opined Hermogenes.

"Not even close," agreed Ashot. "What you're hearing is about a hundred little brawls and set-tos. Ambrose is losing it completely."

Hermogenes glanced sideways at Antonina. "He'll sally tomorrow. Bet on it."

Ashot nodded. "He's got to. He can't let Antonina sit out here, rotting his army out from under him."

"How many will he still have, do you think?" she asked.

Ashot shrugged. "His cataphracts. The most of them, anyway. Those aren't Egyptians. They're a Greek unit, from Paphlagonia. Been here less than a year. They won't have much in the way of local ties, and all of their officers—down to the tribunes—were handpicked by Ambrose."

He tugged his beard. "Six hundred men, let's say. Beyond that—"

Tug, tug. His eyes widened. "Mary, Mother of God. I think that's *it*."

Eagerly, now: "I could bring up the Thracian bucellarii. Those fat-ass garritrooper shits'd never have a chance! We'd—"

"*No.*"

The gaze which she bestowed on Ashot was not icy, not in the least. The past few days, if nothing else, had restored her good temper. But it was still just as unyielding.

"My grenadiers I said it would be. My grenadiers it is."

Ashot sighed, but did not argue the point. Antonina was wearing her armor at all times, now, except when she slept. True, the sun was down. But the many candles in her pavilion still shined off her cuirass, making her seem—

Jesus, he thought, *how can any woman have tits that big?*

✧　　✧　　✧

As the night wore on, the sounds of fighting within the fortress waned. Then, at daybreak, a sudden outburst erupted. Rapidly escalated to the sounds of a pitched battle.

Antonina had prepared the grenadiers the night before. By the time the battle within the fortress was in full swing, Antonina was already out on the street, in armor, on horseback. Ashot and Hermogenes sat their horses alongside her.

Ahead of them, drawn up and ready for battle, stood the Theodoran Cohort.

Three hundred of them were now armed with John of Rhodes' new handcannons. The handcannons had barrels made of welded wrought-iron staves, hooped with iron bands, mounted on wooden shoulder stocks. The barrels were about eighteen inches long, with a bore measuring approximately one inch in diameter.

The guns were loaded from reed cartridges with a measured charge in one end of the tube and a fiber wad and lead ball in the other. A hardwood ramrod recessed into the front of the stock was used to ram the charges down the barrel. The handcannons had no trigger. The charges were ignited by a slow match—tow soaked in saltpeter—held in a pivoting clamp attached to the stock.

As handheld firearms go, they were about as primitive as could be imagined. John of Rhodes had wanted to wait until he had developed a better weapon, but Belisarius had insisted on rushing these first guns into production. From experience, he had known that John would take forever to produce a gun he was finally satisfied with. The Malwa would not give them that time. These would do, for the moment.

Primitive, the guns were. Their accuracy was laughable—and many a bucellarii did laugh, during the practice sessions in Rhodes, watching the Syrian gunners miss targets at a range that any self-respecting Thracian cataphract could have hit with an arrow blind drunk. But it was noticeable that none of the scoffing cataphracts offered to serve as a target. Not after watching the effects of a heavy lead bullet which *did* happen to strike a target. Those balls could drive an inch into solid pine—and with far greater striking power than any arrow.

The formation into which the Cohort was drawn up was designed to take advantage of the hand-cannons. Half of the gunners were arrayed at the Cohort's front, in six lines stretching across the entire width of the boulevard, twenty-five men to a line. Squads of Hermogenes' infantry were interspersed between each line of gunners, ready to use their long pikes to hold off any cavalry who made it through the gunfire.

The other hundred and fifty gunners were lining the rooftops for fifty yards down both sides of the boulevard, ready to pour their own fire onto the street below. The rest of the Cohort, armed with grenades, stood in back of the gunners, their slings and bombs in hand.

The sounds of the fighting within the fortress seemed to be reaching a crescendo. For a moment, the gates of the fortress began to open. Then, accompanied by the steel clangor of swords on shields, swung partially shut.

"Christ," muttered Ashot. "Now that poor bastard Ambrose has to fight his way *out* of the fortress. What a mess that's got to be in there!"

Suddenly, the gates of the fortress opened wide. Seconds later, the first of Ambrose's cataphracts began spilling out into the street.

It was immediately obvious that the enemy cataphracts were totally disorganized and leaderless.

"That's not a sally!" exclaimed Hermogenes. "They're just trying to get out of the fortress."

"Fuck 'em," hissed Antonina. *"Euphronius!"*

The Cohort commander waved, without even

bothering to look back. The nearest cataphracts were not much more than two hundred yards away. Well within range for his best slingers.

"Sling-staffs!" he bellowed. "Volley!"

Twenty grenadiers standing in the rear wound up, swirled in the peculiarly graceful way of slingers, sent the missiles on their way.

His best grenadiers, those twenty, with the most proficient fuse-cutting wives. Only three of the grenades fell short. None fell wide. Only two burst too late; none, too soon.

The crowd of cataphracts jostling their way out of the fortress—perhaps four hundred, by now—were ripped by fifteen grenades bursting in their midst. Then, a moment or so later, by the belated explosions of the two whose fuses had been cut overlong.

The casualties among the cataphracts themselves were fairly light, in truth. Their heavy armor— designed to fend off dehgan lances and axes—was almost impervious to the light shrapnel of grenades. And while that armor provided little protection against concussion, a man had to be very close to a grenade blast in order to be killed by the pure force of the explosion itself.

But their *horses*—

The armor worn by the cavalry mounts was even heavier. But it was concentrated entirely on their heads, chests, and withers. The grenades—especially the ones which exploded near the ground—shattered their legs and spilled their intestines. And, most of all, threw even the unwounded beasts into a frenzied terror.

Ambrose's cataphracts had been nothing but a mob, anyway. Now, they were simply a mob desperately trying to get out of the line of fire. More cataphracts piled out of the gates, adding to the confusion. Another volley sailed their way. More horses were butchered.

Another volley of grenades landed in their midst.

Ambrose's loyalists dissolved completely, then. There was no thought of anything but personal safety. Breaking up into small groups—or simply as individuals—the cataphracts raced their horses down the streets of Nicopolis.

Going where? Who knows? Just—somewhere else. Anywhere else.

Anywhere common soldiers weren't rising in mutiny.

Anywhere grenades didn't rupture their bodies.

Anywhere the hot sun of Egypt didn't blind them, glancing off the great brass tits of a giantess.

Anywhere else.

Antonina captured the would-be Emperor two days later. In a manner of speaking.

After negotiating safe passage, a small group of Ambrose's subordinates rode up to the Prefectural Palace where Antonina now made her headquarters, accompanied by perhaps a dozen cataphracts.

And a corpse, wrapped in a linen shroud.

Ambrose, it was. The former commander of the Army of Egypt had been stabbed in the back. Several times.

He made us do it.

Loyal Romans, we are. Honest.

He made us do it.

And we'll never do it again, neither.

Neverneverneverever.

We promise.

Antonina let it pass. She even welcomed the "loyal officers" back into the ranks of the Army of Egypt. Reduced in rank, naturally. But even that punishment, she sweetened. Partly, with an explanation that room needed to made for the *new* officers whom the *new* commander had brought with him. Mostly, with a peroration on the subject of the future riches of Roman soldiers, from Malwa booty.

The officers made no complaint. They were glad enough not to be hanged.

The only grumbling at her lenient treatment of Ambrose's cataphracts, ironically enough, came from the other soldiers in his army. They were disgruntled that the same louts they had battled in the fortress— the stinking bums who had threatened their wives, even *shot arrows* at one of them—were let off so lightly.

But they didn't do more than grumble—and rather quietly, at that. Their own position, after all, was a bit precarious.

Best to let bygones be bygones. All things considered.

Someone, of course, had to pay the bill. Ambrose himself being dead—which didn't stop Antonina from hanging his corpse, and leaving it to sway in the wind from the fortress' battlements—the bill was presented to Paul and the former Prefect.

Both men had been found, after the cataphracts fled, huddling in one of the fortress' chambers. Paul, still defiant; the Prefect, blubbering for mercy.

Antonina hanged the Prefect immediately. His body swayed in the wind at the great intersection at the center of the city, suspended from one of the tetrastylon pillars.

Paul—

"No martyrs," she pronounced, waving down the bloodthirsty chorus coming from all her advisers except Theodosius. "An executed prefect is just a dead politician. Nobody gives a damn except his cronies, and they won't grieve for more than a day. A religious leader, on the other hand—"

She straightened in the chair which, for all intents and purposes, served as her throne in the audience

chamber of the Prefectural Palace. Officially, of
course, authority was in the hands of the new Prefect. In the real world—

He was standing in the crowd before her. One
among many.

Her officers almost winced, seeing that erect, chest-
swelling motion. But there was no blinding flash, this
time. Antonina had stopped wearing her cuirass. Just
the firm posture of a small woman. Voluptuous, true.
But no giantess.

Not that the sight of that familiar, very female form
led them to think they could oppose her will. Giantess
or no, brass tits or no, on *that* matter the question
was settled.

Seated on her "throne," Antonina decreed.

"No martyrs."

Theodosius sighed with relief. Seeing the little
movement, Antonina turned her gaze onto him.

"What do you recommend, Patriarch?" she asked,
smiling now. "A long stay on the island of Palmaria,
perhaps? Tending goats. For the next fifteen or twenty
years."

"Excellent idea!" exclaimed Theodosius. Piously:
"It's good for the soul, that sort of simple manual
labor. Everyone knows it. It's a constant theme in the
best sermons."

Off to Palmaria, then, Paul went. The very same
day. Antonina saw him off personally. Stood on the
dock until his ship was under sail.

He was still defiant, Paul was. Cursed her for a
whore and a harlot all the way to the dock, all the
way out to his transport, and from the very stern of
the ship which took him to his exile.

Antonina, throughout, simply responded with a
sweet smile. Until his ship was halfway to the horizon.

Then, and only then, did the smile fade. Replaced
by a frown.

"I feel kind of guilty about this," she admitted.

Standing next to her, Ashot was startled.

"About Paul? I think that bastard's lucky—"

"Not *him*," she snorted. "I was thinking about the poor goats."

Chapter 35

THE EUPHRATES
Autumn, 531 A.D.

"So where's your flank attack?" demanded Maurice. "You remember—the one you predicted was going to happen that very night. About a week ago."

Belisarius shrugged. Reclining comfortably against the crude rock wall of one of the artillery towers on the dam, he returned Maurice's glower with a look of complacence.

"I forgot about the negotiations," he explained.

"What negotiations?"

Belisarius stuck his thumb over his shoulder, pointing southwest.

"The ones that Ormazd has been having with the Malwa, these past few days." He reached down and brought a goblet to his lips, sipping from its contents.

Maurice eyed the goblet with disfavor.

"How can you drink that stuff? You're starting to go native on me, I can tell. A Roman—sure as hell a Thracian—should be drinking wine, not that—that—that Persian—"

Belisarius smiled crookedly. "I find fresh water flavored with lemon and pomegranate juice to be quite refreshing, Maurice. I thank Baresmanas for introducing me to it."

He levered himself into an upright position. "Besides," he added, "if I drank wine all day—day after day, stuck on this misbegotten dam—I'd be a complete sot by now."

"Anastasius and Valentinian drink wine," came the immediate riposte. "Haven't noticed them stumbling about."

Belisarius cast a cold eye on his two bodyguards, not four yards away. Like Belisarius, Anastasius and Valentinian were lounging in the shade provided by the artillery tower.

"With his body weight," growled the general, "Anastasius could drink a tun of wine a day and never notice." Anastasius, hearing, looked down at his immense frame with philosophical serenity. "And as for Valentinian—ha! The man not only looks like a weasel, he can eat and drink like one, too." Valentinian, hearing, looked down at his whipcord body with his own version of philosophical serenity. Which, more than anything, resembled a weasel after gorging itself in a chickencoop.

Suddenly, Belisarius thrust himself to his feet. The motion was pointless, really. It simply expressed the general's frustration at the past week of immobility. Stuck on a dam with his army while they fought it out, day after day, with an endless series of Malwa probes and attacks.

For all practical purposes, the battle had become a siege. Belisarius was a master of siegecraft—whether on offense or defense—but it was a type of warfare that he personally detested. His temperament led him to favor maneuver rather than simple mayhem.

He had not even had the—so to speak—relief of personal combat. On the first day after joining his army on the dam itself, Belisarius had started to participate directly in repelling one of the Malwa attacks. Even before Anastasius and Valentinian had corraled him and dragged him away, the Syrian soldiers manning that section of the wall had fiercely driven him off. Liberius and Maurice, riding up with their cataphracts to bolster the Syrians, had even cursed him for a damned fool.

The general's cold and calculating brain recognized the phenomenon, of course, and took satisfaction in it. Only commanders who were genuinely treasured by an army had their personal safety so jealously guarded by their own soldiers. But the man inside the general had chafed, and cursed, and stormed, and railed.

The general bridled the man. And so, for a week, Belisarius had reconciled himself to the inevitable. He had never again attempted to directly participate in the fight at the wall, but he had spent each and every day riding up and down the Roman line of fortifications. Encouraging his soldiers, consulting with his officers, organizing the logistics, and—especially— spending time with the wounded.

Valentinian and Anastasius had grumbled, Aide had chafed—**rockets! very dangerous!**—but Belisarius had been adamant. His soldiers, he knew, might take conscious satisfaction in the knowledge that their commander was out of the direct fray. But they would—at a much, much deeper human level—take heart and courage from his immediate presence.

In that, he had been proven right. As the week wore on, his army's battle cry underwent a transformation.

Rome! Rome! it had been, in the first two days.

By the third day, as he rode up and down the fortifications, his own name had been cheered. That

was still true, even more so, a week after the battle
started. But his name was no longer being used as
a simple cheer. It had become a taunt of defiance
hurled at the enemy. The entire Roman army using
that single word to let the Malwa know:

You sorry bastards are fucked. *Fucked.*
Belisarius! Belisarius!

Belisarius drained his goblet and set it down on
the wall with enough force to crack the crude pottery.

He ignored the sound, swiveling his head to the
west.

His eyes glared. It being late afternoon, the sun
promptly glared back. He raised a hand to shield his
face.

"Come on, Ormazd," he growled. "Make up your
mind. Not even a God-be-damned Aryan prince
should need a week to decide on treason."

Maurice turned his own head to follow Belisarius'
gaze.

"You think that's what's been going on?"

"Count on it, Maurice," said Belisarius softly. "I
can guarantee you that every night, for the past week,
Malwa emissaries have been shuttling back and forth
between Ormazd's pavilion and—"

For a moment, he began to turn his head to the
south. Squinting fiercely, as if by sheer forth of will
he could peer into the great pavilion which the Malwa
had erected on the left bank of the Euphrates, well
over a mile away. The pavilion where, he was certain, Link exercised its demonic command.

Maurice grunted sourly. "Maybe you're right. I sure
as hell hope so. If this damned siege goes on much
longer, we'll—ah." He made a vague gesture with his
hand, as if brushing dung off his tunic.

Belisarius said nothing. He knew Maurice was not
worried that the Malwa could take the dam by frontal
assault. Nor was the chiliarch really concerned that

the Malwa could wear out the Romans. The steady
stream of barges coming down from Callinicum kept
the defenders better supplied than the attackers. The
Romans could withstand this kind of semi-siege almost
indefinitely.

But—it was wearing. Wearing on the body, wearing on the nerves. Since the ferocious Malwa assaults
of the first day and night, which they had suspended
in favor of constant probes and quick pinprick attacks,
casualties had been relatively light. But "light" casualties are still casualties. Men you know, dead,
crippled, wounded. Day after day, with no end in
sight.

"I hope you're right," he repeated. Sourly.

Belisarius decided a change of subject was in order.
"Agathius is going to live," he announced. "I'm quite
confident of it, now. I saw him just yesterday."

Maurice glanced upriver, at the ambulance barges
moored just beyond range of the Malwa rockets.
"Glad to hear it. I thought sure—" He lapsed into
another little grunt. Not sour, this one. The inarticu-
late sound combined admiration with disbelief.

"Never thought he'd make it," he admitted.
"Especially after he refused to go to Callinicum."

Belisarius nodded. Most of the Roman casualties,
after triage, had been shipped back to Callinicum. But
Agathius had flat refused—had even threatened
violence when Belisarius tried to insist. So, he had
stayed—as had his young wife. Sudaba had been just
as stubborn toward Agathius' demands that she leave
as he had been toward Belisarius. Including the
threats of violence.

In truth, Belisarius was grateful. Cyril had succeeded to the command of the Constantinople troops,
and had done very well in the post. But Agathius'
stance had done wonders for the army's morale, and
by no means simply among the Greeks. For the past
week, a steady stream of soldiers—Thracians, Syrians,

Illyrians and Arabs as much as Greeks—had visited the maimed officer on his barge. Agathius was very weak from tremendous loss of blood, and in great pain, what with one leg amputated at the knee and the other at the ankle. But the man had borne it all with a stoicism which would have shamed Marcus Aurelius, and had never failed to take the occasion to reinforce his visitors' determination to resist the Malwa.

A quiet thought came from Aide:

> **"Think where man's glory most begins and ends**
> **And say my glory was I had such friends."**

"Yes," whispered Belisarius. "Yes."

It's from a poet whose name will be Yeats. Many centuries from now.

Belisarius took a deep breath.

Let us give mankind those centuries, then. And all the millions of centuries which will come after.

Chapter 36

In its pavilion, at the very moment when Belisarius made that silent vow, the thing from the future which called itself Link made its catastrophic mistake.

It had calculated the possibilities. Analyzed the odds. Gauged the options. Most of all, it had assessed the capabilities of the enemy commander so accurately, and so correctly, and in so many ways, that Belisarius would have been stunned had he ever known how well he had been measured.

Measured, however, only as a general—for that was all that Link understood. The being from the future, with its superhuman intelligence, had burrowed to the depths of the crooked mind of Belisarius. Down to the very tips of the roots.

And had missed the man completely.

"ORMAZD HAS AGREED, THEN?"

Link's top subordinates, four officers squatting on cushions before the chair which held the shape of an old woman, nodded in unison.

"Yes, Great Lady Holi," said one. "He will pull his troops out of position three hours after sundown."

Link pondered, gauged, calculated, analyzed.

Assessed the crooked, cunning brain of the great General Belisarius.

From long experience, the four officers sat silently throughout. It never occurred to them to offer any advice. The advice would not have been welcome. And, if Link had none of the explosive temper of the late Lord Jivita, the being was utterly merciless. The officers weren't especially afraid of the huge tulwar-bearing men who squatted between them and Great Lady Holi. Those were simply guards. But they had only to turn their heads to see the line of silent assassins who waited, as motionless as statues, in the rear of the pavilion. Link—Great Lady Holi—had used those assassins three times since the expedition began. To punish failure, twice. But there had also been an officer who couldn't learn to restrain his counsel.

Finally, Link spoke.

"THERE IS A POSSIBILITY. IT IS NOT LIKELY. WERE THE ENEMY LED BY ANY OTHER COMMANDER I WOULD DISMISS IT OUT OF HAND. BUT I CANNOT. NOT WITH BELISARIUS."

Silence followed again, for well over a minute. The Malwa officers did not ask for an explanation of those cryptic words. None would have been given if they had.

Gauged, analyzed, assessed. Made its decision.

"SEND THE KUSHANS FIRST. ALL OF THEM. ON FOOT."

The officers were visibly startled, now. After a moment, one of them ventured to ask:

"On *foot*?"

Silence. The officer cleared his throat.

"But—Great Lady Holi, it is essential that the maneuver be made with great speed. Belisarius will realize what we are doing by sunrise at the latest. Quite possibly earlier. It is almost impossible—even with the harshest orders—to keep such a large body of men from making *some* noise. And we have no control over the Persians, in any event."

Another interjected, "We *must* get the flanking

column upriver as fast as possible. So that they can ford the Euphrates before Belisarius can block their way. That requires *cavalry*, Great Lady Holi."

"BE SILENT. I UNDERSTAND YOUR ARGU-MENT. BUT THERE IS A POSSIBILITY, IF BELI-SARIUS IS CUNNING ENOUGH. I CANNOT TAKE THE CHANCE. THE YE-TAI, AFTER THEY CROSS, CAN RACE UPRIVER TO SEIZE A BRIDGEHEAD. THE REGULAR CAVALRY, FOL-LOWING, CAN BRING THE KUSHANS' HORSES WITH THEM. THEY SHOULD STILL BE ABLE TO REACH THE YE-TAI IN TIME TO HOLD THE CROSSING."

The officers submitted, of course. But one of them, bolder than the rest, made a last protest:

"It will take the Kushans *so much time*, if they cross the river on foot."

"THAT IS PRECISELY THE POINT.

"NOW, DO AS I COMMAND."

All opposition fled. The officers hastened from the pavilion, spreading the command throughout the great army encamped below the dam.

Alone in its pavilion, Link continued to calculate. Gauge. Analyze.

Its thoughts were confident. Link was guided not simply by its own incredible intellect, but also by intelligence—in the military sense of the term. Roman prisoners had been taken, here and there, in the days of fighting. Interrogated. Those of them with personal knowledge of Belisarius had been questioned under torture, until Link was satisfied that it had squeezed every last item necessary to fully assess the capabilities of its enemy.

It would have done better, had it been in Link's power, to have interrogated a Persian survivor of the battle of Mindouos. The man named Baresmanas.

But, perhaps not. Link would not have asked the right questions. And Baresmanas would certainly not have volunteered the information, not even under the knife.

But he could have. He could have. He could have warned the Malwa superbeing that mercy can have its own sharp point. Keener than any lance or blade; and even deadlier to the foe.

Chapter 37

"Finally," hissed Belisarius.

The general was practically dancing with impatience, waiting for his horse to be brought up to the artillery tower where he had made his headquarters for the past week.

He was already in full armor. He had begun donning the gear the moment he heard the first katyusha volleys. As he had predicted, the Malwa were attempting to cross the Nehar Malka on a pontoon bridge. He was convinced that the maneuver was a feint, but, like all well-executed diversions, it carried real substance behind it. Thousands of Malwa troops were involved in the crossing, supported by most of their rocket troughs. By now, an hour into the battle, the scene to the east was a flashing cacophony. Katyusha rockets crossed trails with Malwa missiles. The Syrian soldiers on the rockpile added their own volleys of fire-arrows, aimed at the boats on the canal. The Nehar Malka was lit up by those flaming ships.

In the darkness ahead, he could make out the looming shape of his horse. Maurice, he realized, was the man holding it.

"How long ago?" were his first words.

He could barely make out Maurice's shrug.

"Who's to know? The Persians are being damned

quiet. Much quieter than I would have expected, from a lot of headstrong dehgans. But Abbu's scouts report that they've already moved out at least half of their forces. Due west, into the desert."

Sourly: "Just as you predicted."

Belisarius nodded. "We've some time, then. Is Abbu—"

Maurice snorted. "Be serious! Of course he's in position. The old Arab goat's even twitchier than you are."

As Anastasius heaved him into the saddle, Belisarius grunted. "I am *not* twitchy. Simply eager to close with the foe."

" 'Close with the foe,' " mimicked Maurice, clambering onto his own mount. "My, aren't we flowery tonight?"

Securely in his saddle, Belisarius grinned. It was obvious that the prospect of action—*finally!*—had completely restored his spirits.

"Let's to it, Maurice. I do believe the time has come to reacquaint the Malwa with the First Law of Battle."

He tugged on the reins, turning his horse.

"The enemy has arrived. And I intend to fuck them up completely."

"*What?*" he demanded.

Maurice took a breath. "You heard me. Abbu's courier reports that they're sending the Kushans across first. On foot, all of them. They even dismounted the Kushan cavalry. They've got their Ye-tai battalions massed on the bank, mounted, but they aren't crossing yet. Behind them, Abbu thinks they're forming up kshatriya and Malwa regulars, but he's not sure. He can't get close enough."

Belisarius turned and stared into the darkness, raising himself up in the stirrups in order to peer over the wall. He was on the road at the eastern end of the dam, just behind the front fortifications. For a moment, he plucked at his telescope, but left off the motion almost as soon as it started. He already knew that the device was no help. It was a moonless night, and the Malwa crossing the almost-empty riverbed were a mile south of the dam. He could see nothing, not even with his Aide-enhanced vision.

"Kushans first, and without horses," he murmured. "That makes no sense at all."

He scratched his chin. "Unless—"

"Unless what?" hissed Maurice.

Scratched his chin. "Unless that *thing* is even smarter than I thought."

Maurice shook his head. "Stop being so damn clever! Maybe they want to make sure they don't make any noise crossing the Euphrates. Kushans on foot will be as silent as any army could be."

Belisarius nodded, slowly.

"That's possible. It's even possible that they made arrangements with Ormazd to have horses left for them. Still—"

A little noise drew their attention. An Arab courier was trotting toward them from the western end of the dam.

"Abbu says now!" the scout exclaimed, as soon as he drew up. "Almost all the Kushans are in the riverbed. At least eight thousand of them. Probably all of them, by now. Their first skirmishers will have already reached the opposite bank."

Belisarius scratched his chin.

"God damn it to hell!" snarled Maurice. "What are you waiting for? We can't let those men cross, general! After all our casualties, we don't have much better than eight thousand left ourselves. Once they get on dry land—on the south bank—they can ford upstream any one of a dozen places. We'll have to face them on—"

"Enough, Maurice." The chiliarch clamped shut his jaws.

Scratched the chin.

The general thought; gauged; calculated; assessed. The man decided.

His crooked smile came. He said, very firmly:

"Let the Kushans cross. All of them."

To the scout:

"Tell Abbu to send up the rocket when the Ye-tai are almost across. And tell that old maniac to make sure he's clear first. Do you understand? I want him clear!"

The Arab grinned. "He will be clear, general. By a hair, of course. But he will be clear."

An instant later, the man was gone.

Belisarius turned back to Maurice. The grizzled veteran was glaring at him.

"Look at it this way," Belisarius said pleasantly. "I've just given you what you treasure most. Something else to be morose about."

Glaring *furiously*. To one side, Valentinian muttered: "Oh, great. Just what we needed. Eight thousand Kushans to deal with."

Belisarius ignored both the glare and the mutter. He began to scratch his chin, but stopped. He had made his decision, and would stick with it.

It was a bad decision, perhaps. It might even, in the end, prove to be disastrous. But he thought of men who liked to gamble, when they had nothing to gamble with except humor. And he remembered, most of all, a man with an iron face. A hard man who had, in two lives and two futures, made the same soft decision. A decision which, Belisarius knew, that man would always make, in every life and every future.

He relaxed, then. Confident, not in his decision, but in his soul.

"Let them pass," he murmured. "Let them pass." He cocked his head, slightly. "Basil's ready?"

"Be serious," growled Maurice.

Belisarius smiled. A minute later, he cocked his head again. "Everyone's clear?" he asked.

"Be serious," growled Maurice.

"Everybody except us," hissed Valentinian. "We're the only ones left. The last Syrians cleared off five minutes ago."

"Let's be off, then," said Belisarius cheerfully.

As he and his three cataphracts walked their horses off the dam—moving carefully, in the dark—Belisarius began softly reciting verses.

The men with him did not recognize the poem. There was no way they could have. Aide had just given it to him, from the future. That future which Belisarius would shield, from men who thought themselves gods.

Those masterful images because complete
Grew in pure mind but out of what began?
I must lie down where all the ladders start
In the foul rag and bone shop of the heart.

Chapter 38

The moment the signal rocket exploded, Link knew.

Its four top officers, standing nearby on the platform of the command tower overlooking the river, were simply puzzled. The rocket, after bursting, continued to burn like a flare as it sailed down onto the mass of soldiers struggling their way across the bed of the Euphrates. Ye-tai, in the main, swearing softly as they tried to guide their horses in the darkness through a morass of streamlets and mucky sinkholes. But there were at least five thousand Malwa regulars, also, including a train of rocket-carts and the kshatriya to man them.

The flare burned. The officers stared, and puzzled.

But Link knew at once. Understood how completely it had been outwitted, although it did not—then or ever—understand how Belisarius had done it.

But the being from the future was not given to cursing or useless self-reproach. It recognized only necessity. It did not even wait for the first thundering sound of the explosions to give the order to its assassins.

Across the entire length of the dam blocking the Euphrates, the charges erupted. Almost in slow motion, the boulder-laden ships which formed the base of the dam heaved up. The sound of the eruption was huge, but muffled. And there was almost no flash given off. The charges, for all their immensity, had been deeply buried. Even Link, with its superhuman vision, could barely see the disaster, in the faint light still thrown off by the signal flare.

The officers saw nothing. Then, or ever. The first assassin's knife plunged into the back of the first officer, severing his spinal cord. A split second later, the other three died with him. Still staring at the rocket. Still puzzled.

Link had failed, but its failure would remain hidden. Its reputation was essential to the Malwa cause, and the cause of the new gods who had created Malwa. The officers would take the blame.

The mass of soldiers in the bed of the Euphrates—perhaps fourteen thousand, in all—froze at the sound. Turned, stared into the darkness. Puzzled. The night was dark, and the dam was a mile away. They, too, could see nothing. But the noise was ominous.

Then the first breeze came, and the smartest of the trapped soldiers understood. Shrieking, cursing—even sabring the slower-witted men who barred their way—they made a desperate attempt to scramble their horses out of the riverbed.

The rest—

The wall of water which smote the Malwa army came like a mace, wielded by a god. Untold tons of hurtling water, carrying great boulders as if they were chips of wood. Smashing in the sides of the old riverbed, gouging channels as it came, ripping new stones to join the old.

By the time the torrent struck, all of the doomed men in that riverbed understood. The sound was no longer a distant thunder. It was a howling banshee. Shiva's shriek. Kali's scream of triumph.

All of them, now, were fighting to get out. Their horses, panicked as much by the terror in their riders' voices as the thunder coming from the north, were scuttling through the mud, skittering past the reeds, falling into sinkholes, trampling each other under.

But it was hopeless. Some of the Malwa soldiers—less than a thousand—were far enough from the riverbed's center to reach the banks. Others, caught by the edges of the tidal wave, were able to save their lives by clinging to reeds, or boulders, or ropes thrown by their comrades ashore.

A few—a very, very small few—even survived the flood. A gigantic, turbulent mass of water such as the one which hammered its way down the riverbed is an odd thing. Fickle, at times. Weird, in its workings.

The Euphrates, restored to its rightful place, raged and raged and raged. But, here and there, it took pity. One soldier, to his everlasting amazement, found himself carried—gently, gently—to the riverbank. Another, too terrified to be amazed, was simply tossed ashore.

And one Malwa soldier, hours later and fifty miles downriver, waded out of the reeds. The Euphrates had nestled him in a bizarre and permanent little eddy—like a chick cupped in a man's hand—and carried him through the night. A simple man, he was—simple-minded, his unkind former comrades had often called him—but no fool. It was noted, thereafter, that the previously profane fellow had become deeply religious. Particularly devoted, it seemed, to river gods.

But for the overwhelming majority of the Ye-tai and Malwa regulars caught in Belisarius' trap, death came almost instantly. They did not even drown, most of them. They were simply battered to death.

Twelve thousand, one hundred and forty-three men. Dead within a minute. Another nine hundred and six, crippled and badly wounded. Most of those would die within a week.

Ten thousand and eighty-nine horses, dead. Two thousand, two hundred and seventy-eight camels, dead. Thirty-four rocket carts, pulverized. Almost half of the expedition's gunpowder weapons, destroyed.

It was the worst military disaster in Malwa's history.

And Link knew it. The superbeing was already examining its options, before the wall of water had taken a single life. Throughout the horror which followed, the creature named Great Lady Holi sat motionless upon its throne. Utterly indifferent to the carnage—those dying men and animals were simply facts—it went about its business.

Calculating. Gauging. Assessing.

The officers would take the blame. Link would take the credit for salvaging what could be salvaged.

Calculating. Gauging. Assessing.

Which was not much.

By the time the next rank of officers crept their timid way onto the command tower, Link had already made its decisions.

"WE MUST RETREAT. BEAT THE DRUMS.

"ORGANIZE RATIONING. WE WILL BE FORCED TO RETREAT THROUGH THE DESERT, WITH FEW CAMELS. WE CANNOT RISK A BATTLE ON THIS SIDE OF THE RIVER. BELISARIUS WILL HAVE ALSO COLLAPSED THE STONES INTO THE NEHAR MALKA, RESTORING THE OLD DAM. HE WILL BE ABLE TO CROSS EASILY. AND THERE ARE STILL TEN THOUSAND PERSIANS IN PEROZ-SHAPUR. OUR FORCES THERE MUST KEEP THOSE PERSIANS PENNED IN WHILE WE MAKE OUR RETREAT."

Even with the grim reminder of the slaughtered officers lying on the platform, some of Link's new top subordinates dared to protest.

Through the desert? Many will die, in such a retreat.

"AT LEAST FOUR THOUSAND, BY MY ESTIMATE. THEY CAN BE REPLACED."

And what about the Kushans? There are eight thousand of them in position to attack!

"POINTLESS. THEY HAVE NO HORSES. NO SUPPLIES. AND WE HAVE NO MEANS OF SUPPLYING THEM. OUR OWN SUPPLIES ARE LIMITED.

"BELISARIUS WILL NOT FIGHT, HE WILL SIMPLY ELUDE THE KUSHANS AND WAIT FOR THEM TO DIE OF HUNGER. A WASTE OF EXCELLENT TROOPS—WHOM WE NEED OURSELVES. WE MUST BEGIN THE RETREAT IMMEDIATELY. SEND COURIERS TO THE KUSHANS. THEY MUST GUARD OUR REAR AS WE MARCH BACK TO BABYLON."

The officers bowed their heads. They began to scurry out, but Link commanded them to remain. There were still some calculations to be made.

The officers waited, silently, while Link gauged and assessed.

It did not take the superbeing more than five minutes to reach another conclusion. A human commander, faced with that bitter logic, would have screamed fury and frustration. Link simply gave commands.

"SEND WORD TO OUR FORCES IN BABYLON. TELL THE COMMANDERS TO AWAIT OUR ARRIVAL, BUT THEY MUST BEGIN THE PREPARATIONS FOR LIFTING THE SIEGE OF BABYLON."

A last protest:

Lift the siege of Babylon? But—

"WE HAVE NO CHOICE. BELISARIUS HAS SAVAGED US THIS YEAR, DUE TO THE INCOMPETENCE OF MALWA'S GENERALS. OUR SUPPLY FLEET WAS ALREADY STRETCHED TO THE LIMIT. THIS NEW DISASTER WILL DESTROY MORE SHIPS. WE HAVE LOST TOO MANY MEN, TOO MANY SUPPLIES, TOO MUCH

EQUIPMENT. WE CANNOT MAINTAIN THE SIEGE. WE MUST RETREAT TO CHARAX, AND BEGIN AGAIN NEXT YEAR.

"DO IT."

When the wall of water reached Peroz-Shapur, in the middle of the night, more Malwa lives were lost. Not many—simply those unlucky men among the forces guarding against a sally who had chosen the wrong moment to relieve themselves in the riverbed, away from the foul latrines of a siege camp.

Above, on the walls of the fortified town, Baresmanas and Kurush listened to the river. The Euphrates was back, and with it, hope.

"He has done it," whispered Kurush. "Just as he promised." He turned away, moving with his quick and nervous stride. "I must ready the troops. We may be able to sally, come dawn."

After he was gone, Baresmanas shook his head. "How can such a warm and merciful man be so ruthless?" he whispered. "So cold, so cruel, so pitiless?"

There was no accusation in those words. Neither condemnation, nor reproach. Simply wonder, at the complexity and contradiction that is the human soul.

Elsewhere within the walls of Peroz-Shapur, in the slave quarters where war captives were held, two thousand Kushans also listened to the sound of Malwa's destruction.

Friendly guards were questioned. Soon enough, answers were given.

The Kushans settled their bets.

Those who had won the wager—all but one— celebrated through the night. They had the means with which to celebrate, too. Their guards were in a fine mood, that night. Wine was given out freely, even by stingy Persians.

Only Vasudeva refrained from the festivity. When
questioned, the Kushan commander simply smiled and
said, "You forget. I made another bet. Enjoy yourselves, men."

Grinning, now, and pointing at the amphorae
clutched in his soldiers' hands. "Soon, everything you
own will be mine."

By the end of the next day, the Malwa guarding
Peroz-Shapur began their retreat. Kurush—against
Baresmanas' advice—tried a sally. His dehgans blood-
ied the enemy, but they were driven off with heavy
casualties. The Malwa lion was wounded, and limping badly, but it still had its teeth.

The day after that, the Kushans were sent out to
clear the riverbanks of the multitude of corpses
which had washed ashore. Bury them quickly—no
sanctified exposure to the elements for *those* foul
souls—so that the stench would not sicken the entire
city.

The Kushans did their work uncomplainingly. They
had another bet to settle.

By the end of the day, the count had been
made to every Kushan's satisfaction. And Vasudeva
won his bet.

Many bodies had been buried, and their identities
noted. There was not a single Kushan among them.

Vasudeva was rich, now, for he had been the only
Kushan to dare that gamble. Rich, not so much in
material wealth—his soldiers had had little to wager,
after all—but in the awe and esteem of his men.
Kushans admire a great gambler.

"How did you know?" asked one of his lieutenants.

Vasudeva smiled.

"He promised me. When we gave our oath to him,
he swore in return that he would treat Kushans as
men. Executed, if necessary. But executed as men.
Not hanged like criminals, or beaten like dogs."

He pointed to the river below Peroz-Shapur. "Or drowned, like rats."

The lieutenant frowned. "He made that vow to us, not—" A gesture with his head upriver. "—to *those* Kushans."

Vasudeva's smile was quite like that of a Buddha, now.

"Belisarius is not one to make petty distinctions." The commander of the Kushan captives turned away.

"Your mistake was that you bet on the general. I bet on the man."

Two days later, at Babylon, Khusrau Anushirvan also basked in the admiration of his subordinates. Many of them—*many*—had questioned his wisdom in placing so much trust in a Roman general. Some of them had even been bold enough, and honest enough, to express those reservations to the Emperor's face.

None questioned his wisdom now. They had but to stand on the walls of Babylon to see how wise their Emperor had been. The Malwa fleet had been savaged when Belisarius lowered the river. It had been savaged again, when he restored it. A full quarter of the enemy's remaining ships had been destroyed in the first few minutes. Tethered to jury-rigged docks, or simply grounded in the mud, they had been lifted up by the surging Euphrates and carried to their destruction. Some were battered to splinters; others grounded anew; still others, capsized.

And Khusrau had sallied again. Not, this time, with dehgans across a pontoon bridge—no-one could have built a bridge across the roaring Euphrates on that day—but with sailors aboard the handful of swift galleys in his possession. The galleys had been kept ashore until the river's initial fury passed. As soon as the waters subsided to mere turbulence, the galleys set forth. Down the Euphrates they rowed, adding their own speed to the current, and destroying every Malwa ship they encountered which had managed to survive the Euphrates' rebirth.

There was almost no resistance. The galleys passed too swiftly for the enemy's cannons to be brought to bear. And the Malwa soldiers on the ships themselves were too dazed to put up any effective resistance.

Down the Euphrates the galleys went, mile after mile, until the rowers were too weak to pull their oars. They left a trail of burning ships thirty miles behind them, before they finally beached their craft and began the long march back to Babylon. On the west bank of the river, where the Malwa could no longer reach them.

Between the river and the Persian galleys, over half of the remaining Malwa fleet was destroyed. Not more than two dozen ships eventually found their way back to Charax, of the mighty armada which had set forth so proudly at the beginning of the year.

Other than sending forth the galleys, Khusrau made no attempt to sally against the Malwa encamped before Babylon. He was too canny to repeat Kurush's mistake at Peroz-Shapur. The Malwa lion had been lamed, true. It had not been declawed. There were still a hundred thousand men in that enemy army, with their siege guns loaded with cannister.

The Emperor simply waited. Let them starve.

The siege of Babylon had been broken, like a tree gutted by a lightning bolt. It had simply not fallen yet, much like a great tree will stand for a time after it is dead. Until a wind blows the hollow thing over.

That wind arrived twelve days later. Emperor Khusrau and his entourage, from the roof of Esagila, watched the survivors of the Malwa expedition drag their mangled army back into the camps at Babylon.

That army was much smaller than the one which had set out a few weeks since. Smaller in numbers of men, and horses, and camels, positively miniscule in its remaining gunpowder weapons.

Two days later, the entire Malwa army began its long retreat south. By nightfall, the camps which had besieged Babylon for months were empty.

Khusrau spent all of that day, also, on top of Esagila. Surrounded by his officers, his advisers, his officials, a small horde of sahrdaran and vurzurgan, and a young girl named Tahmina.

Khusrau's more hot-headed officers called for a sally. Again, the Emperor refused.

Malwa was lamed, but still a lion.

And besides, the Persian Monarch had other business to attend to.

"Ormazd," he hissed. "Ormazd, first. I want his head brought to me on a pike, by year's end. Do it."

His officers hastened to obey. Surrounded by the rest of his huge entourage, the Emperor remained on Esagila. For a time, he stared at the retreating Malwa. With satisfaction, hatred, and anticipation.

"Next year," he murmured. "Next year, Malwa."

Then, he turned and began striding to the opposite wall of the great, ancient temple. His entourage began to follow, like a giant millipede, but Khusrau waved them back.

"I want only Tahmina," he commanded.

Disgruntled, but obedient, his officials and nobles and advisers obeyed. Timidly, hesitantly, the girl did likewise.

Once they were standing alone on the north wall of the temple, Khusrau's gaze was fixed on the northwest horizon. There was nothing to see, there, beyond a river and a desert. But the Emperor was looking beyond—in time, even more than in space.

His emotions now, as he stared northwest, were more complex. Satisfaction also, of course. As well as admiration, respect—even, if the truth be told, love. But there was also fear, and dread, and anxiety.

"Next year, Malwa," he murmured again. "But the year after that, and after that, and after that, there will be Rome. Always Rome."

He turned his head, and lowered his eyes to the girl standing at his side. Under her Emperor's gaze, the girl's own eyes shied away.

"Look at me, Tahmina."

When the girl's face rose, Khusrau smiled. "I will not command you in this, child. But I do need you. The Aryans need you."

Tahmina smiled herself, now. Timidly and uncertainly, true, but a smile it was. Quite a genuine one, Khusrau saw, and he was not a man easily fooled.

"I will, Emperor."

Khusrau nodded, and placed a hand on the girl's shoulder. Thereafter, and for the rest of the day, he said nothing.

Nor did he leave his post on the northern wall of Esagila, watching the northwest. The Malwa enemy could limp away behind his contemptuous back. Khusrau of the Immortal Soul was the Emperor of Iran and non-Iran. His duty was to face the future.

Chapter 39

Days later, Belisarius and Maurice surveyed the Nehar Malka from what was left of the rockpile on its north bank. Most of those rocks, so laboriously hauled out by the Kushans, were back where they came from. Once again, the Royal Canal was dry— or almost so, at least. The crude and explosive manner in which Belisarius had rebuilt the dam did not stop all the flow.

The Roman army was already halfway across what was left of the Nehar Malka. On their way back to Peroz-Shapur, now. After destroying the dam, Belisarius had retreated north, in case the Malwa made an attempt to pursue his still-outnumbered army. He had not expected them to make that mistake—not with Link in command—but had been prepared to deal with the possibility.

Once it became clear that the enemy was retreating back to Babylon, Belisarius had followed. They had reached the site of the battleground just two hours before.

"Enough," he said softly. "The Nehar Malka's dry enough. I don't think Khusrau will complain."

"Shouldn't think so," muttered Maurice. The chiliarch was not even looking at the Nehar Malka, however. He was staring at the Euphrates.

Not at the river, actually. The Euphrates, to all appearances, was back to its usual self—a wide, shallow, sluggishly moving mass of muddy water.

No, Maurice was staring at the banks of the river. Where the Malwa had abandoned their dead. It was not hard to spot the corpses—hundreds, thousands of them—even hidden in the reeds. The vultures covered the area like flies.

"Jesus," he whispered. "Forgive us our sins."

Belisarius turned his eyes to follow Maurice's gaze. No expression came to his face. He might have been a simple village blacksmith, studying the precision of his work.

When he spoke, his voice was harsh. "A man told me once that war is murder. Organized, systematic murder—nothing more, and nothing less. It was the first thing that man said to me, on the day I assumed command as an officer. Seventeen years old, I was. Green as the springtime."

"You were never as green as the springtime," murmured Maurice. "Day you were born, you were already thinking crooked thoughts." He sighed. "I remember, lad. It was true, then, and it's true now. But I don't have to like it."

Belisarius nodded. Nothing further was said.

A few minutes later, he and Maurice turned their horses and rode down to the bank of the Nehar Malka, ready to join the army in its crossing.

The job was not finished, not yet. Neither of them knew when it might be. But they knew when a day's work was done.

Done well. They could take satisfaction in that, at least, if not in the doing.

Craftsmen at their trade.

EPILOGUE

A throng and its thoughts

From her position on the dais against the east wall, Antonina surveyed the scene with satisfaction. The great audience chamber of the Prefectural Palace was literally packed with people. Servants carrying platters of food and drink were forced to wriggle their way through the throng like so many eels. The noise produced by the multitude of conversations was almost deafening.

"Very gratifying," pronounced Patriarch Theodosius, seated on a chair next to her.

"Isn't it?" Antonina beamed upon the mob below them. "I think the entire Greek aristocracy of Alexandria showed up tonight. As well as most of the nobility from all the major Delta towns. Even some from the valley. The Fayum, at least, and Antinoopolis."

A slight frown came.

"Actually, I'm a bit puzzled. Hadn't really expected

such a massive turnout. I thought for sure that a good half of the nobility would boycott the affair."

Theodosius' eyes widened. "Boycott? A public celebration in honor of the Emperor's ninth birthday? God forbid!" The Patriarch smiled slyly. "Actually, Antonina, I am *not* surprised. Left to their own devices, I'm quite sure that half of Egypt's Greek noblemen would never have come. But their wives and daughters gave them no choice."

He nodded toward the middle of the great room, where the crowd was thickest. At the very center of that incredible population density, a cup of wine in one hand, stood a handsome young Roman officer.

"Egypt's most eligible bachelor," stated the Patriarch. "The merarch of the Army of Egypt. Newly elected to the Senate—and already quite rich on his own account, due to his share of the spoils from Mindouos."

Antonina stared at Hermogenes. A bit of sadness came to her, for a brief moment, thinking about Irene. The host of women who surrounded Hermogenes were all younger than Irene, and—with perhaps one or two exceptions—considerably prettier.

"Put all their brains together," she muttered, "and they could maybe match Irene. When she's passed out drunk. Maybe."

"What was that, Antonina?" asked Theodosius.

Antonina shook her head.

"Never mind, Patriarch. I was just thinking about a dear friend." Sigh. "Who will never, I fear, find a husband."

"Too pious?" asked Theodosius.

Antonina bit off a laugh. "No, no. Just too—*much*."

She rose from her seat. "I will take my leave, now. The event is clearly a roaring success. I think we can safely conclude that Alexandria and Egypt have been returned to the imperial fold. But I'm tired, and I don't think *that* crowd will object to my absence."

Theodosius suppressed his own humor, now, until after Antonina had walked out. Then he did laugh, seeing the mob below heave a great collective sigh of relief.

The Patriarch was quite certain he could read their minds, at that moment.

Thank God! She's gone!

No real woman has tits that big.

Satan's spawn, that's what she is.

The Whore From Hell. Ba'alzebub's Bitch.

But they kept those thoughts to themselves. Oh, yes. Discreet, they were. Reserved.

"Very proper folk," said Theodosius approvingly, turning to the man seated to his right. "Very polite. Very noble. Don't you think so, Ashot?"

A charitable interpretation, from a man of God.

Less charitable was an Armenian cataphract's response.

"Scared shitless, that's what they are."

A king and his fears

"You are not thinking of *marrying* that woman?" demanded the negusa negast of Axum. The sovereign of Ethiopia leaned forward on his royal stool, his thick hands planted firmly on powerful knees, his massive jaw clamped shut. He frowned ferociously upon his youngest son.

Prince Eon bolted erect on his own stool. His jaw sagged. Dropped. Plummeted like a stone.

Standing behind him, Ousanas burst into laughter.

"Excellent idea, King of Kings!" cried the dawazz. "Certain to shrink overconfident fool boy's head into a walnut!"

Eon finally caught his breath. Enough, at least, to choke out, "Marry—*Irene?*"

He goggled at his father. The father glowered back. "You seem much taken by this woman," accused the negusa nagast.

Eon's eyes roamed about the royal chamber, as if seeking rhyme or reason lurking somewhere in the stone recesses of heavy Axumite architecture.

"I *like* her, yes," he said. "Very much. I think she is incredibly capable and intelligent. And very witty. She often makes me laugh. A wonderful ally in our struggle. Even—" His eyes almost crossed, contemplating absurdity. "—yes, even attractive. In her way. But—but—*marry* her?"

He fell silent. Again, his jaw sagged.

Satisfied, the negusa nagast leaned back in his stool. He fixed Ousanas with a stern gaze.

"Good thing for you, dawazz. Any other answer and I would have you beaten."

Ousanas looked smug. "Can't. Dawazz not subject to royal authority. Only answers to Dakuen sarwe."

The King of Kings snorted. "So? You think the regiment would hesitate? Just last night, the demon woman took half their monthly stipend, answering all their riddles. This morning, she took the rest. When they couldn't answer any of hers, even after she gave them all night to think it over." The negusa nagast glared. "Dawazz be a bloody pulp, Prince give any other answer. Be sure of it."

The negusa nagast smacked his heavy thigh. "I am satisfied. The Prince is foolish as a rooster, true. Headstrong like a bull. Who else would get me in a war with Malwa? But at least you have kept him sane, dawazz. Sane enough. Delusions of grandeur can be tolerated, in a King, so long as they are merely political. Never delusions in a wife!"

His heavy shoulders twitched, as if a sudden shiver had run down his spine.

"God save us from that fate! Never marry a woman smarter than you. Too dangerous, especially for a King. *That* woman! Smarter than Satan."

He turned his head, looking through the entryway to the room beyond. His library, that was.

"Best collection of books south of Alexandria," he noted proudly. "I have instructed my slaves to make a precise count. They will count them again, before I allow that woman to leave for India."

Eon cleared his throat. "We must leave soon, father."

The negusa nagast nodded his head. The gesture was slow, but certain. As solid as the head which made it.

"Yes. You must. Important to follow up on Garmat's successful mission, and quickly. Give all support to Empress Shakuntala and her cause. Give Malwa no time to think."

Again, the little shiver in the shoulders.

"*Essential* to get that woman on the other side of an ocean."

An empress and her marriage

"The time has come, Shakuntala," stated Holkar firmly. The peshwa leaned forward and lifted a scroll lying on the carpet before his cushion.

"This was brought by courier ship this morning. From Tamraparni."

Dadaji unrolled the scroll, scanning it in the quick manner with which a man reads over a document he had already committed to memory. An odd little smile came to his face.

"Out of illusion, truth," he murmured.

He rolled the scroll back up and handed it to his

Empress. Shakuntala stared at the harmless object as if it were a cobra.

"What is it?" she demanded.

Dadaji's smile faded. "It is a letter from the King of Tamraparni. Offering us an alliance—a *partial* alliance, I should say—against Malwa." He shrugged. "The offer is couched in caveats and riddled with qualifications. But, at the very least, he makes a firm promise of naval and logistical support. Possibly some troops."

He paused, taking a deep breath. Shakuntala eyed him suspiciously.

"And what else?"

"The offer—this is not said in so many words, but the meaning is obvious—is conditional upon your marriage to one of his sons." A wry smile. "His youngest son, needless to say. The King of Tamraparni is willing to risk something, to keep the Malwa at bay. But only so much. Not the heir."

He stopped, studying the young woman who was Andhra's Empress. Shakuntala was sitting very erect, her back as stiff as a board. Her face, if possible, was even stiffer.

Holkar tapped the scroll with a finger. "The King makes allusion to the false way in which we bandied his name about, in Muziris. But he does not complain, not formally. It is quite clear that your seizure of Suppara has changed the situation drastically. You are no longer an 'Empress-in-exile.' You have reestablished yourself on Andhra soil. With a port, here, and one of Majarashtra's largest cities—Deogiri—under the control of your forces. That gives you something far beyond formal legitimacy, which you already had. It gives you power."

He chuckled dryly. "Not much, not much, but some. Enough, at least, that the ruler of Tamraparni is willing to use you to keep Malwa as distant from his island as possible."

He paused. Shakuntala's face was still expressionless. Dadaji suppressed a sigh.

"Empress, we must consider this offer very seriously. A dynastic marriage with one of south India's most powerful kingdoms would greatly strengthen your position. It might well make the difference between Andhra's survival and its downfall."

Still expressionless.

Now, Holkar did sigh. "Girl," he said softly, "I know that this matter pains you. But you have a duty, and an obligation, to your people."

The peshwa rose and strode to an open window, overlooking the harbor. From below, the sounds of celebration wafted into the palace. The governor's palace, once. The Malwa official languished in prison, now. Shakuntala had taken the building for her own.

Watching the festive scene below, Holkar smiled. Suppara was still celebrating, two weeks after its liberation from the Malwa heel. Dadaji knew his countrymen well. The Marathas would have celebrated even if the city were in ruins. As it was, they could also celebrate an almost bloodless victory. Once the cannons which Kungas had seized opened fire, the Malwa warships had been turned into wrecks within an hour. By the time Shakuntala and her cavalrymen disembarked on the docks, the Malwa garrison had fled the city.

Celebrate, celebrate, celebrate.

Malwa is gone. Andhra has returned.

The Empress herself is here.

Shakuntala! Shakuntala! Shakuntala!

Holkar pointed down to the city. "If you fall, girl, those people will fall with you. You brought them to their feet. You cannot betray that trust."

Behind him, Shakuntala's face finally broke. Just a bit. Just a flash of pain, a slight lowering of the head. A slow, shuddering breath.

But it was all very quick. Within seconds, she had

raised her head. "You are correct, Dadaji. Draft a letter to the King of Tamraparni, telling him that I accept—"

A new voice cut in.

"I think this is quite premature."

Startled, Holkar turned from the window. "Premature? Why, Kungas?"

The Kushan was seated on his own cushion, to Shakuntala's right. He had said nothing, thus far, in this meeting of Shakuntala's closest advisers.

"Because," he rasped, "I do not think we should jump at the first offer." He spread his hand. "There will be others. The Cholas, for a certainty, now that Shakuntala has shown she is a force to be reckoned with. And I think their offer will have fewer caveats and qualifications."

He flipped his hand dismissively, almost contemptuously. "Tamraparni is an island. The Cholas share the mainland with the Malwa beast. They have less room to quibble. Their offer will be more substantial."

Holkar restrained his temper. "*If* they offer! I do not share your boundless optimism, Kungas. True, the Malwa press them close. But that is just as likely— more likely, in my opinion—to make them hesitate before offering the Malwa any provocation. Kerala *also* shares the mainland with Malwa, and we all know how that fact led Shakuntala's own grandfather to betray—"

"I agree with Kungas," interrupted Shakuntala forcefully. "We should wait. Not accept this first offer. We should wait. Longer."

Holkar blew out his cheeks. He knew that tone in Shakuntala's voice. Knew it to perfection.

No point in further argument, not now. So, he desisted; even did so graciously. Although he could not help casting an angry glare at Kungas.

No point in that either, of course. As well glare at an iron mask.

✦   ✦   ✦

"What are you playing at?" Holkar demanded, after he and Kungas left the Empress' chamber. "You know how critical this question is! You and I have spoken on the matter before—many times."

Kungas stopped abruptly. Dadaji did likewise. The two men stood in the corridor for a moment, staring at each other. The peshwa, angry. The Bhatasvapati—amused, perhaps.

"Not quite, Dadaji," came the mild response. "*You* have spoken *to* me on this matter, that is true. Many times. But all I ever said was that I agreed that Shakuntala's marriage—whenever and however it comes—will be a decisive moment for our struggle."

Holkar frowned. "Yes. And so?"

Kungas twitched his shoulders. It might have been called a shrug.

"So—that does not mean I agree that she should marry the youngest son of the King of Tamraparni. I think she can do better."

Holkar, scowling: "With whom? Chola? *If*, of course, the Cholas even—"

"Who is to say, who is to say?" interrupted Kungas. Again, that little vestige of a shrug. The Bhatasvapati took his friend by the arm. "You should have more confidence in the Empress, Dadaji. When the time comes, she will know what to do. I am sure of it."

Silence followed, as the two men resumed their progress down the corridor. On the part of Kungas, it was an inscrutable sort of silence. On the part of Holkar, an irritable one.

Had the peshwa known the thoughts of the Bhatasvapati, at that moment, he would have been considerably more than irritated.

Dig in your heels, girl, dig in your heels. Stall. Make excuses. Dither. I will help, I will help. When

*the question of marriage is finally posed, you will
know what to do. Then, you will know.*

The Bhatasvapati shook his head, slightly, thinking
of the strange blindness in the people around him.
So obvious!

A general and his officer

Within a minute of his arrival in Agathius' room,
Belisarius knew that the crippled officer was preoccupied with something. The cataphract was plucking at
the sheets of his bed, as if distracted. The motion
seemed to make his wife nervous. Or perhaps it was
just that the young girl was fussing over her injured
husband, the way she kept fluffing his pillows and
stroking his hair.

Belisarius decided that he should come to the
point. He began pulling a scroll from his tunic.

At that moment, however, Agathius turned to his
wife and said, "Would you leave us for a moment,
Sudaba? I have something I must discuss privately
with the general."

Sudaba nodded. Then, after a last fluff of the
pillows and a quick smile at Belisarius, scurried from
the room. Belisarius was struck by the way Agathius
watched her as she went. Odd, really. He seemed like
a man trying to burn an image into his memory.

Once the Persian girl was gone, Agathius took a
deep breath and looked to the general.

"I need your advice," he said abruptly. "I will have
to divorce Sudaba, now, and I want to make sure—
if it can be done—that the divorce does not cause
problems for you. With your alliance with the Persians, I mean."

He spoke the sentences quickly, but clearly, in the

way a determined man announces a decision which
he does not like but must carry out.

Belisarius' jaw dropped. It was the last thing he
had been expecting to hear.

"Divorce Sudaba?" His eyes wandered about, for
an instant, as if searching for rhyme and reason
hidden away in a corner of the room.

"But—*why*?"

Agathius' face grew pinched. With a sudden, quick
flip of his muscular wrist, the cataphract twitched
aside the blankets covering his body. From the hips
and above, that body was still as broad-shouldered
and thick-chested as ever. A bit wasted, perhaps, from
his long weeks of bed-ridden recovery, but not much.

His legs, however—even that part of his legs
which still remained—were pitiful remnants of the
powerful limbs which had once gripped a warhorse
in the fury of a battlefield.

"Look at me," he said. Not with anger so much
as resignation.

Belisarius frowned. Scratched his chin. "It does not
seem to me that Sudaba cares, Agathius. Judging from
what I can see, I think she is not put off—"

"Not *that*," growled Agathius. The man's usual good
humor made a brief re-entry. "Far as that goes, I think
she's happier than ever," he chuckled. "I'm here all
the time now, where she can get her hands on me.
And there's nothing wrong with my—"

He broke off, sighing. "The problem's not with her,
general. Or with me, for that matter. It's—it's—" He
waved a hand, weakly. "It's the way things are, that's
all. She's a Persian noblewoman. I'm a fucking
baker's son with a battlefield rank in the military
nobility."

Agathius glanced around the luxurious chamber, for
a moment, as if assessing its value.

"I've still got plenty of booty left, from Anatha—
a damn little fortune, by my old standards. But it's

really not going to last more than a year or two. Not the way I have to live, if I'm to meet her expectations—and, even more, the expectations of her family.

"I've got to face facts, general. I'm a legless cataphract—which is the most ridiculous thing in the world—whose only other skill is baking bread. There's no way I can—"

He gaped, then, seeing his general burst into riotous laughter.

Gaped. That was the last reaction he had been expecting.

With a fierce struggle, Belisarius forced his laughter down. "Oh, God, I *am* sorry," he said weakly, wiping his eyes. "I feel so guilty, now. I wanted the pleasure of telling you myself. I had to come to Peroz-Shapur anyway, to refit the army, and so I thought I'd bring the news personally instead of just sending it by courier."

Agathius' face was a study in confusion. "News? What news?"

Belisarius was grinning now. And there was not a trace of crookedness in that expression, not a trace.

He hauled out the scroll. "As soon as it was clear that we'd driven the Malwa back to Charax, I sent—well, 'recommendations' is hardly the word. Emperor or no, he's still my kid. I gave Photius firm and clear instructions, and, I'm pleased to say, the marvelous boy followed them to perfection."

He handed over the scroll. "Here you are. The official document will arrive by courier, some weeks from now. This is a copy sent over the semaphore line. Doesn't matter. It's as good as gold."

Gingerly, Agathius took the scroll. In an instant, Belisarius' quick mind understood the expression on the man's face.

"You can't read," he stated.

Agathius shook his head. "No, sir. Not really. I can

sign my name well enough, as long as I've got some time. But—"

He fell silent. Not from embarassment so much as frustration.

The embarassment, in that moment, was entirely Belisarius'. The general should have remembered that a man of Agathius' background was almost certain to be illiterate.

The general waved his hand, as if brushing aside insects.

"Well, that'll have to change. Right off. I'll send word to Patriarch Anthony to send one of his best monks to be your tutor. Two of them, now that I think about it. Sudaba's probably not literate, either. Not a dehgan's daughter."

Grinning:

"Can't have that. Not in the wife of a Roman Senator, recently enrolled in the ranks of the Empire's *illustres*. By unanimous acclaim, mind you. I also got a private message from Sittas. He tells me the Emperor's nomination was extremely—ah, *firm*. Sittas himself took the occasion to appear before the Senate in full armor. In recognition—or so he told those fine aristocratic fellows—of the valor of the Greek cataphracts at Anatha and the Nehar Malka."

Grinning:

"The Emperor also saw fit to give the new Senator a grant of royal land, in keeping with his exalted status. An estate you've got now, Agathius, in Pontus. Quite a substantial one. Annual income's in the vicinity of three hundred solidi. Tax-exempt, of course. As an imperial grant, it's *res privata*."

Grinning, grinning:

"Oh, yes. There's real soldier business, too, in addition to all the Senatorial fooferaw. You've been promoted. You're the new *Dux* of Osrhoene. That post carries an excellent salary, by the way. Another four hundred solidi. In addition to the troops stationed in that province, you have complete authority over all Roman military units serving in Persian Mesopotamia which are not directly under my command. You report only to me, in my capacity as *magister militum per orientem*."

Grinning, grinning, grinning:

"As you can see, I've picked up a few new titles of my own. As Dux of Osrhoene, your official headquarters will be located at the provincial capital of Edessa. But I'd really prefer it if you based yourself here, in Peroz-Shapur. I've already discussed the matter with Baresmanas and Kurush, and they have no objection whatsoever. Quite the contrary, actually. They're even hinting that Khusrau will insist on presenting you with a palace. I think they would feel a lot more secure in Rome's allegiance if the commander of the Roman forces was planted right in their own territory. Along with his Persian wife and—"

Grinning, grinning, grinning, grinning:

"—soon enough, I've no doubt, a slew of children."

The grin finally faded, replaced by something which was almost a frown. "God in Heaven, Agathius! Did you really think I'd let one of the finest officers I've ever had go back to baking bread? On account of his *legs*?"

Agathius was speechless.

Belisarius rose, smiling crookedly.

"You're speechless, I see. Well, that's good enough for today. But make sure you've got your wits about you by tomorrow—*Duke*. I'll be coming by, first thing in the morning. We've got a new campaign to plan, against Malwa. You won't be riding any horses in that campaign—you'll be staying right here in Peroz-Shapur—but I'll be relying on you to organize the whole Roman effort to back me up."

"I won't fail you," whispered Agathius.

"No," agreed Belisarius. "I don't imagine you will."

He turned away. "And now, I'll go tell your wife she can come back in. Best thing for you, I think." He left, then, murmuring a little verse.

"Think where man's glory most begins and ends
And say my glory was I had such friends."

A captor and his captives

Two hours later, Belisarius was enjoying a cup of wine with Vasudeva in the barracks where the Kushan captives were quartered. A very small cup of wine.

"The Persians are back to their stingy habits," groused Vasudeva. The Kushan commander cast a sour look around the dingy room. He, along with fifteen of his top officers, were crammed into a space that would have comfortably fit six.

"Crowded, crowded," he grumbled. "One man uses another for a pillow, and yet another for a bed. Men wail in terror, entering the latrines. Leaving, they blubber like babes."

Glumly:

"Nothing to wager on, except whether we will eat the rats or they, us. Every Kushan is betting on the rats. Ten-to-one odds. No takers."

Philosophically:

"Of course, our misery will be brief. Plague will strike us down soon enough. Though some are offering odds on scurvy."

Belisarius smiled. "Get to the point, Vasudeva."

The Kushan commander tugged his goatee. "It's difficult, difficult," he muttered. "There are the proprieties to consider. People think we Kushans are an uncouth folk, but they are quite mistaken. Naturally, we have no truck with that silly Rajput business of finding a point of honor in the way you trim your beard, or peel a fruit. Still—" He sighed. "We are slaves. War captives taken in fair battle. Bound to respect our position, so long as we are not belittled."

From lowered eyelids, he gave Belisarius a keen scrutiny. "You understand, perhaps?"

The Roman general nodded. "Most certainly. As you say, the proprieties must be observed. For instance—" He drained his cup, then, grimaced. "Nasty stuff! I've gotten spoiled on that good Roman campaign wine, I suppose."

He wiped his lips, and continued, "For instance, if I were to bring you along on my next campaign as a slave labor force, the situation would be impossible. War captives used for labor must be closely guarded. Everyone knows that."

All the Kushans in the room nodded solemnly.

"Unthinkable to do otherwise," agreed Vasudeva. "Foolish for the captor, insulting to the captive."

"Yes. But since I will be undertaking a campaign of rapid maneuvers—feints, forced marches, countermarches, that sort of thing—it would be impossible to detail any troops to waste their time overseeing a lot of surly, disgruntled slaves. Who would slow us down enormously, in any event, since they'd have to march on foot. Can't have slaves riding horses! Ridiculous. They could escape."

"Most improper," intoned Vasudeva. "Grotesque."

Belisarius scratched his chin. "It's difficult, difficult."

He raised his hand.

"A moment, please, while I consider the problem."

He lowered his head, as if in deep contemplation. Sent a thought inward.

Aide?

Piece of cake.

❖   ❖   ❖

When Belisarius raised his head, a familiar expression had returned to his face. Seeing that crooked smile, the Kushans grinned.

He gave Vasudeva—and then, the other Kushan officers—a keen scrutiny of his own.

"You have heard, perhaps, that I have some small ability to see the future."

Vasudeva snorted. "You are a witch! Everyone knows that. Not even thumb-sucking Persians will take our wagers on *that* subject. And we offered very excellent odds. Twelve to one."

Belisarius chuckled.

"Slavery is an interesting condition, Vasudeva. It takes many forms. Different in the past than in the present. And different still, in the future. Many forms."

He leaned forward. Sixteen Kushans did likewise.

"Let me tell you about some slaves of the future."

Leaned forward. Leaned forward.

"They will be called—*Mamelukes*."

A message and a promise

When Antonina opened the door, Koutina hurried into her bedroom.

"I was hoping you'd still be awake," said the maid, "even though you left the birthday celebration so early."

Her young face was eager, almost avid. She held out a sheet of papyrus.

"It's a message! A message! For you! They say it came by the semaphore network—all the way from Mesopotamia!"

As she passed the paper over, Koutina added, "I think it's from your husband. I'm not sure. I can't read."

Uncertainly:

"Though it seems awfully short."

Antonina studied the message. Koutina was quite right, she saw. It was a very short message.

Just long enough. Her heart soared.

Next year, love. Next year.

"Yes," she whispered. "I will be there. I promise."

An emperor and his people

The morning after his birthday party, Emperor Photius made his way to the servant quarters of his palace.

Trudge, trudge, trudge.

Some of the nine-year-old boy's gloom came from simple weariness. The birthday party had been a tense, unhappy, and exhausting affair. What with the huge crowd, and the presentation of the Senators, and the ever-critical eye and tongue of the Empress Regent, Photius had enjoyed himself about as much as a sheep enjoys its shearing. Or a lamb, its slaughter.

Mostly, though, his black and dispirited thoughts came from The News.

Theodora had told him last night, just before the party began. Much as Photius imagined a farmer tells his piglet, "How marvelous! Aren't you just the fattest little thing?"

Reaching his destination, Photius knocked on the door. That was the only door which the Emperor of Rome ever knocked upon. All others were opened on his command.

The door to the modest apartment in the palace's servant quarters swung open. A young woman stood in the doorway. She was quite a pretty woman, despite the scars on her face.

"Oh, look! It's Photius!"

She smiled and stepped aside.

"Come in, boy, come in."

As he stepped through the door, Photius felt his melancholy begin to lift. Entering the living quarters of Hypatia and her husband Julian always cheered him up. It was the only place in the world where Photius still felt like himself. Hypatia had been his nanny since he was a toddler. And, though Julian had only become his chief bodyguard recently, Photius had known him for years. Julian had been one of Belisarius' bucellarii.

Julian himself now appeared, emerging into the small salon from the kitchen. He held a cup of wine in one hand.

Grinning cheerfully. The same cheerful grin the man had worn the first time Photius met him, at the estate in Daras. Photius had been six years old, watching wide-eyed from his bed while a burly cataphract climbed through his window and padded over to the door leading to Hypatia's quarters. Cheerfully urging the boy to keep quiet. Which Photius had, that night and all the nights which followed.

"Welcome, Emperor!" boomed Julian.

"Don't call me that," grumbled Photius.

Julian's grin widened.

"Feeling grouchy, are we? What's the matter? Did your tutors criticize your rhetoric? Or did the Empress Regent find some fault with your posture?"

"Worse," moaned Photius. "Terrible."

"Well, lad, why don't you come into the inner sanctum and tell us all about it?" Julian placed a large hand on the boy's shoulder and guided him into the kitchen. Hypatia followed on their footsteps.

The room—the largest in the apartment, by a goodly measure—was crowded, as usual. Two of

Julian's fellow cataphracts were lounging about the huge wooden table in the middle of the kitchen. Wine cups in hand, as usual. Their wives and mothers busied about preparing the midday meal, while a small horde of children scampered in and out of the room, shrieking in play.

As usual.

"Hail, Photius! Rex Imperator!" cried out one of the cataphracts, lifting his cup. Marcus, that was.

The other, Anthony by name, matched the gesture. And the words, though he slurred them badly.

Julian plunked himself down at the table and said, "Ignore them, lad. They're already drunk. As usual, on their day off."

"'S'our right," muttered Anthony. "A whole day wit'out 'avin' to listen t'a fuckin' tutor natterin' a' th'puir boy."

"Photius has to listen to them nattering seven days a week," said Hypatia. Primly: "Don't see him blind drunk two hours after sunrise."

"'Course not!" snorted Anthony. "'E's only eight years—no, by God! Nine years old, 'e is! Birt'day's yesserday!"

He lurched to his feet. "Hail Photius! Emperor of Rome!"

"Don't call me that!" shrilled the boy. "I'm sick of it!"

"Bein' called Emp'ror?" queried Marcus, bleary-eyed.

"No," groused Photius. "I'm sick of *being* Emperor!" He let out a half-wail. "I never asked them to!" And then a full wail. "They made me do it!"

The three cataphracts peered at the boy owlishly.

"Dissagruntled he is," opined Marcus.

"Downhearted'n downcast," agreed Anthony.

Julian bestowed a sage look upon his comrades. "Photius says he has terrible news to report."

It came out in a rush:

"They're going to make me marry somebody!" shrilled Photius. *"Next year!"*

Very owlish peers.

"A'ready?" queried Marcus. "Seems a bit— ah—ah—"

"Early," concluded Anthony. His eyes crossed with deep thought. "Ten years old, 'e be then. Still too early for'is pecker to—"

"Don't be vulgar!" scolded his wife, turning from the stove.

Anthony shrugged. "Speakin' fact, tha's all."

Hypatia sat down on the bench next to Photius. "Who are you supposed to marry?" she asked.

"Somebody named Tahmina," he replied sourly. "She's Persian. A Princess of some kind. I think she's the daughter of Baresmanas, the Persian ambassador who was here last spring."

"The *Suren?*" hissed Julian. His easy, sprawling posture vanished. He sat bolt upright. An instant later, Anthony and Marcus did the same.

The three cataphracts exchanged stares with each other. Then, suddenly, erupted into a frenzy of table-thumping, wine-spilling exhilaration.

"He did it! He did it!" bellowed Julian, lunging to his feet.

"Here's to the general!" hallooed Anthony, raising his wine cup and downing it in one quaff. The fact that he had already spilled its contents did not seem to faze him in the least.

Marcus simply slumped, exhaling deeply. His wife came over and enfolded him in her plump arms, pressing his head against her breasts.

All the women in the kitchen were standing around the table, now. They did not match the sheer exuberance of the cataphracts, but it was obvious that their own pleasure in the news was, if anything, greater.

"Why is everybody so happy about it?" whined

Photius. "I think it's terrible! I don't want to get married! I'm only nine years old!"

His plaintive wail brought silence to the room. Everyone was staring at Photius.

Gently, Hypatia turned the boy to face her. "Do you understand what this means?" she asked. "For *me*? For *us*?"

Uncertainly, Photius shook his head.

Hypatia took Photius' hands in her own. "What it means, Emperor, is—"

"Don't call me that!"

"Be quiet, Photius. Listen to me." She took a deep breath. "What it means, *Emperor*, is that your father has ended the long war with Persia. No Persian—not a *Suren*, for sure—has ever married a Roman Emperor. That peace will last our lifetimes, Photius. And more, probably."

She turned her head, looking at Julian. "What it means, *Emperor*, is that my husband will not die somewhere, on a Persian lance. Our children will not grow up fatherless."

She looked around the room. "What it means, *Emperor*, is that Anthony's mother over there will not have to bury her own son before she dies. And Marcus' wife and children will enjoy a comfortable retirement, instead of grinding poverty on a cripple's dole."

When she turned back to face Photius, her eyes were leaking tears. "Do you understand?"

Staring up at her scarred face, Photius remembered a night when that face had been covered with blood instead of tears. A horrible, terrifying night, when a boy barely four years old had hidden in a closet while Hypatia's pimp savaged her with a knife for refusing a customer.

He had been helpless, utterly helpless. Had only been able to cower, listening to her shrieks. Powerless, to stop the torment of the woman who had raised him while his mother was gone. Powerless.

He lifted his little shoulders, then. Squared them.

He was powerless no longer. He was the Emperor of Rome.

True, the pimp Constans was beyond his reach. Years ago, when Maurice and Anastasius and Valentinian had come to bring Photius and Hypatia to the estate in Daras, they had paid a little visit on Constans. Two years later, after he married Hypatia, Julian and several of his cataphract friends had tendered their own regards to the crippled ex-pimp.

Constans was beyond his reach or any man's, now. But much else was not.

Powerless no longer. He had never, quite, thought of it that way. Had never, quite, realized what that meant. To *other* people. *His* people.

"Okay," he said. "I'll do it."

A new round of celebration erupted, in which, this time, Photius participated cheerfully. He even drank three cups of wine with his cataphracts, and got a bit drunk himself.

And why should he not? He was the Emperor of Rome, after all.

Their Emperor.

A farewell and a parting thought

Baresmanas and Agathius saw him off at the gates of Peroz-Shapur. As his army marched past, Belisarius and his two companions spoke briefly on the prospects for his coming campaign.

Briefly—and more out of habit than anything else. It was a subject they had already discussed at great length.

The time came when friends made their farewells, knowing it might be for the last time. Agathius was gruff and hearty. Baresmanas was flowery and profusive.

Belisarius was simply cheerful.

"Enough," he said. "We'll meet again—be sure of it! I don't intend to lose, you know."

Quick, final handclasps, and the general trotted away to join his army.

Damn right, spoke Aide. Then—

Belisarius broke into laughter.

"What was that last?" he asked. "Sounded like 'those sorry bastards are fucked.' Terrible language! But, maybe not. Maybe you just said—"

Mutter, mutter, mutter.